P9-EEO-583

Runaway Girl

TESSA BAILEY

Tessa Bailey

Copyright © 2018 Tessa Bailey
Print Edition

All rights reserved. No part of this publication may be reproduced, distributed, or transmitted in any form or by any means, including photocopying, recording, or other electronic or mechanical methods, without the prior written permission of the publisher, except in the case of brief quotations embodied in critical reviews and certain other noncommercial uses permitted by copyright law.

TABLE OF CONTENTS

CHAPTER ONE

Naomi

I'M FIFTEEN MINUTES away from marrying the man who ordered me the wrong white wine at our rehearsal dinner last night. There are definitely far better reasons to get cold feet, but the lemony Pinot Grigio clings to all sides of my throat now like a reminder.

He doesn't know you.

I scan my reflection in the mirror, looking for flaws. The smallest thing counts. A flyaway blonde hair, a wrinkle in my custom Pnina Tornai wedding dress, my diamond pendant being slightly off-center. But no. I may as well have stepped right out of a bridal magazine. A real-life Photoshop job, primped, airbrushed and ready to be shipped down the aisle.

That's exactly what this feels like. I've been packaged. My attributes were all selected from a pull-down menu. Pageant queen. Check. Hostess skills. A must for any Southern housewife! Writes a mean thank you card. Why, of course!

After all, I'm preparing to marry the next mayor of Charleston. The rest of my life will be lived beneath the finicky microscope of old money and my own peers, who judge twice as harshly. I've been groomed for this my whole life. Cotillion. Finishing school. Private tutors. Non-stop critiques from my mother. I am in this to win it.

But with ten minutes on the clock, I'm not sure what winning is anymore.

What. Is. Winning?

I fall onto a cushy divan—gracefully, of course—and force air to enter my nose and leave my mouth. In. Out. In the full-length mirror's reflection, I watch my bridesmaids plow through a bottle of champagne behind me, speculating in hushed tones on what my wedding guests will wear to the big day. It's the tip of spring, so yellows, blues and pinks are likely to make an appearance. They talk about it like the weather report. I should get up and join them, right? Any second now, they're going to realize I've been quiet too long. I *have* been quiet too long. Where are my manners? They're here for me. I should be thanking them for their support and handing out their Tiffany charm bracelets, but all I can do is think of Pinot Grigio.

I'm a Sauvignon Blanc girl. Everyone knows that.

A little hiccup leaves my mouth, but I disguise it with a polite cough and stand up once more, smoothing creases from the embroidered satin of my dress. I notice my maid of honor watching me with a wrinkled brow and give her a pinky wave, forcing a smile until she returns to a conversation that has now turned to which of the groomsmen are single.

Five minutes. Oh God.

The sick citrus flavor has now traveled to my stomach, stewing and gurgling. I haven't thrown up due to nerves since my first pageant at age four. I won't start now. I can't. This is a thirty-thousand-dollar dress. A vomit stain wouldn't exactly match the beading. And worse, my friends have eagle eyes. They would definitely notice and they would know. They would know I'm panicking. I can't have that. The future mayor's wife is a cool customer. Unflappable. She makes everything look easy. That is who I am. Not a jittery girl with back sweat.

Years of etiquette classes, a structured diet and a well-rounded social calendar have guaranteed the prominence I will acquire as soon as I say "I do." I should be grateful for the opportunities I've been given, even though there have been moments over the years—moments like right now—when I look around and recognize nothing. Or feel like a mannequin that has been styled and positioned by someone else. Here is an example to follow! Look how she holds her pose!

It has never been harder to hold the pose as it is right now. I can balance a book on my head and tap-dance simultaneously, but walking down the stairs and pledging my future to someone who only knows the mannequin is scary. *I'm* scared.

Because I'm not sure I know the girl trapped inside the mannequin, either. Who is she?

A flash of black outside catches my eye. Not exactly an eye-catching color, but among the pastels, the dark figure crossing the street outside the church draws me closer to the window. It takes me a moment to place the identity of the black-haired woman stomping up the church steps with a defiant expression, but when I do, my feet go from cold to frostbitten.

Addison Potts.

What is my estranged cousin doing at my wedding? Lord knows she wasn't invited. Her side of the family hasn't been welcome at so much as Sunday brunch in decades. I haven't seen her in Charleston since we were in our twenties. Possibly longer than that, since we never ran in the same circles. My circle is currently popping open their second bottle of champagne—and an answering pop happens somewhere in my midsection as Addison pauses outside the church doors. Not hesitating, exactly. Just giving guests a chance to look at her. Encouraging them.

Shaking things up.

A small laugh puffs out of me, creating condensation on the window.

Where has she been? What has she been doing while I prepared to be the keeper of someone's social calendar? She left Charleston for New York years ago, all by herself. That much I do know. Looking at her now, that innate defiance in her every movement...I bet whatever she did since leaving South Carolina, she did it for herself. On her own terms. She's been living. That much is clear.

Addison frowns and glances up at the window, but I duck back before she sees me. My heart beats wildly in my throat. What would Addison see if she looked at me? Exactly what I am. A pampered Southern belle with the appropriate amount of friends. An inner circle of four, an immediate network of thirty-two and a broader outer circle of two hundred and fifty. A blonde beauty queen whose interests include scrapbooking, creating signature cocktails for parties and fancy gift-wrapping. My long-lost cousin would probably laugh at me.

Maybe she should.

When I look back down at the church steps, Addison has disappeared into the church, leaving a stir in her wake. And for the first time in my life, I understand envy. I've never caused a stir. Not once. I've inspired approval. Matching sweater sets don't exactly drop jaws, do they?

"Naomi," calls my maid of honor, Harper. "I promised your mother we'd have you walking down the aisle at three o'clock sharp. We should head down."

A bridesmaid leans a lazy hip against the liquor cart, jostling the bottles. "Yes, let's not cross the woman. I want to make it to the reception with my limbs intact."

Despite the cyclone brewing in my belly, my tinkling laugh fills the room. "Ladies, would you mind terribly if I have a moment alone with Harper? We'll be down in a shake."

"Of course," chirp three bridesmaids, far too brightly.

What am I doing? This impromptu meeting is not on the agenda. A quick glance at the clock tells me I am now late for my own wedding. If my mother has to come up the steps, she will be breathing fire, and that's the last thing I need right now. We don't want to keep Elijah waiting. No. No, we never want to do anything to upset this perfectly perfect ideal life I've landed. This is what I've always wanted. Wifehood to a rich, respected man. A military hero who inspires sighs of envy and pride when he walks down the street.

A good man. An honest man who will stay true to his vows. A kind, compassionate human being. That is Elijah Montgomery DuPont, the next mayor of this fine town. He just happens to think I prefer Pinot Grigio. That's only the tip of the iceberg, though, isn't it? I spent hours getting coiffed for the rehearsal dinner last night and he looked right through me. Sure, he kissed my cheek and nodded as I spoke. Made sure I arrived at my assigned seat without injury or assault. I love Elijah.

He just doesn't love me. And after seeing Addison Potts outside on the church steps, I know exactly why. Where my cousin is vivacious and exciting, I'm a cookie-cutter, boring-as-beige debutante who's never lived outside of the staunch parameters laid out for her. I haven't experienced anything, unless someone planned it for me. I'm not interesting or worthy of anyone's undivided attention. My fiancé is probably standing in front of the altar right now, dreading the next fifty years of eye-glazing conversation about the country club and charity planning committees.

Me. I'm going to be inflicting the boring.

Oh Lord. No. I can't do it. I don't want to do it.

I have to get out of here. I have to save Elijah.

And, more importantly—I think I have to shed my outer mannequin shell and go do some living. I've existed these last two and a half decades for my parents. Now I'm going to dedicate the next five to a husband without knowing what I really have to offer beyond small talk and juice cleansing tips? What do *I* want from the future? I don't even know. But I have to go experience more before I'm sure it's this.

"Naomi." Harper waves a hand in front of my face. "I've been calling your name, honey. What did you want to talk to me about?"

"I'm not going down there," I whisper, wide-eyed.

Well, now. There it is. My first dropped jaw. "What now?"

My gaze bounces around the room, cataloguing everything I need to take with me. Purse. My car keys are zipped in the inner pocket. I definitely need those because my suitcase is in the trunk, my laptop and honeymoon clothes inside. As long as I have those things, I won't need to go home and risk my mother hog-tying me and dragging me back to the church.

I can just…go.

Excitement is building in my chest. I'm really doing this. I should be terrified, but knots are loosening inside me instead. I'm not getting married today. I'm making this choice.

With a shaky swallow, I swish toward the secretary in the corner and scribble out a note with a trembling hand. *I'm sorry, Elijah. I couldn't do it.*

I hesitate before penning the next part. Am I going to completely sever ties with my fiancé? Yes. And no. I need to give Elijah his freedom. It's only fair after what I'm about to do. I can't ask him to wait while I figure myself out. That wouldn't be fair. But I know I could search this entire world and not find a more decent man. So while I'm going to break off our betrothal? In my heart…I'm going to keep hope alive that we'll find our way back to each other. If we're meant to be, he'll forgive me one day, won't he?

I didn't want it to end this way, but it's for the best.

Those final words blur together as I stare down at them, until the clock drags my attention away. I'm now ten minutes late for my own wedding. Unheard of. My mother is probably on the way—no, those are her footsteps coming up the stairs now. I have to move.

I shove the folded note into Harper's hands. "I'm sorry to do this to you, sweetheart, but I need you to give this to Elijah." She starts to shake her head. "You've been a good friend, Harper. I wish I had more time to explain, but right now, I need you to stall my mother while I escape down the back staircase."

"But why?" Harper breathes, fanning herself with the note. "Elijah is just so handsome."

There's no time to answer, though, and I turn from my wide-eyed friend, snatch up my purse and jog toward the staircase door. Not an easy feat in my crystal-embellished pumps I had designed to match Cinderella's slippers—which, heavens, seems so trite and cliché now. It's dark on the way down to street level, making it feel like a dream. Or a mistake. I'm not supposed to be in the dark, I'm supposed to be walking down the aisle adorned in refracted stained-glass lighting. We tested several different positions of the sun before deeming three o'clock the optimal aisle time. I can already hear my mother grinding her molars. We're losing the sun.

Who cares? I laugh as I throw myself through the exit door

and click quickly through the parking lot, purse in one hand, the hem of my wedding dress in the other. There isn't a soul around. No one wants to miss the upper-crust betrothal of the town hero and his trophy wife, do they?

While that harsh thought stings like an angry bee, it makes me move even faster toward my white Range Rover, parked in the valet section. I want to be more than someone's blonde Stepford Wife. I want to be...more like Addison. More like the black sheep cousin who walked with her chin up into a church full of people who dislike her. I want to be brave like that. Before that can happen, I need a reason to be brave. I need to see and learn and do.

Go back, says a voice in the back of my head. *You can't really be doing this.*

You don't have what it takes to survive.

That might be true. But I am doing this, regardless.

I'm a runaway bride.

Within moments, I'm peeling out of the parking lot and gunning it toward the freeway, my veil blowing in the wind. Before I take the on-ramp, though, I pull over and map a sensible route to Florida on my voice-guided navigator.

One ditched wedding does not a spontaneous woman make.

After that, though, I'm on my way.

To what?

I guess I'll find out.

CHAPTER TWO

EndoftheInternet.net
Username: IGotAnswerz9
Did anyone hear about the runaway bride in Charleston?
Did she run away or is foul play involved?
Theories welcome (nothing outlandish please).

ConspiracyCrowd.org
Username: IWant2Believe2000
Has anyone checked the dressing room for alien substances?
No, of course not. Apparently, the truth is TOO REAL for
some people.

Naomi

AROUND THE TIME I hit Jacksonville, I realize several things. All at once. Like a cold bucket of water thrown in my face. One, I have to use the ladies' room—desperately. Two, I'm still wearing my wedding dress, which is going to make relieving myself at a gas station awkward to say the least. Three, I have no marketable skills.

That last one is a doozy.

To my credit, I have a degree in Women's Studies from Clemson. But apart from the annual car wash I ran with my sorority sisters, I've never actually had a job. Holding a sign, showing a little leg and giving my best smile to passing motorists doesn't really count, I'm assuming. Which stings a little, because I was prouder of the nine hundred and fifty-eight dollars we made senior year than I am about most of my accomplishments.

There are several high-spending-limit credit cards in my wallet that say I don't need to work, but going to an ATM or charging purchases to the accounts would alert my parents to my whereabouts, and I've chosen not to do that. Just like I chose to throw my ringing cell phone out the window while speeding through Savannah. My parents will use every ounce of guilt under the sun to make me turn this Range Rover around, which means I simply cannot speak to them. Not until I have a better plan than driving until somewhere looks inviting enough to stop.

Yes, I am officially on the lam.

Which means I'll need money. There's a wad of spending cash in my honeymoon suitcase, but after gas, lodging and food, it won't see me through longer than a week.

My bladder is jostled by a bump in the road and I let out a whimper. All right. I guess I'm doing this. I'm walking into a gas station in a Pnina Tornai and availing myself of the public toilet, no matter the sanitary conditions. Someone will probably film me on their cell phone, the video will go viral, and I won't have to worry about being tracked through my Amex. The internet will just send my mortified parents after me lickety-split.

After pulling over into the closest space to the mini mart connected to the gas station, I take a bracing breath and step out of the Rover—

Snap.

My left heel gives way beneath me and my backside hits the concrete. Ouch.

And Lord help me, I pee a little in my panties. I'm no match for the jostling.

A hand appears in front of me, and I'm hauled to my feet by an older gentleman in a Jaguars cap. "You, uh…doing all right there, ma'am?"

"Yes." I smile and bat the wrinkles out of my dress. "This isn't what it looks like."

The older gentleman's wife stands off to the side, cradling a bag of Cheetos to her chest. "What is it, then?"

"Oh, you know…" I say weakly, bypassing them toward the market. "All my other clothes are at the dry cleaners."

Walking down the halogen-lit aisles of the packed mini mart toward the bathroom, I truly consider turning around and driving back to Charleston. My tailbone is pounding, I think I ripped the seat of my wedding dress—I'm just praying my pee-specked panties aren't visible to all and sundry. My broken heel has left me in a lop-sided limp. Four hours left to my own devices and I already look plain pitiful. And I have no plan.

I pick up a bag of something called Funyuns on the way to the bathroom and open them, shoving a crunchy, onion-flavored ring into my mouth. "Oh," I mumble around the bite, looking down at the bright yellow bag. "These are really good."

When there's no one in the bathroom, I whisper a thank you to the man upstairs and carefully roll up my Funyuns, leaving them on the counter. I'll have to get money out of the car to pay for them, not to mention perform a second walk of shame, but pay for them I will. I might have left a church full of people in the lurch, but I draw the line at shoplifting.

A split second before I close myself in the stall, a young woman about my age walks in and does a double take. "Nice dress," she says, scratching the corner of her eye. "You need some help?"

"That's really not necessary."

She comes forward anyway. "You need help or half of the

skirt will end up in the toilet."

Her bluntness turns my face hot, but manners keep me from declining a second time. "Very well, thank you." We enter the handicapped stall out of necessity, thanks to our need to fit my giant skirt and two full-grown women. It helps that my gas station savior seems very no-nonsense about the whole operation, simply yanking up my skirt while I die a little inside. Because her soft chuckle tells me she's definitely seen the pee spot. "Got a little excited, huh?"

"Something like that," I croak, tugging down the white, silk underwear from the back waistband. Deciding I have nothing to lose, I bury my face in the gathered abundance of my dress and sigh as my bladder gives up the fight. *Oh Lord. That feels good.* "This afternoon, I was getting a pre-wedding massage and doing photoshoots in a rooftop garden," I say, my words muffled. "Now I'm peeing with a stranger in a mini mart in—where are we?"

"Arlington."

"Oh. What a lovely town you have here."

"I'm from Clearwater." I cringe over my conversational hitch and the fact that I am still nowhere near being finished relieving myself. Needing to fill the non-silence, I start to say how unseasonably cool it is when my savior clears her throat. "You need to talk about anything?"

Talking is the absolute last thing I'm interested in right now. Not when I'll only sound like I'm flying by the seat of my...dress. Which I am, but still. This woman might be a stranger, but I wouldn't want her to remember me as a no-plan Nancy. I lift my head and smile, just as my never-ending stream of bodily fluids drips to a halt. "Actually, if you could just tell me how people go about hunting for jobs these days, I would truly appreciate it."

My savior looks surprised. Probably because I'm wearing a

wedding dress in a gas station and employment seems like a problem for another day. "You have a résumé?"

"Why, sure," I lie.

Wanted: Pageant Coach for Temperamental Teen. Email Jason.

NOT THE MOST enticing advertisement I've ever read. It's only eight words, and I swear I can already sense that Jason is blunt, frustrated and lacking in tact. I have no choice but to answer the no-frills call for employment, though. My gas station savior turned out to be a truck driver who must have been sent straight from the lord Jesus himself. She let me sit in the front seat of her truck while she ate a hoagie and I performed my cursory job hunt on her cell phone.

I had a moment of panic watching the blinking cursor in the job search engine. What to type. What to type. I can't very well seek employment as a scrapbooker or gift-wrapper—it's not even close to Christmas. I'm one heck of a party planner, but I have no professional experience or references to speak of. That left my oldest and strongest talent. Pageantry.

Until I left my fiancé at the altar, I was set to move into his extravagant mansion on the Battery as soon as we returned from our honeymoon. Prior to that, I've never lived anywhere but my parents' home and the sorority house, both of which had display areas for my pageant crowns. Forty-eight of them, to be exact. I've been stuffed into more bathing suits, ball gowns and high heels than there are countries in the world.

Did I enjoy a single second of it, though? As I cross the street toward a single-story, red-shingled house with a giant detached garage and a boat out front, I admit I have no idea. I don't remember a time when I wasn't being paraded around for someone's approval—it always just seemed natural. The thing to do.

When I replied to the advertisement for a pageant coach, I had to do some quick thinking due to my lack of résumé. Instead of sending a list of credentials and work experience—um, car washes count, right?—I replied with a cheerful message and some links to pageant websites that listed my name as a past winner. Within five minutes, I received an abrupt reply, which sent me to this address in St. Augustine, Florida, an old-fashioned, palm-tree'd, narrow-streeted town on the water. Hopefully no one in the house saw me wrestling my way out of a wedding gown in the backseat and donning a white linen dress with nude, strappy sandals. That definitely wouldn't do.

I raise my hand to knock on the door and pause when I realize I'm having a hard time swallowing. Buck up, Naomi. A job interview can't be so different from the question round in a pageant, right? Simply smile and give the most diplomatic answer. Shine. Sparkle. Wave. Woo. The Battle of Waterloo was nothing compared to the backstage at a beauty competition. I should be able to handle a temperamental teen and a terse advertiser.

With a deep breath, I knock on the door and wait. Seconds pass before I hear a heavy tread approaching. Very heavy. Kind of ominous, really. Nonetheless, I put on my most dazzling smile as the door is jerked open.

My smile drops, but I yank it back up. Despite the thunderhead of a human being looking down at me from the height of the doorframe. Not a gentleman. Not a gentle anything. Tattoos peek out of the neckline and sleeves of his dirty gray T-shirt. His jaw is covered in coarse-looking black hair, as is his head, which has been the recipient of a ruthless buzz cut. The smell of motor oil and cigar smoke wafts toward me, nearly knocking me back a step, but there's an underlying note of cinnamon that is oddly pleasing layered under the rest of it. And it's the last pleasing thing about him, this man who looks suited to climbing out of a swamp with camouflage paint on his face to the soundtrack of chopper blades. That seems like an unusual thought, until I realize the tattoo on his right arm is the Army logo. Fitting. Although this man is so large and riddled with muscle, he could be his *own* army.

His mouth turns down into an even deeper frown, and I realize I've been counting the unseemly bulges of his abdomen. Are those meant to be seen clear through clothing?

"Good evening. You must be Jason," I say brightly, holding out my hand. "I'm Naomi Clemons. Charmed."

He props a meaty forearm on the doorjamb and shakes his head. "Yeah. This isn't going to work."

I keep my hand extended. Just hanging there, like it has no protocol for being ignored. Can he sense how useless and inexperienced I am? He must. "I'm sorry?"

A single dark eyebrow goes up. "About what?"

His deliberate obtuseness rankles, and I'm surprised to find myself growing kind of irritated. At least it's a welcome change from the insecurity. "I'm sorry, as in, I don't understand what you mean by 'this isn't going to work.' We are midway through introductions, sir. You haven't even taken my hand yet."

"Don't plan to."

"I'll just leave it here," I say, ignoring the growing strain in said limb.

He shrugs a mountain-like shoulder. "Be my guest."

I've never been more tempted to stomp a foot. "Take the

hand."

A sigh gusts out of him. "Fine."

The man takes my hand and gives it a firm squeeze—and promptly covers my palm and fingers in thick, black grease. He revels in it, smiling just enough to reveal a set of strong, white teeth that look absolutely indecent set against his dark beard. He's waiting for me to whine or admonish him, too. I can tell. And it's shocking to have anyone display such impoliteness toward me. Especially a man. Where I come from, men bend over backwards to make me feel welcome. I am the furthest thing from welcome right now. I am distinctly *un*welcome.

I've had a bad day. I'm tired and hungry. Those delicious Funyuns were not enough to tide me over. This unfamiliar town has me feeling like a fish out of water, and I don't even know where I'm laying my head tonight. That has to be the only reason I'm hit with a burst of defiance the likes of which I've never experienced. At least since this morning.

Pasting a pleasant expression on my face, I wipe my greasy hand straight down the front of my white linen dress. *Hallelujah* is all I can think when Blackbeard's smile loses power, enough to hide his teeth. "Well, now. Let's start over." I breathe deeply and square my shoulders. "You must be Jason."

His grunt is apparently the only answer I'm going to get. A tangle of wills ensues. It reminds me of the Battle of Fort Sumter, because once a winner is declared and the loser surrenders, it doesn't feel like it's going to be over. More like, it's going to kick off a whole darn civil war. Thankfully, neither one of us is required to raise the white flag. We're interrupted by another set of approaching footsteps, this one far lighter than Jason's.

"Is that her?" a young girl calls. "Jesus, Jason. Invite her in."

Jason doesn't budge. He's too busy frowning at me and my

grease stain.

"Move," she says, her hands appearing on his sequoia tree waist and pulling ineffectively. "She's the only one who answered the ad."

Having claimed the upper hand, I wink at him. "How surprising, when it was so beautifully written."

"This isn't going to work," he says, repeating his earlier sentiment, before stomping into the house. In doing so, he reveals the temperamental teenage girl outlined in the doorframe, in all her pierced, blue-haired, ripped leather glory.

Lord have mercy. This is going to be a challenge.

What if I'm not up for it?

CHAPTER THREE

ReadtheComments.com
Username: TheRappingTheorist
If you're having girl problems, I feel bad for you, son.
I've got 99 theories and spontaneous combustion is actually a
completely viable one.

Jason

I DON'T LIKE surprises.

Especially in the form of little blonde beauty queens.

Didn't help that I saw her changing in the back seat of her car. In my defense, the windows of her Rover were tinted, and with all the wiggling around, I initially thought some kids were making out in the backseat across from my house and was preparing to go send them on their way. By the time I realized it was a solo, half-dressed woman, I'd already witnessed the whole damn show. That was before I saw her walking across the street in the fading sunset light, one hand holding down the wind-fluttered hem of her skirt, her mouth moving in what looked like a rambling pep talk. What was she saying?

Annoyed at my own curiosity, I follow the girls into the living room. And there she is again. Still here. I've never seen someone arrange themselves on a couch before. That's exactly what she's doing now. Knees pressed together, ankles crossed and out to the side, fingers smoothing out her dress, hair being rested behind shoulders, hands folding together. Watching her glide across the street, I'd had not a single doubt in my mind that my wild child little sister would run roughshod over this smiling Disney princess. Then she'd gone and wiped motor oil on the front of her white dress without batting a single one of her curled black eyelashes.

Well, if Miss Clemons thinks that grease streak is going to make me feel guilty, she's got another think coming. That's what I tell myself. But when I notice she's transferring oil to her other hand, too, thanks to her having folded them like a damn Sunday school teacher, I stomp toward the bathroom to hunt up a washcloth.

This isn't going to work.

Even if she turns out to be a match for Birdie's temperament, this blue-eyed Southern belle can't have the run of my house. Coming and going as she pleases looking like…that. Maybe I should have dug down a little deeper into the links she sent me. I gathered a pageant winner would be attractive, but I didn't expect her. She's not merely attractive. With her glowing skin, soft, swollen mouth and limber-looking body, she's insanely beautiful. How is it that she doesn't have a single imperfection? This house is a fucking mess, due to my profession and lack of shits to give. She fits in here like a square peg in a circle.

In other words, she doesn't.

My time in St. Augustine is limited. The Army gave me an extended leave due to our family emergency, but it's quickly coming to an end. I don't want distractions. I want to keep my head down, push through the next few months to my next deployment and go wheels up. A few minutes around Miss Clemons and I can tell it won't be as easy to switch off my surroundings and go through the motions until I can get back to serving my purpose.

Yeah. She's got to go.

I throw open the bathroom linen closet and grab the first washcloth I see. It would be too rough against skin like she's got, though, so I trade it for one relatively newer. As in, purchased in the last decade. I pinch it in the corner, so I don't get my boat filth all over it, and return to the living room, wondering why the hell she was changing in her car.

"Why the hell were you changing in your car?"

Birdie slaps her hands over her face. "God help us."

Naomi stalls out mid-sentence, gaping at me and the dangling washcloth. "Did you actually...see me changing?"

"Relax. I didn't catch anything important." I toss her the cloth, but she doesn't even acknowledge it when it lands on the couch. "Just enough movement to know what you were doing."

A laugh tinkles out of her. "I think you must be mistaken, then."

I sigh and nudge the washcloth closer. "I don't make mistakes."

She flicks a look at the washcloth. "What am I supposed to do with that?"

"Clean your hands off with it."

"Oh." She smiles and tilts her head at me. "No, thank you."

I growl.

Birdie throws her booted feet up on the coffee table, crossing them at the ankles. "Now this is what I call entertainment."

Naomi dismisses me with a blink of those blue eyes and refocuses on my sister. "Where were we?" She claps her soiled hands together, and I grind my teeth. She's doing this on purpose, isn't she? "Right. You were telling me about the pageant you entered."

"Yeah." The same booted feet she slapped up onto the table

with confidence a moment ago jerk and Birdie sits up straighter. She twines a finger in the rubber band around her wrist, twisting, letting it go with a snap. Day and night. That's my sister. One minute, she's the planet's biggest wiseass, but she can look so small and nervous at the flip of a switch. I hate it. But God didn't exactly bless me with the tools to fix it. "Miss Saint John's County. It's my first and last. I just need you to help me win the one."

"Oh, just the one?" Naomi has a teasing smile on her face— she never seems to stop smiling—but she's watching Birdie fidget with the rubber band, a small crease between her brows. "Forgive me for asking such a frank question upfront, sweetheart, but what made you want to participate in one single pageant?" She sends me a bemused look. "Most of these girls will have been competing since childhood."

"Yeah, I know. I go to school with some of them." My sister rolls her eyes and plows a handful of fingers through her shock of blue hair. "Pastel hell in heels."

"You're going to love my wardrobe," Naomi says without missing a beat. "So entering the pageant is to get a rise out of the...pastel hell girls?"

"No. That's just a bonus." Naomi waits, and I watch the remainder of Birdie's bravado drain out of her in one awful wave, leaving a pale face behind. "My twin sister Natalie wanted to compete in this pageant. She used to go sit in the audience and support her friends. With all the plays she performed in at school and baton-twirling...she just hadn't gotten around to the pageant yet." Her chin levels up. "And now she can't, so I'm going to do it in her place."

A drape seems to spill down around the perimeter of the room. If the situation wasn't so fucked up, I might have laughed at the way awareness creeps over Naomi. She thought she was walking onto the set of *Legally Blonde: The Musical,* but it has turned out to be Shakespeare. And the fact that I know enough to reference Broadway is a true testament to the elephant in the room. My missing sister. Birdie's twin. She was the drama club queen, the one with the all-pink wardrobe and boy band crushes. She would have been in awe of Naomi, but she's not here. Her ghost, however, is alive and well. One look at Birdie's stiff demeanor would clue anyone in, and Naomi is no different. Her blue eyes trip around the room, landing on framed photographs of the twins at various stages of their life. Several ticks pass.

"How long ago did you lose her?"

"Six months." Birdie shakes out her hands, as if trying to distract Naomi from the fresh horror of it. It's an impossible feat, however, seeing as we're living in our childhood home. I've become numb to the loss of Natalie, throwing every ounce of my energy into building a scuba diving business from the ground up. Running a household. Keeping an eye on Birdie. I couldn't protect my own family, and because of that, I'm not sure I've allowed myself to mourn. Some part of me doesn't feel deserving of it. I'm the big brother. The son. I didn't do my job.

There is no way to forget who I'm letting down by being here, either. The backs of the men I no longer have. The sights and sounds and grit of battle that run in my veins. I was overseas with Special Forces so long, I can't process the normalcy of what's around me. So much so that I don't want it, even though I know I'm doing right by Birdie.

It seems that no matter where I am, I'm in the wrong place. But there's only one place I feel adequate and it's so far from here, I have to constantly remind myself it exists and that I'm needed there. Far more than I'm needed here.

"Look," Birdie continues. "I told Nat that pageants were stupid and shallow, but she was so determined to try one before college. That was her. She had this glittery, laminated wish list...and this pageant was at the top." She presses her lips together. "Sometimes we felt what the other was feeling. Twinsense. It would mean something to her, even though she's gone."

Naomi seems frozen in shock, but only in a way another adult would recognize. All Birdie is seeing is concern. I think. I hope.

Why do I hope? A few minutes ago, I wanted this beauty queen out of here. I still do, don't I? If she would stay the hell in one category, it would help me make a decision. Instead, she's already given me adversarial, vulnerable and determined in the space of one encounter.

I'm trained to handle surprises, but this isn't the kind I'm used to.

Naomi takes a notepad out of her purse and settles it in her lap, on top of those squeezed-together knees. This is not the time to imagine my dirty hands prying them apart for a marathon pussy-eating session, but I'm a thirty-two-year-old man with working parts and she's the most incredible thing I've ever fucking laid eyes on. There. I admitted it. The prim and proper attitude she's got is annoying me and turning me on at the same time. A pretty urgent combination, especially when I haven't touched a woman in months, so excuse me if this isn't the time and place. I bet her tight little ass would wiggle around the bed so much, I'd need to hold her still.

Thinking about it will have to suffice, however, because I don't have the time or stupidity to get tangled up with a woman I could be seeing on a daily basis.

When did that become a definite possibility?

"So let's talk about—"

Birdie cuts her off. "You think this is a stupid reason to enter a pageant, don't you?"

Naomi sucks in a breath. "No. No." She opens her mouth, closes it. "I was thinking…I—I've never had any reason at all to enter them. Not that I can remember. I was just kind of put there. And even though, God, even though what happened is so terrible and I'm so sorry, I wish I could want something for an important reason like you. I'm…amazed."

I don't think my sister took a single breath throughout that whole impromptu speech. I'm not sure I did, either. We don't talk a lot about Natalie. Or my parents who couldn't handle grief and parenting responsibilities at the same time, so they split. We don't talk much at all. This woman has been in the house for less than five minutes and she's already ripped off the Band-Aid.

"Jason?" Birdie prompts me. "Can she coach me?"

It's obvious that this woman on my couch is qualified to show Birdie the pageant ropes. Maybe overqualified. But I can't ignore the fact that she changed in the back seat of her car. Where did she come from? Why couldn't she change before leaving for the meeting? This is not a woman who leaves getting dressed until the last second. There's something not quite right about the situation. Before I make a decision, I need to know every detail of the landscape.

It's definitely not because I personally want to know more about her.

"Can we have a few minutes alone, Birdie?"

NAOMI LOSES SOME of her careful composure when Birdie leaves the room. Her knees have zero blood left in them, she's pressing them together so tight, and if she clings to that notebook any tighter, she'll rip it straight down the middle. Her nerves are unsurprising—I'm an intimidating motherfucker. In my line of work, my size and general air of go fuck yourself have served me well. And I don't turn it off for anyone. Even if her fresh, fragile appearance is making me wish I'd at least rinsed off for the interview.

"Coffee?"

She opens her mouth to decline. I can tell. "No, thank you—"

Her stomach growls loud enough that I hear it clear across the room. She claps both hands over her mouth and turns the color of a pink sunset. "Oh sweet lord," she says. Or something like it, since the words come out muffled. "I'd be grateful if you could go ahead and pretend you didn't hear that."

"They heard it in St. Louis. Let's go." I jerk my thumb over my shoulder. "Kitchen."

"No, thank you—"

"Kitchen, beauty queen."

I'm inside the room for a full minute before she inches in behind me, chin up, arms folded over her middle. "I'm guessing you haven't been out of the military long, Blackbeard. Ordering people around seems to come naturally."

My lips twitch at the nickname. "Bossing everyone around came naturally before the military. You like pie?"

"Of course I do." A line appears between her brows. "But I haven't eaten a meal yet."

When I open the refrigerator, I'm grateful for the waft of cool air against my skin. It's the next best thing to a cold shower, and after my impromptu fantasy of separating her thighs, I'm in desperate need of one. What the hell is it about this woman? I don't know if I necessarily have a type when it comes to women, but I know this pretty princess with the Southern twang is not it.

If I came across her in a bar, I would assume she'd gotten lost on the way to a church picnic and stopped to ask for directions. I would absolutely assume she was already married. Naomi is the marrying type.

That certainty has my hand pausing before it can reach the half-eaten apple pie on the second shelf. Changing in her car, starving, looking for employment and most definitely not in South Carolina where the pageant bio said she belongs. Is she running away from a man?

It's a good thing my hands are out of view. She'd probably have questions about the plastic ketchup bottle I'm suddenly squeezing in my fist. I suddenly wish I'd been nicer to her.

At least a little.

"So, what's the story?" I ask in a strained voice. "You've never eaten dessert before dinner?"

She slides onto a stool on the other side of the island, folding her grease-covered hands neatly in front of her. "Do Funyuns count?"

"Maybe on a technicality."

Her whole face brightens, and a hot shiver blows down my back. "Then, yes. I have." She gets more comfortable in the stool. "A bite or two of pie won't hurt."

I slide the pie tin and a fork across the island and lean forward on my forearms. "Have at it."

With a suspicious expression, she picks up the fork. "Why do I get the feeling you're lulling me into a false sense of security? Is this your equivalent of bringing an interrogation suspect coffee and cigarettes before asking the hard questions?"

A laugh tries to build in my belly, but I squash it. "You're pretty perceptive."

Naomi rears back with a gasp. "Did you just pay me a compliment?"

"Don't get used to it."

"Wouldn't dream of being so bold," she whispers, finally finding a spot to dig into the pie and holding a forkful in front of her full, pink mouth. Our gazes connect over the bite and my groin tightens up. So hard I have to turn away. But in my periphery, I can see her guiding the pie home and chewing. "Oh my word," she moans. "This is incredible. Did you make this?"

"Bakery."

I can't help it. Needing to look, I turn back to face her. Her arm has gone limp on the counter, her head tipped back as she chews. She's damn near having an orgasm in my kitchen. And somehow she manages to look innocent and sweet as shit while doing it. Beautiful, too. "You've probably heard enough compliments to see you through the next decade, haven't you?" I don't realize I've said it out loud until her eyes pop open and she lets the fork go on the counter with a clatter. Goddammit, I don't like the way she puts me off-center. "It's a good thing I only care about your ability to coach Birdie."

"Of course," she says quickly, smoothing her hair. "Please. Ask the tough questions."

"Why were you changing in your car?"

"Oh, that one." She wets her lips, attention drifting to the ceiling. "I needed to get away for a while. Can we just leave it at that?"

"No."

She shoots a frown at me. "Maybe you should advertise for a manners coach."

"That's no way to talk to your employer, beauty queen."

"Oooh." She shakes her head. "You're lucky I like your sister or I'd go hunting for gift-wrapping jobs. It might not be

Christmas, but every day is *somebody's* birthday. There must be a demand for skilled wrappers—"

"Are you going somewhere with this?"

Naomi stops mid-sentence and pinches the bridge of her nose between two dainty fingers. When she drops them, I see she's left a grease smudge behind, and honestly, the sight of it makes me want to kick a hole in the island. "I'm sorry. I've had an awfully trying day."

Determined to ignore the way her confession—and apology—sinks into my gut, I move to the sink and wet a paper towel. She watches me warily as I cross to her and flinches as I lift the wet, wadded up square of Bounty. Fuck. Up close, she's even more extraordinary. I had no idea women came this soft and beautiful. If someone laid a finger on this woman to send her packing, they're going to pay. That's a promise. "Stop fidgeting and let me clean your nose off."

"I can do it," Naomi murmurs.

She makes no move to take the paper towel from me, though, so I do it, removing the grease in two swipes and stepping back, hoping she can't hear the rollicking thunk of my pulse. I need to distract her. "What are you doing in St. Augustine?" Before she can give me some rote line of sugar-coated bull, I shake my head. "A real answer."

Time seems to creep past as I wait for her answer. It's not what I'm expecting at all.

"I don't want to be boring forever." She traces the edge of the fork with a polished fingernail. "I've done everything according to someone else's plans. The perfect plans. I want to make my own imperfect ones for a while. I want to surprise myself...and mostly...I want to learn to be interesting." Pink rises in her cheeks, like she's traveled into her own world and forgot I was standing there. "It won't distract me from coaching your sister, Jason. You have my word. I'll do the best I can."

"I believe you," I say slowly. "What's this going to cost me?"

"I...well, I'm certain I have no idea. Someone else always paid my pageant coaches." She chews on her lower lip. "Since I'm not a very experienced coach, why don't we say...two hundred dollars an hour?"

"Are you insane?"

"Fine, forty. Plus the cost of wardrobe, shoes, and any other incidentals." She holds out her hand for a shake. "I'm hired. I'll start tomorrow."

The last word breaks off into a feminine chuckle.

"What?" I ask, my throat feeling raw. This woman just played me. And I liked it.

"I'm doing it already. Surprising myself." She reaches down and captures my hand, shaking it firmly as she comes to her feet. "It's a fine start, don't you think, Blackbeard?"

There are a million things on the tip of my tongue. Mainly I want to ask who gave her the false impression she was boring. But I'm worried where my curiosity will lead. I'm worried there won't be an end to how much I want to know. "My sister isn't easy."

"I wonder where she gets it."

A grunt escapes. I step closer to her, even though I shouldn't. "Are you safe, Naomi?"

I'm still holding her hand in the pretense of a never-ending handshake. Her pulse doesn't skip at my question, genuine confusion marring her brow. "Of course I am."

Satisfied for now that she's telling the truth, I let her go, watching as she rushes to step back and smooth herself. Hair, dress, collar. "Thank you for your hospitality."

"Yeah."

The shape of her hand refuses to leave mine long after she's sailed out the back door.

What have I just set myself up for?

CHAPTER FOUR

ConspiracyCrowd.org
Username: UrdadsMyFave69
You're all reaching.
Runaway Bride looked down the long barrel of monogamy...
...and got the fuck out. Godspeed, my friend.

Naomi

TAKEN FOR GRANTED.

Now there is a phrase I've heard a million times throughout my life, but I never really understood the meaning of it until last night. I've taken so many seemingly small things for granted, only to find out they're not small at all. Buying shampoo, for example. On a budget.

After being hired as Birdie's coach, I ventured into downtown St. Augustine to find lodging. What a kick in the butt that turned out to be. The amount of spending cash I had packed to bring on my honeymoon wouldn't have gotten me through one single night in all of the establishments I tried. At the final hotel—a sprawling, Spanish-style spa—I was not so politely directed to a different part of town.

A little red in the face, I kept my head up and drove...and drove...and drove until I found a place that I could afford. They were even kind enough to put the price right outside on the marquee. Very convenient.

So, fine. The carpeting was scratchy, everything smelled like cigarettes, and the shampoo and conditioner bottles on the sink were empty. At least I went into the office and rented the room myself. Hauled my own suitcase and wedding dress up the stairs. Ventured out and found my own dinner. Three things in one night I've never done before. Four if I include landing a job.

Speaking of my job…

"Jogging?" Birdie's feet skid on the hardwood as I usher her toward the door front. "No one said anything about that."

"The fitness category is a polite way of saying the judges are inspecting your butt. Exercise is part of the gig." My explanation only makes Birdie cringe harder. "It's not fair. I know. There are expectations for a woman's body to be perfect and no one should have to live up to them. Who even sets them?"

Birdie eyes me hopefully. "So that's a rain check on the jog?"

"No dice. The pageant world is unforgiving. When this is all over, you never have to jog again and you'll be perfect, sweetheart. But if pageant-ready is the goal, we have to suffer some." I turn in a circle, searching for a Nike swoosh among the pile of mostly male footwear. "Where are your running shoes?"

"In a Foot Locker. Waiting to be purchased."

"Oh dear. That is an obstacle."

"I have some Converse that might work in a pinch." Birdie growls her way down the hallway toward her bedroom and comes back a moment later with unlaced black and white sneakers. "Hang on, I have to check my blood sugar before we go." She jingles the bracelet around her wrist. "Diabetic in the house."

I try not to show a reaction. "I didn't know."

"It's not usually the first thing I tell people."

Standing in limbo between the kitchen and living room, I

watch as Birdie hops up onto the kitchen counter and pulls two small, black devices out of the cabinet. She pops the top off one and inserts a blue plastic piece, presumably with a needle at the end. In the second device, she shoves in a white test strip, and after pricking her finger, she presses the tip of her digit there, waiting as the meter beeps.

"One twenty-nine. Good to go," Birdie calls, breaking everything down as fast as she set it up. "Hope that didn't weird you out."

"It didn't. I've just never seen it done before."

"Congratulations." Birdie slides off the counter. "Your diabetes cherry has officially been popped."

I let out a choked sound. "I think I'll focus our training on the interview round."

Laughing, Birdie drops down to tie her shoes. "That's probably not a bad idea." She shoots me a look through a dangling hunk of blue and black hair. "How are you so straight and narrow, but you still managed to outmatch my brother?"

Having Jason brought up for the first time since I arrived gives me the urge to search over my shoulders, positive I'll find him lurking in a corner scowling at me. His presence is everywhere in the house. A giant rain slicker hangs on the coatrack, military commendations sit perched on the mantle, cigar smoke and cinnamon linger in the air. "I'm not sure I did outmatch him."

"No? He walked around looking like he'd woken up on Mars last night."

"Oh." Surprise kicks me in the stomach. Surprise…and pleasure. Yes, I did hold my own just a little, didn't I? "Well, next time we'll aim for Mercury. It's closer to the sun."

Birdie sails past me toward the door with a snicker. "Let's get this over with."

We start with a light run when we reach the sidewalk, leaving the nook of Charlotte Place and hitting a left on Marine Street, where we jog along the Matanzas River. Ships bob in the rich blue water, some of them ferrying tourists between the Bridge of Lions in the distance and farther south. Palm trees and ornate lampposts seem to be positioned a uniform distance apart, completely at odds with the kitschy restaurants across the road, beckoning to passersby with bright colorful signs, drink specials, haphazard strings of lights and backyard dining.

Running beside Birdie without talking gives me a chance to study her closer. Now that we're out in the sunlight and the wind is blowing the hair back from her face, I can see just how unique she is, which I already discovered last night. I've never been in the company of someone with such a fighter's spirit. It's there in the stubborn set of her chin and sharpness of her gaze. She sees a lot. Every word directed at her is weighed and dissected, given a worth.

She reminds me a little of the Addison I saw climbing the steps of the church. Ready to take on anything. Anyone. Yes, I don't know the real Birdie, yet, but she strikes me as someone who's been through more than most adults and is stuck in the body of an eighteen-year-old.

"Are you trying to decide if I'm pretty enough to compete?"

"I most certainly am not." I discreetly dab at the sweat on my forehead. "Incidentally, I think you're beautiful. I'd trip a nun on Sunday for those cheekbones."

Birdie's stride hitches. "Yeah?"

"Yes, ma'am."

We go back to running in silence for a few minutes. "I don't care about things like cheekbones. I just want the best chance of winning for Nat's sake."

"Noted." My lips wrestle with a smile. "You've got them all the same. A little contouring and you'll be the envy of Florida!"

"Are you always this upbeat?"

I have to think about it. "I don't know. When it comes to my mouth, yes. In my head, I'm a whole other story sometimes." Birdie is about to respond when she catches sight of something in the distance, her eyes glazing with horror. Before I can ask what's wrong, she snags my arm and drags me behind a palm tree. "What's is it? What's wrong?"

"Pastel hell in heels." She peeks around the jagged trunk of the tree. "Just loitering in the sun with stupid gelato cones. Jesus, they're like a fucking Aeropostale ad."

I grab my own quick glance, deciding they look like a group of normal, everyday teenagers. A lot like my friends in high school. Is this the kind of reaction we inspired in everyone else? "Do you want to go talk to them?"

"I'd rather get Heimlich'd by someone holding scissors."

"Are they mean or—"

"No." Birdie seems annoyed by that fact. "They were just...they were friends with my sister. Some of them do pageants and Nat would go to cheer them on." She falls back against the trunk and crosses her arms. "Every time I run into them at school, there's this split second of disappointment on their faces."

"Why would they ever be disappointed?"

"Because I'm not her." She pushes off the tree. "We all used to be friendly, even though I didn't really fit in with that circle. Now we're just acquaintances. Natalie was the one who brought everyone together. With friends and family. Both. She'd put on a silly play or throw a board game on the floor and whine until everyone picked a talisman. She was the glue. Everything…everyone is apart now because there's no glue." She huffs a breath. "Anyway, if they knew I was doing this pageant shit for Nat, they would probably pity me, and I'd rather be set on fire."

"You know…" I power walk to keep up with her, back in the direction we came. "I'm going to pretend you didn't use the S-H word in reference to my life's best work. Instead I'm going to make a suggestion, if you're open to it."

"We're a mile from my house and I have nowhere to hide. Was that your plan all along?"

"I'm going to let you think so." We fall into step together. "They're going to find out sooner or later. Why not face it head on? Tell them what you're doing. That way you can control the how and when."

"Sorry, I didn't hear you. I was too busy mapping different routes for tomorrow's jog."

"Already planning our next run?" I take a mid-stride leap. "You're having fun. I knew it."

A corner of her mouth ticks up. "I'm going to let you think so."

It takes us just under fifteen minutes to reach Birdie's street. We're both huffing and puffing a little as we turn onto Charlotte Place. Up ahead, I hear the drone of an engine and the scratchy bass of rock music. I want to say Metallica is playing, although I have no idea how or where I learned that information. Probably during one of my mother's cautionary tales about what happens to good girls who let Satan infiltrate their minds. In this one instance, I have to admit she might be right. The music is loud enough to rattle my molars.

"Where is that noise coming from?"

Birdie laughs. "Jason is home."

Don't ask me why I skid to a halt on the sidewalk. It's an

involuntary reaction. I simply didn't anticipate being seen while sweating. I would feel the same way no matter who I was approaching, man or woman. Yesterday morning, I was preparing to marry a man I'd spent years dating. I still plan on being loyal to Elijah, physically and mentally. Even if there was a moment in the kitchen last night, I swore Jason was thinking no-good man thoughts about me. And I am ashamed to admit that I spent an inordinate amount of time last night remembering the way he looked at me. I'm not sure a man has *ever* looked at me in such a manner. As if he wants to see me in my birthday suit—and was good and mad about it.

I let my recalled irritation at him bubble up, although it doesn't exactly feel like irritation. I'm a wary cat approaching the house on the balls of its feet, ready to take a polite warning swipe if needed. When we hit the driveway, I search the front yard—which is littered with engine parts, lifejackets and oxygen tanks—and I see Jason.

Retreat. Retreat.

Before I can stop myself, I'm actually backpedaling on the sidewalk and I have no idea why. It might be the fact that Jason is now visible in the parked, elevated boat. Shirtless.

Not merely shirtless, however. He's indecently shirtless.

There's a lit cigar in the corner of his clamped together lips. Dangerous, considering there's enough black hair on his chest to start a forest fire if one single ember should escape. Lord, I thought men his size only existed in the Bible. Built for fighting lions in dens or carrying giant stone tablets down from the mountaintop. Jason is a modern version of a Bible warrior in a peeled down wetsuit that wraps far, far too low on his hips for decent company. And the tattoos. They're everywhere. Poking in and sneaking out of places they shouldn't. No. No, sir. I'm not getting any closer to that.

To my utter horror, I realize my mouth is open wide enough to catch a battalion of bees. No honey required. *Stop looking at the unruly line of dark hair below his belly button.* I know where it leads. I'm a grown woman. Old enough to know I do not want that zipper to come down any lower. Old enough to know my toes should not be curled in my sneakers right now, too.

Why is he looking at me like that? Is he smirking at me through all that cigar smoke?

"I-I'll see you tomorrow," I say, patting Birdie awkwardly on the shoulder.

"Wait, what?"

I pull my ponytail as tight as it will go, continuing my backward journey on the sidewalk, away from the sight of Jason. "Um. Tomorrow we'll outline the competition and get a better idea of what we need to work on. I'm going to make some phone calls and try to get us some affordable indoor space. We'll need to perfect your pageant walk and—"

"Why can't we do it now?"

"It's a school night."

Birdie looks at me like I'm nuts. Maybe I am. "It's four thirty."

"That is true, isn't it?" Over Birdie's shoulder, I see Jason jump down from the boat and land on bare feet, like some huge, nimble king of the jungle. He starts in our direction, that cigar glowing red between his teeth, and I back up another several yards, horrified to realize my belly is tingling. Nerves. Just nerves. For some reason, he inspires them in me like no one in my experience. "You should speak to your brother about proper running shoes."

"Okay." Birdie looks over her shoulder, coming back with a

knowing look I don't care to interpret. "Do you want me to ask Jason to put on a shirt?"

"What? No. Why would you…what?"

Jason's low chuckle snaps my spine straight.

"I was just about to head home," I say to them both, pretending to be fascinated by a palm tree as I cross the street toward my car. "I'll be back the same time tomorrow."

"Are you sure you don't want to stay for dinner?"

Birdie asks the question, and one glance at her expression tells me she's enjoying my suffering. Maybe if I ask nicely, she'll explain the source of it. Sure, I've never been around such a rough and tumble man, but I don't understand why his appearance should distress me like this. "Thank you so much for the invitation, but I'll have to decline until another time."

Jason plucks the cigar out of his mouth, flicking ashes onto the sidewalk. "See you at six thirty, beauty queen."

I grind my teeth behind a smile. "I have plans."

He's smirking again. He doesn't believe me. "You do now."

With that, he saunters back to the boat, leaving me with a view of his back, which is equivalent to the broad side of a barn. If barns were made of muscle and such. Such being…scars and interestingly shadowed valleys. Running straight down his spine is the tattoo of a dagger, and stretching across ridges of muscle from one shoulder to the other is a pair of crossed arrows, bisecting the dagger. I refuse to let my gaze go any lower.

"He can be a little scary," Birdie says, nudging me. "But he's only killed, like, two out of my last five pageant coaches. The odds are in your favor."

I can only stare as she jogs off toward the house.

"See you tonight, coach number six!"

CHAPTER FIVE

EndoftheInternet.net
Username: IGotAnswerz9
Let me be plain. The only one with a motive to kill Naomi was the mother.
Bridezilla? Ha! Try Momzilla. She wasn't about to let her daughter ruin HER perfect day. Tale as old as time.

Jason

NAOMI ARRIVES AT six thirty on the dot with a chipper smile and a bottle of white wine. My military nature likes the on-time arrival. My male nature likes the white shorts she's wearing even more, but I'm not going to dwell on my chemical reaction to her. After the way she ran off like a scared bunny rabbit at the sight of me in no shirt this afternoon, I'm even more positive that getting physical with this woman just ain't going to happen. She's not my type. I'm even further from hers. And the way I'd like to get down in bed with her would probably give her the fucking vapors.

This afternoon in the driveway, I thought I saw a spark of reluctant interest in Naomi, but I was definitely mistaken. She's holding that bottle of wine in front of her like an exorcist presenting a cross to fend off the evil spirits. Fine enough—it's better this way. Birdie came back from their run this after-noon…excited. I haven't seen her that way since I got home.

Before Naomi arrived on our doorstep, Birdie seemed determined to compete in the pageant for Natalie, but winning wasn't a possibility. I had to sign off on the paperwork, so I know she wrote *for shits and giggles* under the question, "Why do you want to compete in the Miss St. John's County Pageant?" Yet an hour ago, I walked past her room and saw her practicing a runway walk. Maybe having someone in her corner who knows what the hell they're doing is making all the difference. Hell, it's more than she had going for her yesterday when she only had me.

Bottom line. Naomi is giving Birdie a fighting chance and I'm not going to fuck that up. It's all I know how to give my sister. I've failed at protecting the person she was closest to in this world. And thanks to my working hours and lack of warm fuzzies, I've been unable to give her a healthy, welcoming home. On the rare nights we manage to have dinner together, we eat silently in front of the television and part ways with an abrupt goodnight.

I don't have a clue how she's supposed to deal with her grief. I've lost so many brothers, I've stopped taking the time to process the horror of it. Pick up and keep moving. There is always the next job to perform. Prisoners to be liberated. Firefights to win. Intel to gather. It's what I should be doing now. It's what I'm built for—not comforting a teenage girl.

Maybe this is it. Maybe this pageant is Birdie's version of pick up and keep moving. If that's the case, I'm keeping my hands off of this beauty queen from Charleston. I'm just going to jerk off thinking about peeling those prim white shorts down Naomi's legs and giving her the business while she sends me stern, disapproving looks over her shoulder. Again. I've already given in to that fantasy twice since we shook hands in my kitchen last night. The fact that she's made me surrender to a physical weakness twice, while clearly finding me off-putting, makes me want to rattle her the only way I know how. Being an asshole.

I nod at the wine beneath her arm. "Who the hell is going to drink that?"

Somehow she manages to make an eye twitch look graceful. "As a host, the proper protocol is to invite me into your house, then offer me a glass. Are we going to have a sparring match on your porch every single time I arrive, Mr. Bristow?"

"Jason."

"I'll start calling you Jason when we're on friendly terms."

"Is that the protocol?"

"As a matter of fact, it is."

That censorious pout is the exact one she gives me in my fantasy, which is making things pretty confusing and inconvenient for the man downstairs. "Come in. We're having fish."

"Oh, yay." She looks down at the bottle and does a little dance. "I picked the right wine."

"Fish tastes just fine with beer. Better, even."

"Have you ever tried it with wine?"

"Hell no."

"Then how would you know?" She presses her lips together, and I find myself doing the same, so I won't smile. Why does she suddenly look so excited? Why do I like it? "I have a great idea. Why don't you try a glass of wine and I'll try your beer?"

I'd rather drink piss, but I can't bring myself to say it out loud. One, it's a friendly game, and friendly is where I need to be so she'll call me Jason. Why I give a shit is beyond me. Two, I really want to see this Southern belle drink a Budweiser straight from the bottle. "Done."

Naomi bends a little at the knees and pops back up. "Fun." She blinks those blue eyes at me, and I have to command myself not to lean closer. "Technically, this is a beer drinking contest. Of a sort. Isn't it?" She adds under her breath, "That is definitely not boring."

I feel a frown drag my eyebrows together. "Who told you—"

"Jason," Birdie groans behind me. "Let her in."

Until my sister's interruption, I completely forget Naomi is still standing outside. And as she bypasses me into the house, careful as hell not to touch me with so much as a scrap of fabric, my pulse starts to tick faster. I'm probably just irritated over having to drink wine.

Birdie and Naomi sit in the dining room, while I grab the baked halibut out of the oven and separate portions onto plates, alongside carrots and roasted potatoes. When everything is plated, I squeeze lemon over the top of basically everything and add some salt. I'm definitely no chef. I'm complete shit at cooking, actually. Most nights, I pick up food on the way home from the marina— Italian, sushi, sandwiches. Right now, I might as well be blind-folded with both hands tied behind my back.

Moments later, I search for a reaction when I set the food down in front of Naomi. There's nothing but positivity radiating from her every pore when I know it's probably garbage compared to what she's used to eating. Why am I making that assumption, though? On my return to the kitchen to retrieve a beer, a wine glass and a corkscrew, I remind myself I know next to nothing about Naomi. Maybe I should stop making assumptions.

Naomi eyes the open Bud when I set it down in front of her. "Ladies first."

She flicks me a pointed look. "So you do have manners when it's convenient."

I dig into my dinner instead of answering, noticing Naomi has carefully separated the potatoes from the rest of her meal.

"That's your first beer?" Birdie asks, her attention swinging back and forth between me and her coach. "No way."

"Way." Naomi tilts the bottle to her lips, and I stop chewing, watching her throat move as she swallows. Her eyes squeeze shut and she traps the liquid inside her mouth with a napkin. "Oh Lord, that's terrible." A laugh sneaks out of me, and Birdie almost falls off her chair. "You drink the wine now."

"Will it help you recover if I hate it?"

"Yes."

I sigh through the process of opening the wine and pouring half a glass, then I toss it back in one gulp. Cool, crisp, fruity. Not that I would ever admit this out loud, but apparently people haven't been bullshitting when they claimed white wine goes better with fish. "Want to switch now?"

"You didn't even tell us if you liked it," Naomi sputters as I trade her beer for my refilled wine glass, remaining silent as I perform the task. "You did like it," she gasps, turning to Birdie. "He did, didn't he?"

Birdie laughs into a bite. "Good luck getting him to admit it."

"Oh, I will." She takes a dainty bite of fish. "I've set my mind to it now."

I pick up a potato and toss it into my mouth. "What's this about new sneakers?"

"Subtle subject change by Bristow," laughs my sister, edging her hand toward my beer. I catch her wrist, moving it away, and she continues without missing a beat. "Coach number six is making me exercise."

"Coach number six."

"Right. Because you killed or fired the other five. Just play along."

I take a swig of beer and plop the bottle back down. "They had it coming."

Naomi still hasn't touched her potatoes. "I suppose your boat makes it easy to hide the bodies out at sea." When we just stare at her, she stabs her fork into a carrot. "What? You two can be morbid, but I can't?" She doesn't wait for us to answer. "I noticed your equipment today. Are you a scuba diver, Mr. Bristow?"

Her emphasis on Mr. Bristow is impossible to ignore. If she only knew how hot that teasing formality makes me. "I have a company. We do private, guided dives in St. Augustine. Corporate team building. Vacationing retirees." Naomi sets down her fork, clearly finished, so I drag her plate closer and start eating her potatoes. "I was a master diver with the Army, placed with Special Forces. When I was discharged, I wanted to stay in practice for..."

"For when he goes back," Birdie finishes.

My sister won't look at me, so I'm not sure if she was simply being matter-of-fact or if the numbness I picked up in her tone was real. It has always been the plan for me to redeploy, and she's never expressed discontent over it. Overseas is where I belong. In the end, I just nod and continue. "For when I go back, yeah. After Birdie graduates. My vessel is the one I use for dives. I license the Bristow Diving name out to several instructors in the area, though. About seventeen altogether in the fleet."

"It sounds like you're doing very well."

I am. And I shouldn't like her knowing that so much. "What about you, beauty queen? Have you always been a pageant coach?"

"No, this is my first time." She takes her first sip of wine, sighing with pleasure, and I feel that sound right between my legs. "Officially, anyway. I have mentored some friends."

"What were you doing before you left Charleston to become a coach?"

Birdie lets her fork clatter onto her plate. "God, Jason. She's not a suspected terrorist. Stop with the interrogation."

"Just making conversation."

My sister makes her disagreement obvious with an eye roll. "We'll wait here while you get your polygraph machine hooked up."

"No, it's okay," Naomi breathes, holding up peaceful hands. Looking...alarmed. "It's fine. It's totally natural to be curious. Why, I'm practically a stranger."

The almost-argument rattled Naomi, that much is obvious. There's an ever-so-slight tremor in her fingers, and her coloring has gone from cream to pink. She jumped right into playing peacekeeper like an old pro. Needing to put her at ease, I open my mouth intending to drop the subject, but she keeps going before I get the chance.

"I-I mentioned I needed some time away from Charleston and I meant it. I'm sure it sounds awfully trite, but I'm here to...well, discover what I'm made of, I guess you could say." She's talking directly to Birdie now and that's fine, but I need her attention back soon so I'll know I didn't scare her or something. "I've never been out on my own and I wanted to try it. To see if I even knew how. Isn't that something a woman should know about herself?" She waves a hand. "I kept busy while you were in school today, Birdie, walking around St. Augustine and figuring out what to do while I'm in town. Speaking of beer, did you know there's a brewery in town? They teach a beer making course and I'm taking our little contest tonight as a sign that I should go." She rearranges herself in her chair with a nod. "I'm sure they make beers that won't make me want to buy a new mouth."

"So, you're here for, like, an adventure?" Birdie asks slowly.

"Yes." Naomi reaches over to squeeze Birdie's arm. "Coaching you will be part of the adventure." She winks at my sister, who gives her a genuine but grudging one back. "It's just exciting to spend my free time how I choose."

I'd like to explore that last comment, unfortunately I'm still stuck on the beer-making course. "Where is this brewery? Who's teaching this class?"

"I don't know." She turns and digs around in the purse she left hanging on the back of the chair. "There's a group of young men with adorable mustaches on the flyer—"

A grunt comes straight from my chest. "Let me see it."

Her back straightens at my command and I already know what that means. "No."

"Heard of Google? It won't be hard to find out the information."

"Then I suggest you Google it, Mr. Bristow," she fires back, celebrating the final word with a sip of wine. "Let's talk evening gowns, Birdie…"

If you'd told me six months ago I'd be sitting at a table listening to women debate the merits of strapless versus halter dresses, I would have called you a liar. But hell if the time doesn't fly by while I'm watching Naomi grow more and more animated over the top of my beer, her giggle making my kitchen comfortable instead of functional. A place to dwell instead of a place to eat and get the hell out. An hour passes before I know I've blinked.

I worried she'd be a distraction.

As she deigns to look over at me, though, pursing her beautiful lips to find me studying her probably way too closely, I start to think distraction might have been an understatement.

CHAPTER SIX

ColdCaseCrushers.com
Username: StopJustStop
Question: Are you all off of your NUT? She's probably at a
friend's house.
Or having a nice long think. Try it sometime!!!
This is how rumors start and trails go cold, people. Diversions
provided by nincompoops like you. I'm taking a break. I'll be
offline until further notice. Good. Riddance.

Naomi

I TAP THE quarter against the payphone and play a game with fate. If the coin goes into the slot by itself, I'll call my mother. If it doesn't go in, I can wait until tomorrow. Tap, tap, tap.

When I returned to the motel last night, I used the phone in my room to contact the brewery and sign up for the beer making class. It took me fifteen minutes to walk here from the motel this afternoon, but since I'd allotted a half an hour, now seemed a good a time as any to get this dreaded phone call out of the way. I really don't want to make it. So much so that I'm hopping around like I need to visit the little girls' room. Until this moment, it's been possible to pretend my whole disaster of a wedding day never took place. That it was all a cream-and-navy-colored dream. But it wasn't. And the fallout is probably pacing by the golden-mouthed, ivory-handled antique phone in our grand salon back in Charleston.

One might assume I miss the opulence of my parents' home, but Lord, one couldn't be further from the truth. I would rather be at my motel in all its lacking charm, questionable décor and disreputable clientele. Because I can wear what I want, leave to get food or go shopping without being questioned endlessly. It symbolizes the freedom I didn't have before, and I won't give it up yet. It symbolizes choices.

Speaking to my mother doesn't mean I have to go back to South Carolina. But she will use every tactic at her disposal to try and make it happen. Guilt, tears, threats. I know this from experience. Years of arguments at the dinner table between her and my father, just waiting for her to play the trump card. *You had an affair.* The winner to every argument against my father. Every argument I couldn't mediate successfully, that is. Lord, the pressure to calm everyone down before we reached that point of no return—the affair—was so intense, I used to sit down with talking points in my head. Subjects with which to divert their attention. Jokes. Gossip. I even went through a card trick phase in my teens.

Distracted by memories of the past, the coin falls into the slot.

"Gosh darn it," I mutter, poking the sticky keys until I dial the full number, listening as it begins to ring. "Here goes nothing."

"Clemons residence."

"Hello, Martha." Stunned silence. "Is my mother or father at h—"

"Naomi Elizabeth Clemons."

A chill racks my body, and I step into the sun to combat it. "Hi, Mother."

"That's it? That's all you have to say? Do you have any idea what the last forty-eight hours have been like? Where are you?"

"I'm not in Charleston," I push through stiff lips. "I went south. Kind of like the wedding."

Silence. "Is that supposed to be some kind of joke?"

"No. I'm sorry." Still cold, I turn my face up to the sky and let the sun beat down on me. It helps, the reminder that I'm here in this time and place. Because I chose to be. "I called to apologize. About everything. You worked almost as hard as the wedding planner—"

"No, no. No. I worked much harder. I've been working on this wedding since you were a child. I did my job. Made an advantageous marriage, secured the right connections—the kind of connections that allow you to marry the next mayor. A war hero. The son of my best friend. How dare you walk away from this and leave me to deal with the damage, Naomi? How dare you?"

"He doesn't love me," I whisper. "Can't you see that? Can't everyone?"

A beat passes. "Do you think your father loves me, Naomi? You well know what he did." I can hear her struggling to get a good breath. "The child of his former lover—that Potts girl—had the nerve to show up at the wedding. She drove off with your groom. Do you have any idea the kind of humiliation that caused me? Your father's misdeeds are still fresh in everyone's minds, and trust me, no one missed the irony."

My eyes open only to be blinded by the son. "Elijah left with Addison Potts?"

"Don't you dare say her name to me."

"I'm sorry," I murmur, trying to picture Southern gentleman Elijah with leather-pants-and-smirk-wearing Addison. "Do they…did they know each other before the wedding?"

"Oh, don't worry," huffs my mother. "The tabloids are hard at work trying to find out."

I'm so stunned by the unexpected news, I'm not sure how I feel about it. Elijah and Addison. Day and night. An exciting, spontaneous night so different from my sensible nine o'clock bedtime with a cup of chamomile. They would have interesting conversations, I bet. He wouldn't stare straight through Addison as if she's invisible. He'd look. She'd probably drop his jaw. Am I jealous? Yes. Of course I am. I want Elijah to look at me like that, don't I?

A vision of Jason in his kitchen devouring me with a sweep of hooded eyes catches me off-guard, but I shake it off. What a weird time to think of my employer. I shouldn't be thinking about him at all when he's not around. Not even a fleeting brain wave.

"Maybe they're together now? Maybe…"

My mother's snort punches me in the ear. "Do you hear yourself? If you've learned one lesson from my life, Naomi, it's that we are the wives. Potts girls are nothing more than passing distractions. Eventually men tire of the flash and return to the class. Elijah will be no different." She stops for a moment. Dramatic emphasis, I'm sure of it. "You better be back here when that happens, Naomi. Do you hear me? You get back to Charleston and salvage this for us."

I hang up feeling like I've been pulled through a knot hole backwards. My sensible blue sandals gather dust on my way across the brewery parking lot and I almost forgo wiping them off with a moist towelette before entering. There is a crowd of people in the waiting room, some of them toting cameras, their out of state ball caps signaling their tourist status. I'm the only one who's alone, but right now that's probably a good thing. After the phone call with my mother, I'm unfit company.

You get back to Charleston and salvage this for us.

How long do I have here in St. Augustine before the situation with Elijah becomes…unsalvageable? Birdie's pageant isn't for six weeks. With her inexperience, she's going to need every single one of those days leading up to the competition. But I'm guessing my mother will begin expecting me much sooner than that. Like tomorrow. That expectation sits on my head like a boulder as two young men with goatees in leather aprons guide the medium-sized group out of the waiting room and into a warehouse filled with seven-foot-tall metal tanks. The large distillery room reminds me of a greenhouse with sloping skylights that take up almost the entire roof. It's the sunlight, rumble of machinery and low drone of the guide's speech that calm my fussed phone call nerves.

I'm here now. I'm nowhere else. I'm here because I want to be.

I repeat the impromptu mantra until I'm actually able to pay attention to the mishmash of a history lesson and brewing tutorial.

A third member of the guide crew joins us with a tray of mini-pints, handing them out one by one to the sunburned tourists, including me. I'm meeting Birdie later for a training session, so my plan is to only have a few sips—but I'm pleasantly surprised when the cool liquid kicks up hints of chocolate. Chocolate beer. Who knew such a thing existed? Before I know it, the little glass has vanished and I'm staring down at nothing but droplets.

Another tray is brought out, and this time, I'm definitely going to pass. Until a woman to my right gives me a light elbow in the ribs. "You have to try this one. It's infused with wine."

"Wine? They saw me coming a mile away," I murmur, plucking a glass off the tray and giving the guide a disapproving head tilt when he winks at me. "This is definitely my last one, though."

It's not my last one.

I have two more throughout the tour—one with a black licorice undertone and another, nuttier ale. I can't help it, though. It's too heady a temptation to bask in the sunlight with my new friend, an elbow-happy enabler from Tuscaloosa. It's too easy to let my blood warm, my mind drift further and further from the wreckage I left behind in Charleston. Elijah and Addison. If my mother is right and they hit it off...how do I feel about that?

I decide to have another beer and really dig deep for an answer.

The sting of my mother's phone call eases with every sip of the beverage I always thought I'd hate. What is Jason doing drinking Budweiser when caramel beer exists—

Oh shoot. I picked up a sixth mini-pint, didn't I?

Letting the crisp liquid sit on my tongue as I've been instructed, I can no longer keep thoughts of my employer at bay. It riddles me with guilt even letting him creep into my head, but I know it's only mild curiosity since I've never met anyone like him. Men like Jason have only ever existed for me in action movies. I better have a nap and some coffee before my appointment with Birdie later, because he'd take the utmost pleasure in firing me. When the gigantic fellow hired me, he looked like he was spitting nails. No, Jason doesn't strike me as a forgiving man.

Not like Elijah.

As the son of Charleston's longest sitting mayor, Elijah was occasionally approached in the street by those who opposed his father's politics. They weren't always friendly, either. No, they could be downright insulting toward Elijah. But he never lost his temper and always took the time to patiently address their concerns. One such occasion took place while we were on a dinner date. A volunteer at a local community pool had been applying for funding to reopen for several years and continued to be rejected. Meanwhile a *new* community center was being built in a more affluent neighborhood.

A month later, I was watching the news and a segment came on, proclaiming the closed community center was once again opening its doors, thanks to intervention from the mayor. Elijah never once took credit, but I knew he'd run interference.

Most women wouldn't have a chance in hell of gaining a man's forgiveness for leaving them at the altar, but my fiancé is…was? A very compassionate person who puts very little stock in public perception.

My mother is right. It is possible to make what I did right. I'm just not ready yet. I've embarked on exactly one expedition of self-discovery and it has only led to me feeling wobbly on my stool. I'm capable of surviving one day on my own. Whoopeedoo.

"Naomi, isn't it?" The main tour guide—Keith, I believe—brings my head up, as I've been staring into my empty glass once again. "Why don't you come on up here and stir the barley."

"Me?" I clunk down my glass, acutely aware of my tipsy state now that everyone is looking at me. "Why, sure…"

I walk to the front of the room and hop up onto the crate indicated by Keith. He drops a leather apron over my head and almost knocks me off balance, but I recover, returning a thumbs up from the Elbow Queen of Tuscaloosa. I'm handed a large wooden paddle roughly the same size as an oar and begin stirring the contents of a steel turbine. The clockwise circling of liquid and barley is so hypnotic, I don't realize right away that Keith has joined me on the crate. A quick glance over my shoulder tells me he's at the borderline of being too close, but I don't want to interrupt him while he's addressing the room, so I keep stirring. When his body heat moves closer, though, I start to weigh the merits of clocking him with the paddle. A thought that makes me giggle.

Keith's warm breath tickles my ear. "Care to share the joke—"

Hands clasp me around the waist and I'm lifted off the crate, my feet dangling in midair until they land on the ground. At first, I think it's Keith manhandling me, and I freeze in shock, but I twist around to find—Jason?

"What are you doing here?"

My question emerges sounding more like What'reyoudoon—here?

Not that Jason notices. He's too busy glaring at Keith.

And now that I've been discovered drunk in the middle of the afternoon on a workday, I'm too busy wondering if my new boss will make a big or small scene while firing me.

CHAPTER SEVEN

EndoftheInternet.net
Username: IGotAnswerz9
Let me be plain. The only one with a motive the kill was the ex-fiancé.
He's not even trying to hide his "new" lover. Case closed.

Jason

WHAT THE HELL am I doing here?

It's not normal behavior to ignore a startled receptionist and waltz into a tour-in-progress, like the rules don't apply to me. But to my mind…they don't. I've been back on US soil for six months and still, the world around me doesn't make sense. Rules seem arbitrary. I don't want my sister's pageant coach drinking beer with other men, so here I am to collect her. There. Done. Special Forces has conditioned me to follow gut feelings—red tape be damned. Once you've set explosives in the desert or slipped silently into the ocean and swum five miles in the pitch black to do recon, a flimsy gate that says *next tour at four o'clock* is laughable.

I don't have answers to the questions that are sure to follow, though. Naomi is looking up at me with clear confusion. The whole room is staring at me the same way, in fact, and it's making the back of my neck sweat, little winks of light going off in front of my eyes. How many times have I told myself to stop acting without thinking? Is this how a civilian behaves? Is this behavior out of the ordinary? Those are the questions I'm supposed to ask myself.

I'm not supposed to cancel a lucrative, corporate personnel dive at the last minute and drive like a bat out of hell across town to put a claim on a woman who hasn't asked for it. Hell, I don't want to claim her. Do I? My blood is pumping hot, my pulse shaking like a pissed off rattlesnake from seeing the guide standing too close. I barely know the first thing about Naomi.

Still.

What I do know is she's...gorgeous. So fucking gorgeous and sexy in this afternoon sunshine, her eyes a little glassy from the beer she's definitely been drinking. Nothing can detract from the stunning cornflower coloring of them, though. They match her coordinated outfit, starting with the T-shirt-looking dress and ending at her shoes. As usual, her hair is pulled back in a smooth ponytail, and my fingers itch to loosen the knot, let it fall into my palms. Drag it down my lap while she gasps at the growing sight of me.

Much as I'd like this attraction to begin and end with a chemical reaction, it doesn't. I liked having her at my dinner table last night. Liked it way too much. She spun some kind of magic and made me forget for a couple hours that those four walls are missing parents and a sister. That nothing is the same as I remember it and I don't have battle to escape into. Her laughter made it okay not to dwell on the wrong last night. Made things feel okay.

Better than okay.

But this? Me showing up here uninvited is not normal. I can't just stand here in front of the crowded room and stare at this woman, but it's what I do, despite the whispering. Despite the hushed conference between guide and receptionist happening at the entrance. Rules and correct behaviors are lost on me, and I don't know how to get them back. I just know I don't want this woman here right now. Most of the time when this sense of not belonging strikes, I can laugh my way out of it. Or walk away pretending I don't give a damn. I do what I want. Deal with it.

Sometimes I can't, though. Like when I wake from a nightmare and the only way to calm down is to sprint full speed along the water, passing motorists watching me with startled faces through their windshields. Or right now, when I've just barged into a room where I don't belong and Naomi is looking at me with…not horror anymore. She seems more thoughtful than anything, her attention straying to my balled-up fists, the sweat on my upper lip.

Before I can define her expression, she steps closer and takes my fist in her hand. And it's like dropping from the highest point of a roller coaster.

"Everyone, this is my friend Jason. I wasn't sure he was going to make it." She faces the entrance, her face breaking into a wide smile. "Could we sort out his admission fee once the tour is over? I swear on a stack of Bibles he's good for it."

The guide and receptionist exchange a blank look. "Sure," says the guide, signaling his crony who was standing too close to Naomi when I arrived. "Go ahead and get back to it, Keith."

Fucking Keith.

I commit the name to memory, but I'm distracted by Naomi turning her pretty, apple pie and Cool Whip smile on me. Some reflex has me taking my hand back and crossing my arms over my chest. I don't need someone to cover for me—and I let her know it with a look. It makes a dent in her smile, and when she moves past me, giving me wide berth, I wish she was still holding my hand.

In silence, I follow her to the end of a long, wooden table littered with empty glasses and stand behind the stool where she perches herself, crossing those legs tight tight tight. Pink lipstick marks on five of the beer glasses proclaim Naomi as their owner, and I have to admit I'm surprised. After she cringed over a sip of Bud, I didn't think she'd make it through the full tour.

Naomi tucks hair behind her ear and whispers at me over her shoulder. "You can sit, you know."

"I'll stand."

However, I do move closer to her side so I can get a front row seat to her pout. "Fine," she murmurs, watching me. "If you want to make everybody nervous."

I toss a glance at the other members of the tour who are all in varying stages of drunkenness. Whether I liked Naomi covering for me or not, it worked. They already seem to have moved on from my odd entrance. "You're the only one who seems nervous."

"Well I've never been fired before."

"Fired?"

She hiccups and her cheeks go pink. "I'm drunk on a workday. I didn't intend to be, but how was I supposed to know they made wine beer?"

"First of all, that's disgusting—"

"Liar. You're a wine-liking liar. I feel comfortable saying that since I'm fired."

My sigh moves some of the finer hairs on her forehead, a clue that I've moved closer without realizing. "You're not fired, beauty queen."

"Isn't that why you came here? To catch me in my cups?"

She's unintentionally given me an out—no way I'm not taking it. "Yeah, but just for fun. So I could hold it over your head."

"You have a weird idea of fun." She breathes in and slumps a little—which is a whole hell of a lot for this woman. "I probably would have been able to stop at one, but I had a phone call with my mother."

I go still. I've been unsuccessful during our first three meetings to get anything out of Naomi. Apart from her pageant titles and zip code, she remains a complete mystery. I feel almost guilty taking this chance to find out more, since she isn't the textbook definition of sober, but I might not get another opportunity like this, and dammit, my curiosity is growing by the minute. "Oh yeah?" I take a glass of beer off a nearby tray and sniff it, drain it, almost spit it out when it tastes like chocolate. "It didn't go well?"

Naomi catches the chocolate-inflicted suffering in my tone and presses her lips together. "Sticking with Budweiser?"

"I'll never stray again." I stab the table with a finger. "Phone call. Go."

I've learned she doesn't like taking orders from me, but she seems to have drowned that aversion with beer, because she doesn't hesitate to continue. "I bet you think girls walking around with books on their heads only exists in old movies, don't you? Not true. I got so good at balancing *Moby Dick*, I used to forget it was there."

It's a testament to my curiosity that I completely forgo a dick joke. "What does this have to do with your mother?"

A man in an Orioles hat turns to tell us to be quiet but thinks twice about it when I give him a dark look. "Because she's three hundred miles away and I can feel the whale on my head right now."

I swallow the urge to guide my hand over the crown of her head. To let her know there's nothing there. "She puts pressure on you," I say quietly. "Why? About what?"

"Decisions I've made."

"You don't seem the type to make bad decisions."

"I almost walked in here with dusty shoes."

"Well, call the goddamn firing squad."

She laughs into her wrist and something heavy moves in my stomach. "You seem like you're feeling better."

That catches me off-guard. "Who said I wasn't feeling fine?"

"You had the shaky sweats when you blew in here." I'm still trying to decide how to feel about her noticing my weakness and pointing it out—pissed off or less pissed off—when she lays a hand on my shoulder. "My granddaddy used to get the shaky sweats and the only thing that helped was telling war stories. Isn't that ironic? I remember them all like the back of my hand. Do you want to stop trying to scowl me to death so I can tell you one?"

"I'm fine now," I rasp.

"But you weren't fine before and the first step is admitting it." She tucks her hands under her chin and blinks innocently. As if she isn't the first person who's ever been brave enough to call me on...anything. I should get in her face and tell her to back off. Instead, I just stand there staring at her tempting, bow-lipped mouth, waiting for more words to come out. "Let's go with the First Battle of Bull Run—it was the first major battle of the Civil War and it resulted in Stonewall Jackson earning his nickname—"

"Could you please speak a little louder?" Orioles cap stage whispers from down the table. "I want to hear this."

Turns out, so does everyone else. Thirty seconds into the recitation of the battle facts, everyone has turned to face my sister's pageant coach, beers poised in front of their mouths, and Keith is watching her with a dreamy smile, obviously more than happy to be interrupted. I have to grip the edge of the table to keep from snatching Naomi up and taking her to a quiet corner, so I can have the story—and her—all to myself. In the end, though, I just want her to keep going. I'm interested in hearing every last detail. And damn, she's even more beautiful when she's excited. There's a peachy flush on her cheeks from having everyone's undivided attention and being wrapped up in the story herself, although she seems surprised when she finally comes up for air and finds everyone watching in rapt silence.

"'There is Jackson standing like a stone wall. Let us determine to die here, and we will conquer. Rally behind the Virginians.' Brigadier General Bee said that first part about Jackson—that's where he got the nickname." Naomi takes my chocolate beer and drains the reminder of it. "His pep talk didn't really make sense, though, did it? Unfortunately, he was shot through the stomach right after and died the next day. So no one really knows what he meant. Maybe he didn't even know." She stares down at the empty glass. "Did I just drink this?"

"Time to go." I pluck the glass from her hand and set it on the table. "Come on, beauty queen. You're going home."

She's about to protest but thinks better of it. "That's probably for the best." I catch her elbow as she slides off the stool, throwing off her balance with a wave at her adoring crowd. "It was lovely spending the afternoon with all of you. My favorite was the wine beer. What was all of your favorites—"

"You're not finding out today," I say, guiding her to the exit.

"Oh." She gives another flutter-fingered wave. "Next time, then!"

"Bye, Naomi," they chorus as one.

Keith's voice reaches us as we walk out the door. "Storytelling gets you a discount next time you come back. How about Friday—"

I smack the door shut behind us, cutting him off.

We settle up my admission ticket at the front desk, the receptionist still clearly miffed that I didn't respect her authority. Naomi gets her smiling in no time, though, leading to a longer conversation about local boutiques, and it's another fifteen minutes before I get Naomi to my truck. She stops just short of climbing into the passenger side. "Oh, no. Thank you for the offer, Mr. Bristow—"

"Jason."

"But I think a walk sounds lovely."

"Get in."

"That's okay," she says breezily.

My eyes narrow. "Are you nervous about getting into the car with me?"

A hand flies to her throat. "No, of course not. It's just...oh, now you're just making me feel impolite." With a grumble, she climbs into the car and engages her seat belt with a dainty hand. "Happy now?"

I leave her with my grunt and circle to the driver's side, but something still isn't right. For one, Naomi is tense as all get out. Her knees are going to pop if she presses them together any harder. Palms rake nervously up and down her thighs, which is pretty fucking distracting, considering she's wearing a T-shirt for a dress and it's leaving those endless, tanned thighs exposed. The kind of thighs one associates with pristine, white tennis skirts. *Enough with those thoughts.* She's nervous driving with me for some reason, the least I can do is not fantasize about fucking her, now that she's trusted me enough to get in the truck.

The farther we drive, the less I require a distraction for my lecherous thoughts. The route we take absorbs all of my focus. We drive well out of the downtown area in the direction of the interstate. We're on the edge of town when chain motels begin to appear, which I sure as hell don't turn my nose up at, but they grow more and more rundown with every passing block. That's when my jaw starts to bunch, along with my gut. "Beauty queen…"

"Right here is good." She points to the sidewalk of the deserted road and shoulders her purse. "This is perfect, thank you. I can walk the rest of the way."

"You don't want me to see where you're staying." Those bolts in my stomach tighten all the more. "That's why you didn't want to get in the truck."

"I'm proud of my accommodations, but I know you'll want to ask me questions, and…" She bottoms out with a gusty sigh. "I've had too much beer to be cagey. It's just ahead on the right. The Budget Max."

"Jesus Christ." After pulling into the parking lot, I cut off the truck's engine and look around. Peeling paint. Unmarked doors. A sign advertising hourly rates. There isn't a fucking chance I'm leaving Naomi here—but hell if she doesn't already have a defensive chin raise thing going on. It makes me want to drag her across the console and lay bites on that jawline until it goes slack. "I've slept in war zones nicer than this," I mutter, my hands flexing on the steering wheel. "We're about to be neighbors, baby."

"Pardon me?"

"I'd rather saw my arm off than leave you here." I shove open my door and climb out. "Let's go get your shit."

"What?"

She hops out and I spring into action to cover her, my heart clamoring up into my throat. *Fuck. Calm down. Calm down.* There's no immediate threat. I'm in Florida, not Afghanistan.

Talking myself down only helps partially, though. And hell, maybe there is an immediate threat. Her name is Naomi and she looks ready to tear a strip off my ass. Beating her to the first word is the only offense I have.

"Mr. Bristow—"

"Jason. I'm Jason. You're Naomi and..." I'm out of practice being sincere, so it takes me a lot of throat cleaning to continue. "You're going through something and I want to help." My words take some of the fight out of Naomi. "I need to help," I finish quietly.

Her head tips to one side. "Why?"

The truth is not an option here. There's something about this woman that raises the bar on my protective nature. I get jealous thinking of her with other men. I'm attracted to her like crazy. Fuck it, I like her, even when we're taking swipes at each other. She comes off like an ice princess. Then before I can blink she's soft and kind of silly. Getting drunk in the middle of the afternoon and telling war stories. There's something about her. There's a lot about her. But there isn't a chance in hell I'm telling her any of that.

If this afternoon reminded me of anything, it's that normalcy still escapes me. My sense of propriety and social cues haven't returned and they probably never will. Especially since I'm planning to reenlist when Birdie is graduated and independent. Naomi is the epitome of social grace. She's coaching my sister on how to charm, how to be diplomatic. We're like chalk and cheese—which is a moot point, since she's shown no signs of interest in me.

Better to go with a slightly different version of the truth. A valid truth. One that leaves out the fact that I need her where I can see her...because she makes me feel things.

"I was overseas for a long time. I haven't really been able to turn off how I lived. How I operated. I've got all these signs when it comes to you, beauty queen. You changing in your car, living in a rundown motel a long way from home when you clearly come from some kind of money. You don't want to be found. Something is wrong and I don't know how to leave your safety to chance. What I know how to do is fix and protect and prevent bad things from happening."

Unsure if I want to see how my blind stab at sincerity landed, I tip my head back and squint into the sun. "Can you please just let me do that?"

I don't realize she's come closer until she murmurs, "Where would I...reside, exactly?"

The softening of her voice, her nearness, knits a tight pattern at the back of my neck. "There's a guesthouse above the garage. Nothing fancy, but it beats the hell out of this."

"That is so kind of you, but I like being on my own. I like being able to make my own decisions." She reaches out and squeezes my hand. "Thank you for the offer, but no."

"Plan B it is."

Before she can question me, I've thrown her over my shoulder. "Which room?"

"Mr. Bristow!"

"Jason. Which room? You've got three seconds to tell me before I start kicking in doors."

"This is outrageous!"

"Three, two..."

"Second floor. The one in the corner! There's a potted plant. O-or there was before it died...some time ago, by the look of it."

I head for the staircase. "You tried watering it, didn't you?"

"I am not having a conversation about horticulture while

you're carrying me over your shoulder, Blackbeard." Her ribcage expands on a huff against my shoulder. "Did you even mean that whole speech about wanting to fix and protect or—"

"Don't say things I don't mean."

"You lied about disliking my Sauvignon Blanc," she grumbles.

"Is that what it's called?"

"Yes. It's my favorite. I never order anything else. Ever." For some reason, talking about her choice in drink seems to be upsetting her. Even more than me carrying her over my shoulder like the fucking lawless ogre that I am.

Getting her to the top of the stairs costs me no effort—until she starts to wiggle. Holding on to her is the easy part. It's ignoring the way her sexy backside shifts under the thin cotton of her dress that drops the hammer in my pants. It takes a single instant for my throat to grow dry as dust. My hands, which were holding the backs of her thighs to keep her steady on the upstairs trek, are now fighting with the hem of her dress. To keep it down. What I'd really like to do is lift the airy, blue thing to her waist and run my palms over the smooth hills of her ass cheeks. I bet she wears no-nonsense, white cotton panties, just waiting to be torn off in my bare hands. Bet she'd gasp and press those thighs together to hide her pussy.

I bite back a groan when we reach her door. She's still shifting around, trying to get down, and I let her slide off now, steadying her in front of me. Those blue eyes are spitting fire and she's preparing to unload on me when she stops. She stops, clearly interpreting the unchecked hunger on my face. It has been there since she showed up on my doorstep and grown in power every time I've been in her company. Now we're standing outside a motel room in a clandestine part of town, and that alone calls sex to the stage. The thought of it. The possibility of it. And Naomi is thinking about it now. With me. Can't tell if she finds the idea off-putting or appealing, but at least I have her looking at my mouth, my chest, my hands, which have moved of their own volition to grip her elbows.

"You want to be kissed, beauty queen?"

A sound wells up in her throat. "I don't know," she breathes, letting me ease her toward the door. "I-I'm supposed to be mad."

"We can work on that." I drop my mouth to the curve of her neck, letting her feel my breath, a hint of my teeth. "Or you can stay mad. Call me every name in the book if it'll help you stay a good girl afterward."

Her heavy-lidded eyes fly to mine. "Are we still talking about kissing?"

I suck the smooth skin of her neck into my mouth, growling as she sobs and falls against the door. "What do you think?"

Need to get Naomi into the room. Now. I'm too distracted by her taste to keep her safe out here in the open. No cover. Without taking my mouth off her neck, I reach into her purse and close my hand around a key, sliding it into the rusted, brass lock. One wrist flick and we're inside, Naomi flattened against me as I walk us backwards. It goes against my nature to enter a room without searching for threats, though, so as I drag my mouth toward hers, already anticipating the kiss I need more than life right now, I scan the room.

And find a wedding dress hanging in the open closet.

"What the fuck is that?"

CHAPTER EIGHT

ReadtheComments.com
Username: LittleMissMorbid
So, okay. Guys. Not trying to be weird or whatever. At all.
But has anyone explored the possibility that Runaway Bride
was actually sacrificed in a pagan ritual by her bridesmaids?

Naomi

WHAT IS...WHAT IN the world...is happening?

When I was a child, my mean cousins on my mother's side used to blindfold me and spin me around, laughing as they watched me bump into walls. Of course, they were perfect angels as soon as the adults walked back into the room. Ma'am this, sir that. As the youngest cousin, it was explained to me that a fair amount of hazing was par for the course. As an adult now, I recognize what a load of horse hockey it was—and those cousins are still mean as snakes.

Right now, I may as well have been blindfolded and dropped into the spinning teacups at Disneyworld. I've never vacillated between so many emotions in such a short period of time. During the truck ride, I was nervous about Jason seeing my motel. Then I was touched at his open honesty. Ticked off when he tossed me over his shoulder like a sack of laundry. And then...and then I...I don't know what I was.

Was his mouth really on my neck?

Why am I shivering?

It's likely that I'm cold because Jason's body heat is no longer up against mine. I've barely had a chance to process his question—*what the (f word) is that?*—before he's moved past me to the closet, leaving me shaking in the patch of sunlight projected by the window. My stomach sinks down into my sandals when I realize what he's seeing.

My wedding dress is hanging there like a ghost in the Haunted Mansion ride.

Why am I relating everything to Disneyworld?

"Naomi."

"I know."

"You know what?"

"I know it's a wedding dress and you're wondering about it."

He turns with a raised eyebrow. "Thanks for the breakdown."

Oh Lord. I almost kissed Jason, didn't I? His mouth did something rather indecent and, fine, pretty delicious to my neck. All of it was leading somewhere, In a way that I didn't plan or anticipate. My brain wasn't even in control. But common sense is back behind the wheel now and screeching its outrage at me. Rightly so. Am I really so fickle a woman that I could intend to marry one man, then kiss an entirely new one three days later?

No. No, I'm not fickle. I love and respect Elijah Montgomery DuPont. He's a good man. The best man for me. We have the same interests, our families go back generations, we already bought furniture for our home. I chose my meditation room so it would overlook the water. Plans have been made. Yes, my cold feet and impulsive decisions put everything on hold. Maybe when all is said and done, I'll have no chance of getting Elijah back. But I will try. I have no choice, if I ever want to be accepted into the family fold again.

"I fled my own wedding," I rasp—and it sounds so much worse when I say it out loud. My legs give way and I drop onto the edge of the bed, the weight of what I did finally sinking in. Hard. "Everyone I've known since childhood was there, a year of planning and meetings and tastings…and I wrote a note and escaped down the back staircase."

So much silence passes, I have to glance over to make sure Jason didn't teleport from the room. But here's there, all right. Tall, wide, imposing. Intense. Nothing moves apart from a ticking muscle along his bristled jawline. "When?"

"Saturday."

"*Three days ago?*" He points a lethal-looking finger at the wedding dress. "Were you changing out of this in front of my house?"

"Well, I could have worn it, but that would have been an awkward interview."

More jawline ticking. "Not really feeling the jokes right now."

"Sorry." I tighten my ponytail with a brutal tug. "I just knew if I stopped moving before I found a place to stay and a job to sustain me…if I stopped and thought about what I'd done, reality would hit and I'd realize I made a huge mistake and go back to Charleston."

A beat passes. "Was it a mistake?" The room is eerily still. "Do you wish you'd gone through with the wedding?"

"Yes. And no."

He laughs without any trace of humor. "Let's talk about the yes first. Because if this closet door had been closed, we'd be rounding third base on this fucking bed right now, beauty queen, and we both know it."

"Thank goodness the door was open then, because I don't associate with men who use terms like *third base*. And *fucking*." I shoot to my feet in a burst of frustration. "Are you happy now, Mr. Bristow? You got me to say *fuck*."

"Do I look happy?"

"Do you ever?"

His chest expands on a measured breath. I can almost hear him mentally counting to ten and am pleased to be the cause. If only so I can take a moment to square up and prepare for our next round. Although why I am going rounds with this man at all is beyond me. We don't owe each other anything, do we? Why does it feel like we do? When his mouth was on my neck, I can't deny there was a moment of me thinking...finally. As if some subconscious part of me had expected to find myself in his arms. But that's crazy, isn't it? He's mean and vulgar and nothing like men I've admired in the past.

"Explain what happened."

Oh. Oh wow. I needed this. I needed to voice everything out loud to another human being. So badly that the truth comes barreling out like monkeys escaping from the zoo. "I was standing there in my perfect dress, poised to enter optimal stain-glass lighting—"

"You just lost me."

"I couldn't get married. I've never been tested or tried. I'm so lacking in experience and mettle and strength. I'm boring. I'm not ready to be a wife to Elijah when I haven't even lived. Who am I offering him? I don't even know the girl who would have recited her vows." I roll my lips together. "And then I saw her coming up the steps of the church. My cousin, Addison. My father had an affair over two decades ago, but gosh, it might as well have happened yesterday. Addison is the daughter of the woman my father strayed with. The family turned their backs on Addison's mother. Addison, too. But I've never seen anyone so full of…everything. She's lived. She's been tested. I needed that. I need to live. To learn what I can do myself. Otherwise I have no idea what I'm bringing to a marriage.

"My mother has brought up my father's affair every single day since it happened. We're the wives. Girls like Addison and *her* mother are just distractions. She used to say that to me, over and over, before I was old enough to even understand." I shake my head. "I think some part of me believed my mother's nonsense about us being only wife material until I saw Addison. I believed wife material was the goal. But…can't I be a wife *and* a distraction? Can't *she*?" I turn to Jason and find him watching me with shadows in his eyes. "I don't want to be boxed and tied up with a bow."

The silence stretches. "What is your plan?"

"Spend some time learning me. Just…being." I lift a shoulder and let it drop. "Maybe when I go back, Elijah won't look right through me. I have to try, don't I?"

It doesn't feel right, confiding that last part to Jason. Which is why I force myself to say it. The reaction Jason stirs in me is confusing and I can't allow it to continue. It's wrong when such a short time ago, I was pledged to someone else. And could be again in the future.

"You'll go back to him when this is all over."

The question is delivered in such a flat tone, I'm not sure it's a question. Even if it was, it doesn't feel right answering in the affirmative with Jason watching me. So I stay silent and let him interpret my answer. Yes. I can't escape my reality forever.

Jason's hands flex at his sides. "You can come and go as you please just as easily from our place. I won't get in your way." His voice sounds rusted as he drags out the suitcase from under the motel bed, tossing it onto the mattress. "Let me know when you're done packing and I'll carry it down."

With that, he leaves the room, closing the door behind him.

And I'm surprised to find the finality of that click scares me a little.

JASON AND I do not speak on the ride home.

We do not speak as he carries my suitcase up the stairs attached to his garage, where the boat seems to sit in quiet judgment. Or when I walk into the medium-sized studio behind him, carrying the wedding dress of doom over one arm. He leaves my things beside a full-size bed and returns a few minutes later with linens and some towels, setting them on the counter of a small eat-in kitchen with an off-handed grunt.

There was tension between Jason and me from the beginning and I've never understood it, so I'm not going to try now. He's a complicated man with control issues. I've simply been lucky enough to land in his perceived jurisdiction. Enough said.

He rubs a hand along the back of his neck, nods and stomps from the studio, leaving me standing alone among the dust motes and scent of pine air freshener.

I pace to the window just in time to catch him entering the house, the door rattling on its hinges when he slams it behind him. Without a command from my brain, I pick up my right foot and stomp it down hard, a headache creeping in through the back of my skull.

All right, maybe I'll try and unpack the reason for the tension between Jason and me just a *little* before I unpack my suitcase.

Crazy as it seems, I think maybe Jason wants to have sex with me. Might as well lay it out there bluntly. I might be unaccustomed to mating rituals of the super alpha, but after his reaction to finding out I recently belonged to another man—and very well could again—there's no denying his...attraction. I can only assume he finds it unacceptable that I'm not simpering at his feet, grateful for crumbs of attention from the almighty war god.

Listening to my brain lie to itself, I slump down into the single kitchen chair. I remember how he froze up at the beer tour, visibly incapable of explaining his hasty entrance. I remember him outside of the motel, asking me to let him protect me. Jason Bristow isn't the kind of man who accepts attention from a woman as his due. But it's possible he wants mine—and I'm not free to give it to him.

Where would it lead anyway? I'm a Charleston girl. This is only my temporary home. Based on what Birdie said at dinner the other night, this isn't Jason's permanent home, either. He's being deployed once Birdie graduates high school. St. Augustine is only a detour.

A knock on the door brings me hopping to my feet. "Yes?"

"You naked in there?" Birdie calls back.

The tightness leaks out of my muscles, leaving me slumped against the table. "No, I'm decent. Please come in."

Birdie slides in on a pair of striped socks, a backpack slung over one shoulder. "We're officially shacked up, I hear."

"Yes, it's been quite a day." I chew my lip. "Does it bother you? Me staying here?"

"No, I'm just surprised." She hops up onto the kitchen counter. "I kind of pictured you staying somewhere way nicer than this. Ocean view. Room service."

"There was free coffee in the lobby."

"We have free coffee, too, but you have to make it before Jason gets there." She shudders. "He makes it way too strong."

"That doesn't sound like him."

"Your sarcasm is duly noted." She seems to be thinking something over, her mouth moving in time with her thoughts. "Is everything okay? Jason was even less of a sparkling conversationalist than usual when I got home."

"Yes, everything is fine." I press two fingers to my forehead, trying to massage away the mounting ache. "But would you mind if we skipped the run today? I'm not going to lie to you, Birdie, I discovered wine-and chocolate-flavored beer today and everything went downhill from there in deplorable fashion."

That surprises a laugh out of her. "And that downhill slide included my brother clubbing you over the head and dragging you home?"

"You're not far off."

Birdie's ankle starts to jiggle. "I know my brother comes off like an indestructible badass—that's because he is. Being home has been hard on him because of it. It's like throwing the Terminator into a knitting circle. He's out of his element just walking down the street. Now he's obligated to play my babysitter, too."

Picturing Jason looking for danger on a perfectly peaceful street, my heart gives a heavy thud. "You're way more than a simple obligation." She seems skeptical—and also like she wants the subject closed. "Anyway, what does your brother's condition have to do with me?"

She shrugs. "Once he decides you're in his keeping, you get the full Jason."

This is where I should point out that I didn't ask to be in anyone's keeping and I'm just fine on my own, thank you very much. But I manage to keep it to myself. It's not that hard, actually, because I'm nursing a little bubble of sympathy for the man who wasn't physically capable of leaving me at the broken-down motel. "Is he in the habit of collecting strays?"

"Nope. Just the two in this room." She slides off the counter and removes a notebook from her backpack, flipping it open and dropping it on the kitchen table in front of me. Bold, slanting letters are tangled up with rough sketches of dresses, shoes, crowns. It's a work of art that reminds me a lot of Birdie herself. Kind of chaotic at a glance, but smart and focused if you pay attention. "I had some extra time in study hall today and I spent it writing down my pageant vision, like you asked. I figure you'll be able to whip my walk into shape and get me ready for the question and answer round, but I'm stuck on one minor part."

"Which is?"

"I have no talent for the talent portion."

"Um. Excuse me. You certainly do." I pick up the notebook and turn it her way. "I can't even draw stick figures. These dresses you've drawn could have come from the mind of a professional designer."

Birdie snorts. "Doubtful. But either way, it's not like I can draw on stage." She blows out a breath. "Anyway, that wasn't really Natalie's style. She would have done something more traditional like singing or dancing."

"Can you sing?"

Red appears on her cheeks. Likely feeling that rise in color on her face, she paces away, feigning fascination with the wall. "I don't know. I've never sung in front of anyone before."

"Not even Natalie?"

"No. I was more of the listener. Not that I minded," she rushes to add. "You're not going to ask me to sing right now, are you? That would be on par with jogging—on broken glass."

Lord, I really like this girl. I don't know if we have enough time to ensure she wins the pageant, but I'm going to do everything possible to see she does well. No more daytime beer drinking. I'm not sure there was anything adventurous about that anyway. I'm still the same predictable Naomi. No matter, though. I'll start small and work my way up. "I was once told by a pageant coach that when I sing, wine turns back into water. She called my voice the anti-miracle."

"Harsh."

"You don't know the half. She used to follow me around with a tape to check my measurements. If she was feeling particularly mean, she'd wait until after lunch."

The younger girl pulls a face. "What a bitch."

A surprised giggle tumbles out of my mouth. "Language." I wait until I can talk without laughing. "How about I start singing and you join in when you're comfortable?"

She covers her face with her hands, dropping them a moment later. "Oh God. Fine."

I stand up and clasp my hands in front of my waist. If I wasn't still nursing a tiny buzz from the beer, I might be more self-conscious. As it is, though, I've had a terrible phone call with my mother today, sipped past my limit and been almost kissed by Jason. A little laughter at my expense won't hurt. And laugh she does. As soon as the butchered beginning note of "America the Beautiful" leaves my mouth, she doubles over with laughter and I snort on the word *spacious*.

Birdie lets me get almost to the middle of the song before she adds her voice to the mix.

She's as terrible as I am.

I drop into the kitchen chair and she plops onto the ground, both of us holding our sides to contain the mirth. She seems almost surprised to be laughing at all, and it's probably the beer, but for some reason her astonishment sends me over the edge. "You didn't even know you were that bad. I could tell."

"Jesus Christ." She wipes her eyes. "I should have left it a mystery."

"We'll go with a waltz."

Until Birdie flops back on the floor, I don't notice the imposing figure standing in the doorway. It's Jason. I have no idea how long he's been watching us, but it's impossible to read his expression. But I do notice the lines around his mouth seem deeper than they did this afternoon and that observation causes my amusement to die a quick death.

"Dinner's in an hour." He cuts me a bland look. "You coming?"

I want to go. I had fun the last time. Real fun. That's precisely why I shouldn't accept dinner invitations, I think. My mission in St. Augustine is to learn to do, to live, for myself, before I return to the life of duty of tradition I've been groomed for since birth. I can't help but worry that getting too close to Jason and Birdie might make accepting that role difficult. There needs to be some part of myself I hold back.

"Thank you for the offer, but I think I'll spend the night getting situated." I splay my fingers over the surface of Birdie's notebook. "May I keep this for the night?"

Birdie splits a look between me and her brother as she rises to her feet. "Sure." She takes a step toward the door. "See you tomorrow?"

"Count on it."

Jason remains in the doorway for a few beats after Birdie bypasses him, watching me with shadowed eyes before leaving. A while later, there's a knock at my door. When I go to answer it, there's a plate covered with foil sitting on the top step. And a Budweiser.

CHAPTER NINE

ConspiracyCrowd.org
Username: IWant2Believe2000
Runaway Bride's alien abductor was probably a guest at
the wedding.
They operate in plain sight. They are MASTER deceivers.

Jason

I STAND AT the kitchen sink with a beer in my hand, looking for signs of life in Naomi's apartment. Nothing. She and Birdie don't share their rehearsal schedule with me—I just shell out the cash—but since my sister isn't here, I'm pretty sure she's practicing with her coach.

I'm not sure what's worse. Having the beauty queen living above the garage and not seeing her. Or having her live in a dump and bumping into her constantly. Both of those arrangements have their drawbacks. For instance, it has been over a week since we've made eye contact and I'm growing more irritable by the day. I wasn't the only one interested in that kiss. Was I? Did I push too hard like I do with everything else and now she's nervous around me?

That's the worry that has burrowed under my skin since the night she moved in. Forcibly. My style of solving problems is abrasive. Cut and dried logic. The fastest way from point A to B. But I can't expect other people to see my solutions the same way.

I can't expect Naomi to understand that leaving her in an unsecured location would have cost me sleep.

Right. As if I'm sleeping.

Every time I close my eyes, I taste her neck. I haven't been to a lot of exotic places on vacation, but those hints of blood orange and cedar and grapefruit on her neck make me think of boats on a pond, big trees full of flowers. I can see her in a beach house with loose bracelets tinkling together on her wrist. A glass of wine in her hand. And a tuxedoed gentleman to fetch her another one before she even finishes the first. Someone who knows how to make her comfortable and engage her in a normal, non-antagonistic conversation.

Someone with class.

Motherfucker. I should never have performed that internet search.

As if the weird conspiracy theory sites speculating on Naomi's whereabouts weren't bad enough…I can put a face to her ex-fiancé now. All it took was their wedding announcement to know the score. Naomi Clemons, of the Charleston Clemonses, had been preparing to marry the goddamn future mayor. A millionaire with an honorable service history, even if he didn't see the kind of brutal conditions and combat I've been involved in. Very few men have, though. That's why it's impossible for me to forget that kill-or-be-killed battles are taking place now. Now. At any given moment. And I'm standing here drinking a beer, thinking about the neck of a woman who probably scrubbed the spot where my mouth touched.

I slap the beer bottle down on the counter with a curse. Apparently, I've lost my self-respect, because it doesn't seem to matter that Naomi isn't interested. Or that she's set on going back to her fiancé. I can't stop thinking about her. The awkward dance I sense we're doing to avoid each other in the driveway is gnawing at me. Over the course of the last week, I've watched a change happen in Birdie. She still wears the grief of losing Natalie on her sleeve, but she's out the door earlier for school, testing her blood sugar more regularly, eating better. We still don't have a lot to say to each other when we end up in the kitchen at the same time, but I'm paying attention. It's the beauty queen making the difference.

Because of that, I feel the annoying need to make an effort. Naomi doesn't want my mouth anywhere near her? Fine. Doesn't mean she has to sneak up the steps to her apartment, trying not to press down on the creaky middle one. I don't want to make her nervous. If I were a hospitable man, I might even want her to feel welcome.

Caging a growl in my throat, I push away from the window. Right now, I need to get out of the house. It's too quiet. My mind interprets quiet to mean danger, which is why the nightmares creep in during the dead silence of night. Images from last night's dreams project themselves on the backs of my eyelids, only now they're woven through with the pictures I found on the internet. The handsome couple posing in front of a stately home, a soft smile curving the feminine lips I still want to taste, despite everything. Goddammit.

Before I've made a conscious decision where I'm going, I grab my house keys off the peg and walk out the front door.

I seem to recall writing out a check a few days ago to a church. Rental space in their basement? Yeah, I think that was it. I don't question these things, but I'm thankful now for my airtight memory. Birdie's explanation about needing more room to practice her walk went in one ear and out the other at the time, but I dig for the name of the place now. Ancient City? Definitely

Baptist. A quick address search on my phone later and I'm in the truck, headed in the direction of the church. I'm not sure if men are welcome at pageant practice, but I'm about to find out.

The church is mostly empty when I walk in through the front double doors. A woman arranges silk flowers around the centered podium, a custodian with headphones in his ears vacuums the carpet. Neither one of them spares me a glance as I stride down the aisle toward the basement, and my jaw clenches. Good to know the security is on the up-and-up. I should have come with Naomi and Birdie to make sure they were safe.

When I reach the bottom of the stairs, I walk into what can only be described as mayhem. Naomi is losing a battle with a stereo from the nineties and an iPhone adapter. Birdie is fighting an equally difficult war with tears, and a young man I don't recognize is pacing, flushed exasperation clouding his face.

"I don't even have my walk down yet," Birdie says, swiping the back of her wrist beneath her eyes. "Why am I learning the dance already?"

"The pageant is in a month, Birdie. We have to learn them simultaneously." Naomi is facing away from my sister, so I'm the only one who can see her eyes closed, her mouth moving in a silent plea for patience. "The choreography might seem impossible right now, but we will get there. Eventually the waltz will click."

"Not before I break his toes."

The night Naomi moved into the apartment above the garage, I heard her singing all the way in my kitchen. It was so bad, I assumed she was playing a joke. But when I stepped in through the doorway and saw the concentration line between her eyes, my theory was dashed. She's a horrific singer, which I never would have seen coming in a million years, since everything else about her is fine-tuned almost to a fault. Her bearing, her manner, her appearance. While standing on the threshold, I realized Naomi was revealing her flaw for Birdie's benefit. That's why I couldn't walk away without asking her to come to dinner. I just couldn't do it.

While they laughed, still not realizing I stood there watching, I remember Naomi telling Birdie they would hire a partner to perform the waltz with her. I decide I don't like him when he bends down to massage his toes, giving Birdie a pointed look.

Naomi gets the stereo working and the strains of violin fill the basement. "Let's try it again." Her smile is bright and positive. "Positions, please."

Birdie groans. "Can my position be prone?"

Mister Toes rolls his eyes. Yeah, really not liking him.

The first few steps of the routine are impressive. I've never even seen my sister dance, but the instructor must be good because she's got posture and rhythm I wasn't aware she had. After fifteen or so seconds, however, they lose momentum and Birdie's foot slams down on her instructor's foot. With a groan, she plops heavily onto the floor.

Naomi hides her disappointment well as she returns to the stereo in a few quick steps. That's when she notices me. "Oh. Mr. Bristow."

I bite down on the impulse to remind her my name is Jason. "Yeah." Feeling Birdie's surprise, I send her a nod. "Hey."

She stands, wiping the floor's dust from the seat of her jeans, reminding me of when she was a second grader playing Barbies versus Monsters with Natalie in the front yard. Before I enlisted. Long before my parents moved away. So long ago, I don't remember what I worried or thought about back then, besides my first boat and how fast I could enlist.

The sharp focus of before and after catches me hard. Reminds me of what I missed when I left. Those last years of Natalie's baton competitions, school plays and first boyfriends. Birdie getting older and transforming into this quick-witted ball-buster with an iron will. There's also what I'm missing now. The sounds of battle are always in the back of my mind, pulling me. Making me feel utterly out of place and helpless in this stale basement. It's not a feeling I handle well. At all.

"I'm not paying to have you sit around," I snap, attempting to jab a hole in the tension in my chest. The air in the room turns frosty. Naomi slowly sets down the iPhone and crosses her arms. Birdie doesn't move at all. I couldn't give a shit about the partner's reaction...I just know I've fucked up and clearly hurt my sister's feelings. Who am I to criticize her when she's throwing herself outside her comfort zone to honor our sister? All I know how to do is work, provide, repeat. She's not only allowed herself to feel the loss of Natalie, she's leaning into it.

I need to fix this fast. How, though?

Naomi draws my attention. So perfect and pretty in her fluttery yellow top and white jeans. But she's not perfect, is she? No, she sings like a choking cat.

That's what gives me the idea. A terrible one, obviously. Dancing is meant to be graceful and requires the kind of coordination I'm not sure I have, since I haven't attempted to dance since high school—and I was still getting used to my size fourteen feet back then. If I make this attempt, there's a very good chance I'll make a fool out of myself. No, it's a certainty. Birdie is shrinking more and more into herself as the seconds tick past, though, and I have to act.

I can't believe I'm about to do this.

"Show me how to do it." I roll my neck. "Let's give it a shot."

"What?" Some of the ice melts in Birdie's eyes. "Shut up."

It occurs to me too late that if I waltz to make my sister feel better, I'll either have to partner with her. Or Naomi. Considering our resident Southern belle has been avoiding me for a week, I'm pretty sure she'd rather dance with a giant lizard than partner with me. So I'm surprised when the music kicks off again and she steps forward. "I think that's a lovely idea."

Naomi understands what I'm doing. It's there in the softness of her voice. There's no denying my pulse triples when she sails up to me, joining my right hand to her left, placing her opposite one on my shoulder. Christ, I didn't forget how beautiful she is, but her nuances—a scattering of light freckles on her nose, the sexy indent at the top center of her bow lips—they blow me away now. Did I really almost kiss this woman? Was I fucking crazy to try?

"I'm going to lead for the sake of teaching," she murmurs, her blue eyes ticking up to mine. "We'll have to be just a touch closer."

I swallow hard. "Come on then."

There's a momentary hesitation on her part. That tongue skates out to wet her lips, the flyaway blonde hairs around her forehead seem to quiver. One step forward, though, and her tits flatten against my belly, her breath bathing the hollow of my throat. I take the opposite tact and stop breathing altogether, just not fast enough to bar the grapefruit-cedar and blood orange scents entrance to my nose. She feels so small against me, but substantial. Feminine. Alive.

Pull it together.

Now is not the time to lust after Naomi. My sister and that punk are watching me—the exact wrong time to let my dick get hard. Maybe I can make progress here, too. Naomi is giving me another chance to be her...what? Her friend?

I resist the urge to curse as Naomi steps forward. Closer. Our bodies press together so tightly, I can't help but think of dragging her higher, getting her legs around my hips, her tuxedoed future mayor be damned. *I'd fuck you better.*

"When I step forward," she whispers, her face pink. "You have to step back."

"Right," I rasp. "Got it."

She lifts up on her toes a little and I feel her stiff nipples through my shirt. Fuck. A simple, physical response to friction or something more? I can't tell anything from the way she's staring at my throat. "We're moving in a box. One, two, three. Feel it?"

"Yeah," I say, checking the urge to press my cheek to her hair, like some kind of smitten suitor from the fifties. "I didn't mean to snap at her."

"I know," she responds right away. "Look at her. She's forgotten all about it."

She's right. Over Naomi's head, I can see my sister frowning in concentration, doing a pretty damn good job of keeping up with her partner, who clearly is the more experienced of the two. I'd like to point out to Mister Toes that Birdie is the one dancing in high heels, but it's probably better to keep my mouth shut this time around.

My blown-out sigh brings Naomi closer, her fingers flexing where they twine with mine, but I know she's just trying to reassure me. It's not what I want it to be. Maybe what we have is destined to be something else. A unique brand of friendship—and I'll have to learn to be happy with that.

Sure.

I WAKE UP with sweat pouring down my face, my chest. Explosives continue to go off above me, sparks pinging the surface of the water. No, not the water. They're right there in my bedroom, smoke rising on the shoreline. Voices shout, chopper blades whirr above, in place of my ceiling fan. The urge to dive from my bed onto the floor is fierce and I've followed through with it many times before, but this time I dig my fingers into the mattress and breathe. One, two, three, four...

By the time I reach ten, the smoke is beginning to fade, along with the taste of gunpowder and sand. As always, there's a plea repeating itself in the back of my head. *Please let everyone have gotten out. Please let everyone have gotten out.* Long after I'm grounded in my bedroom, though, the mantra continues because I know somewhere, thousands of miles away, it's counting for something. I'm meant to be there. I'm meant to be doing my job.

Unlike the reflex to take cover, the need to punish my body with exertion is unshakeable. I'm out of the bed and shoving my feet into sneakers, rifling through a pile of folded laundry at the same time. Towels. All towels. With a growl, I forgo the shirt and move silently through the dark bedroom toward the door. *Get out. Get out. Move.*

I'm through the kitchen in seconds and twisting the knob to the back door. It brings me out onto the driveway—where I almost mow Naomi down like an ocean liner cutting through a dingy. "What the hell?"

"Oh shoot. Oh Lord." She presses shaking hands to her chest, which is no wonder since I shouted at her like a fucking lunatic. "You scared the life out of me."

"What are you doing out here? It's..." I have no idea what time it is. "Late."

"Early, actually. I couldn't go back to sleep, so I ran down to my car for..." Her gaze drops to my sweaty chest complete with matted hair. "My yoga mat was in the trunk. Did you just come back from a run? I didn't pass you…"

My voice is raw when I answer. "No."

"Do you have the shaky sweats again?" Naomi whispers.

I say nothing. I'm usually through half a mile by now and still nowhere close to normal. Having a conversation is not in my wheelhouse right now. I'm a sweating jumble of nerves and guilt and frustration, while she's fresh and gorgeous in a baby-blue nightgown. God, she doesn't even look real, she's so out of place in my black driveway among my whirlwind of thoughts. But I can't just blow her off. We've started waving at each other through the kitchen window when she passes on the way to her apartment every day. It's better than nothing. I don't want to give that up.

Naomi sets down the yoga mat she's had tucked underneath her arm. I've never felt more oversized and awkward as I do watching her carefully tuck her nightgown beneath her tush and take a seat on my back stoop. She pats a spot on the brickwork beside her. "Did I ever tell you about the invasion of Normandy?"

An electrified spike rises under my skin. My breathing comes faster. She's offering me a kindness, and for some reason, it goes against the very grain of my existence to accept it. I'm not earning it. I've completed no mission. I've done nothing to warrant a favor. "I don't need your help. I didn't ask."

She cups her knees in her hands and waits, the moon making her face look silver, instead of its usual creamy peach. "On my drive to St. Augustine, I pulled over at a gas station in my wedding dress to use the bathroom. I fell on my butt and…" With a sniff, she picks an invisible speck off her nightgown. "I peed myself a little. A stranger saw it and everything. The woman who helped me hold my dress while I relieved myself asked me if I got excited."

The distant blasts that were still going off in my ears when I walked out of the house fade some. I don't want her to be the reason. I want to get rid of the horrible noise myself. "Why are you telling me this?"

"I don't know."

"We're not trading humiliations here. I'm not humiliated."

"I didn't say you were. You shouldn't be." I'm snapping at her and yet, the soft rise and fall of her breasts makes me want to lay my head there. "Do you want me to leave?"

My swallow is thick. "No."

"Okay."

It takes me a full minute to sit down beside her. My veins feel pulled tight and ready to snap, my legs are still aching to sprint until I can't go any farther. Everything else inside me seems drawn to her, though, and that gravitational pull wins. Her usual scent of cedar and blood orange is softer than usual, probably worn off in sleep. The smell of morning dew and saltwater surrounds us as she starts to talk, her light voice carrying on the easy breeze.

"The invasion of Normandy was the largest amphibious invasion in history. You're a diver, so you probably already knew that." She doesn't wait for me to respond that yeah, I know a little, but not the finer details. Not the little nuggets of interesting facts she inserts into her stories. "For a successful invasion, the weather needed to be right. A full moon to illuminate the beach, mostly. The Allied forces couldn't agree on a date for the invasion. The Americans wanted to go on the fifth, but the British were hedging. Finally, an Irish lighthouse keeper on the west coast advised them to hold off until the sixth…"

I'm halfway to getting lost in Naomi's words when her pinkie finger nudges mine. It's so faint, I wonder if I imagined it. But I look down to find her hand right there. Waiting. Without giving my head a chance to talk me out of it, I cover her hand with mine. She turns her palm up and we lace our fingers together. Friendly. It's just friendly. Apparently not harmless enough to stop my eyes from closing, my skin from enjoying the warm grace of her, though. Her recounting wraps around me as the sun starts to rise over the distant houses. And for the first time since coming home, I return to normal without having to break myself. Holding the beauty queen's hand in mine, though, I start to wonder if she's capable of breaking me instead.

CHAPTER TEN

ReadtheComments.com
Username: TheRappingTheorist
Her palms are sweaty, knees weak, arms are heavy...
...and those are all symptoms of pre-combustion, if
you're interested.

Naomi

WHEN I ESCAPED to Florida, I envisioned myself participating in life-affirming feats. Skydiving, cattle roping, standing in the sunroof of a limousine with my arms thrown to the wind. Over the last couple of weeks, though, I've found that having dinner in a restaurant alone is panic-inducing enough. I've never eaten alone in public. Not once. It wasn't something I acknowledged to myself as odd before now. I simply always had company. A reason to be out in the first place, whether it was charity planning, celebrating a birthday or attending a luncheon.

Since moving into the chalet—as I lovingly refer to my studio above Jason's garage—I've been bringing home groceries and trying new recipes out in the tiny kitchen. My creations have become a source of pride for me. Look! Tacos! I can make edible tacos! Growing up, we always had a chef to make meals for us. Occasionally the chef would leave already prepared meals for my mother to pop into the oven and declare herself a cook. Thus, preparing my own food is new to me—and I love it. But I can't allow myself to hide away in the comfort of the chalet. So here I am, pacing back and forth in front of a seafood restaurant. Afraid to go inside.

Ludicrous, isn't it?

Blowing out a quick breath, I scan the menu, which is posted outside in a mounted plastic frame. On the other side of the front window, I watch a waitress drop off a glass of wine at someone's table. I could be drinking that wine. All I have to do is go inside and sit down.

Birdie invited me to dinner again tonight and I'm starting to feel like an awful witch turning down the invitations. If the thought of sitting across from Jason didn't make me jumpy, I would consider saying yes once in a while. As it is, though...I brace myself every time I know I'm going to see Jason. Whether it's through the kitchen window or in the garage lifting weights with a cigar clamped in his mouth, I find my toes curling. Which is a polite way of saying my whole body grows flushed and sensitive, tingles running up and down my arms. He's so intimidating in the daylight. Broad and covered in ink and frowning at whatever I'm wearing.

That's why I get nervous. His demeanor. Not because I'm thinking of that almost-kiss. Or how he spoke to me afterward. *If this closet door had been closed, we'd be rounding third base on this fucking bed right now, beauty queen, and we both know it.* Third base. I had to Google it to be sure I had a clear picture of what he meant. And...wow. That would have happened so fast? Of course Jason has fast, rough sex. Do I harbor any delusions he'd be a gentle lover?

Not to me, obviously. Someone else. Someone available.

An image springs to mind of Jason's powerful, tattooed back flexing as he overpowers a woman on a bed, his mouth rasping inappropriate words in her ears. Acid climbs my throat and sours in my mouth so fast, tears spring to my eyes. I'm sure that's why my curiosity slips past my willpower and I replace the woman with myself. A moaning, messy, straining version of myself, fingernails scraping down Jason's closely-shaved scalp. Down further, traveling over his sharp mountains of back muscle to his—

Mid-pace, I trip over the uneven sidewalk.

What am I thinking?

I'm not. I'm not thinking of Jason. Not like that.

Maybe what I need is a phone call with my mother to remind me I'm on borrowed time. I'm sure she's ready to throw me to the wolves for staying away this long. And it's only going to get worse, because I'm not ready to go back to Charleston yet. Birdie and I have finally begun making progress on her walk. The final turn of the dance is yet to click, but we're nearing a break-through. I can feel it. I am invested in Birdie being successful.

More invested than you are in salvaging your relationship with Elijah?

I let the reminder of Elijah sink in. Since the day I met my ex-fiancé, Elijah was kind and caring, but distant. So distant. Smiling and attempting to respond with the proper remark to whatever I was saying across the dinner table, but never taken off guard. Never peppering me with questions, the way I would try to do with him. Because of this—because I *cannot* imagine him pining away for someone who stoked so little a fire, I haven't wondered overmuch if he misses me. Did I hurt him by calling off the wedding…or was he relieved?

Not wanting to examine that possibility too closely, I lean against the wall of the building and slide my new cell phone out of my purse. I managed to make it almost three weeks without one, but scheduling practice sessions with Birdie was becoming too much of a challenge using the smoke signal method. I haven't synced my email yet out of pure survival instinct, because I'm not ready to read messages with the underlying subtext of: Are you insane? Tapping my finger on the screen for a moment, I open the internet browser instead and search my name. A classic rookie mistake if I've ever heard one, but I promise myself to gloss over anything too negative. While I'm curious to know what's being said about me, I'm freaked about dining alone in a restaurant—I definitely don't need another complex.

When I hit search, all I can do is stare at the screen as dozens upon dozens of websites pop up with variations of the headline: Theories on the Naomi Clemons Disappearance.

Oh dear. That's rather dramatic.

I click the first link. It takes me to a site called Conspiracy Crowd.

Did Naomi Clemons really run from her own wedding? Or was she taken by force? A witness close to Clemons claims she left a note and left of her own accord, but how credible is this bridesmaid? Does she know who kidnapped Clemons?

"Oh Lord," I whisper, clicking over to another site. This one has an old picture of me at a charity event. I'm passing a man I don't recognize, but the angle of the shot makes it look like we're handing each other a note. The photo caption reads: *What had Naomi Clemons gotten herself into? Inside sources hint at an organized crime ring dating all the way back to Prohibition. Debutante or mob shill?* "You can't be serious."

Despite my better judgment, I'm moving on to a third site when Birdie's face pops up on my phone and it begins to vibrate. Still in shock over the conspiracy theories floating around about my disappearance, I answer with numb lips. "Hello?"

"Naomi, can you please, please come home?"

Hearing the tears in the younger woman's voice, I push off the wall. "What's wrong, Birdie?"

She blows out a shaky breath. "Remember when you suggested I tell Natalie's friends about my plans to compete in the pageant?"

"Yes."

"I took your advice and—like, I fucking doubled down for some reason. I was feeling all confident and in charge, which is totally your fault, by the way. And I invited them over. They're coming over. Here. To hang out."

"That's great, Birdie. Good for you!"

"No. They're coming now. Now."

"Oh. So soon. Well, order some pizzas and..." I drop my voice in deference to the people around me. "Tell Jason to wear a shirt."

"He's not even home yet. Naomi, I can't do this by myself." She pauses. "I barely knew how to talk to Natalie, okay? And her friends aren't forced to endure me out of sibling obligation. When I bend over backwards to out-awkward myself, they'll just leave."

"You're not awkward."

"You're not at school. You don't know how everyone looks at me."

Birdie is right, of course. I have no perspective on her high school experience. Mine was exactly as it was supposed to be. Junior committees and homecoming dances and football games. Smiling for yearbook pictures and gossiping between classes. It almost seems like I watched a movie about someone's life instead of living it myself. Birdie lives in an awareness right now that I didn't achieve until I was getting ready to walk down the aisle. There's no one to guide her through this phase of her life, either.

Jason isn't ready to handle teenage drama while he's battling his own demons, is he?

For a moment, I get stuck in that morning on the back stoop when he held my hand and I let his sweat soak clear through the side of my nightgown. I'm not sure I've felt more...real. Vital. Helpful. In a way I've never been before. The fear of getting too close to Jason and Birdie is why I've been eating dinner alone. Why I've been spending my days exploring St. Augustine and getting comfortable in my own company. My own skin. I can't help but feel like I'm about to cross the line I've drawn...but I close my eyes and cross it, anyway, knowing full well I'm making things harder on myself in the future.

"How long do we have?"

I start down the sidewalk with a burst of purpose. Now that I've made the decision to go from pageant coach to slightly more than a pageant coach (read: it's complicated), I'm ready to dazzle these teenagers within an inch of their ever loving lives. Being that I ran away from a life of entertaining and frippery, I shouldn't be so excited to help Birdie play hostess. But I am. Maybe I'm allowed to enjoy making things pretty and being the classic Southern hostess I was trained to be. I'm also allowed to want more. To be more.

A quick stop at the market and I'm standing at the back door of the main house. My hands are full, so I use my foot to tap on the door. "Birdie?"

Jason opens the door while my foot is mid-knock and I almost do the splits right there on the threshold. He catches me around the waist before I drop, though, steadying me on my feet. Amid the tangle of limbs and grocery bags, his fingertips brush the underside of my breast and we both suck in a breath.

"Shit," he grunts, deep gray eyes running over my face. "Sorry."

"It's okay," I say in a high-pitched voice, praying my nipples aren't hard. They feel hard. Oh God, they are. They have to be. Trying to move before he has a chance to notice, I start to sidestep Jason, but he refuses to let me carry the bags, taking them out of my hands one by one. My breath remains poised in my throat as his gaze darkens to the shade of thunderclouds, letting me know he most definitely sees my pointed nipples through the thin, red cotton of my tank top. "I can manage the bags," I whisper. "They're t-tight—light. I mean light."

Without breaking our eye contact, he reaches out with the fist full of bags and sets them on the nearest counter. "You don't carry bags when I'm around."

Why that causes the private place between my legs to cinch up tighter than a girdle, I don't know. It startles me into sounding breathless. "Thank you, Mr. Bristow. That's very gentlemanly of you."

Look out, Scarlett O'Hara. There's a new, simpering Southern belle in town.

"Jason." Slowly, he rubs the inside of his cheek with his tongue. "And it doesn't have anything to do with being a gentleman."

"Oh no?"

"No." His smirk is patronizing—and close, so close—but I'm too flustered to admonish him. "You want to unload, I'm just letting you know I'm here to help you do it."

If I was damp before, I'm growing dangerously close to soaked now, the area below my belly button in a permanent squeeze. He's not supposed to make me feel this way, is he? It's wild and indecent and...I've never experienced it before. "I-I thought we were friends."

"We are." A floorboard creaks as he takes a step closer, his eyes flickering to my mouth. "I'm talking about a shoulder to lean on, beauty queen. What are you talking about?"

"Nothing," I breathe, shooting past him to the soundtrack of his low chuckle. "Have the guests arrived yet?"

"No," Birdie says, stomping into the room and plowing through the shopping bags. "What's all this stuff? Tranquilizers? Please say it's tranquilizers."

I shoo her hands away. "You'll have to wait and see. Is the living room clean?"

Jason reaches over my shoulder to search the bags. I slap his hand away, too.

"Well?" I ask, hands on hips.

"It's decent," Jason says, shrugging. "I was told my only job was to wear a shirt."

I turn to face him and ram back into the counter when I find him a mere foot away. "It's nice to know you own one."

He flashes his teeth. "I own at least six."

Lord, I wish he wouldn't smile. It's disconcerting. I've just gotten used to the permanent scowl. "Next we'll work on an iron."

"Don't push it, baby."

Birdie's groan turns me back around. "BRB while I slam my head in a door to forget I ever heard my brother call someone *baby*."

The conversation is making me anxious. Or maybe it's the giant soldier radiating heat behind me while a T-shirt barely contains his muscle. I don't know. "Birdie, cut these limes up into little wedges. Mr. Bristow, do you have cocktail glasses?

He leans a forearm on the island. "What do you think?"

"Regular glasses will suffice. How many friends are coming

over?"

"Six."

"Seven glasses if you please, Mr. Bristow."

Jason pushes away with a sigh and I hear glasses hitting the counter with little clinks a second later. It takes some fast handiwork, but by the time the doorbell rings, I've managed to whip up seven blueberry Moscow mule mocktails with sugar on the rim, although I leave the sweet stuff off of Birdie's drink in deference to her diabetes. And I add cute pink straws, just because I can. I don't realize I've been holding my breath as I worked. When I step back, though, I find Jason and Birdie watching me with their jaws in the vicinity of the ground.

Birdie shakes her head. "Holy shit. This is the first time I've had the urge to Instagram a food or drink item. You've turned me into a lemming."

"I'm choosing to take that as a compliment." I adjust a slipping lime. "Well. Go answer the door. I'll bring these out on a tray after the appropriate greetings have been made and everyone is seated. They won't have coats to take, being that it's May in Florida. I'll give you a three-minute lead time."

"Three minutes. Okay, I can do that." Birdie starts to leave but turns back around. "What is an appropriate greeting?"

"Comment on the weather. Ask them about school. People love gawking at the insides of other people's houses, so they'll only be half listening, anyway."

"Right."

Birdie jogs from the room and I can no longer ignore Jason's stare. It's been burning a hole in the side of my head since I started making the mocktails. "Yes?"

"You didn't have to do all this."

"I enjoyed doing it."

Jason clears his throat. "They look great. I probably wouldn't have thought to offer them something to drink." He sends a look toward the kitchen door. "Damn, I really don't know what the hell I'm doing. I'm the furthest thing from parent material there is."

I'm beginning to wonder how many complicated layers exist underneath Jason's invincible soldier façade. I've witnessed him twice in the midst of what seemed like a panic attack and I don't need a degree to know he's fighting a serious mental battle due to his time overseas. This man is not used to feeling inadequate, and being Birdie's guardian makes him feel that way in spades. I think that's what he's trying to tell me in his own gruff way.

"You would have thought of something. I just beat you to it."

He narrows his eyes at me. "I liked your wine. That night you came to dinner."

My finger flies on its own to jab him in the chest. "I knew it," I gasp. "Wait. What made you tell me that now?"

"I don't know. When you do something nice..." Jason nods at the tray of drinks. "I get this annoying urge to reciprocate. So knock it off."

"You don't really want me to knock it off."

He crosses his arms, braced like a warrior for battle. "Don't I?"

"No." I hesitate to let him know I've been paying such attention. "You like to keep people safe. Don't you think that's nice?"

A muscle jumps in his jaw. "It's more of a necessity. I can't turn it off."

"Well, it makes people feel secure. Telling me you liked the wine and waltzing for Birdie..." I turn and fuss with the garnishes again. "Those gestures are an extension of making people feel safe. Maybe you're nice after all."

I can almost hear the cranks turning in his head, but it's entirely possible he just wishes I'd shut up. "My three minutes is up." I pick up the tray. "Come with me. As man of the house, you have to make an appearance."

He grunts. "Let me carry that."

"Absolutely not." I twist away, careful not to spill a drop. "This isn't the same thing as grocery bags. This is a presentation."

"My mistake."

He's chuckling as he follows me, and my mouth moves into an answering smile. "I shall let you open the door, Mr. Bristow."

"After you, beauty queen."

We pass through the kitchen door, swing through the dining room and bank right into the living area. Seven teenagers are sprawled in various positions around the room, Birdie standing in the midst of them flipping through television channels. Her shoulders are bunched up tighter than double knotted shoelaces. I'm surprised by a kick of nerves in my own belly. I'm not sure if I'm anxious to make a good impression for Birdie. Or if I've simply gotten to the age where packs of teenagers become more intimidating than a herd of raptors.

"Hello!" I set the tray down on the coffee table, pleased when the teenagers sit up a little straighter. "Who's thirsty? There's no alcohol in these, so don't go ringing the police on me. Not until I do something fun to deserve it. How was everyone's day?"

A smattering of "goods" are issued from around the room. The girls are definitely more engaged than the boys, their phones at the ready to snap pics of my mocktails, although one of them is open-mouthed staring at Jason.

He smirks at me to let me know he notices. I shoot him back a frown.

"Listen, if you all get hungry, just holler. I'm Naomi and this is Birdie's brother, Jason."

I nudge him with an elbow and he coughs. "Hey."

"He's not as scary as he looks," I say.

Birdie snorts. "Have you seen what he leaves in the shower drain?"

Laughter kicks up around the room and her shoulders relax. I don't mind one bit that she broke the ice at Jason's expense, and his nonchalant shrug says he couldn't care less, either.

"Oh my God, these are so good," one of girls groans. "Birdie, your house is the new chill spot. My house is gluten free—our snacks suck."

I barely resist the urge to squeal. "We have chocolate-covered cashews. Should I go grab them?" I throw Birdie a wink. "There might be some gelato lying around, too."

"I love gelato."

"Please. That sounds amazing."

"Birdie, I'm like, never leaving."

The last thing I see when I back into the kitchen is Birdie slipping in between two girls on the couch. She looks a touch uncomfortable but relaxes when everyone lapses into an easy conversation about the school principal's questionable hygiene. And when I hear a roll of laughter coming from the living room, I throw my arms up in a victory V, just as Jason enters the kitchen behind me. We trade a smile over my shoulder and something warm twines down my belly, slithering like a serpent over my thighs.

Not good. I'm barely able to put a name to these distracting sensations he sets off in me and they're only getting stronger.

"I'll just get the gelato..." I manage, moving to the freezer. I'm thankful for the rush of cool air that flows over my bare shoulders, but when the tendrils of white clear away and I reach for the gelato I tossed in earlier, my hand closes around cold, hard glass instead. I pull out the unopened bottle of wine, staring down like a foreign object. "What's this?"

"Been keeping it in there," Jason answers in a gruff voice. "In case you ever decided to come for dinner."

"It's Sauvignon Blanc."

"That's the one you like, isn't it?"

"Yes, but you remembered."

I glance back to find him watching me with a raised eyebrow. As if to say *and?* Oh, and this is very dangerous, this particular gesture. I've tried to limit the comparisons of Elijah and Jason. But this one is too on the nose. In desperation, I try to call Elijah's face to mind, but it won't appear as long as Jason is looking at me. Moving toward me. Taking the bottle out of my hand and putting it back in the freezer. Against my good judgment, I look up and back to find him close. To find his expression has gone from questioning to knowing. He can't know, though. I can't tell him why it's significant that he remembered my favorite drink.

At this point, his knowledge of my relationship with Elijah is limited. That's how it has to stay, right? If I confide in Jason that my ex-fiancé was a good man who unfortunately didn't excite me physically the way Jason does…that revelation could encourage him. To push this carefully balanced friendship into something more.

To touch.

To touch, like he's doing now. Standing behind me, his palms scrape down my hips, his mouth ghosting over the nape of my neck. What is happening? Why am I letting him do this?

My panties are still wet from earlier and even more moisture coats my sex, makes the material of my thin underwear heavy. The freezer is still open and the cold air collides with my breath, creating white puffs in the air, letting me know I'm breathing heavily. I have no choice with Jason's hot mouth poised on my neck to kiss, to move…but remaining stationary. Waiting for a signal. My silence is a signal in itself, though, because we both know I have no problem telling him no. And he has no trouble listening.

I don't say no, though. I can't. His fingertips tighten on my hips and he tugs them back, bringing my backside into the cradle of his lap. Oh my Lord. No. Cradle is a soft word and there's nothing soft happening with Jason. His manhood is long, thick and able where it presses between the split of my bottom.

"Before you tell me I'm nice for buying you wine…" he rasps into my hair. "Understand that I want to drink it out of your belly button. Want to warm it on that perfect skin, sip it into my mouth, then let it drip out all over your pussy. I'd drench that pretty pink spot real fucking good so I could push in rough."

The ache between my thighs is so intense, I can barely speak. "Mr. Bristow."

"Mr. Bristow, what?" His tongue grants me the barest of licks on the nape of my neck, his hot breath coasting over the damp spot. "Take you to bed? Or let you go?"

"I-I don't know."

"You know what you want. It's a matter of admitting it."

"I can't."

His right hand moves to the front of my skirt, splaying just over the waistband of my panties. "Tell me not to squeeze your little pussy." I sway under an onslaught of heat and land back against Jason's chest…but no words leave my mouth. "Can't say that, either, huh?"

I'm not prepared for my reaction when his hand journeys lower and cups me hard through my skirt. Electricity zips along my nerve endings, my nipples bundle into sharp, aching peaks and I...I almost have an orgasm.

"I want you. I want this." His grip tightens. "I want to brand you with a J here."

My eyes are turning glassy and I'm beginning to shudder, because here comes my climax. Can I let it happen? No. No. Who is this woman who so casually casts aside years of a relationship and lands immediately in the lap of another man?

I can't do that. It's not me. It's not right.

My mother's words from our phone call ring in my ears. *I've been working on this wedding since you were a child. I did my job. Made an advantageous marriage, secured the right connections—the kind of connections that allow you to marry the next mayor. A war hero. The son of my best friend. How dare you walk away from this and leave me to deal with the damage, Naomi. How dare you?*

I'm not just tossing away years of building a relationship. I'm forgetting a duty that is so firmly ingrained in me, I don't know where it ends and I begin. I hate that, but it's true.

With a burst of will, I twist away and catch myself on the nearby counter. Jason slams the freezer shut and grips the appliance, as if he's contemplating throwing it through the kitchen window. Watching the violent flex of muscle in his arms, I have no doubt he could. The front of his jeans bulges, thick flesh tunneling down into one pant leg. Those words he said to me, the things he wants to do...I should be repelled by that kind of vulgar talk, shouldn't I? The longer I stand here remembering them, though, the harder it is not to ask for more.

Who am I anymore?

"Go. I'll make the fucking ice cream."

"It's gelato," I breathe, uselessly.

A second later, I'm out of the kitchen and up the stairs to my apartment, feeling Jason's gaze following my every step.

CHAPTER ELEVEN

ConspiracyCrowd.org
Username: UrdadsMyFave69
Good morning, Internet.
Another day, another voicing of my support for Operation
Pussy Freedom.
If you're out there, Runaway Bride, get your freak on.

Jason

EVERY SUNDAY MORNING, I get bagels from the same shop. Always at the same time. I get an orange juice to go and drink it on the way home, even though it's too much of a luxury. I force myself to open the carton and drink from it, though. Force myself to recognize that I'm in a place where letting down my guard isn't going to get me or one of my men capped. It's my version of a baby step, even if I haven't ventured beyond that one simple thing yet. Why should I when I'll need to rekindle my powers of observation in a matter of months? I'll need it.

For now, walking and drinking orange juice is just my way of sanding down a mental weakness and making sure it doesn't get too coarse. Too strong. Because someday—God knows when—I will need the ability to differentiate between danger and safety.

Nearly at the bagel shop, I can't stop myself from searching rooftops, looking into the faces of everyone who passes and trying to determine their intentions. The lack of heavy gear on my body leaves me too weightless and a trickle of sweat beads and slides down my spine. In the midst of this blurring between real and fake, there's a constant, though—which is new. Naomi is real. I know because I've held her in the palm of my hand. Fitted her into my lap. If I close my eyes, I can hear the tiny intake of breath she took when I squeezed.

My thoughts become more depraved with every step I take. They change shape, too. One second I'm dragging Naomi's panties down to her knees, testing her wetness. And the next...I'm simply knocking on her door to make sure she's safe. I'm listening to one of her battle stories. She's taking up every corner of my mind, so when I spot her up ahead in a crowd of milling people, I think my brain is playing tricks on me. But, no. Another step, another, and she's still there. I speed up. It's involuntary. What is she doing out here alone? It doesn't help that she seems...nervous. Why?

I'm caught in the middle of a swallow when I reach her where she stands outside of a packed restaurant. Some remaining strand of common sense reminds me not to be obvious about position-ing her between my body and the wall of the establishment, giving my back to the street. She rejected me in the kitchen a few nights ago and I shouldn't be standing this close, no matter how badly I need it—to smell her, feel her heat—but I'm not in full control of my actions. I'm driven to protect her.

"Jason?" She lowers her silver-rimmed sunglasses. "What are you doing here?"

"Getting bagels." My voice sounds the furthest thing from normal, but I manage to hitch a casual thumb over my shoulder. "I, uh...get bagels and orange juice at Holy Doughers on Sundays. Their cream cheese is better than their name."

"Oh." Her tongue dances out to wet her lips, her eyes not

quite meeting mine. "Okay, well don't let me keep you."

It's clear she wants me to leave. Ignoring the ridiculous shift of hurt in my chest, I run through a laundry list of reasons she'd want me gone so soon. Yeah, I propositioned her up against my refrigerator, but I've made it pretty clear since the beginning I'm interested in sex. I might have put my hands in places they'd never gone, but only after being positive she wanted them there. Before she didn't. What happened aside, it's not like Naomi to be abrupt. Is there another reason she wants me gone?

I'll say one thing for jealousy. It stops the unwanted bout of paranoia in its tracks. When am I not jealous lately? *She's going back to a man she almost married and you're worried about a brunch date?* "Are you meeting someone?"

"What?" Naomi waves off the question with a flutter of delicate fingers. "No. No, nothing like that. I'm just trying to…oh Lord, it's too embarrassing. Could you just forget you ever saw me?"

"Impossible," I say, my tension ebbing so fast I momentarily forget to guard my words. Thankfully, she seems too distracted to notice my slip. I'm not dwelling on it, either, because I'm more interested in why she's twisting her fingers in the material of her skirt, her face the color of cotton candy. "What could you possibly be embarrassed about, beauty queen?"

"You're going to poke fun at me."

My stomach drops. Have I teased her too much? "Swear on my life I won't."

Naomi fidgets for a few more seconds, then apparently takes my vow seriously, thank God. "I looked up the best brunch spots in St. Augustine and made a list of them, weighed the pros and cons. The Speckled Hen has Nutella-stuffed French toast and that moved them to the top of the list. But I got here and…I've never gone into a restaurant by myself. The idea of it intimidates me."

"You've never been to a restaurant by yourself?"

"Isn't that just crazy? I'm always meeting a friend or accompanied by someone. And a reservation has always been made, but the Speckled Hen doesn't take reservations. I'm not even sure I could go in there and sit by myself, even with a reservation. Won't everyone stare at the pathetic loner?" She fans her face. "Look away, Blackbeard. I think I'm starting to sweat."

Not for the first time, I want to ask this creature where the hell she came from. She's not typical. In Charleston or anywhere else. I can say that with total conviction. In this moment, I would give a limb to lay her down and study her without a time limit. Asking her where she came from wouldn't be helpful right now, though. She'd assume I was making fun of her, when in reality I couldn't give her a more sincere compliment. *You're like no one else.*

"It took me a month to walk into the bagel shop. When I got home," I say instead, astonished to be revealing myself out loud. To a woman I'd kill to sleep with, no less. "Too many options. Too many people around me in the line. Standing behind my back. The whole process of ordering and paying was new all over again and I was so sure...no, I'm still sure that everyone thinks I'm acting odd."

Naomi hasn't blinked. "Is all of this true or are you trying to make me feel better? Either way, it's very sweet of you, Mr. Bristow."

"Blackbeard." I massage the bridge of my nose with a laugh. "I mean, Jason."

Her mouth tips into a smile, the pink of her skin fading back into cream. "No one in the bagel shop thinks your behavior is odd. I'm sure of it. They're probably wondering how many bagels you could eat in one sitting."

"Four and a half." I plant a hand on the wall over her shoulder, stopping just short of leaning down to inhale her. "No one in there is going to think you're a pathetic loner."

"It's all in our heads," she murmurs, glancing over at the boisterous line of customers waiting to get in. "Would you judge me if I chew your theory over for a week and try again next Sunday?"

"No, beauty queen. I wouldn't." I'm rarely impulsive, but hell if I'm not taking her hand and leading her through the throng of people to the hostess station before I know my own mind. "We still have to eat, though."

"You're going to have brunch with me?"

"I'm going to have eggs. They don't need a fancy name." I stop at the hostess station and lose some of my momentum. What the hell am I doing? I go to the bagel shop every Sunday because I crave that routine. I've tested the route and eaten the food. Safe. The process is safe. A glance around the Speckled Hen tells me it's packed to the gills and I recognize no one. It's totally foreign to me. I'm sweating under my shirt again. My instinct is shouting at me to carry Naomi out of here and retreat to the house.

She needs this, though.

Hell, I need it, too, I think. Naomi was brave enough to try something new first. Braver than me. I don't want her to retreat, so I can't either.

"Two for breakfast," I say, clearing my throat.

"Brunch?" chirps the hostess, making Naomi chuckle.

"Sure," I mutter. "Whatever you want to call it."

"We have a thirty-minute wait. Or there's space at the bar now."

Naomi gives me a slow nod when I turn to her. "Sure. The bar."

We quickly find out the hostess is either a liar or she has a different meaning of the word *space*. The bar is jammed with locals forking eggs into their mouths—although none of the eggs look like the ones I'm accustomed to. They've been primped, sprinkled with shit and arranged on other shit.

"What the hell happened to scrambled or fried?" I say to Naomi, before glancing down and realizing she's nervous again, trying to avoid waitresses barreling past with trays and customers breezing past while staring at their phones. "Come here, baby."

She lets me guide her to a sliver of daylight at the bar where there's no seat, only standing room. Which ends up suiting me, because I can wedge her into the opening and protect her with my back facing the chaotic restaurant. Unfortunately, the crowded space also brings our bodies close. Really close.

And it might be Sunday morning, but my dick isn't sleeping in.

Having Naomi's back pressed to the bar, the view of us blocked in on either side, I can't help but fantasize about how easy it would be to let my hands climb up beneath her skirt. To get her supple ass in my hands, lift her up on her tip toes and rock that sweet pussy against my lap. I'd whisper in her ear that I'm interested in eating one thing and it isn't brunch. It would damn well be the truth, wouldn't it? She's got every cell in my body buzzing.

The harried bartender sets down menus on the bar, but I wave him off, forgetting to feel out of place in the face of my need. "Eggs for me. Basic, scrambled eggs and a bagel if you have it—"

"Is sliced challah okay?"

I groan inwardly, no idea what the fuck he's referring to. "Sure. She wants the Nutella French toast." I look down at Naomi to find her transfixed by the collar of my T-shirt. "Coffee?"

"Tea."

"Coffee for me. Tea for her," I relay to the bartender. "Thanks."

I let out a breath I didn't know I was holding when the guy walks away, and Naomi smiles up at me. "That wasn't easy for you. This isn't. You weren't lying."

"You could tell?"

She reaches up and taps a finger against the pulse at the base of my neck. "Only because of this." I want to grab her hand and press it there more firmly, but she takes it back like she's touched a stove. "Thanks for coming to my rescue." I want to tell Naomi that she pushed me out of *my* comfort zone. That in a way, she rescued me from my bullshit orange juice routine that might have gone on indefinitely. But she distracts me. "Can I ask you something personal, Mr. Bristow?"

"Shoot."

"Why did you come home to take care of Birdie? Where are your parents?"

I encounter a familiar surge of anger and it takes me a moment to answer. "I got leave to come home for Nat's funeral. It was only supposed to be a week, but I couldn't believe the way my parents looked at Birdie. Treated her. They…" I break off to bite down on my tongue. "They cringed when she walked into the room. And I know it was grief. I understand. But I couldn't leave my sister in that environment. I took an extended leave and told them to get out of St. Augustine until they pulled themselves together. My aunt on my mother's side lives in Dallas, so they found an apartment near her."

"Poor Birdie. That must have been so hard. Her own parents…"

"Yeah." I rub at a kink in my neck. "I think she's dealing with it all right now."

Naomi nods, scrutinizing me with a thoughtful frown. "Have you asked her how she's doing?"

I drop my hand, laughing without humor. "I've reached about the end of my capabilities. I'm not exactly cut out to raise a teenager. Food, a roof, a pageant coach. These are the things I can provide."

She wants to press me. Or disagree. But she doesn't. "Don't forget you can cook a mean halibut," she says, referring to the one time I convinced her to come to dinner.

"Apparently my roasted potatoes need work. You didn't touch them."

"Of course not," she gasps, rearing back. "They're made of carbohydrates."

"You just ordered Nutella French toast," I point out.

"Carbs don't count during brunch. Everyone knows that."

I don't bother subduing my smile. "Who scared you off weeknight potatoes?"

"Well…" Her nose wrinkles. "Potatoes were always on the table at dinner time, but my mother would frown every time I ate one, so I stopped."

That pisses me off good, but I've got her standing close and talking to me. I'm determined not to ruin the moment or send her running. "So it wasn't me and Birdie that scared you away, it was the starch."

"You didn't scare me away." The stilted way she says it tells me that's not entirely accurate. "Why would you think that?"

There's an obvious answer to that—I definitely don't hide my interest, much as she tries to conceal hers—but there's something else I've been curious about since that dinner. "You seemed nervous when we argued."

"Did I?" She smooths her sleeves absently, then frowns over a stray thread. "I suppose I've gotten used to playing mediator." Her attention leaves the thread and she seems to realize what she said. "Um. To my parents. They argued a lot about the affair. Gosh, I still haven't gotten used to talking about it out loud to someone other than my family."

"You made it sound like a big deal. No one in Charleston talks about it?"

"Only the polite way. Behind our backs."

We share a quiet laugh. "Did you mediate out of necessity or because you enjoy it?"

"What an odd question." She shifts side to side, patting her hair. "I don't know. I've never thought it through. Not in that particular way." A beat passes. "Out of necessity, I suppose."

"Yeah?"

"Yes. The fighting scared me when I was a child. I didn't want to be scared," she whispers, cracking my chest in half. "So I did whatever I could to distract them. Sometimes it worked. Sometimes it didn't. And then I got older and it became more of a burden than something that inspired fear. I must just be conditioned to jump in and calm the waters."

"They shouldn't have argued in front of a child. Especially not about that." I swallow, wishing I had the freedom to pull her closer, kiss her forehead. "I'm sorry. It's not your job to calm the waters. I might not be…thrilled you were getting married the day you ran away, but I am glad you made the waves this time. Good for you, baby."

"Thank you," she breathes, looking up at me, like she's seeing me for the first time. We remain suspended there for long moments, before she visibly snaps out of it and stands up straighter. "Here's what I know. Next time, I'm going to eat enough potatoes to choke."

"Good girl."

The dose of heat in my voice brings her eyes back snapping up to mine and there's no help for it, I have to get closer. This woman is not available to me, but I want her anyway. I can't imagine anyone else having her, frankly. Especially when she's moistening her lips, clearly aware I need to kiss her. Christ, she's such an impactful combination of vulnerable and funny and brave and empathetic. And seriously, since when does empathy make my cock hard? If I pushed forward with my hips, Naomi would feel the erection she conjured up with her nearness. Again.

"You're a good man for staying home with Birdie," she whispers, forcing me to lean down to hear. "For giving up your calling and focusing on hers. You might not even be aware of the difference you're making, but I am."

I'm going to kiss her. I'm going to kiss her ex-fiancé out of her mind. Her eyelids droop a little more with every inch I close in. She wants it—

There's a clatter of mugs in saucers on the bar behind Naomi and she jolts forward, her tits flattening on my stomach. On reflex, I reach out to steady her, but she's already cradling my hard cock, her lips popped open in surprise.

"Come on, baby, you knew it was there," I rasp into the crown of her head, my hands shifting the dress up her thighs. "It's always there, hoping you'll need it."

Naomi seems to gather her will, whirling to face the bar. But that only drags her ass into my lap and I feel the moan pass through her. Hear the low answer of mine, right as the food arrives. It's indecent and it's fucking torture, but that's how we eat our meals. The crowd grows, pushing us closer together. Closer. Naomi's tight little backside rests against my cock, one of my hands gripping her hip, the other operating my fork. Hell if I taste a goddamn thing when I'm more turned on than I've ever been in my life.

I can feel every inhale and exhale she takes. Can feel her swallowing, can hear her breaths. I'm salivating to bite and lick the back of her neck, but I sense she's looking for any reminder she's doing something bad. Any excuse to pull away and be faithful to someone else. That only makes me want to fuck her more. Claim her.

We eat in record time and I dig into my front pocket, grazing the curve of her ass as I retrieve my wallet. Another moan shakes her, but the spell is broken when I toss money onto the bar and we're forced to separate. It's agony. Agony not having her curves on my lap any more. I need to know she's suffering, too, but she doesn't look at me as I guide her to the exit. I walk home beside her in a fever state, the flesh angry and neglected in my pants. The closer we get to home, the more obvious it becomes that I'm going to suffer alone. She's composed and serene where I'm hot and bothered. She proves me right by running up her apartment stairs as soon as we hit the driveway.

I curse vilely, all but ripping the door off its hinges getting into the house. As soon as I determine the house is definitely empty, I unzip my jeans and take my cock in my hands, jerking root to tip, root to tip as I stumble blindly into my bedroom, groaning the name of my torturer.

"Naomi."

CHAPTER TWELVE

ColdCaseCrushers.com
Username: StopJustStop
This is what happens when I leave the Internet.
All hell breaks loose. Well I'll leave you to it, you big pack
of lunatics.
I'm taking a break. I don't need this!!

Naomi

I PACE MY apartment fanning myself. What just happened?

Have I lost my mind? Eating a meal in a public place while shamelessly pressed to a man's intimate parts. Tempting him when I know darn well nothing good can come from a physical encounter. How wrong of me.

But my body seems bound and determined to be thrilled.

I tempted. I was a temptation.

My nipples pull into tight beads and I rub them with restless palms, pressing my thighs together. Thanks to years of stringent Sunday school sermons and the libido-dampening reality of living under my parents' roof, I don't touch myself frequently. I have no choice right now, though, do I? I'm going to explode into tiny particles unless I find release. Already I'm so wet, I wonder if I didn't orgasm in the restaurant solely from the feel of Jason's thickness, that big paw on my hip, tugging me back. Tugging, tugging.

Rolling his hips. Breathing into my neck.

"Lord," I sob, bending forward over the kitchen table, reaching back to pull up my skirt. My few and far between masturbation sessions were usually in the dark under my goose feather duvet. But after having Jason behind me for what felt like hours, I want this position. I need to simulate being taken from behind, even though I have no idea what that's like.

I've never even done it this way. Sex with Elijah was infrequent due to his busy schedule and when it actually happened, we moved like strangers, not speaking, rarely making eye contact. I always sensed he physically held back with me, but I was too afraid for confirmation of that—and a subsequent explanation of *why*—that I never brought it up. No, I simply gave him what I thought was expected and hoped it would be enough. When it was over, he would smile and go back to being a perfect gentleman, making it easy to tell myself I was being silly.

I wasn't, though, was I? Sex is supposed to be like I feel right now. Like I'm going to die unless someone takes the ache away. *Now.* Not just someone, though. A specific man.

My eyes land on something sitting on the table. It's the newspaper I found on the steps this morning. It landed there early and I didn't want to wake up Jason or Birdie bringing it to them. There's a subscriber sticker on the roll. Jason Bristow, along with the address. Suddenly there is a devil on my shoulder telling me I should return the newspaper. Now. Anything to get back in his proximity. My body is begging me. I'm not thinking clearly at all. I'm a servant to the memory of that hand on my hip, the offer of something…hot. Hard.

I'm already calling myself ten times a fool as I snatch up the newspaper and move on shaky legs back down the stairs.

"What are you doing?" I whisper. "What are you doing? Go

back."

A growl of pain comes from inside the house, snapping my mantra in half. Someone's hurt. No, Jason is hurt. I only left him a few minutes ago—what could have happened in such a short time? I don't know, but he obviously needs help. Hastily setting aside my selfish neediness, I drop the paper on the driveway, letting myself into the house.

"Mr. Bristow?" I call. "Are you okay?"

Panting drifts down the hallway. Loud. Rasping. Urgent.

I move toward it, already trying to figure out where Jason would keep his first-aid kit. Under the bathroom sink? The kitchen?

When I reach his bedroom door, I hesitate a moment. It's an intrusion, but surely an emergency excuses this breach in manners. Yes. Surely it must. I push the door open.

Jason's broad, tattooed, at least six-and-a-half-foot frame silhouetted in the window, his packed muscle chest rifling up and down. Standing. Corded thighs flexing. So his injury must not be too bad—

I slap a hand over my mouth to trap my gasp.

Jason's head whips toward the door, his body turning to half-face me. I don't move. How can I move? Buttocks tensing and loosening, thrusting hips, an expression of utter pain…and his hand. Jason's hand is paused mid-way through its progress up his huge…huge. His erection is huge. Jason watches me through narrowed eyes for a few beats before continuing to stroke, his thumb rubbing over the veined head.

My back bashes up against the doorframe. "I-I thought you were injured."

"Might as well be," he grates, dropping his head forward, his hand pumping faster, faster. "Never been in this much pain, baby, and I'm sorry. You caught me at the point I can't stop, so either shut the door or come help me."

"Help you?"

I can't even believe I'm still standing here. The second I realized Jason was pleasuring himself, I should have slammed the door, run for my Range Rover and driven straight to a monastery. Yes, a vow of silence and years of self-reflection are the only way I'm even going to get over this sight in front of me. This private male ritual that is so much more...raw and arousing than I ever realized.

Because it's Jason performing it, whispers a voice in the back of my head. *Help him.* Oh Lord, that devil on my shoulder is back and it's talking nonsense. There's no way I could go closer, let alone participate. Unfortunately, my thighs are writhing and when I wasn't looking, my hands started creeping toward my breasts. Breathing. When did my breathing get so shallow?

"Naomi," he groans through his teeth. "Go. Or get over here."

I can't believe I'm doing this. But I'm back in that state of suspended reality, just like in the restaurant, trying to make excuses for doing something purely because my body wants it. Yes, before I can stop myself, I'm walking on shaky legs toward the bed. Jason's head flies up, his nostrils flaring. Primal. Hungry. It's intoxicating and exciting to have someone look at me like that.

Someone? Or Jason?

I can't answer that. Not now, not ever. Maybe I can give myself this one pass, though. Like carbs at brunch. As soon as I get within reaching distance, he snags the back of my dress with his free hand, pressing me toward the bed. Into that position I need so badly. So badly that I whimper, falling forward onto my elbows, presenting my bottom to him. It's indecent. It's amazing.

Jason flips up the back of my dress, lifts, leaving it gathered at my waist. A hoarse sound leaves him. "Goddamn, Naomi." His rakes his hands over the cheeks of my bottom, squeezing. "You're the most incredible thing I've ever seen."

"Please..."

I have no idea what I'm asking him, but somehow he interprets. "You're not ready for me to strip off these little panties yet, are you?" He runs a finger under the narrow strip of cotton hiding my most private flesh, grazing my clit with a knuckle and making me suck in a breath. "You curious enough about my cock to come closer, but not enough to take the pounding."

"I don't know. I don't know."

"It's too big for I don't knows, baby." His open mouth travels up the center of my bottom, his teeth nipping at the small of my back. "You want to get off without the guilt of letting me help? Then touch yourself, Naomi. I'll even let you pretend afterward that I had nothing to do with satisfying that pussy." He tucks my backside into the cradle of his hips, giving me a hard, punctuated thrust. "We're just two people accidentally fucking ourselves in the same place at the same time."

Lust blankets my brain, my world, my senses, and I can do nothing, nothing in the wake of those sexual words but touch myself. I brace myself with my left hand and slide the fingers of my right into my panties, whimpering when I make contact with my swollen clit.

"Fuck, baby. Fuck. Good girl." I hear the wet strokes of Jason's hand up and down his erection, faster than when I walked into the room, accompanied by guttural grunts. "Let me pull your panties down so I can see, woman. *Woman, please.*"

Woman. So base. So elemental. My answer is a moan and

cool air greets my cheeks, carrying a heightened awareness of our positions. I'm facedown on the bed, this insanely strong male masturbating to the sight of me. Watching the desperate fondling of my fingers against my clit up close. Abusing his flesh harder and harder the closer I get to orgasm. Lord oh lord oh lord. It's decadently sinful. I couldn't have conjured a scene like this in my wildest fantasies and I wonder if I've been living at all. I've definitely never needed to climax so badly my thighs trembled, like they're doing now.

"Put a finger in that gorgeous pussy and make my fucking life," Jason says unevenly, instinct telling me he's close. Just as close as I am. "Go on, baby. Let me see it disappear into that pretty pink slit."

I'm sexy. I'm ruinous. I'm a goddess in that moment. With a curl of my mouth, I invade myself with a finger, rolling my eyes back in my head. The rush of sensation that has been gathering inside me pops and I wail for God into the bedclothes, my body jerking as it is pummeled by spasms. One right after the other. Wetness lands on the backs of my thighs, my bottom, the strangled groans of the man behind me like the crescendo of a symphony. I reel hard, my lungs seizing as I draw frantic breaths, my lower body continuing to be a battleground for fulfillment and greed. More?

Yes, I want more. I want him inside me, filling me, gratifying both of us.

Another more startling realization is that I want him to gather me close and be my anchor just as badly. To hold me, rock me, fall asleep beside me. I want to forget the obligations I put on hold, let them become distant memories. That realization is what sends me flying back into the present where I've fallen limply to Jason's bed, my panties bunched mid-thigh, the product of his hunger drying on my backside.

I start to stand, stopping and closing my eyes as Jason dries me off with a towel and gently lifts my panties into place. Our breathing is still harsh in the sealed room, and Lord help me, the sound is already getting me turned on again. I have to get out of here before I'm tempted to turn this moment of weakness into a recurring mistake.

Keeping my features schooled, I straighten, letting my dress flutter down around my thighs. "I-I…well…as I said, I thought you were injured—"

His rumble of humorless laughter cuts me off. "Like I said, we were just two people getting off at the same place, same time." His tongue presses to the inside of his cheek as he takes a step closer, close enough that the backs of my knees hit the bed. Warm breath ghosts over my face, a mixture of coffee and cigars. "Any time you want to accidentally make me come so hard that I can't see straight again, baby, I'll be right here waiting."

I walk out of the house in a trance on legs made of jelly. How am I supposed to get a moment's rest with that offer on the table? *Ignore it, Naomi.*

Before I walk into my apartment, I look back toward the house and find Jason watching me from his bedroom window. Ignore anything relating to Jason?

Easier said than done.

CHAPTER THIRTEEN

ReadtheComments.com
Username: LittleMissMorbid
So, okay. Without getting too dark, has anyone tried checking
the walls of the church for a body?

Jason

TODAY'S DIVE WAS an easy one. My group was experienced and didn't need a lot of guidance, just someone to take them out on the water. I'm not talkative on my best day, so it's a good thing the four men only needed a basic outline of the underwater landscape before dropping in with the instructions to be back at the boat within thirty minutes. If they were new divers, I would have brought a crew member to monitor oxygen levels from the boat while I joined the divers, but their experience let me remain solo in the boat today.

Maybe not such a good thing, because the stretch of quiet gives me a chance to dwell on the hottest jerk-off session of my life. I could live nine lifetimes and never get the sight of Naomi out of my head. I almost wish I could forget her taut ass, her spread thighs. Her finger pushing into the smoothest, juiciest-looking pussy I've ever laid eyes on. Christ, even before she fingered herself on my bed, I was sick with lust from the moment I woke up until the second I fell asleep at night. Now I'm a walking, talking hard-on. She's been avoiding me the last few days, but I can still feel her. Sometimes I swear I can hear her moving around in her bedsheets from across the driveway. Been sleeping with my window open hoping for it.

When did I become such a masochist?

I *need* this woman who is devoted to someone else. Someone whose idea of courtship probably doesn't include having to wipe her down afterward.

With a disgusted curse, I check my watch and cross the deck to make sure the oxygen levels are where they need to be. I make a quick notation on my dive log and resume pacing.

Dating and women and sex are not foreign things to me. I've been in relationships, albeit short ones, thanks to my restlessness, inability to communicate and chosen career. During those brief blurs of shore leave while with the service, I met women. I'm not some wet behind the ears kid in the throes of his first crush. I've simply never had a woman get to me like this. I want to hold, kiss her and get inside her head almost as bad as I want to sleep with her—a mind fuck if I've ever heard one.

Wedged in between the moments I'm thinking of getting her naked, I'm thinking of her breezing into my living room looking like a hot to trot housewife, bubbly and determined to make my sister's first friend date a success. I think of her screeching like a barn cat and calling it singing. I think of her leaning across a table full of empty beer glasses and telling war stories.

I'm going to admit it. I've got a serious thing for the beauty queen.

And I have no goddamn clue what to do about it.

The group of divers make their way onto the boat, one by one, and I guide the vessel back into the marina. I started this business because diving is in my blood and I wanted to stay in practice for when I redeploy. I deadlift in my garage, run, dive, stay focused, so I don't miss a beat when I go back. Being a weak link is not an option for me. That's what I am here. Maybe not weak, but I'm the link that doesn't fit.

You like to keep people safe. Don't you think that's nice?

I mishandle a rope when Naomi's voice tinkles into my mind like a crystal-clear bell. I've never thought of nice from that perspective before. Nice is making fancy drinks and smiling and picnics at the beach. Shit I will never find myself doing. But what if Naomi is right and I have my own way of being a...strong link for my sister? Right here in Florida?

There's no way I could ever be as effective here as I am overseas, but maybe I should try talking to Birdie more. It can't hurt, right?

Footsteps approach me from behind and I brace, checking the urge to reach for a weapon that definitely isn't there in my peeled down wetsuit. It costs me an effort, but I turn slowly, nonthreateningly, to meet whoever is coming—and I rock back on my heels when I see who it is.

"Musgrave?"

"Fuckin-A." One of the closest friends I have in my assigned Special Forces group slides off his mirrored sunglasses, raising a shaggy blond eyebrow. "Took my life into my own hands sneaking up on you like that. Guess I'm missing the action."

"You and me both." I put my hand out and we shake hard, a count longer than normal because we're glad to see each other but definitely not comfortable with hugs. "What are you doing in St. Augustine?"

"Don't know. Can't sit still—you know how it goes." He rolls back his shoulders. "Decided to take a drive down from Nashville for the weekend. Get some air."

"Long way to come for some air. Something up?"

"You going to pry into my affairs or buy me a fucking beer?"

As recently as a couple of weeks ago, the prospect of going out into a crowd and sitting at a bar with my back turned would have given me a lot of pause. Sitting among strangers, no control over the endless variables. No weapon or plan. It would have made me sweat and probably suggest grabbing a six-pack and heading home instead. Yeah, having Musgrave with me makes it easier, but it's more than that. Going to brunch with Naomi broke the seal. I got through it, even though the eggs had cilantro in them. I'm more capable now...thanks to her.

"Beer sounds good." I jerk my chin toward the dock's locker room. "Let me go throw something on and we'll head. Don't steal my boat while my back is turned."

"You remember my specialty, then," Musgrave says on a hearty laugh. "Hey, man. When you've got two minutes to meet the bird or get left in the weeds, you improvise."

"Never did return that boat to the owner, did you?"

A lazy shrug. "Didn't hear you complaining over the fast exit. Ain't that the mission you took a knife to the back?"

"It was." Just acknowledging the injury makes the pulse beat harder in that particular section of my back, right above my left shoulder blade. "Did I ever say thank you for getting me to the medic?"

He gives me a look to remind me I would—and have—done the same for him. "Fuck you, Bristow. Go change."

We're both laughing as I move along the dock toward the office. I feel more like my old self than I did two minutes ago, just being around Musgrave who's been the same places I've been. Skirted landmines, risked life and limb, engaged in hand to hand battles with men. Men just like me, fighting because we've been ordered to. Men with families just like me, but who I'll never know beyond those brief, brutal encounters. It's hard to be normal after that.

I shoot a text to Birdie letting her know I won't be home for dinner and to use the cash in my money clip to order a pizza. This isn't the first time I've missed dinner, but it's the first time I've felt guilty about it. I should be home with her, making more of an effort than I have been. Hell, I haven't even really talked to her about the pageant. It's the biggest thing in her life right now and I don't even know if she's nervous. Or optimistic. Doesn't she need dresses for the competition? Have I funded those yet?

Thirty minutes into happy hour with Musgrave and I've drowned most of those worries in Budweiser, but they remain nonetheless, reminding me I need to be home at a decent hour. Need to be up in the morning making breakfast for my sister. Need to be at the window when Naomi floats down the steps in whatever outfit she's chosen to drive me crazy in for the day.

"You heard from Wallace? Hirschberg?"

I shake my head. "Not since I've been on leave. Then again, I don't think any of us are on fucking Facebook. I'm assuming they'll just show up some day like a rusty penny. Sound familiar?"

Knowing I'm referring to his impromptu visit, Musgrave smiles. "Old habits die hard. I still don't like telegraphing my moves." His beer bottle pauses on the way to his mouth. "You know what I mean?"

There's a pinch in my middle. "Yeah. Doesn't feel natural being in one place this long."

The other man seems deep in thought for a moment. "You still planning on going back?"

"Always." My answer doesn't have quite as much conviction as it once did, I'm surprised to find. "Feels like I'm on duty sometimes and just ignoring orders."

"I was like that for the first year. Still am sometimes. I mean, I just drove half a day on a whim because life felt too comfortable."

"And bad things happen when you get complacent. I hear you." We sip in silence. "My couch is yours for the night. I got a…tenant right now. Or else I'd offer you the apartment for as long as it takes to get right."

"A tenant?" He plants an elbow on the bar and turns to face me. "Have to say, that doesn't sound like you, Bristow. You once made Wallace test your shampoo in his hair before you'd trust we didn't put leg hair remover in it."

"Yeah. And he wouldn't test it. Because there was leg hair remover in it."

His crack of laughter draws attention around the bar. "Still, you have to admit, you've got some trust issues."

Okay. So we're going to have this conversation. "Her name is Naomi. She's my little sister's pageant coach."

"Former pageant girl or stage mama type?"

An image of Naomi moaning into my mattress with her ass in the air forces me to clear my throat. Hard. "The former."

He waggles his eyebrows. "She single?"

"No," I answer on instinct. She's off limits to everyone, including my friend. I don't care if it's rational or not. Acid churns in my stomach, though, because I can't physically lie to my teammate. It goes against my nature and training. "Yeah, she's single. But not in the traditional sense."

Musgrave studies my face for a moment. "Fuckin-A. Sounds complicated." Humor flashes in his face. "Single or not, I'm getting a vibe from you that says if I flirt with her, you'll rip my spleen out through my armpit."

"That's eerily accurate."

He whoops a laugh and takes out his wallet, signaling the end of the night. "Well, hot damn. Let's go meet her."

I know Musgrave too well. There's no way out of this.

Getting my own wallet out and throwing money on the bar before Musgrave can, I sigh and begin to wade through the crowd toward the exit. "This should be interesting."

I have no idea how right I am.

CHAPTER FOURTEEN

EndoftheInternet.net
Username: IGotAnswerz9
Let me be plain. The only one with a motive to kill was Naomi's father.
She was threatening to expose his illegitimate child. Textbook!

Naomi

BODY PAINT PARADE.

Who knew such a thing existed?

I scroll through the bright images of people—naked ones—in nothing but artwork to keep them modest. In some cases, painted flowers cover breasts. In others, elaborate designs wind head to toe, covering every inch of the subject's skin. My mouth hangs open in awe. What kind of confidence would a human being need to walk down the street without clothes?

I'm in a lull. I've been so focused on the pageant and taking baby steps in my quest to live on my own terms that time has become an issue. In other words, I don't have enough of it. If I return to Charleston having mastered nothing more than buying my own shampoo, making tacos and eating in a restaurant without a reservation, this whole mission will have been for nothing. I need to try harder. I need something way outside my comfort zone. Maybe the body paint parade is exactly what I need. After all, I won't be alone, will I? Thousands of people participated in Daytona Beach last year…and it's only a couple hour drive from St. Augustine.

Maybe getting out of St. Augustine for a day or two would give me some peace. I haven't seen Jason since I…well, I can't even believe what I did. Let him act as an audience while I touched myself. *Honestly, Naomi.* Shame is what I should feel. Unfortunately, every time I think about that afternoon, vines wrap around my thighs, climbing, climbing until I'm trapped in a pulsing, forbidden garden of need. It's indecent and…I shouldn't want to do it again. I shouldn't lie in bed night after night, wishing my doorknob would turn, Jason would walk in and drop all that tattooed muscle on top of me.

I frown when I realize I'm fanning my face.

Yes, getting out of town for a while is a smashing idea.

Resolving to make a pro-con list before the parade next weekend, I close the window on my web browser. I tap my index finger on the click pad for a few seconds, chewing the inside of my cheek, before opening a new window and signing in to my email.

Four hundred and ninety messages.

I almost shut the laptop, content to live in blissful ignorance for the foreseeable future, but something stops me. What if Elijah emailed me? Don't I owe him a response?

With a blown-out breath, I scroll all the way to the bottom of my inbox, recognizing the names of several friends and acquaintances, all of the subject lines overrun with question marks. News outlets and a couple of those ridiculous conspiracy theory websites are attempting to get in contact, too. But no Elijah. A thickness builds in my throat as I scroll back to the top to find a new email from my mother, subject line: Are you enjoying yourself?

"We've moved into the passive-aggressive phase, have we?" I murmur. Knowing I'll obsess about the contents of the message all night unless I read it, I click.

> *Dearest Naomi,*
>
> *By all means, please take your time coming back to Charleston. Your father and I are faring well, despite the relentless questions from our friends and unwanted attention from the press. The important thing is that YOU are happy. Our quality of life is of little importance.*
>
> *I've been in close contact with Mrs. DuPont and been assured that Elijah is eagerly awaiting your return home but has elected to give you space to figure things out. Isn't that the kind of unselfish behavior we all hope to see from our children?*
>
> *Signed,*
> *Your mother*

A tremor passes through me. "Right on target, as usual, mother," I say with a tremor.

I am selfish, aren't I? All my life, everything has been handed to me. Walking down the aisle, despite knowing I bore my fiancé to tears, would have been my way of showing gratitude. For all my parents have given me. That would have been the behavior of a dutiful daughter, which is what I've been raised to be. I'd be married to a man who would give me everything...

But no. I wouldn't have been able to give Elijah everything. No excitement. Nothing unique. Isn't that why I'm here? As much as I want to learn what I'm capable of, I want to return to Charleston with experiences under my belt. This time away is meant to break me out of the Mattel box I've been living in. So I can be a better wife, mother. Person.

Though it hurts, I force myself to read the email from my mother again. Have things between Elijah and Addison gone south so soon? Disappointment sinks in my belly. With a bemused head shake, I realize somewhere deep down I must have been rooting for them. Lord, I am the least devoted ex-fiancée on this planet. I really must work on that before going home.

For now, I can't let my mother get to me. I do, however, need to make contact with Elijah. The note I left him at the church was pitiful and desperate—plus, I left it almost a month ago. He deserves to know where I am and that…I'm thinking about him.

But when I open the fresh email and type his address into the top bar, it's not Elijah I'm thinking about. It's Jason. Goose-bumps crawl up my neck, as if he's standing behind me, observing me as I email another man. He wouldn't like it. At all. Guilt has my fingers going still on the keys—for two reasons. One, my whole body reacts to the mere thought of Jason, my nipples gathering into painful peaks, my thighs shifting around on the seat. Not the kind of state I should be in while contacting my ex-fiancé and thanking him for being patient. Two, after what Jason and I did in his bedroom…I do feel as if I'm being untrue to my complicated employer. And that's terrifying.

Voices outside distract me from my thoughts. Men. One of them is Jason, but I don't recognize the second. I push away from the kitchen table with a frown and move to the window, finding Jason opening the back door to his house, calling for Birdie. There's something different about Jason and I'm so intent on figuring out what it is, I don't realize the second man is staring up at me from the driveway. I recover with a jolt, sending him a tentative wave, which he returns while shaking his head and laughing.

Birdie comes out of the house in pajama pants and a hoodie,

shaking hands with the second man. Altogether they move toward the stairs and I realize they're coming here. To my place. "Oh shoot." I hop back from the window with a squeak, throwing off my silky pink honeymoon robe, trading it for the blue maxi dress I wore today. A couple of pinches of my cheeks in the mirror and they're already knocking. "Some notice would be nice," I mutter, padding to the front door and pasting on a smile. "A simple phone call. Anything."

"I don't have your number," Jason drones through the door.

I bury my face in my hands for a beat, then pull the door open. "Hello!" Without waiting for an invitation, Birdie sails past me and hops onto my kitchen counter, leaving Jason and the unknown man standing in the doorway. I extend my hand to him and he takes it, squeezing warmly. "Naomi Clemons. It's a pleasure to meet you."

"Kyle Musgrave at your service." He smiles charmingly, and I realize he's quite handsome with his cleft chin and light, sun-scorched hair. The antithesis of Jason's dark, could-be-man-or-could-be-bear appearance. "Sorry for the last-minute visit," he says. "It's a pleasure to meet you, too."

There's no help for it. I have to send Jason a prim look. *See? A proper greeting isn't so hard.* "Think nothing of it. Please come in." I step back with sweep of my arm. "I gather you're a friend of Mr. Bristow?"

He smirks at Jason, who sends him back an eye roll. "Mr. Bristow and I were in the service together. I showed up unannounced at the marina today and he's been kind enough to put a stray dog up for the night."

Jason's frown is fixed on something and I have to turn in a circle to find out it's my silk robe in a heap on the floor. Maintaining my smile, I scoop it up and toss it into my bedroom, closing the door behind it. Thinking about it out of place makes me antsy, though, so I slip into the bedroom, hang it on a peg and reemerge to Jason's shaking head. What is it about him that's tugging at my curiosity? After a moment, the smell of beer reaches me and I realize he's been…out. Drinking in a bar. These two rugged warrior men have been out on the town. A vision of Jason surrounded by dancing women rises unbidden in my mind and I shake my head to loosen it. It's none of my business where he's been.

Yet the back of my neck remains tighter than a pickle jar.

"Can I offer you gentleman something to drink?" Telling myself it's ridiculous to be miffed with Jason for enjoying his evening, I enter the small kitchen area and open the fridge. I hesitate a moment before sliding two bottles of Budweiser out of their sleeve in the cardboard six-pack holder. Jason's gaze nearly burns a hole in my back, but I manage to snick open the bottles without fumbling the play. "Would you like a Coke, Birdie?"

Her bare feet bump the lower cabinets in a low rhythm. "I'm good."

I turn and hand off the beers to the men, catching my breath when the pads of Jason's fingertips brush mine. Is it my imagination or did Jason grow several inches since yesterday? Maybe seeing him shoulder to shoulder with another, regular-sized man drives home exactly how large and intimidating he is. *Don't look at his hand around the beer bottle and remember what you saw it doing. Don't…too late.*

He winks at me, as if reading my mind.

I frown back. "Where do you reside, Mr. Musgrave?"

"Please call me Kyle."

"Save your breath," Jason mutters. "We've known each other for a month and we're still not on a first-name basis."

While Jason and I engage in a very impolite stare down, Kyle takes a long pull of his beer. "Mind me asking why that is?"

My chin lifts all by itself. "He gets his way far too often."

Jason snorts. "We both know that's not true."

I'm pretty sure my face is the color of cotton candy. Lord, I'd like to smack him. "So. *Kyle.* You were saying you reside in…?"

"Oooh," Birdie croons behind me. "She went there."

Jason's eyes smolder at me down the neck of his beer.

Kyle looks like it's killing him to hold in his laughter. "Nashville, ma'am. Music city. That's where I grew up—my mother was a country singer. Daddy played bass in her traveling band."

"I don't have to ask if they were lovesick fools for each other. It's right there in your voice," I say, reaching out to squeeze his arm. "Did they take you on the road with them?"

"First ten years of my life were spent in the back of a converted yellow school bus." He gives me a charming smile. "Probably why I can't sit still now."

"Well, your affliction is our gain. It's so nice to meet you."

"Christ, is this how you'd have been talking to me this whole time if I'd—"

"Answered the door like a gentleman and not smeared motor oil all over my hands?" I pick a speck of imaginary lint off my shoulder. "It's likely. Yes."

Jason hoists his beer. "Thank god I'm not a gentleman, then."

My gasp is rife with outrage.

"Are they always like this?" Kyle asks Birdie.

"Only on days that end in Y."

Jason saunters in one direction around the table, moving in that slow, king-of-the-castle manner I've noticed before. Loose and casual, while somehow projecting a wide array of lethal abilities. He's got even more of that deceptive swagger going tonight than usual because this is obviously not his first Bud-weiser. Not that he's drunk or slurring his words, but his energy is more relaxed.

"Place looks different," Jason remarks. "You've been busy."

I'm not sure if that's a compliment or a complaint, so I say, "There's a lovely indoor farmer's market just off of King Street. I've gotten in the habit of picking up fresh flowers."

"They're nice." When our eyes meet, I see his have softened and a shiver goes through me. I don't know which side of Jason alarms me more. Sweet or sour. He's about to say something more, but his attention drops to the screen of my laptop and whatever he sees there darkens his expression faster than a bolt of lightning. "Looks like we interrupted your work." Before I can respond, he's already draining his beer and setting it down on the table with a thunk. "We should leave her to it. It's not exactly standard protocol for the landlord to drop in on a tenant with guests, is it?"

The way he refers to me as a tenant is like a hot poker to the midsection. That distance, the separation of them and me is what I tried to achieve in the beginning, but it was unrealistic. It didn't work, because I care about Birdie. And it's impossible to hold someone's hand in a moment of weakness, the way I did with Jason, and not…become a concerned party, right? We've traded confidences. That's why my throat feels raw in answer to his dismissive attitude.

A light goes off in my head.

The email. He saw the email I started to Elijah.

My symptoms increase tenfold, the bolts tightening on either side of my throat, my stomach caving in. Guilt. "Can I talk to you for a minute, please?"

I'm not sure why I make the suggestion. What could we possibly say to one another here? But he's already striding for the door. "Yeah."

"Excuse us," I breathe, following. As soon as the door is closed behind me, I'm pinned to it. Not by Jason's body. No. By the pure anger he directs at me. "I'm sorry you saw that."

The words come out in a blind rush.

They give him pause. They give me pause. He takes a purposeful step closer. "Why?"

"I don't know," I say honestly.

"You beautiful, little liar," he pushes through his teeth.

Jason calling me beautiful threatens to derail my focus, but I hang in there. "I'm not lying. We have th-this relationship that consists mostly of arguing. We needle each other constantly...and because of that...the non-fighting moments in between make no sense to me. Where do they come from? Are you always like this with a woman you..."

"Want to fuck? Nah, baby. That would just be counterproductive. But I'm not usually looking to get tail from a woman who's got her sights set elsewhere."

His words are meant to be a slap, but I feel the sting for another reason entirely. "Is that what you were doing tonight, Blackbeard?" I whisper. "Prowling for a woman?"

Oh Lord. I can't believe I asked that. It's the least important part of the statement he just made. And I have *no* right, especially after he saw the beginnings of my email to Elijah. Something inside me calms nonetheless when Jason's angry expression turns to one of utter disbelief. "It's a testament to how deep you've gotten under my skin that I didn't even look, isn't it?" He presses his hands to the door above my head, dropping his mouth to the space just above the curve of my neck. An inch away so I can feel his heated breaths. "Jealous. Aren't you, beauty queen?"

I give a slight nod, unable to do anything but be honest when my body is practically humming out loud, giving me away. I am jealous. And a hypocrite.

"Good," he rasps in my ear, his tongue brushing the sensitive lobe, his teeth worrying that same spot until I'm preparing to be taken against the door. "Try sleeping jealous. I've been doing it for weeks."

Jason backs away and raps twice on the door. "Musgrave. Birdie," he calls, still looking at me. "Let's go." Then just for my ears. "You want to stop tossing and turning and come claim responsibility for this hard dick, you know where to find me."

CHAPTER FIFTEEN

ColdCaseCrushers.com
Username: StopJustStop
Good gravy. Next thing I know, you'll be throwing out
Bigfoot theories.
I'm out of here. Good bye, Internet, forever. And I mean it
this time!!

Jason

THE JOKE IS on me. Despite taunting Naomi last night about tossing and turning through her jealousy, I barely slept a goddamn wink. Several times, I had to talk myself out of kicking down her door and apologizing. Or possibly starting another argument. I probably wouldn't have made up my mind until she answered the door. If she'd had the nerve to answer my knock in that silk, pink robe, though? In the wake of seeing her email to another man? I might have put her over my knee. Shredded that thin, pink tease of a garment in one hand and spanked her yoga-tightened butt rotten with the other.

This is it. I've lost my fucking mind.

Because I know damn well if Naomi answered her door a second time with that vulnerable expression she was wearing when she admitted to being jealous, I would have gotten down on my knees and asked for forgiveness. The fact that she might have spent a night unnecessarily jealous makes me want to quit my morning run, lean over the ocean wall and lose my breakfast. And I feel this way even though she's planning on returning to another man.

I'm pretty sure that makes me a damn fool.

Or I've been horny for this woman so long, my self-respect is waning.

Could be both.

If I could go back and do last night over, I wouldn't have walked away so fast. I would have checked my own jealousy and talked to Naomi. She exposed herself by admitting there's something between us, and I played dirty instead of taking the opportunity to get inside her head. Now the progress we made is lost in the rubble of the fight.

And when the hell did I start believing progress was possible?

When did I start to want it?

An unfamiliar row of houses brings me up short and I realize I've missed the turn for our street. With a curse, I turn and kick up my pace to a sprint, wanting to get home before Birdie leaves. Last night, she stayed up late playing poker with Musgrave and me—until she fell asleep facedown on the table, chips stuck to her forehead. When I carried her to bed and threw the covers over her, I remembered my earlier resolve to talk to her more. Attempt to be more of a brother, rather than a last-ditch guardian. I woke up after my one hour of sleep even more determined to try. Saturdays are pageant cramming days, so she's usually up and out the door by eight, running with Naomi or practicing in the church basement. Maybe I have time to catch her.

I glance up at Naomi's apartment as I slow to a halt at the backdoor, fishing the house key out of my sweatpants. No sign of her. God, I'd give anything for her to turn her nose up at me through the window right now, so I'd know where we stand. This whole wondering if she's got hurt feelings business is going to give me a stroke by noon.

The house is mostly quiet when I walk inside, apart from the music traveling down the hallway from Birdie's bedroom. I grab a towel out of the linen closet and mop off the sweat drying on my back and chest, falling into a kitchen chair with a glass of orange juice moments later. As I'd guessed he would, Musgrave took off this morning before we woke up. Didn't even bother to leave a note, the bastard. He'll probably do this again in a year or so. Show up long enough to reminisce without getting too deep, then hit the bricks.

You won't be here in a year.

I wait for the sense of purpose to flood in—the one I usually get when I think of throwing myself into another seemingly endless round of deployments. This time it's more like a trickle, though. I'm distracted from my confusion when Birdie trips to a stop at the end of the hallway, high heels tucked under her arm. "Hey." She looks around. "Did Kyle leave?"

"Off into the sunset. Knew he wouldn't stick around long."

"Seems to be a running theme with you guys."

"Yeah." I clear the new discomfort from my throat. "I'm here now, though. What's, uh…what's going on?"

She raises an eyebrow at me from the coffee pot. "Huh?"

"What are you doing today?" I nod at the heels that now sit on the kitchen counter. "You have to wear those when you practice walking?"

"Always. They never come off. I might as well have them welded on."

"That sounds tough."

"It's…" My sister does a double take at me, as if she just

realized we're having a conversation. "Um, it's not so bad. I kind of got used to them and now I feel fancy."

"What about the dance? How's that coming?"

She dumps some milk into her mug. "Why are you so interested?"

"Hey, I showed up to watch you waltz."

"You showed up to watch my coach." She holds up both hands. "Totally understandable. Not judging. She looks like two angels had a baby, but some of the devil's DNA snuck in and gave her really nice boobs and legs just to fuck with you." That left turn has me shifting in my chair, sending Birdie into a fit of laughter. "This isn't going as you planned, is it?"

"No." I do my best to stop thinking of Naomi's tits. It's not easy. "I guess I've been pretty obvious about, uh…"

"Wanting to couch the coach?"

"Jesus, Birdie."

"Sorry." She smiles into a sip of coffee. "This is the longest you've talked to me since you got home and I'm ruining it."

A weight presses down on my chest. "I don't want that to be the case. I need to do better."

Her eyebrows knit together. "Need to or want to?" She lowers her coffee revealing the tugged down corners of her mouth. "I know you're not here by choice. I don't expect you to magically be a happy camper. Mom and Dad were like, here you go, Jason. Here's your awkward and disturbingly emotional sibling. Good luck."

"That's not how it went down and that's not how I see it." I stand up and her eyes shoot wide, as if terrified I might try to hug her. "I wanted to be here with you, okay?" Worried I might be throwing to much brotherly love at her at once, I jerk my chin toward the cabinets. "I picked you up some sugar-free chocolate syrup. You still like to drizzle it on your cereal?"

"Yeah. Natalie used to gag every time I did it."

Thinking back to Naomi's story about her mother's frown stopping her from eating potatoes, I make a mental note to never comment on what a woman chooses to eat. One dumb move and an entire food group can be ruined for them forever. "I've eaten expired MREs in a pinch, kid. I'm gag-proof."

Birdie nods, watching me out of the corner of her eye as she goes through the process of testing her blood sugar and injecting insulin.

"When was the last time you saw the endocrinologist?"

She tidies up the scraps of paper and disposes of the needle. "Um. A few months ago?"

I frown. "Did I know about it?"

"No, I just went. I've been going alone since high school started." In the process of removing cereal from the cabinet, she sends me a smirk over her shoulder. "It's pretty fucked up that I have the only disease where the doctors don't hand out lollipops after an appointment, right?"

"Yeah. It's fucked up." I'm not talking about the lollipops, though. My sister has been shouldering a lot on her own, without complaint. And I've been oblivious to it.

Naomi chooses that moment to breeze into the kitchen, looking incredible in some gauzy green shirt that has little cutouts for her shoulders. "Oh." She smooths her hands down the thighs of her white jeans. "I saw you leave for a run. I thought…"

"It's fine," I say. Because suddenly I'm one hundred percent devoted to reassuring women. Hell if it does me any good, though—I can't tell a damn thing from Naomi's schooled expression. "I was just going to ask Birdie about her plans for the day."

Naomi's eyes flicker to mine. "Oh," she says softly. "We're going dress shopping. Time to haggle over prices and cry and swoon. It's the big event."

"Want to come?" Birdie asks me that—and seems shocked to have done so. "I'm totally kidding, obviously. This would be your exact hell on earth."

"I think I'll live."

"What?" Birdie holds her breath, letting it out in a giant rush. "You're coming dress shopping?"

I stop trying to hide my smile when it becomes impossible. "Looks like I am."

Birdie turns to Naomi. "Can we wait for him to shower?"

The pageant coach is watching me thoughtfully, and the more we neglect to look away, the more my pulse starts to weigh down with a now familiar thickness. One that's only ever been inspired by this one woman who comes with a shit ton of complications. "Of course," she drawls. "Try not to clog the drain."

"I make no promises."

I leave them laughing in the kitchen, feeling lighter than I have in a while, save the impossible-to-slake ache in my sweatpants. Two hours later, though, I realize I had no idea what I was getting myself into when I agreed to go dress shopping.

IT'S ABSOLUTE BEDLAM.

There's a thirty percent off sale on ball gowns happening at the department store, and while I appreciate Naomi's attempt to save me money, I would have gladly paid full price to avoid the screeching of hangers on clothing racks and squealing. There is so much squealing.

None of it is coming from my sister. I've seen her expression before, usually worn by men on the wrong side of an ambush. She's trying to talk herself out of retreating, but keeping one eye on the exit. Naomi has a deceptively casual arm around Birdie's shoulder, ushering her through the endless racks of sparkly, poofy dresses, and I know she's prepared to tackle my sister if she tries to run. Not that you could gauge it based on her composure, as if she's shopped for dresses in a veritable sanitarium every day of her life.

I'm following them around a circular rack, trying to ignore the curious looks and whispers I'm getting from the other shoppers. "What exactly are you looking for?"

"We'll know when we find it," Naomi breezes. "But I think Birdie is a winter."

"Come again?"

"Her complexion will pair well with winter colors. Navy, violet, mulberry...even a shocking pink could—"

"Help me look less like a goth who strayed from the pack?" Birdie supplies, scrubbing at her blue hair.

Chuckling, Naomi pulls my sister close. "Now, Birdie. You're gorgeous in jeans and a sweatshirt, but just you wait. Ball gowns are a higher power. They boost things up, tuck others away and smooth creases in between—"

"Of all the days to join you, I choose this one," I mutter.

"But it's more about the way a gown makes you feel, though. The right one will bolster your confidence." She adds in a murmur, "If we find the right one, you'll finally see what I see."

"Pink." Birdie squares her shoulders. "Natalie would have chosen pink."

"What color do *you* want?"

I'm grateful when Naomi asks the question because I was about to do the same. When Birdie came to me wanting to compete in the pageant in Natalie's memory, I hoped it would give her something to focus on. A positive way to remember her twin. Did I do the right thing? She seems almost single-minded in her determination to make this experience exactly what Natalie would have chosen. Is she losing sight of herself in the process?

"I want pink, too," Birdie says with a tight smile. "The shocking kind."

Naomi lets her arm fall as Birdie walks away, scooting around a trio of mothers toward another rack. After a minute, Naomi goes back to sifting through the offerings, but there's a wrinkle of concern between her brows.

"What is it?"

She hums, lifting up a blue dress covered in at least nine thousand sequins for inspection. "It's odd. She's doing all of this because of Natalie, but she's only spoken to me about her sister on one occasion. Other than that, it's what you heard there. Natalie would want this or that." She chews her lip a moment, before glancing up at me. "Do you know what their relationship was like? Before it happened?"

"No clue." I scrub at the cold that surfaces on the back of my neck. "I remember them as kids, mostly. They were late additions for my parents. I left when they were still in elementary school." I swallow something heavy. "Every time I came back they were taller, had new haircuts, sounded different."

"It must have been strange. To get to know Birdie as an adult."

"I don't think I have yet," I admit, watching Birdie pick up a Pepto-colored creation and promptly hang it back up. "Not even close."

"Is that why you came today?" Naomi asks softly.

My nod feels stiff. "Probably too late. It's already been six months of going through the motions. She has no reason to think I'd want to change that. Only that I'd feel obligated."

"Which is the truth?"

"I want to," I say firmly, meaning it.

"Trust that she's smart enough to see that."

We both look down to find her hand on my arm. I know she's going to snatch it back before she actually does it, so I catch her wrist. "Hey."

Her pulse jumps under my fingertips. "Yes?"

"I don't like the way we left things last night."

"You don't?"

If I wasn't intent on straightening things out, I might have laughed over her breathy, little answers. "No. I don't like the way we leave things any night, frankly. But last night was worse because you, uh...I upset you." I notice a woman watching us over the top of the rack and raise an eyebrow at her until she keeps moving. "Friendly fire is all well and good. But I don't like upsetting you."

She shifts, and I actually hear the seam of her jeans rasp together, turning my mouth dry. "Could have fooled me. I accept your apology, nonetheless," she whispers, searching my face. "You're different today. Did you have some sort of middle-of-the-night epiphany?"

"Didn't sleep much, so I definitely had time." Our eyes stay locked for several beats. "Hard to explain, but...I'm trained to see things from the perspective of my teammates. Could be that having Musgrave around made me take a look at myself."

"And having him around made you realize you shouldn't say *dick* to a lady?" Naomi's hand flies out of my grip to smack directly over her mouth. "I did not just say that."

Laughter builds in my chest. "Now you've done it. The ball

gowns heard you and everything. You've scandalized the sequins."

"Stop it." She smacks me in the arm. "Don't tell Birdie. I've just gotten her to stop saying the F word every time she breathes."

"Which F word is that?"

"Oh no. You won't trip me up twice, Blackbeard." With an exaggerated eyelash flutter, she starts to give me her back in favor of the dress rack, but turns to face me again with a serious expression. "I'm glad Musgrave's visit nudged you into getting more involved." She wets her lips. "It means a lot to Birdie that you came today. I can tell."

"Musgrave being here made me take notice that I'm missing out on sweet Naomi by being an asshole." My hand moves out of the need to touch her, my fingertips dragging up her bare arm. "Realizing I need to get more involved with Birdie…that's your doing, beauty queen."

I walk away before I do something stupid like try and kiss her in the middle of pageant dress hell. And I head over to take my place among the long-suffering gentlemen in the seating area outside the changing room. Jesus, she's not available for kissing. When is the rest of me going to accept what my mind already knows?

Naomi

"BIRDIE, IS EVERYTHING okay in there?"

Silence ticks by. "Er. Yes? I don't know."

The woman assisting her daughter in the dressing room beside ours passes me a curious look. I send her a baleful glance in return that immediately reminds me of my mother.

"What was that groan about?" Birdie calls.

"Genetics." I shake myself. "I'm coming in."

"My turn to groan."

Ignoring her theatrics, I ease the curtain aside just enough to sneak in—and my mouth falls open. Birdie is standing on the small pedestal in a rose-pink strapless gown, hugging her elbows with a pale face. Her awkward posture doesn't take away from the dress's influence, however. I've been watching girls walk in and out of these dressing rooms for half an hour and none of them have taken my breath away like Birdie. Yes, I'm biased. She is stunning in the gown, though—yet she seems more distressed than elated.

"Birdie Bristow," I breathe. "It's incredible. You're incredible. How does it feel?"

"I just want to take it off."

The tremor in her voice stirs alarm in my belly. "Okay. Let's take it off. We can try the blue one." She doesn't move. And when I try to slide my hand beneath her arm to reach the side zipper, she stiffens and doesn't budge. She's frozen. "Birdie, what's wrong?"

A hiccup tumbles out of her mouth. "I can't do this." Tears fill her eyes where none existed before. "I look just like Natalie in this dress, but I'm not her. I can't be her."

"You don't have to be. No one wants you to be anyone but Birdie."

"You're wrong. They would have stayed if she'd been the one to live." The words are delivered between chattering teeth and I can barely make them out, but I do and my heart wrenches up to my throat. She has to be talking about her parents. Oh Lord. There's so much more here than a girl who doesn't like a dress. How long has she been holding these damaging thoughts inside of her? "Get me out of this thing. I'm like a cheap knockoff."

"No. That's not true." With shaking hands, I finally get to the zipper and tug it down, wincing as she heaves a breath. "Please look at me."

She tunnels both hands through her hair and sits down on the pedestal in a slip, the dress still in a tangle around her ankles. "I'll be fine. Just give me a few."

"Honey, you can talk to me."

Birdie's voice goes up several octaves, bringing a hush down over the rest of the buzzing dressing room. "I don't need to talk."

The curtain opens behind me, and Jason's reflection appears in the mirror. His frown deepens when he sees his sister in obvious distress. "Birdie?"

He bypasses me in a single stride and stops just short of his sister, clearly unsure of what to do. His fingers flex at his sides, chest lifting and falling. Finally, he goes down on his knees and slowly wraps her in a hug. Their stilted body language tells me it's their first hug in a very long time—and I should leave and let them have the moment. I am leaving, but Jason's eyes find mine in the mirror and implore me to remain. *I don't have this*, they tell me. *Stay.*

"I'm trying to do this in a way that would make her proud." Birdie's face is turned into Jason's shirt, muffling her words. "It's too much pressure trying to make her kinds of choices and decisions. It's like a fat fucking reminder I never could. She was always better."

"Not better, Birdie. Different," Jason rasps. "When you were kids, Nat could never hula hoop as long as you. She threw herself facedown into the grass once, crying about it. Remember?"

She sniffs. "Vaguely."

"You walked first. You won a spelling bee in fourth grade and Nat came dead last. I'm embarrassed I remember this, but you were better at braiding doll hair." He pulls her tighter into the embrace. "People shine at different times. Maybe she was having one of her moments right before she died, so you'll always remember it that way. Remember how you felt less...bright. But she was headed for a valley. We all head there eventually—and then we come out of it. Just like you will. You'll shine, too. You're shining now."

Jason's words make my pulse skip. Twice. Three times. It won't stop fluttering all over the place, listening to him find the absolute perfect words for his sister. And they're perfect because they're not rehearsed or contrived. He didn't try to tell Birdie she was just as wonderful as Natalie. He was honest. Maybe one sister was standing in the sunshine and one was in the shade—and maybe the best way to get through today is to acknowledge that truth and stumble forward toward the next obstacle.

"Let's go home," Jason says, ruffling Birdie's streaks of blue hair. "You don't have to sneak a beer after I go to bed tonight. I'll let you have one free and clear. One."

Birdie bursts out with a watery laugh. "You knew?"

"One beer never hurt anybody." He stands and helps Birdie to her feet. "Get dressed. Take your time. We'll meet you outside."

She eases down onto a velvet stool with a deep breath. "'kay. See you in five."

My emotions are playing leap frog as I lead Jason out of the curtained stall. I'm worried for Birdie. For the direction I've taken with her coaching. I missed so much behind the scenes. What if I did more harm than good by not recognizing the pain she hides behind the humor? It's possible I'm not equipped for this at all.

In a twist, it's Jason that's up to the task of comforting his sister—and my admiration for him in this moment is endless. That's the emotion leaping right past my self-doubt to take the lead. He was amazing in there. Glancing back at him over my shoulder as we walk past the rows of dressing stalls, I see he's questioning how he handled Birdie, just as I'm doing to myself. He's totally oblivious to the fact that he saved the day.

My pulse bongs in my ears with the need to show him. To wipe away his expression of uncertainty. I stop walking and turn, searching right to left for a place to talk alone. But as he draws closer, I see Jason needs reassurance. Nearness. Needs to be grounded. My actions take place all on their own, as if my body has no choice but to compensate for what Jason is lacking. I pull him into an empty dressing room and yank the curtain closed.

And his mouth is on mine before I've secured a breath.

He wrestles me back against the wall, our mouth slanted and suctioned together, his hips knocking into mine and pressing, pressing. "Please, baby," he groans into my gasping mouth, his face pained. "Please."

"Yes."

The kiss is a downpour of rain you can't see through, powerful and hypnotic and intoxicating. It's that first trip around a Ferris wheel, only we're moving at a hundred miles an hour. I'm instantly dizzy at the taste of him, tobacco and coffee and mint toothpaste. I throw my arms up around his neck and cling, letting him smash me into the unbreakable wall of his body while his mouth bears down on mine again and again. He slants our lips together, sipping at me, changing directions, punctuated air leaving his nose, like he's out of control. Snapped.

Just like that.

The first time our tongues touch, we break apart on strangled moans, Jason's hands like vises on my hips. They slip lower to my bottom and lever me up so I can wrap my thighs around his hips. The changing room wall shudders with the force of his drive and I bite down on my lip so I don't scream. He's so thick and ready and right there. Right where I need him.

Our mouths tangle again and this time, there's more exploration. We're fighting for ground, trying to best one another with the most thorough taste. I can't get enough. I can't—

"Easy," he pulls back to rasp at my mouth. "Easy, baby. You can't kiss me like that when I can't have you. It's just cruel."

I nod, common sense dawning slowly but surely. "I j-just…" Lord, his mouth is so sexy. And it's right there, masculine and wet. He's looking at mine, too. "You were amazing in there. You were a hero." I drag my attention to find his eyes. "I'm proud of you."

"So this is some kind of…what? Reward? I don't deserve one. It's what I should have been doing all along." There's conflict in his face, but he lets it go with a curse. "Hell, I'll take what I can get from you." He leans his forehead against mine and we breathe together. Once, twice. "I wasn't sure if I said the right—"

"You did."

"I'm not good with that kind of thing."

"Bull honkey."

His laugh warms my whole body, head to toe. "This is the part when I have to set you down and walk away, isn't it?"

I nod, afraid to admit to myself it's the last thing I want. I drop my legs from around Jason's hips and he eases me to the floor with a wince, adjusting himself in his jeans. He shakes his head and growls at me as I back through the curtains…and find us the object of rapt interest to every pageant mama in the changing room. Birdie picks that moment to exit her stall, raising an eyebrow at the disapproval being leveled at us.

"Jason tried to light a cigar. Right there in the middle of the department store," I blurt the lie, linking arms with Birdie and ushering her out of the dressing room, my chin in the air. "Do you believe the gall of him?"

A glance back over my shoulder tells me he's fighting laughter, but his smile smooths out fast into something hotter and we mimic each other with a slow release of breath. His hungry expression is one that will probably stay with me for days. A lot like that kiss.

Oh, who am I kidding? It'll be a lot longer than that.

CHAPTER SIXTEEN

ConspiracyCrowd.org
Username: IWant2Believe2000
Is Bigfoot an alien? I have a better question for you.
Is Bigfoot NOT an alien? Think about it.

Naomi

I NEED TO get away for a while and clear my head.

No better distraction than marching naked in a parade.

Yes. I am going to the body paint parade today and will be joining as an active participant. I've already chosen a design and a local artist. No sense in being spontaneous without a little planning first, right?

Especially since everything else in my life is suddenly up in the air.

After Birdie's meltdown in the department store dressing room yesterday, I'm not sure where we stand as contestant and coach. Competing might be too hard for her in light of her revelations about Natalie. If that's the case, I will gladly bow out, wish her well and be on my way. The last thing I want is for her to continue training if it could affect her health and well-being negatively. I'll miss her. I'll be sad she never got the chance to compete, since I think she's better than she realizes, but I won't push.

Not too hard, anyway.

Every coach-contestant partnership hits a wall at some point. When I was seventeen, I pretended to have the chickenpox for a week so I wouldn't have to practice. It took a very specific combination of mixed together pink and brown paint to make those spots convincing and they were the very devil to get off. In the end, I was found out. My parents confiscated my car keys for two weeks, leaving me to walk to and from pageant practice. To this day, I still think the punishment was worth lying in bed for a week and watching that *Glee* marathon.

While I won't pressure Birdie, I'm certainly not going to let her think I've given up on her after one bad afternoon. No, ma'am. Somewhere around midnight last night, it hit me. We've been approaching this pageant all wrong from the beginning. We have more than enough time to do it right, if Birdie is game. I guess I'll find out soon enough.

Walking out my front door and proceeding down the steps would be a good first move.

Laptop cradled in my arms, I sway side to side in my sandals. *Any time now, Naomi.*

I've always been nervous to run into Jason. The difference now is…I know why.

Those feelings I admitted—silently to myself—did not dissipate overnight and I have no idea what to do about them. Every time I sit down to make a mental pro/con list on the merits of having romantic feelings for Jason, I keep getting lost in that moment in the dressing room. What a magnificent hero and brother he was. In so many ways, Jason is the same man who answered the front door with a scowl. In others, he's changing for the better.

Listen to yourself. I've been making a pro/con list about merely having feelings for the man. If I decide it's okay to have feelings for Jason...what then? Nothing, that's what. Yes, we shared a kiss, which was somehow more intimate than hoisting my booty into the air in his bedroom and pleasuring myself. It was...well, if I was more fanciful, I might even call it magical. However. Even if he was planning on staying in St. Augustine—which he's not—I am bound for Charleston as soon as the pageant is over.

That's if Birdie even plans on competing anymore.

I could be going back to Charleston a lot sooner than expected.

Finally, I open the front door purely to distract myself from the growing knot in my chest. Laptop in one hand, the bottom of my skirt in the other so I won't trip, I make my way down the stairs and across the driveway, which smells of lingering cigar smoke. Pungent and sweet. When I walk into the kitchen, I'm surprised to find Jason and Birdie sitting at the kitchen table staring into their mugs of coffee. Birdie is in a long nightshirt and Jason is wearing only board shorts as usual, his network of tattoos looking sharp and blue in the morning light. How anyone is supposed to have a relaxing cup of coffee with his nipples staring back at them is beyond me. Thankfully I already had mine. Coffee. Not nipples. And while I've been thinking about nipples and coffee a full fifteen seconds has passed, the three of us looking at each other.

"Am I interrupting?"

"No." Birdie starts to stand up but sits back down. "I was worried I scared you off with my meltdown yesterday."

Jason leans back in his chair like a lazy lion, bringing his coffee mug to his lips. Lips I have now kissed. "I told her you wouldn't scare off so easily."

Relax. He can't hear your pulse racing. This is just like every other day. Nothing has changed. "Jason is right. I—"

His coffee mug hits the table and he slowly sits forward. "What did you just call me?"

Oh Lord. Everything has changed, hasn't it? My mouth won't cooperate now that I've admitted to…having complicated feelings for this man. "Yes, well…once you go dress shopping with a person, it's only right to be on a first-name basis. I'm not sure how you do things here in Florida, but…that's the system. And if it's not broke don't fix it." Ignoring Jason's open scrutiny, I slide into a kitchen chair. "Now then, Birdie. You're not getting rid of me that easy. I spent the night thinking you'd send me on *my* way. I was checking traffic on my route to Charleston just in case."

Birdie deflates with relief. Jason turns a pale shade of green and slides his coffee away.

"Birdie, do you still want to be in this pageant?"

She takes a swallow of coffee. From the way she's moving, I know her leg is jiggling beneath the table. "I think so."

"Do you want to know what I think?"

"Yeah."

I reach across the table and take her coffee-warmed hand. "I think we've been so focused on winning this pageant for Natalie, we forgot to remember she's not the one competing. You're the one putting the work in. We can find a way to honor your sister and you at the same time." I squeeze. "You both deserve the win."

Birdie doesn't respond for so long, I'm not sure she ever will. "What's with the laptop?" she asks finally.

"I'm glad you asked." I splay my hands on the lid and lift. "You're an original. There was nothing in that store yesterday good enough. So I did a little searching. Fell down quite a few rabbit holes. Did you know there's a whole duct tape prom dress trend? Anyway, I ended up digging through alternative gowns, handmade designs. Things like that." The tab I saved last night opens and I turn the screen to face her. "How about something like this?"

She sits forward, gaping at the retro, red and black checkered dress I found at the bottom of the internet last night. "Whoa."

Pleasure sifts around inside me. "You like it."

"If I pretend it's not called Punk Rockin' Pretty, I can definitely get behind it." She seems afraid to smile. "Will they even let me compete in something like this?"

I shrug. "If they tell us no, we'll send your brother after them."

"Happy to help," he says in that rusted morning voice. "The dress gets my vote, too. Looks like more your style, Birdie."

"Yeah." She releases a long exhale. "Thanks, Naomi."

"Just doing my job." I click the laptop shut and fold my hands on top of it. Trying not to show how relieved I am. It's more than that, though. I'm pleased with myself. There was a problem and I found a unique solution. Maybe Birdie doesn't have to be the first and last girl I coach. Would I be crazy to think I could do this as a full-time job with some success?

Setting aside that thought for later, I return to the here and now. "Would you like to choose something different for the talent portion?"

"No, let's stick with the dance. We're having a hard enough time getting it down without changing this late in the game." A line forms between her brows. "I like the new dresses and making it a little about me. But I still want it mostly about Natalie, okay?"

"Of course. We'll balance it however we want." I pat her arm. "I left open all the websites I found, so why don't you hold on to my laptop for today. Let me know which ones you decide on and we'll order them."

"Awesome." Birdie gathers her hair and shoves it to the opposite side of her head. "Can we please change the subject now?"

Jason taps a fist on the table. "I'm taking the boat out today. Who's coming?"

Birdie brightens. "Yeah? You going to let me dive?"

"Once we get through a full lesson and you understand the safety precau—"

"Yes or no, bro."

"Yeah." He looks over at me, that brow raised almost in challenge. "You coming?"

I want to say yes. There are so many reasons to say yes. I've seen Jason cleaning his boat and walking around most indecently in his half-zipped wet suit, but this could be my only chance to watch a Special Forces diver move expertly in the water. He's staying true to his word and making an effort with his sister and without him saying a word, I know he's hoping I'll come along to help. I *want* to help. I want to watch them grow closer. To top it all off, scuba diving in Florida would be an adventure. Something completely outside my comfort zone—and I wouldn't even have to get naked for it.

"Smoke is going to come out of her ears pretty soon," Jason drawls, winking at me.

It's the wink, followed by the burn that climbs my inner thighs, that reminds me why I can't say yes. I need time away from the gravity of this man. To regain my objectivity and common sense, so I can attempt to keep the limits on our relationship. I definitely won't reclaim those limits watching ocean water roll down his big hairy chest.

"I'm so sorry, I would have loved to come diving," I say in

my most cheerful Miss Manners voice. "But I stopped by early for a reason. I'm heading to Daytona Beach for an…art festival this afternoon. Art." Wincing on the inside over my awkwardness, I stand, using my hip to nudge in the chair. "Birdie, we'll meet Monday night after school, as usual. In the meantime, I'll order the dress."

"Yes, coach."

"Well, now. Have a great time," I say, sailing toward the back door. "Bye!"

A scrape of the chair says Jason is following me out of the house and I walk faster, hopping off the porch instead of taking the stairs.

"Naomi."

I pretend not to hear the warning in his voice, turning with a neutral expression. "Yes?"

"You driving alone?"

"Yes. And before you warn me of the dangers of a woman driving alone, please remember that's how I arrived here."

"Noted." A muscle pops in his jaw. "Where are you staying?"

"Mr. Bristow."

"Oh, no. You're not going back to that shit." He saunters closer and I catch a waft of no-nonsense body wash and the faint hint of cigar. "Say Jason and we'll continue."

"Sometimes it's hard to remember which one of us is the coach."

He waits.

I grind the back of my teeth. "It was a slip-up."

He crosses his arms.

"Oh, fine. Jason."

One corner of his mouth goes up. "With your accent, it sounds like Jyson."

His comment, delivered in a low, satisfied pitch, throws me. "That's how it sounds in my head."

"You say my name a lot in your head, baby?"

If the insides of my thighs heat up any more, they're going to catch on fire. "This conversation is getting away from me." I back up and immediately feel the bite of cool morning air, such a contrast to his body heat. "I'll text Birdie the name of the hotel in case of an emergency."

The farther I get from him, the more his amusement fades into something that looks more like panic. "I know it's not...normal to be so worried." He rubs the back of his neck. "But I don't know how to stop."

Sympathy rocks me. My instinct is to cancel, but I can't do that. I wouldn't be doing Jason a favor by giving in to fear on his behalf. And I would be doing myself a disservice by setting aside what I want for someone else. I came to Florida to do the exact opposite. "Everything is going to be fine," I say. "I'll check in later, okay?"

His anxious expression stays with me on the whole drive to Daytona Beach.

Jason

SOMETHING IS ON my sister's mind.

A more pressing something than usual.

We're driving to the marina and she's chewing on her lip, fidgeting in the passenger seat. Granted, we haven't really hung out like this since I came home, a fact that leaves a bad taste in my mouth. But she shouldn't be nervous about going somewhere with me, right?

"What's up?" I nod at her bouncing knee. "You're going to wear a hole in the foot well."

"Oh. Sorry." She tucks her hair behind an ear. "I've just never been scuba diving before."

"Yeah." I clear my throat. "I'm sorry about that. All my dives have been business related lately, but that's no excuse. I should have taken you out."

"It's no big deal." After a moment of silence, she turns to me with a half-smile. "Natalie would have nagged the shit out of you. Given you the silent treatment until you took us. Then she would have sent Google calendar alerts to everyone's phones and had T-shirts made. Bristow Diving Day 2018."

My mouth turns down at the corners, even though I'm trying to smile. "She did tend to make an event out of everything. From what I remember."

Birdie nods. "What do you remember about her?"

This is the second time today Birdie has brought up Natalie, and I think she needs to talk about our sister. That's what she's trying to tell me, in her own way. "I remember she hated getting her hair cut. She would scream bloody murder if they brought the scissors anywhere near her. Was it long...at the end?"

"Yeah. She was watching these braiding tutorials on YouTube obsessively. A new type of braid every day. There would be ribbons threaded through and..." She trails off. "She made us all watch them and I complained, but I kind of liked it. The way we'd all smoosh together on the couch and zone out, listening to her chatter and critique everything."

We've reached the marina now and I pull into my usual space, leaving the engine running so the air conditioner stays on. "She used to make color-coded lists on Christmas morning," I say, pulling memories out of the basket like strings of yarn.

"Columns and all. Just to keep track of which presents came from who."

Birdie's smile spreads and ebbs. "How can someone like that just…not wake up one day? How is that possible?"

I swallow hard and stare out at the water, remembering how confused I was to get the news. And how that confusion gave way to frustration over how a healthy, seventeen-year-old girl can go to bed feeling fine, then experience cardiac failure overnight. No pain, no warning signs. An irregular electrical impulse upset the rhythm of her heart. Her heart stopped. Sudden Death Syndrome. I didn't even know it was a thing. So easy, yet impossible to come to terms with. "There's no good answer for why it happened, kid. I just know it isn't fair." I'm not sure where it comes from, but suddenly there's this expansion inside of me. It's like a bubble with tough outer skin, pushing at the inner corners of my chest and venturing toward my throat. My mouth is the only release valve for the pressure and it escapes in the form of a hoarse gasp. My little sister is gone. "I'd have taken her place. In a heartbeat."

"I know." Birdie rubs at her knees. "I know, Jason."

"I'm sorry I wasn't here."

I hear the click of Birdie's seatbelt and then she's scooting across the seat, laying her head on my shoulder. She doesn't say anything. Doesn't tell me it's okay or try to make me feel better. And I'm glad. I'm being hit hard for the first time since I got the phone call that Natalie was gone. I'm finally processing the reality of never seeing her again and acknowledging the gap she left in the atmosphere. The lack of her has been obvious every waking hour of the day, but I've kept my head down and plowed through. She deserves better than that, though.

In the front seat of my truck, with the air conditioning rumbling and Birdie's shoulder, I close my eyes and give Natalie what I've been resisting. I grieve.

I'm not sure how much time passes while we sit there, but I open my eyes to find Birdie's feet crossed on the dashboard, her expression thoughtful. "Let's save the dive for another day."

"Yeah," I say, my voice rusty. "You pick the date and we'll get it scheduled."

"I should probably practice my walk, anyway. I'm finally beginning to look less like a T-Rex in heels and more like one of those green, blow-up car dealership guys."

Chuckling silently, I put the truck into reverse and pull out of the parking spot. "I'm sure you look like neither of those things."

She snorts her disagreement. "Also, I have some online dress shopping to do." Just like on the drive to the marina, she's back to chewing her lip. "Already had a little peek at the tabs Naomi left open on her laptop, matter of fact."

Hearing the name of my tormentor makes my hands flex on the steering wheel. "Oh yeah?"

"Yeah. Definitely a good idea to move diving to another day, because I've been meaning to tell you..." That knee starts bouncing. "Some of those tabs Naomi left open are...curious. Yeah. Curious is the right word."

"Out with it, kid."

"I think Naomi might be at a nude body art parade."

I slam on the brakes and the truck skids to a rough stop, a roar climbing my throat. "*What?*"

CHAPTER SEVENTEEN

ConspiracyCrowd.org
Username: UrdadsMyFave69
I volunteer to search the nation's nudist colonies for
Runaway Girl.
I promise to leave no stones unturned.

Naomi

I OPT TO leave my underwear on. That decision is validated in spades when I see how up close and personal the artist gets to my lady region. He's on his knees now with an airbrush, spraying a swarm of butterflies onto my skin, starting at my ankles and ending at my neck. From my vantage point, it looks like splatters of color, but the man assures me it will all come together in the end. Not for the first time, I glance surreptitiously at the clock. When is the end? I'm a brutal shade of pink, and if it weren't for the two college girls getting the same treatment across the room, I would be hiding under the covers in my hotel bed.

Oh Lord. He's moving around to the back side now. I chose a very brief pair of briefs, trying to be considerate in giving the artist more canvas. I must have been in denial of the fact that more canvas meant more butt cheek. Now he's right on level with them. I don't think anyone has ever been this close to my bottom before, save my pageant coach with her measuring tape.

And Jason.

A little squeak leaves my mouth when the cold paint lands on my lower back. "It's a little cold is all," I say, striving for casual. "Have you been doing this long?"

His head peeks around my thigh and he tugs a headphone out of his ear. "Sorry, what?"

"Oh nothing." I'm talking to a man who painted butterflies on my boobs. "I didn't realize you were listening to music."

"It helps me focus."

I pat him on the shoulder. "Then by all means, listen away."

He starts to put the bud back in, then seems to think twice about it. "This is your first body art parade, isn't it?"

"Is it that obvious?" I force myself to stop smoothing my hair. "I didn't realize people did them over and over. Seems like something you'd get out of your system after just once."

"Oh no. It's addictive." He moves the airbrush over my hip, leaving a trail of magenta behind in the shape of a wing. "Walking around free like that is...symbolic in a way. For one, there's nowhere to carry your damn cell phone, which kind of cuts the world off. It's just you. Everyone is naked, so we're on the same level. That's how it should be."

"I hadn't thought of it like that," I murmur, mentally repeating what the artist said so I won't forget when nerves eventually strike. "I was mostly hoping to shock myself out of my comfortable little box, but the bigger meaning is even better."

"Oh, it's good for that, too. I can guarantee you'll never have that dream again where you show up for the first day of school naked."

"Because it's not scary anymore."

"Exactly."

Over the course of our conversation, I've managed to forget I'm standing here naked. But I remember when he taps my thigh and asks me to bend forward. "I need to get under the crease of your butt."

I put my hands against the wall like I'm being frisked. If only my mother could see me now! "Oh, of course."

"Perfect."

Biting down on my bottom lip, I try to stop the flow of nervous chatter, but it won't be deterred. There's something that has been on my mind since I left St. Augustine this morning and the artist is so easy to talk to. "How fast do you think someone can form a bad habit? Does it take one time? Two?"

"Depends what you're talking about. Drugs, Chick-Fil-A..."

"Running away when something scares you."

He sits back on his heels. "That's a tough one. But in my inexpert opinion, I would say that particular habit forms pretty fast. It's like instant gratification."

I hum in my throat, once again thinking of Jason standing in the driveway, watching me walk away. Is he on the boat with Birdie right now? Are they connecting? An unexpected wave of yearning rolls through me, so dense I have to breathe thought it.

"Um, can you unclench, ma'am?"

My forehead hits the wall. "Finally found something worse than another woman seeing the pee spot on the front of my underwear."

"What was that?"

"Nothing," I mutter.

Fifteen minutes later, the soft whirr of the airbrush machine cuts out and the artist stands, wiping his hands on paint-stained jeans. "This might be my favorite ever. Come on." He jerks his chin toward the changing area. "Let's take a look in the mirror."

"Okay," I say, letting a pent-up breath leave my lungs. The college girls smile at me as I cross the room and I send them the universal *how do I look* face. They send me thumbs ups in return, so I'm feeling confident when I step in front of the full-length mirror. I'm not prepared for the intricate beauty of the design, though. "Oh. Oh, this is amazing. I had no idea..." I asked for butterflies in various shades of pink, but I didn't expect to be transformed into this moving piece of artwork. I look like a patch taken straight out of the most beautiful garden. "How will I stand washing this off?"

The artist laughs. "Just come back to me next year. Starting with a blank canvas is half the fun."

"If I get through today, I'll consider it. Thank you," I breathe as he walks away to clean his station. Unfortunately, the confidence wanes as I consider the front door.

In the end, it takes me almost an hour to leave the shop once the artist finishes. I hang out in the back with the staff under the guise of drying far longer than necessary, and by the time I get the nerve to walk out into the parade, it's in full swing and the sun is setting.

My heart drums in my ears as I take my first step onto the pavement. In no clothes, save a camouflaged pair of panties. Yes, from a distance it looks like I'm wearing a colorful costume, but up close I know my nipples are visible through the pink paint. Thanks to the design extending to every inch of me, my underwear is weighed down with paint and molded to my core, leaving nothing to the imagination. For all intents and purposes, I'm in public wearing nothing but flip-flops.

And I feel exactly how I used to feel walking in a pageant. Isn't that a kicker? My heartbeat is rollicking and my lips won't stay wet. I'm positive I'm sticking out like a sore thumb—and I've done this hundreds of times in my life. Been on display. The difference is I'm in control of this. I chose this and...there's no one judging me this time. Yes, that's the major game changer here. I can walk from one end of this parade to the other and I'm in competition with no one. Not even myself.

A smile tickles my lips as I move to the center of the street and walk straight down the dotted white line, the sound of Caribbean music floating on the warm wind around me. I reach up and let out my ponytail, shaking it loose. I'm glad I waited until the sun was dipping, because the atmosphere of the parade is enthralling, electric. Most everyone has a drink in their hand and I don't hesitate to join them, untucking the twenty I stowed in the hip of my panties and buying something fruity and green off a street vendor. Alcohol burns down my throat and sugar sweetens my lips. It's terrible and way too strong, but I drink the whole thing just because I can.

I don't want to stray too far from the shop—it's where I left my clothes. So after about ten blocks, I hook around and find a group of women in butterfly wings to walk with. Taking me under their wing, so to speak, they convince me to have another awful green drink, but it must be an acquired taste. This one goes down much smoother...until I start to think of Jason. That's when the alcohol's heat turns inconvenient, seeming to fan down from my belly, making me hyperaware when my thighs brush together. Might as well admit it. I like my boobs. Looking down and seeing them decorated in pink makes me want to touch and cup them. Squeeze.

No. No, that's not true. I want bigger hands on them. Demanding ones.

Don't I?

There's no sense in lying to myself. In the middle of all this freedom, I'm a prisoner to my own thoughts. I can't tone them down or ignore them. Especially since human nature is in full swing around me. As much as this parade is about self-expression, those nobler intentions are slowly giving way to human nature. The sexual kind.

In the darker sections of the parade, nude, painted bodies press close, mouths move as one. I find myself watching couples kiss far longer than is polite, my endorphins popping wheelies south of my belly button. My hands move of their own accord, trailing up my stomach, following the curve of my hips. The music pumps louder and my breathing matches the pace, sounds of laughter and drums joining together to form white noise in my ears. The sense of anonymity adds to the riot of sensations, too. No one knows me here. I'm just a body.

A body that suddenly needs pleasure so bad, it's aching all over.

Jason.

I swallow.

Jason's hands. Touching me there. His foul words in my ear.

Stop. I'm making myself damp.

I hear whispering behind me a second before a hand catches mine.

A jolt of fear has me pulling it away and spinning around. "Excuse—"

It's him. Jason is...here? Is that him standing in a sea of colorful nudity, putting everyone to shame by being ten times as compelling? No, there was something in those green drinks and I'm hallucinating. Oh Lord. I should never stray from Sauvignon Blanc. "You're not really here."

He's pissed. Angrier than I've ever seen him. His jaw is bunched and ticking, that huge, sculpted chest rising and falling beneath his gray T-shirt like white caps during a storm. That anger is cut with something much more intoxicating, though.

Lust. It's the lighthouse in the middle of a hurricane, guiding me in its direction when I should avoid it, well aware it's surrounded by jagged rocks and surefire ruin.

Dark eyes envelop me in a long head-to-toe sweep, that rapt attention lingering between my legs, raking up my stomach to devour my breasts. "If you need proof I'm here, baby, I'll give it to you." Jason grabs the back of his collar and whips the shirt off over his head, earning whistles from several directions. He doesn't seem to be aware of any of them, which shouldn't turn me on more than I already am. But it does. He's like a bull standing in the center of a flower patch and I'm the red flag. I'm so overwhelmed by the authenticity of him, I can only stand there as he drags the T-shirt down over my head, not even bothering to help my arms through the proper holes. "I thought those conspiracy theories about you being a nudist were exaggerated."

My gasp turns several heads on the street. "How dare you read those without telling me? They're complete and total nonsense!"

"Are they?" Jason steps closer. "You're two seconds away from being kidnapped by Bigfoot."

"Excuse m-me, miss," stutters a man to my right. I turn to find a bespectacled man in bike shorts with a dragon painted on his torso. He's half the size of Jason and at least fifteen years his senior, but he's leveling a frown up at him anyway. "Is this big jerk bothering you?"

"Listen up, motherfucker..." Jason fumes, before he trails off into a sigh. "That took balls. If I wasn't here and a man was harassing her, I would want someone to intervene." He passes Dragon Man a nod. "Thanks."

Dragon Man sniffs and tugs up his shorts.

Jason turns his attention to me, and I almost blister under the heat and tenderness of it. "Naomi, please tell this man I would willingly lay down my life to keep you from injury."

"He would," I whisper.

"Without hesitation."

"Without hesitation," I repeat, shivering.

We must stare at each other for longer than I realize because when I zone back in, Dragon Man is long gone and Jason has come closer. Closer, until he's lifting me into his arms. A wicked combination of dread and anticipation is booming in my ears. No. No, the pulse is everywhere. Under my skin. Shooting down to my toes. My sex is heavy and throbbing, my nerve endings in such heaven from being pressed up against Jason's safe chest, I almost moan. I should be screaming at him to put me down. I should demand to know where he's taking me, but I don't care. He's given me permission to stop making decisions. And it's exactly what I need. I need to be absolved of my conscience.

I can barely look away from the determined set of his jaw to absorb my surroundings, but I see we're traveling away from the crowd. Moving down a side street, turning one way, then another until we're on a brief strip of cobblestones between two restaurants. Both establishments are in full swing, music and laughter spilling out of their doors, but we exist in the empty alley between, visible if a passerby looked close enough but far back enough from the street that the darkness swallows us whole.

Jason sets me upright, but by no means does he let me go. We move as one as he walks me backward, tilting my face up with a less-than-gentle hand. "I'd like to do a lot of things right now, Naomi. Like ask if you were sent to drive me fucking crazy. Or go back to the parade and fight every man who had a chance to see you naked before me—the guy who's been beating off thinking about your tits for a month. Yeah, I'd like to do a lot of shit right about now."

"Why don't you?"

He shoves our mouths together but doesn't kiss me. Just breathes, breathes, bares his teeth. "Because you're wet for me, aren't you? Saw you back on that road. Crossing your thighs and arching your back for me. You finally going to let me throw you up on this cock and bounce you on it until you get vocal fry?"

"Jason, you can't just..." My words are muffled by his hard mouth and they're followed by a moan as his hands circle my waist, his thumbs massaging the indent of my belly button. "You haven't kissed me yet. There's an order to these things and I'm confused enough—"

"Come on then, beauty queen," Jason grates. "Taste me."

Our lips brush.

I'm instantly swept up. Mentally and physically. It happens so fast.

One second, my feet are on the ground and the next, my toes are even with Jason's knees. It's the feeling of being strapped into a roller coaster, braced on all sides—safe—with my stomach missing in action. Carried away in a flutter of wings. If I had any delusions that I'd be the one to issue this kiss, that notion dissolves faster than my journey off the ground. Into Jason's hold, up against his chest with a big hand fisted in my hair, the opposite arm supporting my backside, keeping me indecently close.

A shudder rolls through him. "Kissing you fucks me up worst of all, baby. Permanently." He backs me up a pace, settling me against the wall, pressing our foreheads together. "Christ. Look at you. I'm going to do it anyway."

His mouth slants over mine before I finish speaking, his tongue raiding my mouth in a claiming stroke. There's nothing polite or reserved about the way Jason kisses me. It's earthy. Messy. He's hungry and my femininity is his dinner. He feasts on it with purposeful drives of his tongue, the turning of his head in a dance with mine so our mouths are forced to reposition, mate again, sink into a rhythm, stop and do it all over. A growl hovers in his throat as we move, straining closer with every passing second, seeking relief for the pressure built by the joining of tongues, the tight pressing of bodies. Panting. We break only to pant, before joining together with breath sucked in through noses and moans for each other's ears alone.

My mouth has never been this open. I've never wanted to open it so wide and allow so many courtesies. Jason's hand has left my hair and met the second one at my backside, molding the flesh there without asking permission. And he should. He should ask permission. I know that. But I'm moaning into his mouth and my own fingertips are scraping through his short hair, pulling his face closer for more of the glorious ravishing he's giving me— and my demanding body language is nothing if not a resounding *yes, please, do whatever you want to me.*

"Haven't gotten my fill of kissing this sweet mouth by a long shot." He sucks my lower lip into his mouth, slowly letting it go. "While I'm trying to do the impossible, tell me what's next up on the so-called order of things."

"I don't keep a list," I gasp as his teeth rake my neck. "But there must b-be a proper progression."

"Why don't I start by touching you everywhere those butter-flies are painted?" His expression is sexual, challenging. "Then we'll move on to that pretty place they're not."

"How do you know?" The darkness, the drinks, the freedom I experienced during the parade has made me bold. It could just be Jason. He's goaded me into surprising myself since I showed up on his doorstep. "Maybe they're everywhere."

A warning ticks in his eye. "Push me a little more and I'll have no choice but to find out."

Adrenaline is spinning inside me like the wheel on a paddle boat, faster and faster. Jason's hands give my backside a final, rough squeeze, then circle around to my belly, sliding higher and stopping just beneath my breasts. I want to be touched all over and I don't want to wait anymore. The order of things is pointless when it comes to this man. He'll keep me safe no matter what, won't he? I might feel like I'm about to jump off a cliff, but the confidence I have in him is like wings attached to my back.

Throwing caution to the wind, I take Jason's hands and guide them to my breasts, his gruff curse making my nipples peak tighter. "I can't remember where the paintbrush went, Jason." I whisper, helping him squeeze me. "I don't know if there are butterflies under my panties or not."

His body falls into mine, pressing me to the wall as his hands rake down my sides, fingers tucking into the sides of my underwear. Tugging, almost ripping in their haste to peel them down my hips. Jason makes strangled sounds in my ears, his chest shuddering when gravity takes over and the panties slip to my knees. "Either way, I'm going to tongue fuck the shit out of you, baby. No butterflies mean no one else saw that pussy and I'll let you come faster. That's the difference."

Drawing breath is almost impossible as Jason leans his upper half away and lifts the gray T-shirt so he can look at my sex. *So he can look at my sex.* Am I really doing this? Letting a man take liberties with me in public? Yes. Yes, I am. And I don't have a choice in the matter anymore, because if he stopped touching me right now, I think I would go the way of my scruples and evaporate.

"Not a drop of paint on this beauty. Good girl," Jason rasps, hunkering down until he's eye level with the most intimate part of me. I'm partial to my blonde landing strip, even though it's outdated, and Jason seems to like it too. Oh Lord, does he ever. He presses his face against me and inhales, robbing me of a gasp. One hand finds the inside of my thigh and rides higher, higher until only an inch separates him from my core. "Wishing I was inside this pussy of yours has cost me a lot of fucking sleep," he says, easing his tongue out to nudge my feminine lips. Light. So light. But a bomb might as well be going off inside me. "Ready to make nice now?"

Is he talking to me or my vagina?

The answer is yes either way, but I'm not given the opportunity to find out, because Jason pulls me close, urging my legs over his shoulders and…he stands up. My back hits the concrete wall—much higher up than before—of the alley, and the warm friction of Jason's tongue bathes me between the thighs. "Jason," I heave, grabbing for his head, intending to push him away, but dragging him closer instead. "Oh my goodness."

I've never been a fan of cunnilingus. It's always been kind of a formality. A way for the gentleman to assure himself he's doing the right thing before the main event. But I've always been too self-conscious to enjoy it. Am I making the right noises? Did I miss a spot while shaving? What in God's name is he thinking about? None of those questions occur to me now, because I'm quite simply being eaten. Jason mouth moves as if he's savoring a ripe orange, determined to reach every part of me with his tongue, his hands on my bottom pulling me closer for his attention.

He stays on the surface, laving that bundle of nerves with the flat of his tongue until I'm pressing my head back into the wall and crying out, the muscles at the juncture of my thighs clenching tight. And he watches me like the pleasure is all his. As if he's selfish for my taste. His obvious enjoyment cuts the final string on my reservations and lets me sink into the moment. Let's me stop worrying about what happens next and whether or not I look, sound, taste sexy enough. Jason's hunger for more is blatant. I'm more than enough…I'm exactly what he wants.

Exhilaration rides down my spine and settles there, turning my hips restless. Oh. Oh, this is moving so quickly. My nipples ache so badly I can do nothing but feel myself up through the gray T-shirt, pinching the tight points between my knuckles. The action starts a wicked tug between my legs, right where Jason is licking me, and the need for relief swells another story higher. He watches me play with my nipples and growls, jerking me closer to his mouth by my backside, and I scream inside my throat when his tongue slides inside me deep. The intimacy of it starts a tremor somewhere inside me that has never been discovered. Oh Lord. It's happening. I've never actually had an orgasm this way. Getting to that point usually takes a lot of finger work and mental commands to stop obsessing…not this time.

"Jason. S'happening."

Did I just say that?

His only response is to find my clit and flicker his tongue against it, hooded eyes on me…and then his middle finger slides inside, easing in and out slowly, before moving faster, faster. An unfamiliar crescendo builds, the pressure divine and a curse at the same time.

"No no no," I chant, tilting my hips toward his mouth like an offering. "Yes. Almost. Please."

The tip of his finger brushes a magical spot inside me and I tumble off the cliff into the storm, gleefully allowing myself to crash onto the rocks. Only they're not jagged, they're welcoming. They crack me open with the sharpest, most intense pleasure I've ever been given, leaving me in pieces on the shore, my spasming flesh making me feel like I'm still soaring up in the air. My body shakes, but I'm warm. So warm. Jason has let one leg drop at a time, carefully cradling me against the wall with his big body, his labored breaths loud and telling above my head.

The instinct to comfort has my hands lifting, trailing down his stomach toward his waistband. "Don't," he barks, snagging my wrists. "I need a fucking minute after watching how hot you get off. Naomi…Jesus. That pussy is the sweetest little thing I've ever tasted." His jaw bunches, nostrils flaring. "You touch me and I'm going to come like a goddamn college kid."

"I want to see that," I breathe, rocked by the desire to see Jason lose his composure. I'm positive I've never wanted anything more in my life. "Please, Jason."

"Playing dirty using my name." His forehead falls to mine. "I love you saying it so bad."

Being worshipped by this man, having him admit to things in the dark he would never say in the light, turns a crank in my chest. There's bravery, too, crackling in my belly, just knowing I drove him to this breaking point. My right hand strays lower to lock around his erection, teasing him with gentle squeezes through his jeans, drawing a broken groan from his mouth that echoes down the alley. "Jason," I whisper, going down on my knees. "Jason."

"Naomi," he grits through his teeth. He closes his eyes a moment, then braces one hand on the wall, the other going to his zipper. "The hell with it. I want that fucking mouth."

I've spent my life in ball gowns and having men ma'am me to death. I've walked stages and been praised for being a classy

Southern lady. And yet I've never felt more like a woman than right now, watching Jason jerk down his zipper with a shaking hand, needing to get himself inside my mouth. The insides of my thighs are damp, I'm wearing nothing but a T-shirt and my mascara must be running, but somehow I'm the most desirable woman in Florida. Jason makes me feel that way. I want him to feel that way, too.

From this vantage point, Jason is the sexiest, most powerful man I've ever witnessed up close, his body mapped with tattoos and hair, his expression fiercely...possessive. Of me. But also desperate. At my mercy. That combination turns me on all over again. If someone told me I'd be licking my lips for the feel of a man in my mouth, I wouldn't have believed them. Here I am, though, excitement simmering in my blood as he takes his huge, swollen arousal out of his jeans, dragging his fist from root to tip. "Oh my God."

"Yeah. You make it this way, baby." He pumps his flesh a few quick times, groaning. "Come get a suck."

I don't even flinch now at the way he speaks to me, because his actions tell a different story. One of respect and protectiveness. This is about sex. That's the language he's speaking. I want to speak it with him. "Come get it."

A low curse vibrates out of Jason and he walks forward, erection in hand, pants around his knees. He cups my chin in one hand and pulls it down. Firm, commanding. Needy. A second later, his smooth head glides across my tongue and the taste of salt travels down my throat.

"Son of a bitch." He tugs himself back out of my mouth, face contorted in pleasure/pain, before dipping the thick weight back inside, inch by inch. "Fuck, I can't believe I've got you on your knees. Thought I'd just be dreaming about it the rest of my life."

My breath catches at his admission that he's been dreaming about me. Needing a distraction from the pinch in my chest, I wrap my hands around his girth and stroke him toward my mouth, licking around the head in one slow revolution. "What do I do in these dreams?"

"Baby, you *are* a fucking dream. In a pinch, I can get off thinking of you in yoga pants and your pouty lower lip." He steps closer, his booted foot bumping my outer thigh. "You sorry for making me suffer so long? Show me. Show me how you make nice."

Keeping my eyes on Jason, I relax my throat and let him guide his hard flesh deep, blinking when he meets the back. It might have been uncomfortable with someone else, but I'm too mesmerized by Jason to register the tears that jump to my vision, the ground abrading my knees. No. His harsh grunt and another taste of salt make it worth the reflexive pressure of my throat. His flesh jumps inside my mouth as he retreats, thickens as he pushes deep again. Again. Again. Again. The way I'm affected, he might as well be inside me. My folds are slick, a lust-dazed feeling creeping over me, blocking out the entire world. The noise of the parade in the distance erodes, leaving nothing but the wet, sucking sounds of my mouth and Jason's erratic breathing.

"That's so good, baby, baby, such a sweet fucking mouth. You've got me so horny or I'd keep tapping the back of that throat." He wraps my hair in a fist and turns up the pace of his thrusts, each of them punctuated by a curse. "Ahhh, Jesus. Going to come. You want it?"

I hum around Jason's erection and tighten my lips on a down stroke, walking on my knees to get close as possible, reveling in him, inhaling his musk. Want it? Yes, yes, I do. With my entire being. I'm the one that got him to this point—I want the proof.

The reward.

His fist grips the base of his length, rubbing up and down in time with my bobbing lips, working in perfect tandem for tense moments before the dam gives way. A groan rips from Jason and he erupts in my mouth, his hand a blur of motion as he frantically relieves himself into my mouth, down my throat. I watch him, absorbed, triumphant in the arch of his neck, the vein standing out in his temple, the sweat beading on his forehead. He's wrecked. A servant to his own body and the way it jerks, shudders as it empties.

When he's finished, a strange peace comes over me. I've needed this kind of contact with him for weeks, haven't I? The stress of not touching Jason or having him touch me has kept me pulled tight as piano wire, but the wire is cut now and I fall to one side, catching myself on a hand.

"Come here, beauty queen." I'm hoisted off the ground and squished up against his chest, my toes brushing the ground. "Damn. Never thought I'd say this after a month of hell, but you were...you *are* worth every minute of the torture."

Still captured in my dazed state, I let him sway me. My body is slack, but his words have made my pulse boom wildly in my ears. There are worries just out of reach and I can already feel them sneaking back to the fore. *Go away.* "So are you, Black-beard."

His fingers pause in their sift through my hair. "Any time you wanted me, baby, I'd have moved mountains—"

I put my fingers over his mouth before he can go any further. The words he's saying to me are beautiful, like balm on a scrape I didn't even know I had. His arms feel so right around me, his heart beating against my ear. But we're making too many admissions. Where does this lead? Nowhere. It can't go anywhere.

I'm afraid of us admitting too much and not being able to take it back. "Can't we just have the moment a-and—"

"And what? Go back to St. Augustine and pretend this didn't happen?" Using a fist full of my hair, he tugs my head back, his face hovering over mine. "Pretend I didn't drive here at ninety miles an hour because I can't stand the thought of another man looking at or thinking about you?" His voice drops. "Pretend I don't know your pussy melts like warm sugar on my tongue?"

Heat careens through me. "Stop."

"No, Naomi. It's not convenient to want each other this fucking bad, but here we are." He looks away and something hostile passes through his eyes. I'm not prepared to balance myself when he lets go of my hair, but he holds me until I gain my footing. "You haven't completely cut ties with your last relationship, but if you can kiss me the way you did, as far as I'm concerned, they're fucking cut. *I want them cut.*"

"It's not that simple. Legacy and marriage and commitment and bloodlines. Those things are important to my family. I've allowed myself to be selfish, but I can't stay this way forever."

The word *forever* falls between us like a boulder.

"How can you ask me to make huge decisions that will affect my life when you're leaving?" I whisper in a shaky voice. "We both are."

Silence stretches so long, I'm not sure he'll ever respond. Then, "If we've only got a couple of weeks, so be it." It takes him a moment to look at me. When he does, I can't help but think he's holding something back. "Until you go, though, I want it all. I want you in my bed every night. Fuck it, I want to hold your hand and take you out. All or nothing."

"Jason…"

"You want an adventure?" He takes my face in his hands. "Let me help give it to you."

I'm almost dizzy from the rapid pounding of my heart. He can't really be asking me to make a decision when I still haven't come down from what he did to my body. What I did to his. I've barely given myself permission to acknowledge that I have feelings for Jason and he wants more. He wants it all.

Temporarily.

Will I be able to walk away when it's all over?

"Think about it." Jason lays a lingering kiss on my lips. "But please don't take long."

We don't speak as Jason hails a cab and brings me back to the studio to collect my clothes and purse. When I'm dressed, the same cab brings us to the hotel. Jason holds my hand on the way through the lobby and I notice how everyone reacts to him. Men nod, like they can sense his heroism and want to pay their respect. Women duck their heads or full-on stare. He doesn't seem to notice any of it, but I know he does notice, don't I? I know he's not aloof or uncaring about how he presents himself—he told me about the bagel shop. I know him. And with my hand tucked so tightly in his grip, I feel known, too. Protected and appreciated. By Jason. By the time we reach the elevators, my nerves are like tiny bottle rockets. Is he going to stay the night with me? Am I actually going to let him?

Who am I kidding? If he kisses me, I won't be able to say no. Just having his commanding presence so close to mine has me vibrating head to toe. My brain won't stop replaying all his admissions. He's dreamed of me. I'm worth the wait. I taste like sugar. But won't spending the night together be as good as a yes to his proposed temporary arrangement?

"Um…" I stop at the hotel door and turn. "I-I'm not sure—"

"I know, beauty queen." He lowers his head and gives me a

kiss that spins me in a web, my head going so light I think I'm floating. "I want to stay. I need to stay and make you moan all goddamn night. But I can't exist on a half measure of you anymore, Naomi. Stolen moments that end too fast. Give me all, for just a little while." Another lingering kiss, followed by a rough exhale. "Come home to me safely tomorrow."

I can only stand there on knees made of rubber as he walks away, biting my lip so I won't call him back. It's not until twenty minutes later when I'm showering off the butterflies that I realize he called St. Augustine home. And I didn't even question it.

CHAPTER EIGHTEEN

EndoftheInternet.net
Username: IGotAnswerz9
*Let me be plain. The only one with a motive to kill Naomi was
Getaway Girl herself, Addison Potts. Classic love
triangle situation.*
Next!

Jason

THE FLORIDA HUMIDITY must have driven me goddamn
crazy.

That's the thought that ran through my head on the drive
home from Daytona last night. Actually it's still there, pinging
around like a nickel in the dryer. It's ten o'clock in the morning
and I'm pacing the driveway in a cloud of cigar smoke. Restless as
a pitcher in the bullpen waiting for the green light from his
manager.

Or rather, from a blonde with a dream mouth.

It's Sunday morning. She doesn't have pageant practice
scheduled with Birdie. It would be totally natural for her to laze
around in a fluffy hotel bed, browse Daytona for...whatever
women browse for and come back later in the day. Here I am
again, though, hobbled by having her safety out of my control. It
seems like years have passed since I found out Naomi was
sleeping in that shit bag motel, but I can still recall the feeling of

fear. Fear that she might reject my offer to live above the garage and stay. Being helpless to convince her otherwise.

This restlessness inside me is stronger now. But it's different.

Last night, when I found her walking mostly naked down the street, my first reaction had been total and utter denial. That couldn't be her. This couldn't be happening. Who the hell got close enough to paint butterflies on her tits? How fast could I get her away from everyone with a cock? Typical man concerns. I'd been ready to read her the riot act.

Until she'd turned her head and I'd seen her profile. She'd been...blooming. A light shone down on her from some unseen source—maybe my imagination—and I realized I'd never seen her like that before. I've been caught up in my never-ending need to fuck her, being frustrated and confused and amused by her. Because of that, I've missed how she's changed. Until last night. She'd told me in her own words that she'd come to St. Augustine for an adventure and she'd gone out and had one. She's been having them.

I sit down on the bumper of my boat trailer and grind out the cigar stub under my boot. I check my watch for the ninth time in as many minutes. The street was always too quiet for my taste. In my line of work, quiet meant loud was about to happen. With Naomi's exhilarated expression in my head, I want to hear a Range Rover turning the corner. I want to be the one to make her look like that next time. Eating her pussy in an alley was all I'd had to work with on short notice, not that I'd heard any complaints. The need to do better is relentless, though.

The screen door slaps against the house and I turn to find Birdie wandering out, hair in disarray, mug of coffee in hand. "She's not back yet?"

My jaw pops under the pressure. "Nope."

Silence passes. "So you're just going to be sitting here like the post-transformation Hulk when she pulls up?" She pauses with the coffee mug on her lips and sing-songs, "Creepy."

"I don't like…" I blow out a breath. "The unknown. I don't like having no gauge on the situation."

"You're used to having coordinates and commands and an AK strapped across your chest."

"Yes." Birdie sits down next to me on the bumper and lets me take a sip of her coffee. I watch her hover over the rim, marveling at how well she reads me when I'm positive I give nothing away. I've been marveling over her a lot lately. "I know we're in Florida. Logically. But I've been there to see how fast it can end. It's just…" I snap my fingers and feel an answering jolt inside of me. "I know I can't prevent bad things from happening to people, but it's fucking torture not being allowed to try."

The side of my face warms where Birdie studies my profile. "I'm sorry."

That cocked trigger in my chest eases back to the safety position. "That actually helps."

We sit in silence for a while as she downs her brew. "Do you worry about me like that?"

As soon as she sees my incredulous expression, she looks away. "Of course I do, Birdie. I've got our house locked down like Fort Knox. If it was just me, I'd probably leave the doors unlocked, hoping someone would break in and give me the fight I need."

That was revealing. Even to myself. But Birdie just nods, a smile playing around her edges of her mouth. Her question seems to still be lingering in the air, though, so I keep talking.

"You didn't have me here to look out for you and Nat. For a long time. Didn't make it my concern." A warm breeze picks up my words and carries them around the driveway. "Does that make you skeptical now that I care as much as I say I do?"

"Yeah," she says without hesitating.

"That's fair." I clear my crowded throat into the silent morning. "It's easy to get caught up in the belief that you're a superhero. Especially when you're twenty-odd years old and you've been recruited for a specific purpose. Because you were noticed, picked ahead of everyone else. You're avenging mankind, fighting on behalf of the greater good." I'm saying things as they occur to me and time seems to slow. "But there's more than one kind of greater good. It doesn't have to be a whole country or even a town. Sometimes it's just a house." I swallow as she leans into my side. "Or my sister. In that case, she's greater than good."

"Thanks." I can't see her face, but I sense she's not smiling. "Do you think you'll forget about the other greater goods when you leave?"

That jolt is back again, but this time it burns. Naomi's butterfly-painted body and look of wonder dances through my head, along with the moving image of Birdie slow dancing. "No. I won't forget this time."

"Good." Her side leaves mine as she stands, swirling the remains of her coffee inside the mug. "So…are you going to tell me what happened when you found Naomi last night?"

"Nope."

She laughs. "Oh shit. Good or bad?"

I press my tongue to the inside of my cheek to keep from smiling. "Not answering."

"Give me something!" Her eyebrows waggled. "Was she naked?"

"There were some strategic butterflies."

Birdie stumbles in a circle, holding her sides and giggling.

"Did you flip out?"

"No," I say quietly. "It almost came to that, but…she *needed* to parade naked down the street in body paint. I didn't want to ruin it."

After a few beats of silence pass, I look up to find my sister watching me. "You're starting to realize you don't hold the controls to the universe."

"Maybe."

I don't realize Birdie has gone back inside until the screen door whaps off the house again, but I'm still thinking about what she said. What we spoke about. I can't dictate how everyone lives their life. I couldn't even dictate the rescue or loss of life when I was a superhero with a weapon at the ready. Not every single time. There are forces outside the control of normal human capabilities. God, do I really have such an inflated ego that I'm struggling to admit that I'm human?

It's impossible to resist another check of my watch. Almost eleven o'clock now. It's not just Naomi's safety that has me sitting here, though, is it? I want my answer. I need to know if she's willing to be with me…for now. More than anything, I want her to pull up in her Rover, step out and run to me. Fuck. I've never wanted a romantic entanglement before. Never in my life. I've wanted to remain free of them. I want Naomi to tangle me the hell up, though. Messy, ill-advised, potentially ruinous. None of that matters when it's weighed against touching her, the end of my stay in purgatory. The end of us stopping conversations before they become too much. I want to push for more. Want her to push *me* for more.

I meant what I said last night. I want to wake up beside Naomi, give her my cock before she's rubbed the sleep from her eyes. Smear her scent on my body, my sheets, my mouth.

Immortalize it. I want to stop resenting her adventure because it brings her closer and closer to leaving. I want to help her revel in it, whether this time together comes to an end or not.

Do I already feel myself preparing to rage against that ending? Yes.

Will my potential loss of that fight prevent me from giving in to this insanity?

No. Nothing will. I need her. I want to fucking drown in her.

I almost think it's my imagination when her car turns the corner at the end of the block and slowly pulls to a stop along the sidewalk. Relief hits me first, a cool river that puts out the fires my concern started. Then this wild anticipation pounds inside me like fists on a drum. *Want to see her.* I'm craving the sight of her face. Her chin that's somehow graceful and stubborn at the same time. That freckle perched on her cleavage. Those eyebrows that arch when I say something inappropriate. At least they used to. She's grown accustomed to me.

That realization makes my chest heavy as Naomi steps out of the vehicle, her flip-flop dangling from her right foot a little before it touches down. God, she's sexy this morning in a long dress. One that ties at the back of her neck. I'm looking everywhere but her face, because I can already sense she hasn't made a decision yet. That reality blew over my skin as soon as she pulled up.

Help her. She's here for something bigger than you.

"Hi." Her keys jangle nervously in her hand as she approaches, blue eyes vulnerable. "Have you been sitting here all night?"

I step forward trying to catch some of her body heat, barely avoiding a groan when it hits me. "Just about stopped myself."

Naomi closes her eyes, her fingers itching in the material of her dress. "Oh."

We're being awkward. My arms are aching to wrap around her and confirm she's really safe and standing in front of me, my mouth wants to press up against her ear. To tell her she looks like she needs a good lick from my tongue. Another one. I don't have the green light to do any of that, though, so I move past her and collect the bag from the back seat.

A little sandal keychain with Daytona Beach splashed on the bottom in pink script hangs from the zipper. She's going to collect memories and have adventures with or without me. Do I want to help her make positive memories or not?

"Thought I'd take you out for a dive today," I say, turning back around. "Since you couldn't make it yesterday."

She wets her lips. "I don't know if that's a good idea." The sun catches an extra blonde strand of her hair. "I went to Daytona for the parade, because…it was getting to be too much here. Even before. Before…"

"Before we went at each other like animals."

The soft skin of her cheeks flames. "Yes."

"And you're not sure being alone with me is a good idea." I hitch the bag over my shoulder and stop in front of her, letting my interest wander to her mouth, still slightly swollen from sucking my cock. "Because you know next time we're alone, we're not going to stop until I'm bucking inside you. It's going to be impossible now."

Her breath catches. "It didn't seem impossible on the ride home."

"Naomi, let me bring you out on the ocean." I lean in and exhale near her temple. "Let me give you something. I need to give you something. And fuck it, I'm greedy and I want to see you outlined in blue. As if you could get more beautiful."

"This is impossible," she breathes, voice awed. I drop the bag, prepared to haul her up against me and show her how not impossible it would be to give in to the gravity gnawing on my bones. But she steps back out of my reach. "Jason, we're not in the alley anymore."

"I'm going to be that guy from the alley in the daylight or the shade, beauty queen." I take her hand and bring it to my mouth, razing her delicate inner wrist with my teeth. "A couple of weeks, Naomi. Give them to me. Give yourself to me."

I trail my tongue down the inside of her forearm and she pitches forward, catching herself on my chest. Immediately, I hook an arm around the small of her back, drawing her forward so she can feel my erection.

"Say yes to the dive," I rasp against her tipped back chin. "Let me show you what I do."

"Fine. Yes."

For just the briefest of seconds, her nails curl into my chest, sending shockwaves through me. My growl is left hanging in the air as she picks up her bag and climbs the stairs to the apartment. She pauses at the door, looking down at where I still stand in the driveway hungry enough to fight an army for the taste of her mouth. We don't break eye contact until she passes through the doorframe and I'm already counting the minutes until we're alone again. There's a voice in the back of my head whispering, *make it count.*

Make it count.

CHAPTER NINETEEN

ReadtheComments.com
Username: TheRappingTheorist
Go Naomi, it's your birthday.
We gonna party like someone finally took my combustion
theory seriously.

Naomi

I KNOW AS soon as Jason's eyes roam over my bathing suit-clad body that coming on this boat was a mistake—and I'm going to pay. My dress shivers to the floor of the vessel, leaving me in the white bikini I purchased to wear on my honeymoon. It's a brief amount of material for me, giving my breasts the barest coverage, the waistband riding low toward my sex. Instead of material ties, the sides are held together by silver and gold beads, which bite ever so slightly into my hips.

The boat rocks under our feet, groaning. The movement of the water beneath us is a blatant simulation of sex, like the ocean is urging us on. *Do it. Give in.* And he's in no hurry to look away, either. He tosses the wet suit in his hand over the covered engine, rubbing his hand across his bearded jaw. Lord, he's tall enough to seem like a fixture of the sky, his wide shoulders blocking out the sun, leaving me in the shade but far from cool. Quite the opposite, actually. When his tongue glides along his full lower lip, I'm remembering the way his head felt between my thighs. How invincible he looked from my knees.

Playing dirty using my name. I love you saying it so bad.

It's probably too late to hide the effect his attention is having on my body. My nipples are gathering in a rush of euphoria, my libido probably thinking it's going to get relief like last night. Is it? God knows I need it. I've never needed sex. Not like this. Not like I might not have a choice but to go get it. Receive it.

Mouth dry, I reach for the wetsuit Jason indicates with a slow chin jerk, bending forward to step inside and tug it up my legs. On my way up, I can't help but notice the distinct bulge inside his wet suit and he makes no move to hide it. When I finally make it into the ocean, it's going to rise in temperature. Scientists will be baffled.

My manners prod me to fill the silence. "When did you know you wanted to be a diver?"

To his credit, he doesn't so much as smirk at my threadbare voice. "When I was sixteen, I went on a school field trip. Snorkeling, not diving. But it was the first time I..."

"What?"

He scrubs at the back of his neck. "First time I heard the silence under the surface," he says, as if he's never said the words out loud. "I was never big on school. The classrooms made me feel confined, but it was the same at home. I didn't know how to grab hold of my own thoughts. I loved Birdie and Nat, but they were younger and loud." The corners of his eyes wrinkle in response to my quiet laugh. "Snorkeling blocked out every sound for a while and I just felt this new type of ease. Once I started taking diving classes, I felt less confined in school. I could be more...present at home."

"You needed your own place."

Jason nods. "It's not my only place now. I've got running."

His eyes roam over me lazily. "Better yet, I've got a beauty queen who tell me stories in the middle of the night."

I'm incapable of doing anything but basking in the glow he leaves on my skin. My tongue is too tied to respond, though—what would I say?—and he eventually has mercy on me.

"Number one rule is to check your gear, make sure it's functioning properly. I've already done that, but for the future…." Jason's voice is thick as it resumes, contrasting with the white fluffy clouds. He disappears into the front of the boat for a moment and I use the opportunity to quickly jiggle myself in an undignified fashion into the remainder of the suit, zipping it up to my collarbone. Jason emerges with a life jacket in one hand, an oxygen tank in the other. He sets down the tank on its side next to me, slowly stepping into my space, now blocking out the whole sky. "This is a buoyancy control device. It looks like a life jacket, but the difference is, you can control the amount of air inside. You want more on the surface than you do underwater."

I almost moan as he leans in to wrap the vest around my back, sending sea salt, male and pungent cigar smoke drifting over me. It occurs to me that I'm about to do something completely outside my comfort zone, but I've never felt safer in my entire life.

"We're in shallow water, so you can take it nice and easy," he continues gruffly, inches from my ear. "A slow descent is important. Drop too fast and you'll get decompression sickness. Your body has to handle the depth in degrees." His mouth brushes my ear. "One inch at a time, beauty queen." I'm left swaying as he circles around behind me, securing the tank to the back of my jacket and connecting a series of lines. He's saying words like *regulator set* and I should almost certainly be listening and asking questions, but I'm too aware of the hammering of my pulse, the liquid weight rushing to my loins. "I'll be right beside you, making sure you're moving at the right pace."

"Um." I clear the hoarseness from my voice. "What are we going to see down there?"

"This shallow? Sand. Rocks." He moves in front of me in time to wink, reminding me of a sea captain I read about once when I stole a paperback romance novel from my grandmother's library. "Might bump into some grouper or mullet."

"That would be lovely."

Hearing the simpering belle quality to my voice, I order myself to pull it together. Easier said than done when he's got that wolfish expression. I've been living across the driveway from this man for over a month and yes, there's been an often unbearable attraction...but I've been getting by lucky. He's actually trying to seduce me now and at this rate it's going to work. If he brings that mouth around my ear one more time, I'm going to reach such a temperature that this wetsuit will melt and harden right onto my body. And then no one will be having sex because I'll be mummified.

"Naomi."

"Yes?"

"I already have a hard enough time deciphering your thoughts. Get your finger off the fast forward button."

A laugh puffs out of me. "What are you thinking about?"

"Besides what I've been thinking about non-stop since last night?"

"Yes," I croak.

"Diving safety." An edge of his mouth ticks up. "Don't trip over all the excitement."

More tummy flips. He's flirting with me. I...like the way it feels. Like the way he enjoys me, seems to savor and look for layers in everything I say. There *are* layers. There's more than what's visible on the surface. I'm not sure I believed that before coming to St. Augustine. "I do think it's exciting, actually," I rasp, sounding like a fallen woman. "This is what you love."

"Yeah." His jaw ticks as he looks at me. "What I love."

I tip my head to one side and let the sunshine bathe my neck. "Scuba diving. Thousands of people do it only once. Out of that thousand, you were the one who it drew back. Your purpose found you." His fingers run over my vest, inspecting it, but his touch seeps through and warms me, tickles my nipples. "It doesn't do that for everyone."

"Pageant coaching found you, didn't it?"

"In a way. I looked for the job at the exact time you needed me. O-or someone like me," I rush to add, and our eyes clash. "I wouldn't call it my purpose, though."

"Do you love it?"

"I...love Birdie."

His fingers pause on my vest and it takes him a moment to respond. "I love the ocean. Scuba is just a means of getting there." Finished inspecting, his hand lifts, hesitates, and cups my cheek. "Maybe it can be about the contestants for you and not the..."

"Frippery?"

"Ceremony," he returns, eyebrow raised.

"Nice save."

We stand there for a moment, rocking on the water, our bodies separated by nothing more than a few reaching rays of sunshine. "You can do anything, Naomi." I'm going to kiss him. I'm going to kiss—but he clears his throat and steps back, hoisting on his own vest, complete with tank. "Speaking of the exciting world of safety. Do not hold your breath. That will be your instinct at the beginning, but you need to trust the equipment to do its job. Trust *me*. We're going to work on it here, before we dive."

I nod and we get started, applying defogger to our masks and putting them on. Jason is right—I definitely would have held my breath, thinking the water would steal it. Learning to breathe through the mouthpiece feels unnatural. But after a few minutes, I get used to relying on the tube to feed me oxygen. There's a steady whoosh sound effect that stops being foreign and turns comforting, reminding me to continue the in and out pace. That and Jason's unreadable eyes, shaded even in the sunshine. They hold mine, daring me to look away. Asking me not to. By the time Jason leads me to the panel attached to the back of the boat, I'm breathing a little faster than I was in the beginning, but he waits, giving me grounding instructions as we poise ourselves to step off into the blue.

The boat sways underneath me and the water seems to rise, beckoning. Dry snowflakes whip through my arms and legs, twirling around my bones. I'm doing this. Am I really doing this?

His hand encompasses mine, small in big and he squeezes, lifting it to his bristled cheek, since his mouth is occupied by a mouthpiece. That simple gesture settles the riot inside me, dropping the snowflakes into a haphazard pile. *I won't let anything happen to you.* He doesn't have to say it out loud. The sentiment is there in every line of his hard body, barely contained in the shiny black of his wetsuit. Outlined by the sun, he looks like something that rose out of the water holding a trident and my God, my God I've never been more attracted to anything in my life. My blood sings toward him, even as my mind tells me I've got to conquer the blue in front of me.

I nod at Jason with as much confidence as I can muster and pride bleeds into his eyes, making me ever more determined. I have this. No, I'm not having this experience, I'm taking it.

We step off into the water.

It's over my head faster than expected, and my first instinct is to kick back to the surface, but I beat the reaction and let myself sink, let the increasingly colder temperature surround me. My eyes are closed. It takes me a second to realize that and open them…

The first thought that springs to my head is *The Little Mermaid*. The strains to 'Part of Your World' begin to play and an underwater snort sends bubbles twisting and lifting around my face. What I'm looking at is incredible. Eye-piercingly colorful. Greens and blues of every description blend and shift, shafted with sunlight. There's a rock formation to our right, just existing in the silence, welcoming a school of tiny silver fish, steady in the drift. A glance at Jason tells me he's watching me from behind his mask, that sensual mouth wrapped around black. Despite the incredible display of nature around me, I can't help but stare back, hearing my heartbeat rap in my ears. No conflicts exist down here. Just us.

Finally, with a visible effort, he nods at our surroundings. *Make yourself at home.* Timing my breaths in my head like he taught me, I turn and thread slowly through the dense blue, my fins alternating slow kicks behind me. A sense of wonder tugs at my throat, tears springing to my eyes behind the mask. A yellow fish glides past and my hand automatically lifts and reaches out, coming within inches of an animal that's been here all along. Living its own life while I ditched my wedding and paraded naked down the street in body paint.

It's all so much bigger than me or my personal drama.

The whole world is so much bigger.

Bigger than pageants, my mother's expectations, always having the correct response.

When a woman comes across something in this life that she feels compelled to take...when her soul yearns for it...what's the worst that can happen if she leaps? If she makes an honest grab for it? This ocean will still be here in all its glory. The sand won't shift based on my decisions. Only my insides will. I'm ready for that. I'm ready for a seismic shift.

I'm ready to take what I want. What I need. And he's right behind me, watching, needing me back. Ready for his own seismic shift. Maybe. Maybe I'm that for him, too. There's no telling how we'll handle the resulting terrains inside of us when it comes to an end, but I'm not going to hesitate out of fear. Not when I know I can be this brave.

I run my hand over the rock formation, gasping internally when three more yellow fish wiggle out of a crevice, dancing past my face. Needing to share the moment with Jason, I turn...and at first I don't believe what's in front of me. Surely my mind is trying to scare me at my strongest moment. Trying to drag me back into uncertainty. There's not supposed to be a shark moving in slow, back and forth ticks between Jason and me.

It's on the small side. I think. Compared to Jaws. That's all I have to make a comparison. But its teeth are deadly. Sharp. My eyes fly to Jason, who is motionless on the other side of the creature. The time I comforted him in the middle of the night, I thought him tormented, but that was nothing compared to this. He's terrified. This invincible giant of a man with battle scars and enough courage to fill this ocean looks like he's being tortured alive—and that chills my blood until I'm trembling. Jason shakes his head slowly at me. *Don't move.*

Apart from the necessary glide of my fins, I couldn't move if I wanted to. My heart has climbed into my throat and I'm lightheaded from forgetting to breathe. Remembering the importance of breathing Jason impressed upon me, I kick back into my rhythm, though, mentally begging the big, silver animal to keep on its merry way without leaving any bites behind to remember him by.

It seems to take fifteen minutes, when in reality it was only one, but the shark finally vanishes into the distant dark, fish scurrying out of its path and bubbling past me. Jason reaches me before I find the wherewithal to move again, wrapping an arm around my waist and kicking us toward the top, wild eyes searching mine. Seeing God knows what. Because I have no idea what's happening inside me. As soon as we break the surface, my fear is replaced by careening adrenaline. It bashes off my ribs and tickles my neck, filling me with almost unbearable buoyancy.

Jason lifts me onto the wooden platform and I rip off my equipment, gasping for air, trying to live through the blast of energy that's overtaking me. The potency of the rush has me grabbing for the zipper of my wetsuit, yanking at it, needing to ease the pressure on my chest. How can I feel this light and this weighed down at the same time? Water laps against the boat, echoing in my head, but I can't focus on anything until I'm unfettered. When I finally get the wetsuit off and tossed limply into the boat, I slump against the back of the vessel, confused to find the tension still lingers, my blood pumping a thousand miles an hour.

"Baby." Jason is in front of me, blocking out the sun, his hands molding my face. "Jesus Christ, that's never happened in water this shallow. I don't know what the fuck happened. I don't know what the fuck…" He breaks off in a wheeze and I notice for the first time his big shoulders are shaking. Worse than after his nightmares. Worse than anything…for me, too. I can't stand him being upset. "I couldn't get to you. I couldn't get to you."

"Shhh. I know," I rasp, clasping the sides of his face in my hands. Jumpy. I'm so jumpy. And…exhilarated. The energy inside me expands until I feel like I'm going to burst out of my skin. "Jason, that was a shark. I was inches away from a shark."

His fingers plow into my wet hair with a guttural sound. "You think I somehow forgot? I can't stop seeing it. I'm going to see it every time I close my eyes for the rest of my life."

"But I'm fine. Look." Another spike of adrenaline has me shooting to my knees. "A couple months ago, living dangerously meant wearing competing patterns. I just survived scuba diving and a shark encounter." I let go of his face and shake out my hands, a laugh bubbling up and bordering on hysterical. "Oh my God. I feel crazy."

Jason studies me with shadows in his eyes. Shadows and increasing awareness. I'm dancing around on my knees in front of him, no idea if my bikini is in place and not caring. Not caring about anything but freeing this overwhelming fullness inside me. Giving it a home. "You're coming down," he says gruffly. "After a mission, I have energy to burn, no matter how tired I am."

"How do you burn it off?"

"I run most times." His gaze slides down my throat, over my chest, heating, his tongue emerging to wet his lips. "I jerk myself off. Whatever it takes."

Lord, I'm feeling daring. Out of my skin. The soaring sensation is amazing. Nothing is off limits right now. I'm powerful and liberated. "What did you used to think about when you jerked yourself off?"

CHAPTER TWENTY

ConspiracyCrowd.org
Username: IWant2Believe2000
*Of course they couldn't park the alien aircraft in the church
parking lot.
It was probably MILES away. Am I blowing your mind yet?*

Jason

I'M IN LOVE with this woman.

Not just because she's asking me about my masturbation practices. Not that her interest in that direction hurts. I'm thick and ready inside my wetsuit in a way that's going to make unzipping a very delicate process. No, I knew I loved Naomi when I saw the shark. Knew I'd loved her for a while, because the idea of something happening to her made my life flash in front of my fucking eyes.

This thing between us will stall out before it starts. We both have places to be. Places we're needed. Imminently. She's not in my league, either, this goddess who can't stop gasping and shaking in the aftermath of what happened down below. Christ, she's always, always so gorgeous it's painful, but with her eyes bright and unfocused, lips parted on labored breaths, hair in disarray, I'm captivated. I'm a goner. I'm her servant. It doesn't matter what's stacked against us when she's in clear need of an anchor. Right now, in this moment, I couldn't stop myself from being that anchor if I wanted to. It's a force of nature.

I blink and the memory of her face paling in the pool of murky sunlight takes hold. The way the shark blocked her face as it slithered past, hiding her from me, stopping my heart in my chest. Unacceptable. Horrific. If something had happened to her, I wouldn't have bothered kicking back to the surface. How could I let this happen? I'm supposed to protect her. I—

"Jason," comes the murmur of her voice, weaving in and out of the sunlight that falls all around her, turning her into a fallen angel. "Do you need a battle story?"

"No," I manage, swallowing, leaning in to press our mouths together. Needing to touch her, reassure myself she still has breath in her lungs. "No. I need you." Her breath catches against my lips and I can feel her being attuning itself to mine. Click. Slide. My fingertips drag up her stomach and meet at her chest, tugging aside the triangles of her bikini top. "And to answer your question, I can't remember what I used to think about when I fucked myself. You've replaced every image in my head. When I take myself in my hand now, it's Naomi's tight pussy. Naomi's shy tongue." I squeeze her nipples between my knuckles. "Naomi's beauty queen tits."

The sound that comes out of her is desperate. Almost wounded. Every cell in my body responds, whipping into a frenzy. Preparing to please. "I want this." Her hands slap down on my chest, fingers searching for my zipper. "I need you now. Hard. Please, please, please. I want you to throw me down and use me."

The unexpectedness of that is like a fist clamping around my cock and stroking. I double a little at the waist, my groaning mouth sliding along the side of her neck, nearly coming in my wetsuit. "You need to understand how bad I've wanted you, baby, and respect it." I close my teeth around her pulse and bite down, my hands shoving into the back of her tiny bathing suit bottoms to grip her ass. "Respect that my dick is on a goddamn hair trigger where you're concerned. Getting you to an orgasm before I go off is going to take all my concentration, so keep the begging to a minimum for my sanity, huh?"

She arches into me, gasping when I get nice and rough with her bottom. "*Yes, Jason.*"

I jerk her into my body, rubbing my aching cock against the little, wet scrap of material covering her pussy. Can this really be happening? Or is this just another one of my fantasies? "Jesus, even that. Yes, Jason in that belle of the ball tone of voice. You might as well be taking me to the back of your throat."

Eyes glazed, she stares at my mouth while beginning to lower my wetsuit zipper. "Sorry," she whispers, her expression not the least bit contrite, and I nip at her bottom lip in reproof. "Kind of."

I growl, already anticipating how hard I'm going to fuck her. No way to hold back when I've been hungry this long. Both of us have been—that's plain in the way she can't catch her breath, her bare tits lifting and falling on hurried shudders. When we reach my cock, she stops unzipping, letting her fingers drift down over the distended neoprene, grazing my throbbing flesh with teasing touches. I swell to the point of pain, my balls climbing into my stomach. "You trying to earn a slap on the ass, baby?"

Her pupils dilate. "Maybe."

Fuck. I almost can't take this. Can't take this bold, incredible Naomi on top of the brave, blossoming one I've been falling in love with. She's so much wonderful at one time. My heart is going to pound straight out of me. Love and lust shoot up inside me like a rocket, making me bare my teeth. Without taking my eyes off her, I yank down her bathing suit bottoms and deliver a stinging smack to her taut cheeks. She sucks in a rendition of my name and we dive into a kiss that demands payment in the form of my soul. My everything.

My hands slide up the curve of her back and bury in her hair, because I need to steady her. Need to steady myself under the cataclysm of sensations. She's untamed as our tongues surge together, lips straining wide and angling, noisy intakes of air from my nostrils as Naomi climbs me, wrapping her legs around my hips, kissing me from above while I can do nothing but worship her from below with my head tilted back, my hips rocking in time with the ocean beneath the boat. She breaks off the kiss with a whimper, and I attack her throat with my lips, tongue and teeth, groaning at the writhe of her pussy on my imprisoned dick. I've never been more regretful for leaving on my wetsuit. I'd already be thrusting into her like a madman if I'd hadn't been so mired in the aftermath of almost losing Naomi to take it off. And that's what she wants, isn't it? My hardest fuck.

"Jason, Jason, Jason…" She tears at my hair, her lower body moving in an increasingly disjointed way that tells me she's going to climax before I even get my cock out. Yeah. Not happening. I've been suffering day and night for this woman and I'm not going to let her come unless I'm deep enough to feel every little shake and squeeze I wring out of her. "Now. Please."

"I hear you loud and clear, baby. Believe me," I grind out against her mouth, standing up on the platform and carrying her clinging body into the boat. She makes a sound of protest over me stealing her rhythm, hitting me with a frustrated look as she yanks the sides of my wetsuit wide, baring my chest. Drags it as far as she can down my arms. The move—and the frustrated seductress look on her face—is hot enough. But then she buries her teeth in the meat of my right pectoral and pressure surrounds my cock from all sides, my head falling back on a roar.

Liquid heat seeps out of me. So hot. A warning shot. I'm on the edge already and I'm not even inside of her yet. Jesus Christ.

Letting Naomi go for even a second goes against every instinct in my body. Need her skin. Need her heat. But I have no choice. I settle her on her feet by the captain's chair, snagging her mouth in a kiss borne of utter starvation. While my chest tightens at the perfect taste of her, I free my cock as carefully as possible from the clinging material of the suit and rip it down my hips and thighs, letting my feet do the rest. After what seems like a goddamn millennium, I'm naked and Naomi is perusing me openly, panting through swollen lips, her hands racing up to play with her nipples. "Oh my God. All of you at once is pretty…potent."

I fist my dick, watching her cheeks turn pink as I choke a drop of moisture from the tip. "Return the favor."

It takes no effort for her to swipe the bikini top over her head since her tits are already out. I'm transfixed as she slides her palms down her lithe body, hooking a single finger under the beads on either end and easing the bottoms down, gravity taking them to the floor. I'm seeing the world in different colors by the times she's naked below the waist, my pulse hammering in every erogenous zone in my body. How am I going to survive this? I've never wanted anyone more in my life. Never even come close to a fraction of this kind of lust. This kind of desperation to give and get pleasure.

I lunge forward and she comes, scaling my body, our mouths poised in the moment before a kiss. "Fuck," I rasp. "Drenched, aren't you? Tell me you're horny for me."

Her ankles lock behind my back and she arches, tempting me with her incredible tits. "I'm horny, Jason. I'm dying for you."

With a sidestep, I fall into the captain's chair, gritting my teeth as she lands in a wet slide on my lap, our sexes pressing together, rubbing. I make a blind grab for my gear bag, which I slung over the back of the chair earlier. Condom. Front pocket. I snag it between two fingers, rip the foil with my teeth and roll it down my cock. "You'll get your hard fuck, Naomi. I'll ride you hard enough to make you feel used as many times as you want." I stroke greedy hands down her ass and find my erection again, guiding it to the place I've been dreaming about, whether asleep or awake. "I don't trust myself not to blow when I've finally got you on your back, though. Take what your pussy needs now, baby. Take what I need to give you."

I see legitimate stars when I get a couple inches inside of her. And when she whines in her throat and takes the full length of me, hips working to make it happen, I'm lost in an entire solar system. My life ends and starts at the same time. I'm a conqueror and conquered. Her snug pussy is already milking me in a damning tempo, threatening to break me.

"You're big," she whispers brokenly, eyes glazed as they meet mine, her fingernails restless in my chest hair. "Oh my God, you're so big."

"Do something with it," I say through clenched teeth. "It's there for you."

Prickles cover every inch of my skin when she twists her fingers in my hair. Hard. She faced a threat under the surface and survived it. Now she feels like a badass and I love it. I want to help her believe that to be true all the time, not just right now. "Just for me?"

"Goddammit, yes. I'm hard and dripping for you. That's how you've kept me. Horny and unsatisfied for months." I lift her with my hips and drop down hard, satisfied with her closed-mouth scream, turned on by the bounce of her tits. "Feel what a mean girl you've been?"

"Yes," she breathes, her expression somehow contrite and thrilled over my suffering all at once. "I've been hurting, too. I ache all the time."

I lay a hard spank on her ass, soothing it with the heel of my hand. "Prove it."

A look of intense concentration steals over her features, a wrinkle forming between her brows, teeth sinking into her lower lip. For all the buildup, she's suddenly moving with hesitation, as if she's not sure I'm going to like any damn way she chooses to ride my cock. This close, she can't hide her vulnerability from me. Mentally, it brings me to my knees. I've always sensed a lack of confidence when we've lost the battle with our attraction and gotten physical. This confirms what I've sensed under the surface. She has no idea how sexy she can be. No one has ever told her. Made her believe it.

That ends now. Can't she see she's killing me with every twist of her hips, every dig of her fingernails into my shoulders? It's taking every ounce of restraint inside me not to come.

I lean in and take her mouth in a slow, thorough kiss, enjoying the way her hips roll faster, betraying how turned on she is by the kiss. *My woman.* "How did you appear out of thin air and do this to me, huh? Get me so hard. Get in my head. Make me so fucking hot." I bat her right ass cheek with my palm, listening to her moan as the smack lingers in the warm sea air. "Look at you. Sexiest woman on this fucking earth," I grit out with absolute sincerity. "Every time you move, I get closer to coming. You're pulling on every hard inch of me with every tight, little inch of you. Feel it, Naomi?"

Her nod is unsteady as she does exactly that, forcing a roar up the back of my throat. "Y-yes."

"Do you?"

Blue eyes land on mine. Pools of lust and uncertainty warring together. "I want to drive you crazy, but I'm not sure how."

My heart twists, ripping my voice to shreds. "Watching you get off is what's going to drive me crazy. Every time." I'm connected enough with Naomi to know she needs me to be confident enough for both of us right now. To take charge. She's begging me to do it with her eyes, and on the verge of losing my seed to the sexy glide of her pussy up and down my cock, I can't keep my dominance at bay for another second. "Beautiful, sexy woman." I kiss her until she's gasping into my mouth. "That feel like a cock that needs you to take it easy?"

She shakes her head, breath accelerating. Thighs widening, hips scooting closer.

"Nah. It's big and sturdy for you, isn't it, baby?" I bite her bottom lip and drag it through my teeth, ticking my hips up, up, up. "Thick enough to fill you. Hard enough to pump your hips on it as fast and long as you want." I smack her ass hard. Once. Twice. "My maker put it there for your pleasure, baby. Go get some. I love you fucking me. I love it."

Her right hand leaves my shoulder and hesitates between us, a moan already resting on her lips. "I want to touch myself. I want you to see me do it."

My lower body surges up without orders from my brain, lifting her and plunging back down on the seat, the bottom of my spine twisting like wire around a spike. "Do it. Oh God, do it. Rub your clit while sitting on my dick. Tell me what it feels like."

I know the moment the pad of her finger makes contact because her pussy seizes up around me, her head falling back and exposing the column of her gorgeous throat. I'm caught between needing to look down and watch her fondle herself and licking every inch of her neck. In the end, I alternate between the two, rolling my hips as her pace picks up, her fingers creating a furious friction right where she needs it. In no time, she's riding me like a fucking cowgirl, her pointed nipples moving in a delicious up and down bounce inches from my mouth. I'm groaning in an uncontrollable way, my rasp of her name unrecognizable. "Naomi." I raze her chin with my teeth. "Talk to me."

She heaves a strangled sound and plasters herself closer, taking her fingers from her clit in favor of wrapping both arms around my neck. "I'm going to come," she hiccups, grinding herself on the base of my cock. Hard. Without shame. Totally abandoned and so beautiful I can't get a decent breath. Watching her in awe, I bite down on my lip and command myself not to bust. "You're smooth and thick. It's so good." Her voice shakes against my mouth, her sexy ass pumping in my hands. "You could overpower me, but you're not. So big and rough underneath me, letting me. Just *letting* me...God."

Naomi's scream sounds like a miracle, shattering the breeze and making the sunshine seems brighter, hotter. The pressure around my cock turns rhythmic, hot moisture leaving her and coating me—and if I wait another second to give her what she asked me for, it's not happening. I stand on legs that feel strong and brittle at the same time, searching through a haze of lust for somewhere to pin her ass while I fuck her into another dimension. Need to. Need to. The boat engine is covered by a leather-covered hatch and I lunge for it, slapping her backside down on it, bearing down on her while she's still in the midst of her orgasm, earning myself more screams.

I rear back with my hips and pull out, just to the tip. God knows where I'm finding the willpower to hold back and tease when I'm on the verge of emptying myself, but I do it, leaving myself poised for a plunge at her entrance while I lean down and suck her nipples, one by one.

"Jason!"

"Don't worry, beauty queen, I'm going to let you have it back." I wrap a hand around her throat and squeeze lightly, shaking my head when her lips pop open with a feminine sigh of pleasure. Anticipation. Goddamn, she's a wonder. "You still want to be used? I've got that for you."

Her belly lifts and hollows, her back arching as I lick the flat of my tongue over her nipple. "Yes. Yes, please. Please, Jason. Now." I ram into her and she orgasms again. That pussy milks me like a dream, her thighs around my hips in vise grip. Her hand flies out to smack me across the face, connecting hard, but not enough to faze me. It's a reflex she doesn't expect, because even as she shakes through her climax, her eyes are wide, searching on mine. "I'm sorry, it's just…so intense, I didn't mean to—"

I lick a path up to her mouth and take it in a bruising kiss. There's apology in the way her tongue tangles with mine, but I won't allow that. She's got needs and I'm her safe place to express them. "You want to goad me into losing control. You want that hard fuck you requested from your man, don't you, baby? Do it again."

She breathes hard for a moment, then lays her palm against my cheek. The slap is light this time, but when I pull out and thrust deep with a growl, she does it harder, her blue eyes flaring with excitement. Maybe a little disbelief at her own actions.

"Good girl. Get excited for this cock." I capture her wrists and pin them out wide on either side of her. "You're my tight little sacrifice now. Aren't you?"

Naomi nods, her eyes unfocused, face bathed in sunshine. "Please."

"Wrap your thighs around me and hold on." My hips begin to slap down in time with my grunts, my neglected cock tunneling in and out of her wet heat. "I don't come like a gentleman."

Her naked body slides up and back on the leather engine cover, vibrating with each savage drive, faster and faster, the give of her pussy blowing my mind. Jesus Christ, the pain in my stomach increases to the point of agony, the buildup of heat in my balls forcing me to grit my teeth on a shout. So slick and snug. I want to live here. I never want this to stop, but I'm at the end of my rope, desperate for relief. Relief that's going to be so sweet and fulfilling, I can already sense it in every nerve ending, every fucking hair follicle.

I love you, baby. The words clog my throat, but I manage to keep them inside in favor of chanting her name like she's my own personal savior and I was sent to appease her one earthly weakness. My mouth finds hers and I taste her breath, revel in her moans, memorize the incredible texture of her tongue, keeping myself balanced on the edge of orgasm while I fuck her in a frenzy, screams building in her throat, eventually releasing into the air and clashing with animalistic smacks of our sexes. "Fuck. Fuck!"

I take her right hand, which I'm pinning, and smash it against my cheek. Naomi's head is thrashing from side, incoherent words falling from her mouth, but she takes the hint and connects her palm to my cheek, the exhilaration on her face driving me higher. "You're not going to stop me from taking what I need from this pussy." I release her other pinned hand and capture both knees, jerking them wide as I change the angle to grind on her clit, surprising her into a back-arching sob. "Such a lady. So sweet and polite. Until her pussy gets stroked the right way, huh? Now she's just a greedy girl with her thighs open for Jason's cock."

Her hands burrow in her blonde hair, strands wrapping around agitated fingers. "Oh my God. I can't. I can't..." Blindness steals through her eyes. "Harder. Please. It's too much."

The final ounce of control I was holding on to is obliterated when she hits that third peak, her voice hoarse from overuse. Knowing I gave that satisfaction to her, seeing how unusual it is for her to get this much pleasure from a man, it sets me fucking loose. Mentally, physically. I'm flying. My body flattens her on the engine cover, my knees wide, planting on any purchase they can find while my hips hit a wild pace, pounding her without mercy as her screams echo in my ear.

My release is a flood that roars through me, creating a rush of white noise in my ears. My muscles tighten to the point of snapping before they unlock and I shudder violently, my lower body a war zone of pleasure and pain. Need and fulfillment. There's a harbor in the storm, though, and her body is already wrapping around mine, needing me back, making the violent pleasure we've inflicted on our bodies a glorious thing we share, instead of something to combat. God, it's so good. My cock is still jerking with aftershocks, moisture spurting from the tip while I groan into her hair, my hips still moving in fucking motions all on their own. Her lips move over my cheek and I turn into them, inhaling through a long kiss, sensing her need for an anchor and giving it to her. Giving everything to her.

How am I ever going to let this woman go?

CHAPTER TWENTY-ONE

ReadtheComments.com
Username: LittleMissMorbid
I'm not trying to be a downer, guys, but they should probably
drag the bottom of the closest lake, right? Guys?
Guys?

Naomi

I'M GOING THROUGH the motions of making dinner, but I feel like I'm watching the movements of my hands on a movie screen. I'm only half conscious of the knife sinking into the asparagus, cutting on the purplish-white ends. Rinsing them. Putting them in the sauté pan. I have a roasted chicken in the oven and a lemon risotto on the back burner, too, a feat I never would have been capable of accomplishing a month ago. If only I could relax enough to enjoy it.

When I reach up to retrieve olive oil from the cabinet, the sore muscles of my stomach pull and I stumble forward against the counter with a closed-mouth moan. Oh my God. My hot shower did nothing to soothe my aches, apparently. I really did have sex with Jason on the boat. I am actually now in his kitchen, waiting for him to clean up while I get dinner started. Sex is likely to happen again. I am in this reality where it's understood that I'm going to bed with a big, bad Special Forces diver with a secret tender heart.

Sex. Going to bed. Ha.

Ha.

What happened on the boat was not sex. It was...

What the heck was it?

It was a claiming. It was unapologetic fucking. Yes, fucking. Grunting, vigorous, worshipful, ruthless fucking. He was hot for me. My body. The way I tweaked my hips made his jaw drop, made his eyes go molten. My words alone almost brought him to climax. My breasts made him growl. He was so incredibly hard between my legs. Hard for *me*. Naomi Clemons. I've never been so confident in my abilities to please a man, because the results were right there on display where I could devour them with my eyes, catalogue them in my memory bank.

Spank bank.

I snort into my wrist, laughing at the wayward thought. Not so long ago, I wouldn't have allowed an acknowledgment of something so inappropriate. I definitely wouldn't have applied it to a situation involving me. But here we are. I have a spank bank now. It's a done deal and I wouldn't mind making another deposit. I snort again and propel myself into drizzling olive oil. It's one thing to acknowledge my spank bank, another to dwell on it when there's dinner to be made. The silly smile lingers on my mouth until I realize my pulse is still bobbing and weaving.

It fades and I swallow. There was more than sex today. There was connection. A meeting of something far deeper inside both of us, and I think that's why I'm walking shell-shocked through Jason's kitchen with my ears ringing. I'm too afraid to explore what made tears leak from my eyes today when it was over and Jason was holding me close in his huge embrace. So close. I'm too afraid to examine what made my heart feel like a helium balloon in my chest when he held my hand as we drove home in silence, our eyes meeting every so often across the truck's interior.

My life can't change course because of Jason and this thing between us. I'm already so far off the original track that it's going to be a struggle to get back on. Daughterhood. Possibly wifehood. Socialite status awaits me in Charleston, in case I forgot. I have a little bit of time left in the hourglass, though. I'm not down to the final grain yet. So can't I put off thinking about reality a little bit longer? Is that so bad?

Jason is leaving. My life is elsewhere and vastly different from this one. We are both aware of these truths. They are not changeable. So what is the point of stressing over them now when the next week and a half can be a fulfilling close to my adventure? Maybe…maybe I was meant to be an adventure for Jason, too. That possibility makes me feel a little breathless. If I go back to Charleston with the confidence in myself that I can be someone's adventure, my purpose for running from the church will be achieved.

Will that ever be close to enough after Jason?

The kitchen's back door opens and Birdie walks in, forcing my troubling thoughts away. Hesitating in the doorway, she sends me an arch look. "Hi."

"Hello! How did you keep busy today?"

She closes the door slowly, chin tucked into her chest. "I might have…met some friends for gelato." When I stare back at her with an open mouth, she gives me a grudging half-smile. "So…you're cooking for us."

"Yes, well…" I gather my hair and throw it over a shoulder. "I didn't get a chance to run to the store today and Jason…when I saw him in the driveway a while ago…he mentioned he had ingredients just lying here unused. And frankly, I was flat-out sad thinking of you having to eat his cooking day in and day out—"

"It finally happened, didn't it?"

My cheeks smart, spatula frozen in my hand. "Beg pardon?"

Birdie leans on bent elbows over the island, eyebrows ticking up and down like a hungry cartoon cat. "You and Jason finally did the damn thing."

"Birdie Bristow."

Her laughter rings through the kitchen. "Must have been good if you're cooking him dinner."

If I harass this asparagus any more, we'll have to eat it in shreds. "This is simply not a conversation we should be having." I set down the cooking utensil and turn, trying to look casual. "Just out of curiosity, what gave you the impression that the damn thing was done?"

Birdie's lips jump. "You have beard burns all over your neck."

I smack my hands over the offending skin, knowing my face is red as cherry pie filling. "It could have been sunburn."

"But it's not. It's Jason burn."

I groan up at the ceiling and try not to giggle. "Doesn't it make you uncomfortable to talk about your brother in such a manner?"

She shrugs, ducks her head. "A little. But I'm happy enough to get over it."

"Happy?"

"Yeah." Vulnerability flits across her features. "I guess I'm pulling for you guys."

My stomach hollows out. "Birdie...I have to leave after the pageant. Nothing is going to change that." I swallow. "If there was a world where I could stay, you would be enough on your own to tempt me into it."

Her smile warms in degrees and stays there. I return it across the island, marveling over how close I've become to this girl who was a stranger to me until recently. This amazing girl I never would have known unless I'd taken a leap. This is proof that following your gut is never wrong. I'm going to keep on taking leaps, I vow to myself. No matter what happens in this life. No matter where I go or what commitments I make, I'm going to keep this one to myself. I'm never going to settle for being unhappy. I'm never going to be someone who is settled for. I'm more than that. The girl looking back at me believes I am...and I hope I've helped convince her of the same.

Down the hallway, the door to the bathroom opens and the bottom drops out of my stomach. Jason's heavy footsteps eat up the distance to the kitchen and he comes into view shirtless, board shorts riding low on his hips. His gaze swings from me to Birdie. Back to me with a slow wink. "Need some help?"

Birdie props her chin on a fist. "You could get her some cream for her Jason burn."

Pausing in his reach for a beer inside the fridge, his low chuckle reaches my ears a second later. "Maybe I like it right where it is."

Jason's sister lets out a crack of laughter.

I whirl back toward the stove. "You two are..." With a creeping smile, I change tactics before I know what I'm about. "Exactly right. It compliments my eyes. I think I'll leave it."

An arm wraps around my waist and I'm lifted up on my toes, a laughing male mouth finding the curve of my shoulder, a bearded kiss warming me there. Tingles ripple down to my toes, leaving me weightless and covered in goosebumps.

"Hey, hey, whoa. Being aware of the goings-on and seeing them are two different things," Birdie whines from behind us, although I can hear the amusement in her tone. "I'm launching a formal protest."

I wiggle out of Jason's grip and try to subdue my smile. It doesn't work whatsoever, so I face the stove and continue to mutilate the asparagus. "Not so cocky now that I've called your bluff, are you?"

A glass of wine is set down on the counter beside the stove and I look up to find Jason's absently returning the corked bottle to the fridge. "Oh," I breathe in a simpering voice I used to have reason to feign. Not anymore. I'm in full simper mode. "Is that…"

"Don't ask me if it's the right wine, beauty queen," he drawls, without looking at me. Like a cool cowboy. "Just assume."

"Oh," I breathe, hot moisture pressing behind my eyes. "Thank you."

My voice wobbles on the *you* and Jason's head snaps up. Tilts. There are a thousand things in the way he looks at me. He knows the wine is important, but he's a little irritated that I still didn't expect him to get it right yet—which is so this man's personality. Or maybe he's irritated that I have cause to get emotional over someone remembering what I like. What I choose. Or it could be he hates the fact that I'm crying at all. Mainly, the way he looks at me says he's totally content trying to figure it all out. Just content to stand there with me and get to the bottom of everything in my universe. I've never felt more seen in my entire life.

I don't realize my fingers have stopped working until the spatula drops on the floor. And then I'm kissing him. Initiating without hesitation. Jason's eyes flare, then close, his arms opening to greet me. Hold me tight. It's the full-on movie kiss I've always dreamed about. He turns a little to give us privacy, resting the back of my head on his bicep. His mouth slants over mine in a slow roaming of tongues, his thumb sliding along my cheek.

Dropping away. I feel him grip the counter against my hip and register how hard he's clinging to it. His mouth is casual, but the rest of him is not. There is nothing casual about the deafening rap of his heart against my ear.

Nothing about us is casual during an unplanned kiss in his kitchen. Or about how it makes me feel. Like I'm slipping into impossible territory.

That thought forces me to break the kiss and step back.

Dark eyes watch me go, that white-knuckled grip still on the counter.

Searching for a way to break the tension, I seek out Birdie and find her covering her eyes with both hands. "Is it over?" she asks. "I've learned my lesson. Swear."

"Good. And yes, the threat has passed." I clear the sex from my voice, highly aware of Jason moving behind me to take over dinner preparations, his energy snapping like a rubber band against my skin. "One lesson done, on to another." A light bulb goes on over my head and I reach for my purse, taking out the flash cards tucked inside the inner pocket. "Only a week away from the pageant. Let's do some question round prep."

Birdie throws up her hands dramatically. "Haven't I been punished enough?" She makes an air bubble in her cheek. "Fine, maybe a couple. Just don't ask me where I see myself in five years. I hate that one."

Relenting, I flip to the next card. "If you could wake up tomorrow and have gained one ability, what ability would you choose?"

"Flying is the only answer. Everyone else is lying." She taps her fingers on the table and I decide to let her off the hook with that informal answer. "What about you, Jason?"

He only takes two seconds to respond. "The ability to be two places at once." Silence passes while I read between the lines of that. "Naomi?"

Same answer, I want to say. But it would lead to what ifs we can't afford. "I was asked this question once during a pageant and I said I wanted the ability to always know the correct course of action that would benefit the greater good." I blow out a breath. "What I really meant was…flying."

Our laughter fills the kitchen.

CHAPTER TWENTY-TWO

ConspiracyCrowd.org
Username: UrdadsMyFave69
Fine, I'll be serious, everyone. Calm down.
Seriously, though. Has anyone checked Runaway Girl's
web history?
I could really use some new porn suggestions.

Naomi

THERE IS NO way to get this kitchen any cleaner. I've scrubbed the counters and now I'm going to town on the small appliances. Dinner ended forty-five minutes ago, Birdie retreated to her room as soon as she ate her last bite, mumbling about homework. Jason cleared the table and helped me load the dishwasher. Then he vanished, too, leaving me alone in the kitchen. Does this mean he's waiting for me to leave?

My heart drops and I set the sponge carefully on the sink ledge, trying not to make a noise. If he's waiting for me to take off, that would be fine. Fine. Just because we slept together this afternoon doesn't mean it's assumed I'm going to spend the night in his bed.

Actually, sleeping in Jason's bed is a terrible idea.

It's bad enough that I'm spontaneously kissing him and staying for dinner. Getting accustomed to his arms around me in the dark could be that final factor that makes leaving impossible. I definitely don't need that. I don't need to be a willing victim to my tipping point.

What am I still doing here?

Laughing semi-hysterically to myself, I pick up my purse and leave, my chin lifting higher with every step toward the chalet. Look at me! Doing this casual thing! Maybe we'll see each other tomorrow. Maybe we won't. It's an honest-to-goodness mystery!

I close the door behind me, refusing to acknowledge the pair of scissors opening and closing in my throat. Who wanted to have sex tonight? Not me, that's for sure. I haven't even really processed my shark encounter. I'll just have a nice sit-down and let the excitement of the afternoon wash over me. Maybe I'll go out for a run. The night is young—

The door of my chalet swings open and Jason strides in, letting it bang off the wall. In the wake of the echo, he just keeps coming, stroking a hand over his beard. A giant, shirtless man on a mission. God help me, my vagina contracts with such force, I could juice a lemon.

"I'm busy, Blackbeard," I breathe, sinking and floundering. "What do you want?"

Jason doesn't answer me. I didn't really think he would. Instead, he stoops down and throws me over his shoulder, turns and stomps for the door, kicking it shut behind us. The air expels from my lungs and I stutter through the beginnings of nine different protests. Except I'm smiling. I'm smiling at his dimpled lower back and flexing behind like I've lost my mind. Someone wants me enough to pick me up and take me. I'm wanted this badly and it's better than I ever dreamed it could be, so I close my eyes and revel in it as we walk into the house.

Moments later, we enter Jason's bedroom and he lifts me from his shoulder, laying me in the center of his no-frills, king-sized bed. Last time I was in here, it was shrouded in shadows and I barely got a chance to look around. I want to catalogue every single item in the space, but he's above me, knees planted on either side of my thighs, taking up my entire universe. "What do I *want*?" Absently I notice the scent of lavender and wrinkle my nose, but he demands my attention when he presses a hand to the lowest point of my belly, dragging it up between my breasts, flattening it over my heart. "I want back inside of you, beauty queen. Want it like I've never wanted anything." His touch shifts and a thumb drags over my nipple, blurring my vision. "Barely made it through dinner after that kiss."

"I want you back inside me, too," I whisper, lost in the feeling of being trapped between soft and hard, curls of hunger heating and twisting in my stomach and thighs. Lord, I just want him to press me down and never let me up.

"Yeah? Why did you leave, then?" He takes my breast fully in his hand, massaging it rhythmically, creating a wicked thrum south of my belly button. "Give me a glimpse of what goes on in that head of yours, baby."

"You go first."

With a sigh, he lies on his side to my right, his hand continuing its mission of arousal by ghosting over my breasts, only squeezing when I begin to squirm. "I'll admit to some wishful thinking this morning before the dive. That's why I had the, uh…"

"Protection?"

"Yeah. Had it for a while with our name on it, but it's not usually stashed in my gear bag." He leans down and breathes against my hard left nipple, brushing his lips over it and making me shudder. "Remembered the condom, forgot to clean my room." Another brush of lips, but this time they're smiling.

"Maybe I was afraid to hope you'd ever end up here."

Light, languorous amusement dances inside me and I thread my fingers through his hair. "You were cleaning your room for me?"

He angles himself away so I can view his efforts. "Even snuck a candle out of Birdie's room when she was brushing her teeth. If she notices, I'll never live it down."

The bed shakes with my silent laughter. "Your secret is safe with me. And it smells lovely." Knowing he went to such an effort makes me want to roll over and squeal into the bedclothes like a teenager. Although, I was never made to feel like this as a teen, was I? Never like this. "I thought you were trying to send me a hint," I say, shaking my head. "Like today was nice, but it was enough."

His jaw flexes. "And now you know how ridiculous that is?"

"Yes."

"Next time, talk to me."

"Next time, tell me you're just tidying up," I murmur, knowing full well there might not be a next time. He's having the same thought, his expression tightening. But I don't want to lose the moment, so I search for a subject change. "I liked watching you today. The water is your second home. You were standing in front of the ocean and I couldn't believe I hadn't seen you there before. Like you've been walking out of frame the whole time I've known you."

"Out of frame. Yeah. That's how it felt for a long time after I got home." He seems to catch himself, brow furrowing. "That's how it feels, I mean. When I'm away from the water. Even now, taking strangers out on a dive is not the same as fulfilling an actual purpose while I'm down there. Carrying out orders."

I graze his scalp with my fingernails, moving them in lazy

circles. "When you resurface, does it feel like you forgot something?"

"Yes. That's exactly it." His gaze homes in on me. "Not today, though. I couldn't have gotten further from that feeling. I had everything I needed."

My breath gets trapped in my throat. He can't say these things to me. How will I live with these words in my head? "I was happy to have all my limbs," I say, trying to dispel the intensity between us. It doesn't work, but he relents after a hard stare, leaning in to kiss behind my ear, his hand gathering the hem of my dress in a fist. Dragging it higher. Slowly.

"I know what you're doing," buzzes his voice against my sensitive skin.

Cool air creeps up the inside of my thighs as he exposes them, calling attention to how damp my panties already are. "What am I doing?"

"Trying to keep this light." His warm, calloused hand glides up my inner thigh, his teeth traveling along the curve of my ear. "But there's nothing light about us, baby. Is there?"

I shiver. "It doesn't feel like it," I confess.

His mouth finds mine, tempting me into a long kiss. Thorough enough to burn down all my weakened defenses, even if his hand didn't wedge firmly against my core, palming me there, pressing down on my clit. "Then let it be heavy while we have it," he pulls back slightly to rasp. "Okay?"

As if I could say no to anything he asks me right now. And I want to say yes. I want to throw myself into this risky emotional situation and give no thought about how I'm going to climb out. I want to feel every single thing he's offering and damn the consequences. "Yes."

He grips me between the legs, pressing his tongue into my

mouth and licking away my moan. "Good girl." To my absolute dismay, he trails his hand up to my hips, leaving my flesh aching and clenching. Needing him. "Tell me what a day looks like for you in Charleston."

"Uh…" I shift on the bed, trying to get comfortable—so not happening—frowning at his smirk. "Before I left or when I go back?"

"When you go back," he says thickly. "Leave him out of it."

I feel the command in my womb it strikes so deep. This is not the first time Elijah has invaded a moment between us, but it is the first time since we gave in fully to the attraction. To the connection we share. "There is a gala coming up," I say, clearing the rust from my voice. "There's always a gala because my mother is involved in several charities, as am I. Community outreach efforts, memorial funds and landmark restoration. Funny though, all these charities seem to raise money by having thousand-dollar-per-plate dinners. We never really get our hands dirty, so to speak."

He strums my hip with his thumb. "You sound like you want to change that."

"I do. I…can." Saying it out loud makes it concrete, makes it real, and while I enjoy the feeling of purpose and know most of the charities are for worthy causes, I also know I'm going to find it hard to be passionate about the same things when I go back to Charleston. "Anyway, there will be a dress fitting," I say, and God, it sounds so foreign to the life I've been living for well over a month. "Then the Naomi Clemons apology tour will commence. I'll need to say sorry to my relatives and bridesmaids. The wedding planner and catering company." An unwanted laugh flutters in my throat. "My hand is going to cramp from writing notes."

I leave out the most important apology I need to make. To my ex-fiancé.

Jason watches me silently. "And when the tour is over?"

Lying this way with him watching me so intently is the ultimate exposure, but I've felt more comfortable telling someone what I want. What I need. Is it because I'll only be with him another week, or has he become so important to me without me noticing the trajectory we were on? "I want to keep coaching. Girls like Birdie, though. Not girls like me who had the opportunities and training from a young age." A squeeze of my hip encourages me to keep going. "I was thinking…well, I was thinking there must be girls everywhere who would love to try competing but don't know where to start. Or there could be money issues. Not everyone has a generous big brother."

"And I only had to remortgage the house twice," he says, deadpan, before his expression sobers. "It was worth it. She's…woken up since you got here. You could do that for other people, Naomi. You enrich everything. You do it naturally as breathing."

"Jason," I say shakily, my heart pumping like I ran ten circles around the block. "I know you said to let it be heavy, but you say these things a-and it's going to be so hard."

His eyes flash. "That's the first time you admitted it's going to be rough to leave."

"Do you want it to be rough for me?"

"I can't help wanting to stick inside you." He pulls me tight against him, my side to his chest, his voice low in my hair. "You're going to stick in me. No help for it."

It takes me a few moments of measured breathing to center myself. I'm only halfway there when I say, "What will a day look like for you when Birdie graduates and you go back…"

"To wherever they send me?" He eases back, a line forming between his brows. "It doesn't always look the same. There's a strict order to everything we do, and some weeks, it's just an endless cycle of surveillance shifts or patrols. But if we're on a mission, decisions are often made on the fly. Shit never fails to hit the fan. Plans change in seconds. There might be a pick-up time and coordinates where we'll meet the helo. It won't wait for us. It can't, most times, thanks to a volatile environment. Or enemy fire. So we've got a limited amount of time to complete the mission and get our asses to the pick-up, or we're up shit creek."

Jason's explanation rolls so easily off his tongue that he has no idea my metaphorical jaw has dropped. I can't move as he casually explains the danger he faces on a daily basis. Lord, I'm an absolute idiot that the magnitude of life-threatening danger in his profession never fully occurred to me. I'm frozen as he continues on, his hand roaming up and down my thigh as if he's not devastating me with every word from his mouth.

"Other days I might work solo. Kind of comes with the territory of being a diver. Hours of silence seem to pass while I'm swimming, rationing my air. More silence when I hit shore and scout the target location for—" He finally notices what must be total horror on my face. "What's wrong?"

"Nothing," I blurt, smacking my hands over my burning eyes. "I guess I didn't realize how easy it would be for something to happen to you."

Jason tries to pry my hands away, but I resist. He sighs. "Christ. Not that easily, Naomi. I'm good at what I do." A beat passes. "But yeah, the possibility is there. Great men, friends of mine were lost and they were damn good, too."

I drop my hands away and let him see my unspilled tears. "I don't think I'm going to be comforted by battle stories anymore."

His voice is hoarse when he speaks. "I like your stories."

My chin goes stubborn, but I feel it wobbling. "Too bad."

Jason's eyes shut, a muscle working in his cheek. "You're in my bed crying over something possibly happening to me, Naomi." His lids lift and his mouth descends on mine, pausing an inch away, his harsh voice resonating deep in my belly. "Never complain to me again about making it too heavy."

This is it. This is the kiss I'll think about for decades to come, maybe longer. I can feel it ruining me with every mash of his lips against mine, every seeking sweep of his tongue. The taste of tears. The unsteady breath that drifts up his throat that slides down mine. I'm getting every ounce of man. His passion, his frustration, his lust, his fierce spirit. How he feels about me. It's being communicated with the sounds rumbling in his chest, half growling beast, half dying man. It's almost too much to withstand, until his fingers tuck into my panties and begin a determined massage of my clit, as if he knew I needed some of my attention diverted before my heart exploded.

Yes, my heart.

That brief acknowledgment that I'm in too deep is all I'm afforded before need covers everything in an avalanche. Jason is still plundering my mouth and now his fingers do the same to my flesh, his thumb rubbing laps around the sensitized nub he's become an expert on in such a short time. Lord. I drag my mouth away from his on a gasp, looking down my body at the scene we create. His thick, flexing arm bent over my hips, muscles shifting while his hand works inside my underwear. My thighs are spread in a shameless V, both of them jerking when he pushes two fingers inside me, his mouth getting busy on the side of my neck.

"Oh my God. Oh my God. You're everywhere at once. I can't..." He sinks his teeth into me and I whimper, something sparking in my chest when he licks the spot and makes a gruff, protective sound. "Please, I need you."

Jason eases his fingers out of me and I cry out, panting, aching as he rises to his knees, unbuttoning his board shorts and shoving them down. "I can't remember when I didn't need you," he says, looking me over head to toe, as if deciding where to start his meal. "I love the way you scream when I fuck you, but we can't have that tonight. I should cover your mouth and take it slow, but you've been working me up for months. Slow isn't happening the first time I take you in my bed. I've been lying here tortured."

"I'll be quiet," I sob, scrambling to my knees, not totally positive if I can keep my word. Jason is the only one who has ever made me scream. Or slap another human being, for that matter. And this afternoon, I had control over exactly none of those things. I'm out of control and that lack of restraint is already proving addictive.

I raise my arms up over my head, feeling wild and uninhibited. With a quirked lip, Jason whips my dress off over my head and we face each other, kneeling. Inevitably, my attention is drawn to his huge erection, where it protrudes from the opening of his shorts—I can't exactly miss it since the thickness is bridging the distance between our bodies, the head resting on my belly, making a damp indent. Taking it in my grip makes me moan, because I can feel the ripple of anticipation that passes through him, the veins beating where they run up the sides of his hard flesh. Wanting me.

"You're thinking of climbing me again, aren't you?"

"Yes," I breathe into a laugh.

He smiles in a way he's never done in front of me. I know what brings it on. I'm indulging his need to be needed. I have no choice. It's the most authentic impulse I've ever experienced. Needing this man. He takes care of our protection, then slaps his ridged stomach, causing moisture to build between my thighs. "Do it, baby."

There's nothing ladylike about the way I walk forward on my knees and loop my arms around his neck. I'm laboring to breathe as I pull myself up, watching his nostrils flare as I wrap my legs around his waist, putting myself on level with his mouth. His shaft flush with the wet material of my panties. "Like this, Jason?" I murmur, meeting his eyes through the sweep of my eyelashes, because apparently I'll never get rid of this demure streak. It's too firmly ingrained. And that's okay. Pressed to this man, I'm nothing but the sum of my parts and he's aware of them all. Likes me better for them.

Jason's flesh swells against me, a shuddering breath leaving him to ghost over my mouth. "Why don't we see how long you can stay prim and proper..." His hands mold my bottom in a rough grip, sliding me from root to tip along his smooth arousal. "While I'm riding you up and down my cock. Never a hair out of place on my Naomi, huh? You don't know how often I thought of making a mess out of you."

I think of the first time I saw Jason shirtless, cleaning his boat with the cigar stuck between his teeth. How our stark differences and the errant thought of opposites colliding made me weak, hot. Now I know it turned him on, too. "I don't like messes," says an old version of myself, chin lifting. "I like neat and polite."

His big chest rises and falls. "That right?" I try to keep my features schooled as he reaches behind me, guiding his flesh between my thighs. "Why don't we find out for sure?"

He uses the head of his erection to push aside the swath of nude cotton and tucks himself inside of me. One inch, two, before wrenching my hips down the rest of the way, filling me completely with a male grunt. An ocean of waves crashes in my ears, pleasure yanking on undiscovered ropes inside of me. I throw myself forward and whimper into his shoulder, not checking the impulse to bite him. Because Lord, Lord…there's nothing like having him occupy me. That moment of creating one person from two. It's real. And he wouldn't want me to hold back. No, he'd be pissed about it if I did.

That thought almost curls my lips into a smile, but it disappears into an O when Jason uses his hold on my bottom to lift me, lowering me down at the same time his hips pump hard.

"Oh." I lock my thighs tighter, rocking into the pressure. "Jason. Jason."

"Shhh. Again?" Forehead pressed to mine, he clucks his tongue. "Could get messy."

I start to respond, but he jerks me up and down, his shaft leaving and filling me in a brutal invasion. A strangled plea flies up my throat. All of it is too much. The intensity of the pleasure. The easy way he's lifting me, how effortlessly he scrambles my brain. And all the while, he watches me through narrow, concentrating eyes.

"Are you sure you don't want my mess, baby?" Jason leans back, leaving me seated on the ramp of his powerful body. His thighs widen beneath me, muscles bracing, and then he's thrusting into me from below, the incredible strength of him bunching and rolling, his head falling back on a tight-lipped groan. "Feels like you want it pretty bad."

I don't know how I thought I could keep up my prissy pretense in the face of Jason Unleashed, because I can barely keep a thought in my head that doesn't relate directly back to his penis. Every time he drives those hips up, it's like cresting on a wave, glimpsing the shore. Relief. The show he's unintentionally putting on for me is propelling me toward the end already. The veins in his neck stand out, his stomach flexes…and oh God. I shouldn't have looked down at the place he enters me, my panties shoved to one side as his erection slides in and out, made wet from my body. As if sensing my eyes there, his thumb edges beneath the veil of my panties and strokes my clit.

I look up to find his tongue tucked in the corner of his mouth, eyes blazing. "You have no idea how hot you look. Tits bouncing, watching us fuck and blushing like a schoolgirl."

His coarse speech breathes that intoxicating need to be his counterpoint back into me. With a twist. "I won't like it any harder," I say, barely recognizing myself as I reach down and brush my fingers over the place where our bodies join, bringing the moisture back to my mouth. Touching the tip of my tongue to the saltiness. "Yes, this is just right."

"Naomi. Fuck," Jason growls, surging forward and rising on his knees, bringing me along with him. I'm impaled and riddled with lust, incapable of doing anything but sucking in breaths and waiting for him to retaliate. "You little dick tease. You think you won't like it harder?"

I shake my head. "Uh-uh."

He snags my mouth in a savage kiss, his teeth catching my lower lip, dragging it. But I pull away on a sob when he begins bouncing me, up and down, my inner thighs sliding in the building sweat on his hips, my body welcoming him over and over. I'm seeing nothing except blurred colors, feeling nothing but the plundering of my body by Jason's almost indecent size. I cling to his broad shoulders, my head tossed back to gasp at the ceiling as my orgasm looms shiny and potent in the atmosphere.

"Your pussy is calling you a liar, baby," he rasps, nipping my chin with strong teeth. "Tell me the truth now. Tell me you've wanted this all along."

"Yes." He takes hold of my backside, driving up into me harder, faster, and I open my legs wider for this man, giving and taking in equal measure. "I needed you. I needed this."

"Shhh, baby. Shhh. I know. Dammit, I know all about it."

Even as he reminds me to be quiet, our flesh slaps together and a cry builds in my throat. Lust has me in a death grip and it's too intense, impossible to subdue. Our gazes lock and he sees I'm losing my grip on reality—and that reality is we're not the only people in the house. There's a flash of tenderness amidst the fury of his need and before I know it, I'm being turned and pressed onto my stomach.

How is he still inside me? I don't have time to question the logistics because Jason draws me forcefully onto hands and knees, gripping the headboard and thrusting into me with renewed power. "Use the pillow," he grits out, nudging my knees wider with his own and falling forward, aligning his chest with my bowed spine and fucking me. "Jesus Christ, Naomi, you're so goddamn tight. Tell me this beauty queen pussy only gets wet for me. Say it."

His fingers find my clit and rub it gently even as his thrusts increase their pace, their ferocity. "Only for you," I manage, after a shaking scream into the pillow. "I've never done it like this. This is just for you, too."

Jason's hips hitch, a shocked rumble sounding in his chest. In the matter of breathless seconds, his mouth finds my neck and ear, kissing them in turn, his body continuing its relentless drives into mine. "You're incredible. The most beautiful thing I've ever seen or felt, Naomi. Heard, touched or known." The heel of his hand strokes over my swollen nub, moving side to side, pushing slowly until I almost black out from the mind-blowing sensation. "I never want to be inside anyone else," he whispers in my ear, his thighs creeping up around my hips, muscles bunching. "You're it. You're fucking it."

"Jason," I gasp, my heart threatening to splinter inside my chest. The declaration drives me higher, bringing my peak into imminence and I know that's dangerous. I know it, but I can't stop pushing back into his pumping hips with my own, meeting him in the middle. It's coming for both of us…that final death…

Our fingers lace together on either side of my head, holding tight. So tight. "Whose pussy is this, woman?" Jason grinds out into my ear, his bulk ramming me from behind, clacking my teeth together. "Who do you get on your hands and knees for?"

"You," I scream into the pillow.

"Who would get on his hands and knees for you?"

"Jason," I sob, much quieter. But it's loud. So loud.

Finally, he lets out a tortured rendition of my name and several heated drives later, he draws me back tight with a forearm, his big body shuddering through such an intense physical release, I can't believe I caused it. He struggles to breathe, his mouth open on my back and I do the same into the pillow until the strain eases in my muscles. His, too. I feel the tension lessen in us both, little by little, leaving nothing but blissful satiation.

Arms closed around me, strong and reassuring. I'm on my side, absorbing Jason's heat where it's offered from behind. Demanding to be used. My heart orders me to trust the safe feeling. I'm safe right now. Right now is the only time where I want to exist. So I bury the possibilities held by the future and let Jason's kisses in my hair lull me to sleep.

CHAPTER TWENTY-THREE

ReadtheComments.com
Username: TheRappingTheorist
I don't dance now...
*I literally just sit in this chair and try to find one other person
interested in spontaneous combustion.*

Jason

I'M SITTING ON a folding metal chair in the church basement and there's nowhere else in the world I want to be. My sister is about to begin her tenth attempt of the day to get the waltz right, but she still can't get that final turn down. Since I've been knocking off work early for over a week to attend pageant practices, I have the damn waltz memorized, even finding myself humming the notes while cleaning the boat or showering.

Naomi turns and sends me a secret smile from her position at the stereo. It's like someone turns the volume up on my heart, the jagged pounding reaching my ears. And when she twists her hips in that way—that I'm-thinking-of-how-you-banged-me-in-the-shower-this-morning-big-daddy way—my dick thickens in my briefs. Christ, I'm addicted to this woman. Full-on addicted, no way out, no cure.

In other words, I am royally fucked. But I'm not thinking about that yet. Not until tomorrow.

Pageant day.

I swallow the panic that rises in my throat. I've never been one to live with blinders on, but the reward of doing so has been keeping me distracted. I've been one half of a couple since the day I took Naomi diving. The three of us eat breakfast in the kitchen before Birdie goes to school, I fuck the bejeezus out of Naomi as soon as the door closes behind my sister. Then I race through work to get back to her. Sometimes we lie on the couch, her head on my chest, and talk about our favorite things. Memories. Other times we watch movies. Naomi cries at the end of every single one, whether they're action or comedy. At least she cries the rare time we make it to the end of a movie without me trying to get her panties off.

We walk along the water holding hands. She opens her arms to me in the middle of the night when I wake up in a panic, flashbacks ripping through the seams of reality around me. I can't imagine sleeping alone anymore. Or not having her in the kitchen laughing along with Birdie and me at the end of every day.

It's an unconventional family we've formed, but in a short space of time, it's become home. I'm at home here in this place for the first time.

But Naomi is days from ending her time here. And I'm a little over a month from returning to active duty. No more stalling. It's time to admit to myself that hope has been building inside of me. Growing and solidifying by the day. Simply put, I've stopped believing I have no choice but to give up Naomi. My entire being is repelled by the very thought. Send her back to another man? I'll end up in a straightjacket in a padded room. I'll go legally insane, no exaggeration. The thought of another man's fingertips on her skin makes me shake with powerlessness and fear and rage. She's mine.

She's mine. And I'm hers, mind, body and soul.

Across the room, Naomi's smile has disappeared, probably because my expression is feral. Possessive. If we didn't have an audience, I would pin her to the closest wall and fill her up with my hard cock. No. No, I'd get on my knees and pleasure her until she came with her thighs wrapped around my head, just to remind her who handles her needs.

I lunge to my feet and give in to the need to pace, ducking into the hallway so my torment won't be on full display. Even though it feels as if I wear it on my sleeve, twenty-four hours a day. Out of view from the main room, I plant my hands on the wall and breathe in and out through my nose. What the hell am I going to do here? I'd just as soon flay the skin from my body than give this woman up, but the fact remains that we're going in opposite directions.

The service has always been a commitment to me, but it never felt like one until now. Never felt like something that could cause a major drawback in other areas of my life. It *is* my whole life.

No, it *was* my whole life.

Serving my country will never be a responsibility I shirk or take lightly. But it's no longer the only purpose driving me. I have love to offer Naomi. So much of it. I need to protect and serve her. I need to make her happy. Her own happiness is in direct relation to mine now.

My sister is not completely healed from the loss of Natalie, either, despite the progress she's made. When I came home, everything was temporary. Babysitting duty. I still thought of Birdie as a child. That's no longer the case. I don't want to miss what she does after graduation. I don't want to come home every six months and play catch up. I want to see it all in real time. Never in a million years would I have thought myself capable of mending her pain, but I think I might be. Naomi made me believe in that hidden part of myself.

I've already committed to another tour of duty, though, and I won't back out. That kind of wishy-washy behavior isn't in me. Once I make a promise, I keep it. Always. Am I out of my mind to think Naomi would wait for me? When she's returning to a whole heap of money and comfort in Charleston…and potentially the arms of a man whose feet could not be more firmly rooted on US soil. A fucking mayor. Do I have a hope in hell?

Yes.

I close my eyes and let that single word roll through me. This relationship between Naomi and me isn't make believe. I know her flaws and strengths. What makes her laugh and cry. She's the first thing I think about in the morning, last one at night. I'm so in love with her, the feeling would keep me warm in a blizzard. Would melt the fucking snow before it hit the ground. The way she gives herself over to me when we're making love isn't a mistake. I catch her looking at me sometimes like I'm already gone. There's something there. I'm not alone.

In my line of work, risks are par for the course. I've never taken one that would have this much reward. Or potential to fucking maim me.

With a steadying breath, I push off the wall and walk back into the room, just as Birdie messes up the final turn. Again. My chest constricts when I see the frustration on her face. I wish there was something I could do to take it away. Her partner looks irritable as all hell, spearing his fingers through his hair. He holds his tongue, however, when he sees I'm back in the room. I've been enjoying having that effect on him.

"Hey," Naomi says, approaching from the left. Cool comfort settles around my neck, balancing the hunger that snakes into my belly. God, what this woman makes me feel. I look down to find her searching my face with anxious blue eyes. "Is everything okay?"

"Yeah." My blinders have allowed me to keep thoughts of her leaving at bay, but they rush in now and topple my sanity, turning me desperate. I cup the back of her neck in my hand, sliding it up to bury it in her hair, which she always wears down now, loose around her glowing face and slightly sunburned nose. Damn, she's so beautiful. My throat closes up and I have no choice but to lean down and kiss her, letting her sweetness soothe my singed edges. Not gone yet. She's not gone yet. "Baby," I mutter between kisses. "Baby."

"Jason," she says back, warming to the kiss, going up on her toes and opening her mouth for me. I have the presence of mind to turn my back, so we're not making out with an audience, but Naomi absorbs all of my focus after that. I've seen how cruel this world can be, but taking her away would be another level of cruelty. Her taste is so familiar to me already, but the more used to it I get, the more of it I need. My pulse is hammering in my temples as I tug her chin down, getting my tongue in deep. Memorizing her. And yeah, seducing her, because I want her to fucking rip my clothes off when we're alone.

"God, you taste perfect," I groan quietly, breaking the kiss. "I know where you taste just as delicious, though, don't I?"

Pink paints her cheeks. "You have to stop. I c-can't conduct pageant practice with these things staring back at everybody."

She waves a hand around to indicate her hard nipples. Laughter cracks out of me, not just because of her predicament, but because I love that she's comfortable saying these things to me now. A month ago, she would have denied the existence of her nipples if I'd asked. "Think of something that turns you off."

"They're not like…penises." I almost propose marriage to her when her blush deepens even more, her full lips tipping up at either side. "If our two body parts were exactly alike, you'd get an erection every time you walked into an air-conditioned room."

"That would get pretty interesting in Florida." She laughs and my smile grows. "I can't believe you said *erection* and *penises* to me in the space of a minute."

She looks down at her still-hard nipples and sighs, crossing her arms over the offenders. I already miss them. "It's safe to say you've corrupted me, Mr. Bristow."

"Not nearly enough," I growl, leaning in and bringing our mouths together, making contact with just the tips of our tongues. "And you'll be calling me Mr. Bristow tonight when I get you alone. Just sealed your fate."

"If you're trying to render me useless for the rest of the afternoon…" Her hips cinch forward, her belly pressing lightly against the snap of my jeans. Too lightly. "Two can play at that game, you know."

"Oh yeah?" I say, hoarsely, knowing I shouldn't. Naomi making the most basic attempt to seduce me would bring me to my knees. Does she even realize that?

"Mmmhmm." She slips on that sweet, Southern belle expression. Delicate but composed. Anticipation hums in my veins as I try to figure out what's coming. "I have some repairs that need seeing to in my apartment. Could you be a dear and come by with your toolbox later, Mr. Bristow?" Cool eyes run from the notch of my throat down to the snap of my jeans, her accent even more of a drawl than usual. "I'd be very grateful."

Heat rushes to my groin like water through a busted dam. "Ohh, beauty queen. You're in deep trouble with me now."

"Why, I don't know what you mean."

We're in public, so I can't do what I need to do to Naomi. I tickle her instead, digging my fingers into her ribs. With a yelp, she twists and I pick her up off the ground, blowing a raspberry into the side of her neck.

"Jason!"

I'm laughing when I set her down, her look of outrage setting me off even more. Naomi joins in, springing forward to tickle me back. I've never been tickled in my life, so I'm not prepared when it gets to me, a weird, goosey sensation making me yelp. Me. I yelp. Loudly. Naomi stares back stunned and dissolves into stiches. I can only watch as she doubles over, laughing louder than I've ever seen her, tears glazing her eyes. Across the room, Birdie falls to the floor, holding her sides and rolling around. Even Mister Toes—Turner, I've learned is his actual name—is battling a smile.

"Oh my goodness," Naomi says, pausing for another giggle snort. "I've completely lost control of this rehearsal and we only have one more day." She shoos me back to my corner of the room with an exhilarated smile, giving me a nice view of her ass when she faces the stereo. "From the top?"

The instructor sends her a nod, prompting Birdie to get off the floor and into position. They create a frame with their arms and take deep breaths as the familiar melody fills the room. He pushes forward and Birdie retreats, signaling the start. I lean back against the wall and count off the steps, noting the determined set to my sister's chin this time. Tension builds in my shoulders the closer they come to the end. That damn turn into a dip, it's—

Birdie nails it.

The notes of the song jangle to a stop and the song cuts off. All of us stand frozen in the stillness of the church basement, the couple still posed in that final position. Pride rips up my throat and erupts in a shout, colliding with Naomi's victorious cry of *hallelujah*. We both move toward Birdie—who basically just looks stunned—and smash her between us in a hug.

"You did it," Naomi squeals. "It was beautiful. You did it."

"I'm proud of you, kid," I say, smacking a kiss down on top of her head. "Congratulations, you made me give a shit about waltzing."

She lets out a watery laugh into my chest. "I had to get it right. I got sick of watching you guys moon over each other across the room." A beat passes. "I didn't mean that. It's actually pretty cute."

"Cute? Jesus." I ruffle her hair one more time and step back. "I better do something manly for the sake of balance."

Naomi is still beaming at Birdie when I throw her over my shoulder and head for the exit. "How's this?"

The gorgeous blonde draped over my shoulder makes a sound of protest, but I can tell her heart isn't really in it. Especially when she pinches my ass. Hard.

For the second time this afternoon I yelp and we walk home laughing, Birdie performing dance steps on the sidewalk, Naomi's hand tucking into mine when I finally set her back down. I want to stop a million times to kiss her, but I know I need to focus on what's ahead. Funny enough, my little sister getting that final turn right has given me that final boost to ask Naomi to be with me. Permanently. Always. There will be a lot of compromises and obstacles to jump over if she says yes, but there's nothing more worthy of an effort than this woman.

I just have to hope and pray she believes the same is true about me.

We round the corner into the driveway, still debating what to make for dinner when I feel Naomi's hand turn to an icicle in mine. And when she tugs it away, the action tears the breath out of me. My attention flies to her face and finds her pale, staring at something in the driveway. An older man. A rich man—not a distinction I would normally feel compelled to make, except this man is pocket-square, winking-cufflinks, shiny-black-Mercedes-parked-along-the-sidewalk rich. There's no way around it.

One of my most vivid memories of battle is kicking to the surface after completing a mission to plant explosives on the border of ally and enemy territory. Looking up through the dark glass and seeing the telltale flares of a firefight in progress. Knowing my waning oxygen gives me no choice but to breach the surface and enter the fray immediately. That early morning of my memories is all I can compare this moment to. It feels like I'm about to come out of the calm into a fight and there's nothing I can do about it. No way to control the outcome. And somehow, I already know I'm at a distinct disadvantage.

"Daddy?" Naomi whispers. "What are you doing here?"

Naomi's father. Here, at my home. I've barely wrapped my head around asking Naomi to stay and what that would entail. Meeting her parents isn't something I've even allowed myself to imagine. But I'm damn certain this isn't what I'd want. Naomi being caught off-guard. Me in an old-ass T-shirt and faded jeans. No preparation. No clear plans on how I'll keep his daughter and make her happy for the rest of her life.

The man's sharp gaze zips to me, down to the hand he clearly saw his daughter holding. She didn't want him to see her holding it, did she?

Christ. Have I lost already?

"I have a better question, Naomi," he returns, culture rolling off him like expensive fog. "What are you doing here?"

CHAPTER TWENTY-FOUR

EndoftheWeb.net
Username: BlueHairedBirdie
She's in Florida working as a pageant coach.

Username: IGotAnswerz9
Worst theory I've heard yet.

Naomi

I FEEL LIKE a child being sent to their room. What is it about fathers that can reduce their daughters to infancy in a matter of seconds? I can argue with my mother until I'm blue in the face, but the second my father chimes in to disagree with me, it's like being slapped, hot humiliation burning behind my eyes. I've only been disciplined a handful of times throughout my life by my father, but they are easily more memorable than any of my mother's punishments.

As we turn from the stilted introductions my Southern manners compelled me to make between Jason, Birdie and my father, I think back to the last time my father expressed his disappointment in me. It was after yet another debate between my parents that escalated into an argument about The Affair while having after-dinner drinks on the back patio. I was sixteen and—looking back—in the midst of a hormonal know-it-all phase. Having listened to my mother use the indiscretion against him countless times since I was a child, I'd lost my composure and suggested she have an affair to even the odds.

I can still remember the regret of those words leaving my mouth, the sick, heavy feeling that invaded my stomach at their horrified expressions. After spinning from the patio and hiding in my room, I'd waited for the eventual footsteps, thinking it would be my mother who came to deliver my sentence. No cell phone for a week. No parties. No shopping.

Instead, my father had knocked and entered, without waiting for permission. He'd sat ramrod straight at the very corner of my bed, not looking at me.

Naomi, he'd said. Don't behave like trash.

That was all. Five words had sent me sobbing into my pillow for hours. I can still taste the salt of those tears and hear the irrational vows I made to myself that I would never go downstairs again. That I would live in my room forever.

My thoughts are in that same drastic category as I climb the stairs to my apartment, my dad following at a sedate pace behind me. Jason's gaze is like twin brands burning into my back, but I can't turn around and look at him. I'll have the need to reassure him that I'm fine, but I don't know if I am. This is the end of the road. I knew it as soon as I saw my father standing in the driveway, so out of place among the greasy boat parts and modest house. I've rarely seen him without a newspaper partially covering his face, a drink in his hand or glad-handing at a community function. Being the focus of his attention is polarizing. I'm caked in dread.

I wait until my father joins me in the chalet, catching just the barest hint of the intensity Jason is projecting from below, before I shut the door. Silence falls hard and I observe the small space from his point of view. Tiny kitchen with crooked cabinets, a twin bed in the corner, the vases of flowers sitting on various surfaces like lipstick on a pig.

The spark of embarrassment is what changes everything. It makes me angry at myself. I have nothing to be ashamed about. My spine fills with lead as I think back to how helpless I was when I arrived. How I barely knew how to cook my own meals. How little I knew about the cost of lodgings and toiletries. Since that time, I've learned how to be a pageant coach. After today, I'm a successful one. I think. I hope. I've participated in a parade wearing nothing but paint. I scuba dived with a shark. I've...I've had the most insanely satisfying orgasms of my life, not that I'm going to impart that information to my father, but the fact remains. They were so, so satisfying. And the man who gave them to me...navigating the way he makes me feel has quite possibly been the greatest feat of all. We've become friends, confidants. Lovers. I've become important to Jason and he's become important to me and this apartment is part of him, so I will not be embarrassed. I'll be proud of it, along with myself.

Oh God. I'm thinking of this sabbatical in Florida in the past tense already and panic spirals in my stomach, forcing me to brace a hand on the wall. My father catches the action and frowns. He's not going to speak first, is he? He's still waiting for me to answer the question he posed in the driveway. *What are you doing here?*

I don't know how to answer that in a way he would appreciate.

I've been living.

"How did you find me?" I ask.

His lips pinch together. "Your car." He dusts off the kitchen counter before leaning against it. "When you called your mother from the payphone, we knew the area code. I called in a favor with Charleston PD, who asked the department here to keep an eye out for your license plate. I've known for a couple weeks, actually." He tilts his head. "I was giving you a chance to do the right thing."

Pressure catches me around the throat, but I clear it. I'm a grown woman who has amazing orgasms and paints her boobs with butterflies. I'm not a sixteen-year-old girl who falls apart over criticism, veiled or otherwise. "I was planning on coming home tomorrow night."

"Doesn't look like it." He blinks. "Who is that man?"

"Jason," I rasp. "Jason and Birdie. I rent this room from them, but they've...I've become close with them."

His stare is hard. "Your fiancé is in the midst of a dalliance that has captured the public attention and it's proving quite problematic for your mother. I've come to bring you home. This has gone on long enough."

I want to ask about Addison and Elijah. Are they together? Are they happy? But I'm stuck on the way he sneered through the latter half of his statement. "What exactly do you think this is?"

Surprise registers on his only lightly lined face. I've never spoken to him with anything but deference. "The truth?" I'm already regretting it when I nod. "I think you've been overindulged. You had only to repeat some simple vows and you'd have lived in comfort the rest of your life. Comfort and respectability. You've known nothing but those things from birth and they lost their value. You have no idea of your own luck."

"I do, though," I breathe, coming off the wall. "I do know I'm lucky. But I didn't want to live my life in a holding pattern. Wake up, look pretty, entertain, express tasteful opinions over lunch, repeat. I didn't know how to do or be anything else. Or...or if I was meant to repeat that pattern over and over.

Comfortable or not, it's like living someone else's life. I couldn't. I couldn't start another chapter of the same without knowing what I'm capable of. Or knowing that my husband thought me capable of anything but being arm candy."

Time ticks past. "Do you have any idea how selfish you sound?"

A weight slams into my stomach and I lose steam. A lot of it. I can actually feel it leaving my fingertips. "I know I have amends to make. I think about it all the time—"

"Oh do you, really? Do you think about the humiliation you've caused your family? Hiding for almost two months while we endure the questions from our friends and the media says otherwise. How about your fiancé's embarrassment? Do you honestly care about that? Because holding hands with this tattooed fellow seems to prove otherwise."

"Yes, I…" I'm being violently shaken awake from a dream. It was all a dream. I've been living in this fantasy world while others dealt with the consequences of my actions. How could I have done this? "We—this wasn't supposed to happen. With Jason." I know I shouldn't voice my next question, but it escapes me before I can prevent it I'm so desperate to appeal to my father. "Of all people, you must understand, right? I tried to help how I feel about him, but—"

"Do not throw my past indiscretions in my face, young lady," he snaps, the lines in his face growing more prominent. "Well, well, well. How like your mother you are, Naomi. You will not turn this around on me."

"That's not what I was trying to do—"

"I've had to answer for my actions for decades. *Decades.* Now the woman's illegitimate child is being pictured all over Charleston with Elijah. Speculation about her parentage is rampant.

Your absence has made it seem like the past happened yesterday."

"I'm so sorry," I whisper, meaning the apology for my father as well as Addison. To know so little about who fathered her and having the press throw it in her face must be terrible. "I couldn't have known she would come to the church. I haven't seen her in so long...and who knew she'd form this relationship with Elijah—"

"Call it what it is. A transgression with someone completely unsuitable." He scrubs an agitated hand against the back of his neck. "It seems you're both dead set on ruining your family names."

"It doesn't sound like Elijah to create a stir or bring negative attention to his family unless it was unavoidable. Maybe he loves her." Is it crazy that I feel nothing but hope for them, if the rumors are true? There's no jealousy or sense of loss. Just...bittersweet hope.

My comment makes my father livid, though, the sunshine coming through the windows highlighting the spittle flying from his mouth. "You would love that, wouldn't you? It would excuse everything you've done and you could continue your affair with some muscle head—"

"Don't you dare say another word about him. Don't you dare." If I had a baseball bat handy in this moment, I would bash the kitchen cabinets to smithereens. "He's the most honorable man I've ever met. He's been serving overseas while we all sat in air-conditioned parlors and wore stupid hats to parties." I almost laugh when my hat comment brings an affronted expression to his face. "Jason came home to raise his sister and feels guilty that he's not off somewhere almost dying every day. He's honest and heroic and protective of the people he loves. He pays attention to the small things and likes my battle stories...and..."

And I'm in love with him.

Deep, deep, inescapable love.

That realization must be showing on my face, because my father doesn't speak for a long time, his expression turning weary. For a split second, I think I even glimpse some understanding, and it makes me wonder if he was in this kind of love with Addison's mother. All of his compassion vanishes in a big sweep, though, and he advances toward me.

"Listen to me, Naomi. This little rebellion has gone on long enough." He jabs a finger in my direction. "If you're not home by tomorrow, you will be disowned and disinherited. Your mother and I took great pains making this decision and we've agreed. I wouldn't suggest testing how serious I am about this."

That threat...no, that promise hits me like a ton of bricks. Disowned. I've heard of families turning their backs on black sheep. My own family did it to Addison. Her mother and grandmother. But this sounds formal. Jarringly real. His eyes tell me he means it, too. They would absolutely disown me for causing them this humiliation. Needles pound down like typewriter keys in my chest, the pain reverberating in outward waves, turning my limbs to jelly. My parents would refuse to see me ever again. We've had a difficult relationship, but I love them. They love me, too, don't they?

As far as being disinherited...money has never been a concern. Even while working, earning a paycheck and buying my own food these last couple months, the fact that I could return to my own life and be comfortable again was always in the back of my mind. I was never truly broke. It was all an illusion. But this is real. This possibility of going from wealthy to a pauper in the space of one day is terrifying.

"You've been molded from childhood to settle into a comfortable life, Naomi. Working for a paycheck is not in your DNA. How long do you think you'd be able to keep this up? You want to be a pageant coach? Do it in Charleston from the comfort of our home. Or your husband's home. It's a hobby, not a business. Not for you. You have no business experience."

How many blows can I sustain before falling over? I've been a good daughter. I've always done what is asked of me. Expected of me. I've treated my father with respect, but right now all of it seems like a waste. He thought so little of me all along. What was the point?

He sighs, his demeanor growing weary. "I give you credit for lasting this long. I do." He raises an eyebrow at me. "But were you ever truly out on your own? Or did you just find someone else to take care of you?"

There it is. The knockout punch. I sway on my feet, feeling strangled. Somewhere in the back of my mind, I know I stood on my own since arriving in St. Augustine. I found a place to live, a job. I paid my way. The relationship I developed with Jason was on my terms. My father is wrong. I am not being cared for by a man, no matter how much that man insists on being my protector. Right now, however, in the face of my father's verbal assaults, my self-confidence is teetering. Everything I've accomplished seems silly. So I learned to cook for myself. So what? So I taught a girl how to walk a stage. So what, Naomi?

"You're beginning to see sense." My father nods, sliding his car keys from his pocket with a jingle. "I'll let your mother know to expect you home by tomorrow. We'll have your room aired. Once you've gotten some sleep, we'll sit down and sort through this mess."

"I have a commitment tomorrow," I manage, my blood icy as I realize my words constitute an agreement to my father's orders.

Yes, I was planning on going back to Charleston anyway, but that was my decision. Now it's his. "Birdie's pageant. I won't miss it."

He stops at the door, jostling his keys in his palm a couple times. "Then you better drive fast if you want to make it home by midnight."

There's no telling how long I stand there once the door closes. Hours? No, minutes. I hear the purr of my father's Mercedes leave the curb and a breath wrenches up my throat, followed by a sob. I cast a look around the chalet, the neatness I took such pride in before mocking me now.

He's right, isn't he? Everything my father said was right. I got lucky with this arrangement. Jason and Birdie were godsends for a helpless woman. If I hadn't fallen blindly into this perfect situation, I would have gone back home the day after I fled from the wedding. I have no skills to take care of myself or make a sustainable income. I'm useless. Jason knew it, too, didn't he? That's why he retrieved me from the ramshackle motel and brought me here. That's why he's never charged me rent. Pity. It was pity.

I'm pitiful. All this time, I thought I'd come to Florida to have an adventure and figure out who I am down deep at my core. Well I found out, didn't I? I'm an embarrassment to my family and myself. Jason takes pride in fighting for his country. My parents take pride in building charities and being pillars of their community. What do I take pride in? Flowers in the center of my table. Going scuba diving once. Not an adventure. Not important.

I stumble toward the bed, clenching my teeth so hard my jaw aches. I fall onto my knees and drag the suitcase from beneath the frame, walking on my knees to the small dresser. Packing my clothes in heaping handfuls of colors. Clothes tastefully picked out for the perfect spring honeymoon. Such attention paid to every pleat, every stitch pattern. Stupid. So stupid.

When the dresser is empty, I march to the closet and throw it open, yanking my wedding dress off the pole by its hanger. The beading looks like alien crop circles. How did I never notice that? I run my finger over the circular patterns and dig deep. I dig deep for the extraordinary confidence I felt this morning. This self-doubt burns. I don't want it...but it won't go away. I've been ripped to shreds.

The door to my apartment opens and there stands Jason, his gaze going from curious to turbulent when he sees me holding the wedding dress, caressing it with my fingertips. I love him. So much that my heart starts beating at a different tempo, my arms dying to close around him, face wanting to bury itself in his neck to inhale, rub, revel. Mine.

That instinct is what traps me in a bubble of resentment. *But were you ever truly out on your own? Or did you just find someone else to take care of you?*

Heat smarts my cheeks, the dress turning abrasive in my hands.

Powerless, I can do nothing but try and take some of my pride.

CHAPTER TWENTY-FIVE

ReadtheComments.com
Username: LittleMissMorbid
Not to be weird or anything, guys, but…have they pulled her
dental records yet? Just to save time?

Jason

AMAZING AS IT seems, I'd forgotten about the wedding dress hanging in her closet. I'm not sure how, since it represents something wholly unacceptable to me. Naomi married to another man. If she'd gone down the aisle in the thing and recited her vows, I never would have met her. We never would have crossed paths. Or if we had, she would have been off limits to me. I hate that fucking dress with every fiber of my being and she's handling it like a newborn baby. Hell, she seems irritated that I interrupted. I'm on shaky ground already after having her father dismiss me with a rich guy sniff and not being privy to their conversation—an important one, I'm sure of it. So her snapping eyes hit my chest like shock paddles. She needs something from me, I just don't know what it is yet. Only that I need to provide it.

"What are you doing?"

"Packing."

That single, defiant word catapults a boulder into the center of my chest. Her plan was to leave after the pageant. Her packing shouldn't catch me off-guard like this. But it does. How can she leave when I can't imagine a day without her? For the first time, I notice the open suitcase on the bed. It's full of her clothes.

No. Uh-uh. I'm rendered helpless in an instant and I need to shake it. Now. I'm not a man who can exist long in a state of helplessness. Not during battle, not even at the supermarket. But sure as hell not when the woman I love is on the line. "Put down the dress and let's talk about what happened with your father."

Her eyes flash. "Don't tell me what to do."

"Fine." My voice is actually hoarse with the need to get that dress out of my sight. Away from her. "Can you please put it somewhere I don't have to look at it?"

For just a second, Naomi from this morning is back, her expression softening. She turns in a rigid circle, searching for a place to stow the garment, before finally hanging it back in the closet and shutting the door. "I have a lot to do before the pageant tomorrow night. I won't be able to have dinner or...I'll be busy right up until the competition, actually." She's still not facing me. "Just leave me to it, Jason."

Could she really go that long without me so easily? I couldn't. Having her send me away when I'm prepared to lay my fucking heart on the line is unacceptable. "Leave you to what? Your stuff is already in the suitcase. Unless you're planning on packing the appliances, you're done. Come down to the house with me."

Naomi whirls, hands fisted at her sides. "What part about *don't tell me what to do* didn't you understand?"

I massage my brain through my skull. Calm. Keep calm. It must have been a hell of a fight between Naomi and her father. I'm coming in blind and I need to be patient. "I'm sorry. I just want to help."

"Yes, I know. Poor little Naomi is always in need of help, isn't she?" She cuts through the apartment, collecting knickknacks as she goes and stuffing them into her suitcase. "Jason, let me ask you a question. Do you really think I could start my own pageant coaching business, or did you just say that because you wouldn't be around when I found out you'd lied?"

Thrown for a loop, it takes me a second to catch up, but that negative, helpless part of me rebels hardest at being called a liar by the woman I'm crazy about. "Christ. What are you talking about? I've never lied to you, Naomi." I can't have this conversation with furniture between us, so I advance closer, my neck tightening when she backs toward the windows. "What the hell did your father say to you?"

"Nothing that probably...nothing that isn't true." She stares into space for a moment, breaking the spell with a jerky shrug. "He has the family's best interest at heart. Unlike me. I've been down here having a complete break from reality. I'm not the only person affected by my bad decisions—"

"Am I a bad decision?"

Her mouth snaps shut, her eyes regretful. But she doesn't make a denial and a fire spreads in my sternum, ripping through my city and burning down skyscrapers. "Do you think if I'd landed on someone else's doorstep that I could have lasted this long on my own?" Naomi asks instead, her vulnerability plain.

The answer is right there on the tip of my tongue. A vision of her smearing motor oil across the front of her white dress drifts through my mind. It's replaced by her determined marches past the kitchen window, groceries in hand. The way she saved the day when Birdie invited friends over for the first time. How she made it easier to go into a crowded restaurant because I witnessed her bravery first. *Yes, of course, you could have made it on your own. You're amazing. You're dynamic. You adapt in a heartbeat and you refused to let me in until you'd settled into yourself. We both watched it happen.*

But I hesitate. I hesitate because I desperately need acknowledgment that I'm important to her. I've never been a needy person, but goddammit I'm needy in the face of her packing up and getting ready to leave me. Implying I'm a bad decision. If she can just give me a glimmer of hope that I was good for her, I'll have the courage to ask her to stay.

"Having me around to protect you wasn't the worst thing. Was it?"

"No." I can hear her swallow. "Thank you for being tactful, at least."

It's clear that I've fucked up. She doesn't look pissed off anymore, just defeated. Her shoulders sag because of what I said. And God, that spirals me into a panic. I'm losing her. Did I ever have her? "It wasn't a bad thing to have me around, but you would have found a way to last, baby. I'm positive of that."

Too late. My confidence in her came too late. It's diluted by my hesitation. She's not listening. "Thanks," she bites out. "I really need to get back to what I was doing."

"So this is it, huh?" My tone is raw, just like my insides. She's dismissing me. Ending this prematurely without any deliberation. "We're done. A day ahead of schedule, even. Efficient."

She squeezes her eyes closed. "We both knew this was temporary."

That might be true, but my heart never believed that bullshit. She was my woman from the moment I saw her. Mine. How could she have made the same love in the same bed and still classify this as temporary? Casual. Panic and anger clog my windpipe, making it difficult to hide how desperate I'm feeling. She's leaving. If I ask her to stay, she'll say no. What do I have to work with? What do I have? "Wow. After everything, Naomi.

After this whole adventure-seeking mission and all your attempts to be a big girl, you're ready to pack up and run back to daddy at the drop of a hat, aren't you?"

I've never known regret like the kind I feel as soon as those words leave my mouth. She gulps a breath, her arms wrapping around her in a protective hug. Guarding her against me. Oh my God. I hate myself in this moment.

"I didn't mean that, baby. I'm just standing here watching you leave and—"

"You did mean it. You both did."

That revelation that I've echoed something her father said is abhorrent. I want to heave. And God help me, in the wake of my defeat, I'm still obsessed with the possibility that she could go back to another man. It's going to rule my every waking thought when she's gone. The knowledge that she's going to be in the same town as Elijah is a manacle around my neck and I just need...I either need to tighten that manacle until it strangles me. Or I need it loosened.

"Did you keep that dress because you think you might wear it again?"

Again, her silence is as good as a yes.

"Will you go to see him?" I rasp.

We stare at each other across the expanse of the room for long moments, but I can read nothing in her expression. She's totally closed off to me, except for maybe her fingers twisting in her skirt. "Don't ask me that," she finally whispers.

That's as good as a yes, isn't it? Rage and misery claw my stomach, leaving nail marks. If she wasn't standing inside this structure right now, I think I could tear it down with my bare hands. But her safety and happiness are still the most important thing in my world. *Tell her you love her.* In the movies, that sentiment solves everything, but I can see it won't make a difference right now. It won't even make a dent. Love can't change the fact that our lives are taking different paths and she's not interested in finding a way for them to intersect. Hell, maybe it's impossible, anyway. Maybe it always was.

With my head on fire, I leave her standing there, the truest three words I've ever left unspoken fighting to leave my mouth.

I WAKE FROM a nightmare dripping in sweat, my fingers tearing at the sheets. My usual routine of reminding myself I'm in my room in Florida is useless, though, because it's not the recurring dream. Being underwater with no oxygen, blasts going off overhead.

No. It's the shark. My worst nightmare is now Naomi in the path of the shark.

I throw my legs over the side of the bed, doubling over into a coughing fit. One second she was there, the next she was gone. Not so different from reality, is it? She's as good as vanished. Lost to me. Going somewhere I can't protect her. Love her.

Frustration sends me lunging to my feet, stripping off my soaked boxers and sweatpants, leaving them draped over my open windowsill to dry. Have to run. Energy crackles in my veins, turning me jumpy. I drag on a new pair of sweatpants, not bothering with a shirt. With moisture still forming on my forehead even in the air-conditioned room, I shove my feet into sneakers and leave the house, unable to resist a look up at Naomi's dark window. How dare she sleep while I dream of her being devoured right in front of my eyes? At the same time, I savor this last night of knowing she's safe in bed, close by.

My feet eat up the pavement, carrying me farther and faster than ever before. I don't even recognize the neighborhood I've ended up in when I force myself to turn around and go back. Not a single car passes me as I sprint home, already knowing the run isn't going to be enough to stop the thoughts of another man's hands on my woman's skin. Thoughts of waking up every morning for the rest of my life and knowing she's out of my reach. That she always will be.

By the time I skid to a stop in the driveway, I'm a snarling beast. My shoulders are bunched up at my ears, hands in fists. No way I can get through the day like this. I can't even make it through the next hour. I'm preparing to leave the driveway and go for another run—farther this time—when the door opens at the top of the stairs. Naomi's door. She steps out into the night, her white nightshirt a beacon in the darkness.

Hunger takes flight inside me. Maybe it was there from the moment I woke up and I disguised it as something else. My need for this woman is monstrous on a regular basis. Throw in the fact that this is the final night she'll be near to me? I need to be inside Naomi so bad, my cock is already turning thick and ready in my pants, sweat molding the material to my growing flesh. And when Naomi starts to descend the stairs in a hurry, her blonde hair flying out behind her, a growl of relief and stupefying desire leaves me.

Proof she needs me, too. I want to drown in it.

We meet at the bottom of the stairs and I haul her up into my arms, almost falling to my knees at the sublime fit of her. Somehow I remain standing as her legs lock in place around my waist and we fall headlong into a kiss. It's noisy and wet and we're both breathing heavily—it's heaven. It's heaven. I delve one hand into the back of her panties to get a good handful of her ass, my other hand tangling in her unbrushed hair, tilting it left and right as I demolish her mouth. The sounds I'm making into her mouth barely sound human, but I don't care. I care about nothing but getting as close to Naomi as possible and to that end, I stumble in the inky blackness of the night, searching for a place to get inside of my woman.

She gasps up at the sky a second later as I throw her up against the side of the house, my mouth finding her neck and licking straight up the smooth column of it. Her pussy clenches where it presses to my erection. I can feel her response right through the wet material of my sweatpants. I'm damp all over from running, I remember vaguely, but she seems disinclined to care, her fingernails already ripping a path down my back. She needs this cock as badly as I need to give it to her. Thank God. There is something here. Maybe it's only physical for her, but goddammit, I'll take anything I can get.

"Nightmare?" Naomi breathes as I return to the kiss, twining our tongues together, pressing her chin down with my own so I can get it deep.

"Yes," I grate, thrusting my hips into the cradle of her thighs, driving her up against the house. "You were there and then gone, baby. The shark took you and I couldn't stop it. I tried and I couldn't." The truth comes out of me in a rush, so fast I'm unable to stem the flow. Maybe it's the complete darkness, the fact that we can barely see each other's faces. Or maybe it's the animalistic nature of what's happening right now. We've fought, she's broken off what's between us, but our bodies aren't done. If it seems like our bodies are communicating something deeper, I have to ignore it now. I can't take having my hope smothered one more time.

"Jason," she murmurs, her dreamlike voice, our surroundings, making me wonder if I'm still asleep. Imagining all of this. "It wasn't real."

"Is this real?"

Without answering me, she peels off her T-shirt and pulls me tight against her, skin to skin. She twists side to side a little, rubbing her bare tits against my sweat-covered chest, tugging a choked groan from deep inside me. "You're always a little dirtier in the dark, aren't you, baby?" I give her ass a final squeeze, then curl my fingers around the waistband of her panties, ripping them off her sexy body, purely because I can't stand the thought of her those legs lowering for even a second. "Tell me you were missing me up in your bed."

She feels me tugging down the waistband of my sweats and whimpers. "I was missing you."

I drag the head of my freed dick through her slickness, making sure she's ready for me...but I hesitate to drive into her. Something is different. Planting and rubbing myself in her heat is always incredible, but there's a slippery friction now that hardens my balls, blowing an invigorating shiver up my spine. "Condom, baby. Don't have one on me. Goddammit."

Her mouth seeks mine out, breathless and whining. I feel her misery down to my soul and answer it by trying to fulfill her with my tongue, sliding it in and out, capturing her lower lip with my teeth. And all the while, I tease her clit with the bare tip of my cock. Around and around until her thighs are trembling around me, her tits heaving against my chest. I'm lost. I'm so fucking lost for this woman, I swear the ground is quaking under my feet, the organ in my chest on the verge of ripping free it's beating so urgently. I'm not sure how I end up inside of Naomi. Her hand is on mine and we're both guiding my dick closer, closer until I'm penetrating her sex and ramming deep, slamming her up against the house.

"No, no...yes." I breathe heavily against her forehead, trying to withstand the intense pleasure of being inside her without a rubber. All that sweet, wet pressure is bearing down on me from all sides and I could live here. I could fucking live here forever. "Yes. Yes."

"Yes. I know. Yes," she babbles beautifully into my neck. I cinch my hips back and pound into her, grunting as her teeth bite down. "Jason. Yes."

Even as the most insane satisfaction of my life approaches at a rapid rate, I tell myself I can't get this woman pregnant. I won't be able to let her go. Won't be able to live with the possibility of it unless we're together. So I tell myself she's part of the dream. I excuse the way my lower body pins her repeatedly to the house, jarring the thighs wrapped so tightly around my hips. I draw her knees up as high as I can and fuck her harder than I ever have before. And every time I drive deep, my good intentions blur into something primal. No help for it. I can't lie to myself with my defenses stripped away like this, so I admit the truth. I want her to take a piece of me with her when she leaves. I never want to let her escape me, and if that makes me a bastard, then so be it. I love her. I love her.

On some level, she wants this, too. She's working her pussy on me, grinding down, matching my movements, moaning my name. There's no condom. We both knew it when I sank into her. I'm too afraid to hope that means she loves me back.

No, Naomi letting me take her raw is just proof that I satisfy her. That our attraction transcends common sense. I'll take it. I'll take whatever I can get.

With her ass in a brutal grip, I thrust deep and pin her hard between me and the house. "No man's cock is ever going to feel this right inside of you. Only mine." I absorb her sob with a nasty kiss. "You remember that. You remember Jason and how he fucked you like the world was ending. Maybe it is."

She wets her lips. "J-Jason—"

I shhh her, beginning a slow bump and grind, my right hand sneaking over her hip so I can stroke her clit with my thumb. "Your pussy is going to miss me. Going to cry for me in the middle of the night, wondering where its new daddy went."

Naomi's body jerks with shock, and moisture floods around the pumping length of my cock, her back arching like she was electrocuted. "Oh m-my God." She's not seeing me, because of the orgasm she's spiraling through, because of the darkness. But I'm seeing her, watching her come from the treatment of my body and my mouth—it's the most exquisite vision I'll have stored in my memories for the rest of time. "I can't, I can't—"

"Feels like you can." Gripped by my own need for release, I rear back and begin tunneling in and out of her snug sex again and again, letting my climax approach, no more holding back. I can't believe I've held on this long without a barrier of latex separating us. "Listen to me, Naomi," I rasp against her ear. "You're never going to get it like this again—and I'm never going to give it like this again. Never going to give myself like this again. So take it all, baby. Take it and run away."

I sink into her one last time and cut loose, my heart squeezing when she wraps her arms around my head and pulls me close, kissing my face and mouth through the tumult of mind-numbing sensation. *Mine, mine, mine.* It's a claiming and a letting go at the same time. How is that possible? Fuck. The experience of filling her with everything inside me, holding back nothing…and leaving the outcome to fate has me sucking in droves of air, crushing her to my body while my cock continues to spasm, my hips jerking with disorganized movements.

I'm not sure how long I hold Naomi, but it's not enough. She slips out of my arms and finds her shirt, her flushed and sated appearance gorgeous in the build of morning light. Once she's covered and my sweats are back in place, we stare at one another, the distance between us yawning wider even though we're unmoving.

When she turns and flies back to the staircase, floating up them like a fairy—like the dream I'm convinced I just had—the finality of what just happened settles in and I turn and level a punch at the wall.

Over. It's over.

CHAPTER TWENTY-SIX

ConspiracyCrowd.org
Username: IWant2Believe2000
To quote The X-Files, *"Sometimes the only sane answer to an insane world is insanity." Definitely supports my Bigfoot is an alien theory.*

Naomi

I JUST HAVE to get through today. I'll worry about tomorrow tomorrow.

It's a mantra I've been repeating since I woke up from one hour of fitful sleep and forced myself through a shower and a breakfast of oatmeal and sausage. My body is sore all over from the way Jason wrenched my legs wherever he wanted them and attempted to bury me in the house last night. I'm afraid for those twinges of pain to fade. Afraid to lose this proof that I'm not breakable. That there's someone out there who knew it, treated me like I was durable, fuckable, strong. Is that what he intended?

Stop.

Stop replaying every moment of making love in the darkness and all the words that were spoken in heat. In frustration. If I dwell there, I will never get through this day. I'll never do what needs to be done. And I have no choice but to do the responsible thing or life as I know it will never be the same.

Ignoring the questioning voice in the back of my head wondering if a shift wouldn't be so bad...if it would be scary and glorious—I slip a final bobby pin into my hair and smooth my hands down the bodice of my dress. Old Naomi stares back at me from the small bathroom mirror over the sink. The same woman who stared back at me on my wedding day, nothing more than a lump of clay molded in her parents' hands. There are subtle differences to her, though. Her nose is pink from the sun, her neck has whisker burn.

My eyes mark the biggest difference, though. There's a weight to them that wasn't there before. My heart beats faster the longer I look. Perhaps my intentions were frivolous, but they weren't all for naught, were they?

A lump rises in my throat and I turn from the mirror before hope or satisfaction creep in. I don't have room for those things today. All I have is duty.

Although, the pageant doesn't feel like a responsibility. Not at all. I'm excited. I'm nervous on Birdie's behalf. I'm afraid I didn't do enough. Or didn't give her a strong enough chance to succeed. I'm also...confident I did my best. My best is not just adequate, either. In only a couple months' time, I've helped transform a total pageant rookie and—

Again, the hope that I could be something more, something of my own making, begins to inflate, but I shove a pin in it and leave the bathroom, smacking the light off with an impatient hand. Across the room on the bed, my suitcase is packed and closed, my purse sitting neatly on top. I'm going to leave straight from the pageant, so this is my last time here in this room. This room where I've been free to get dressed how I choose, eat what I make, stay in bed past a reasonable hour. This room where I resisted falling in love and failed.

I press a hand to my stomach and breathe deeply, mentally

placing my personal turmoil on the back burner. Today I am one thousand percent focused on Birdie.

And I have the distinct desire to help her kick some ass.

I can feel eyes on me as I carry my suitcase down the stairs, all the way to my Range Rover, where I stow it in the back. So much for putting turmoil on the back burner. By the time I close the hatch, my entire body is covered in goosebumps and I'm having a hard time swallowing. Perhaps ironically, I dig deep for my own pageant poise and walk toward the house, pausing when Birdie and Jason pile out, plastic-covered dresses draped over their arms, tote bags likely containing makeup and shoes slung in the crooks of their elbows.

It's almost impossible, but I avoid eye contact with Jason and paste a broad smile on my face, reaching out to take some of the burden. "And how are we feeling today, Ms. Birdie?"

"Er...vomity?"

"That's perfectly natural." I shoulder a tote bag and reach for more. "There will be vomit receptacles backstage."

Birdie blinks. "You're kidding."

"I never joke about vomit," I say, winking, feeling like an actress in a play about my life before Florida. But it's working. It's pushing me from point A to B. Encompassing Birdie and an inscrutable Jason with a brisk look, I turn on a heel toward my Rover. "I'll bring this stuff in my car and meet you there. Let's go make magic!"

As soon as I'm behind the wheel with the engine started, I deflate a little, then perk back up. Keep going. Keep moving. It's a twenty-minute drive to the pageant venue and we arrive in the parking lot at the same time. Jason insists on carrying the entire haul of clothing and beauty equipment to the rear entrance, Birdie and I taking over from there. In a scene straight out of my memories, backstage is a chaotic whirlwind. Teenage girls huddle in half-naked groups, their overly caffeinated mothers trying to apply makeup from awkward angles, unplugged curling irons tucked under their arms like weapons. Ready to be plugged into the closest outlet and used at the drop of a hat.

Two girls I recognize as Pastel Hell in Heels jog past, stopping to drop kisses onto Birdie's cheeks, wishing her good luck. She repeats well wishes back to them, her shouldering relaxing somewhat at their easy acceptance over her being there. I want to run after them and smother them in hugs, but I'm distracted by the pageant director marching through the fray with a clipboard. She rattles off call times and answers questions with her pen lifted gracefully.

"Is it too late to back out?" Birdie drones.

"Yes. Come on."

We weave through dozens of brightly made-up girls who stare at Birdie with open curiosity—and it's no wonder, since she's wearing a Guns & Roses T-shirt with the sleeves cut off so wide, the sides of her bra are visible. "Why is everyone ready so early?" She whispers to me as we pick our way to our assigned preparation area, complete with beauty station and changing room. "The pageant doesn't start for two hours."

"To socialize. Network. Learn each other's weaknesses. Maybe catch sight of the judges on the way in and gauge their moods. Anything to gain an advantage."

She falls into the padded chair. "You didn't think we'd benefit from any of that?"

I wink at her. "No one benefits from waking you up early, Birdie."

"Not even I could sleep with Jason pacing back and forth until the sun came up."

My hands pause in the act of removing Birdie's beauty kit from the tote bag. "Oh." My heart has shot up into my mouth, but I settle the case on the smooth, lacquer surface and brighten. "Can I get you a coffee before we get started, then? Have you eaten? We want to make sure we keep your blood sugar in range."

Birdie gives me a measured look. "Excuse me, but this is fucked."

"Birdie Bristow," I admonish without heat. "We really do need to get you ready."

"I'm no masterpiece, but we totally don't need two hours." She tugs on the neck of her shirt, her movements restless. "You came here for a new perspective. An adventure. Didn't you find that? Didn't you have one?"

"Yes," I whisper.

"And you're content with that? Finding something and somewhere that makes you happy and being satisfied just to know it exists." She shakes her head at me, like I'm a difficult math problem. "I don't get that. I don't get why you wouldn't hang on to something that makes you happy. Won't you miss it?"

"Every day."

"Then don't." Her eyebrows slash together. "Don't miss it. Hold on to it."

"It's not that easy."

"Why can't it be, Naomi?" Silence stretches between us, filled in by the muffled chatter of other contestants. "Why can't it be as simple as keeping what and who makes you happy?"

"For me? For me...my happiness has the power to make others unhappy."

"Well, fuck them."

It feels so good to laugh. To have this honest moment after falling back into my old self for the last hour by sheer force of will. "*Them* are my parents." Emotion makes my cheeks feel heavy and stiff. "If I don't go back to Charleston tonight, I'll be...removed from the family. I'll have my inheritance taken away."

She jolts in her seat. "That's what your father came to tell you?"

"Yes," I say, reaching for the dresses Birdie is still holding and beginning to hang them up in order of the schedule. "Among other things."

"Did you tell Jason?"

"No." Urgency rises in my middle like a tide. "And I don't want him to know. First of all..." In the tangle of my heartache, I was only partially aware of my reasoning for keeping my father's threats from Jason until now. But the truth flows out, inescapable and real. "Jason left home at eighteen, made his own way. Joined the Army. Rose to the top of his profession and still he's not satisfied he's done enough. I can't...I want him to remember me as my own woman who lived without restraint for two months. Not a girl whose parents still have the power to discipline her. That's just sad. You know?"

"I mean, I get that? I get what it's like to have your parents make it look so easy to be separated from you." She's quiet for a moment. "But I can't help but think if you were just honest with my brother, you guys could work it out. Find a way for you to stay and..."

I can see her running into snags in that plan, just like I did. Or would have if staying was ever on the table. "He hasn't asked me, Birdie." My mouth does its best to form a reassuring smile. "Jason knowing why I have no choice but to go home won't change anything. It's where I belong. He's going back overseas when you graduate." I give a jerky shrug and lie straight through my teeth. "I'm good with everything. I'm good."

Birdie scrutinizes me while I finish hanging dresses, a robe and her fitness category outfit. Next, I lay her makeup out on the table and begin applying foundation. We don't speak again during the whole process of doing makeup and styling her hair, but I can feel her demeanor tensing as the clock ticks past, making mincemeat of two hours. The pageant director stops by to give us our specific call times, clearly curious about Birdie, who she hasn't seen on the local circuit. This is where I'm able to shine, though, and the woman is laughing and giving us gossip on the judges by the time the applause sounds from the theater, the host having begun his spiel.

"Okay, this is it, Birdie," I say, kneeling down in front of her as the director sashays away. "The pageant is going to feel interminably long while it's happening, but when it's over, you'll swear you didn't blink once. That might be fine if you did these all the time, but this is your only pageant. Just this one. So I want you to slow down and remember why you decided to do this in the first place. Okay? We found each other for a reason, didn't we?" Birdie nods, continuing to resemble a deer in headlights. "Forget everyone else in the theater. You're not here for them. You're here for your sister. We're here for her." I reach for my purse and take out a slim jewelry case, handing it to Birdie. "Here's a reminder in case you get overwhelmed out there and forget."

Birdie stares down at the box for several beats before popping it open. She doesn't cry when she takes out the charm bracelet. Or when she reads the inscription, "For Natalie," on the dangling heart charm. Instead, her spine straightens and she gets some fight back in her eyes. I don't think I've ever had more pride in anyone in my entire life. She's extraordinary.

"Thank you," she says, handing me the bracelet so I can clip it on. "Can you look out at the crowd and let me know where Jason is sitting? Just in case I need to focus on a friendly...and hairy face?"

"Yes," I murmur, standing. I take a look at the clock on the wall and hand her the fitness category outfit. "Introductions and fitness are up first. Wave and walk. Smile with teeth. One side of the stage to the other. Make eye contact with the judges. Easy-peasy, just like we practiced. We didn't suffer through all that running for nothing."

"Got it."

"Visualize it in your mind. I'll be back before they line you up."

"Okay."

I can hear Birdie repeating my words back as I enter the hustle and bustle of pageant girls and moms, dipping out the back door and hurrying along the side of the building. Spectators are still filing into the entrance, trying to combat the Florida heat by fanning themselves with their tickets. I say a quick prayer that the side entrance is unlocked, but it's not. Someone inside hears me jiggling the handle and opens it for me, though.

"I promise I'm not sneaking in without paying," I reassure the grandmother wearing the Cayleigh is My Shining Star T-shirt. "Just trying to find someone..."

I spy Jason leaning against the back wall about twenty yards away. His arms are crossed over his mighty chest, and Lord, if he doesn't look more uncomfortable in his surroundings than a bear at the opera. As if sensing me, his gaze cuts in my direction and stays there. He doesn't wave, smile or come to meet me. We just watch each other through the excited conversation of the crowd. It goes against everything inside me not to run to him, but I understand what he's trying to communicate. Last night was our goodbye. No sense in making it any harder.

My legs are unsteady beneath me as I turn back toward the side exit and shove through, out into the heat. It raises the temperature of my chilled skin somewhat, but nowhere near enough. My only hope is I appear confident as I rejoin Birdie in time for the director to start calling names.

"He's against the back wall. Just to the right of the entrance."

Birdie exhales. "I knew he wouldn't sit."

"He's fine. Focus on the intro."

Watching Birdie walk through the curtain from the side of the stage minutes later is almost surreal. She's wearing black workout gear with silver studs running along the seams…and a pair of red Converse. On stage, the spotlight bathes her and she smiles radiantly into the white beam while her name is trilled over the loudspeaker, along with her hometown, her age, her hobbies—avoiding organized social activities—and the fact that it's her first pageant, which draws murmurs from the crowd. When Birdie told me she'd omitted any mention of her sister in the paperwork, I worried it would be a mistake. That she'd want that recognition for Natalie when the time came. I can see now why she did it. Why she decided to hold that mission close to herself. It's too sacred to share with a room full of people who didn't know the weight Natalie carried. They would forget it by tomorrow.

True to my own word, the next hour is a blur. After the introductions, we strip Birdie out of her fitness outfit and zip her into an asymmetrical, black and purple sequined gown with a retro vibe. I comb her hair to one side and clip it, curling the ends while she reapplies eye shadow, completing the look. Some of the girls in the room have a hair stylist and makeup artist, in addition to their mothers, but I think Birdie would have gone crazy with that many cooks in the kitchen. Or at least I tell myself that so I don't feel so woefully inadequate.

"Jesus. You need a glass of Sauvignon Blanc."

At Birdie's words, I take my first breath in what must be an hour. "You know my drink of choice, too?"

"Jason stores the case of wine he had delivered in my closet." She blots her lipstick. "Probably so you won't see it and realize he's been a goner since your job interview."

Time slows down, my pulse walloping me at all the crucial pressure points. "Why did you have to go and tell me that?"

"You're right. That was mean." She visibly braces when her name is called from the stage entrance. Not for the first time, I notice Birdie seems kind of distracted, instead of nervous. Like she's trying to work out a puzzle. "Um. Okay, coach. We are go for the evening gown portion."

I snap back to the here and now, just as the music begins to pump in the theater loud enough to shake the walls. Little pockets of cheers go up as contestants begin walking the stage and Birdie rushes to the stage entrance to wait in line. "Dazzle them," I say lamely, trying furiously not to think of the fact that Jason ordered me a case of wine. What is the deal with my composure falling apart over wine? *Honestly, Naomi.*

Before I know it, the evening gown portion is over and we're backstage, changing Birdie's dress once again for the question and answer round. Her dance partner, Turner, has texted me that he has arrived and is waiting in the area designated for men, so I tick that item off my list of things to stress about. He might have been kind of a jerk, but at least he's completing his end of the bargain. Probably because I have his final payment in my purse.

Around me and Birdie, mothers quietly read practice questions from flash cards while daughters shake out their limbs, close their eyes and try to get in the zone. It's so familiar to me, I get a knot in my throat and I give myself a moment to look around. I enjoy this world. It's a lot like me, in a way, isn't it? Pretty, frivolous and kind of silly on the outside, but behind the scenes, there's a whole host of insecurities and pressure to say the right thing, be what everyone expects. Most of the girls scattered backstage have flawless grade point averages and interests that extend far beyond pageants. They're here to rack up scholarship money and if people find that frivolous then they can go stuff a sock where the sun doesn't shine.

Against my will, I think of conducting practices in a space designed and decorated by my own hand. Tasteful white walls with silver and bright poppy-red accents. Gleaming red wood floors and gauzy curtains that would float around during consultations, letting the girls dream of their shining moment on the stage…

I swallow hard and command myself to focus and stop being fanciful. It's so hard to do that now that I've let myself imagine possibilities, though. Imagine more than a life of following the dictates of others. Showing my face where I've been asked to show it. Making phone calls to assist local Charleston charities, but not really putting in the time and effort to personalize them. To put my own unique stamp on something. Isn't the effort behind Birdie's pageant what will make it worthwhile?

I shake myself. "Want to run through some practice questions?"

Birdie is staring back at her reflection in the mirror.

"Birdie."

"Huh?"

"Is everything okay?" I hunker down beside her chair. "You're doing incredible out there. If I didn't know this is your first pageant, I wouldn't believe it."

"Thanks." She nods and sits up straighter. "Yeah, I think it's going well? Hard to tell. I can't see anything out there. Just vague outlines of heads."

"Every pageant is different. Some of them don't have spot-lights." My forehead tugs with a frown. "Maybe we should have—"

"Rented a spotlight for practice? Jason would have loved that expenditure."

Hearing his name sends a wave of longing down my back. "So. Practice questions?"

"Bristow."

Birdie and I trade a smirk at the director calling her name. "Too late." She doesn't seem to realize she's rubbing the bracelet between her thumb and forefinger. "Here goes nothing."

My pulse pounds thickly in my ears minutes later as I watch Birdie approach the microphone, pose and smile at the host. To strangers, she probably doesn't appear timid, but I can see the fingers out of view from the audience rubbing at her skirt.

"Miss Bristow. Where do you see yourself in five years?"

I slap a hand to my forehead and somewhere in the back of the theater, I swear I hear a low, disbelieving chuckle. Silence ticks past. One second, two. Oh my God, she isn't going to answer. I should have forced her to answer this practice question. Why didn't I—

"It's important to have plans. Goals. It's just as important to know when your plan needs to change, though. Life…requires change. Five years ago, I wasn't planning on competing in a beauty pageant. I don't even like wearing dresses." The host and audience laugh. "You have to decide what's worthwhile and adapt, even if it's new or you didn't expect it. Maybe it's just as productive to live without a five-year plan. Or to start with a five-day plan and see where it takes you."

The buzzer peals.

Birdie's words strike deep, but I'm all about her as she glides toward me and falls through the curtain into my arms. "Shit. Did that even make sense?"

"Yes. Yes." I squeeze her tighter. "Perfect sense."

A full minute passes. The next contestant takes the stage, but Birdie still doesn't let go. "I thought I would feel her," she whispers. "I thought there would be some part of Nat here, but there's nothing. It's just a microphone and lights and..." She steps back with a hiccup. "I just wanted her to be proud or close. Just close one more time. But she's not. She never will be again, will she?"

This is why she's been distracted. She was waiting for a full circle moment and it hasn't come. "That's not true."

"Please don't tell me I carry her in my heart." Birdie moves past me in a rustle of fabric and I catch the sheen of moisture in her eyes. "Can you get Turner? Let's get the dance over with and go home."

Defeat weighs me down as I turn to do what Birdie asks...but something stops me. Birdie's words echo back from that first run we took together. *Natalie was the one who brought everyone together. With friends and family. Both. She'd put on a silly play or throw a board game on the floor and whine until everyone picked a talisman. She was the glue. Everything...everyone is apart now because there's no glue.*

An idea occurs to me. A crazy one.

I have one shot to make this pageant what Birdie needs, though. Who cares if we win? It was never really about winning, was it? No, it's about family.

After throwing a quick glance at the clock, I sprint out the backstage area, urgency pumping my legs faster than I thought possible. On the way out of the exit, I pass Turner and skid to a stop. "Uh…you can go home. I'll mail you the check."

He salutes. "You don't have to tell me twice."

"It's been real," I shout over my shoulder, then throw the metal door open and run smack into Jason. He catches me by the elbows, not budging a single step even though I've essentially just hit him with my full weight. All the breath in our bodies seems to escape at the same time, softening every line of where we connect. *Then* he stumbles a little, his arms sliding up to my shoulders, into my hair. Oh God. How am I going to survive without him?

"What's wrong?" He searches every inch of my face, tilting it for a better look. "She seemed a little off in that last round."

"She is." With a willpower I didn't know I had, I untangle myself and ease away. "You have to dance with her."

No reaction. "Say what now?"

"Birdie. The waltz. It has to be you." I make a frustrated sound, knowing I'm getting ahead of myself. "She wanted to honor Natalie with the pageant, yes. But it was more. It was about *feeling* your sister again. Connecting to her in some way. You're that connection she needs. To make this pageant about Natalie, all of you, and nothing else. This is Natalie bringing you together, the way she used to. That's where Birdie is going to feel her." I grasp his forearm. "Please. You're the only one who can do this."

"Naomi…" He scoffs, but understanding is dawning in his face. "I can't. This is crazy."

"You can. You can be her hero."

Whatever protest he was going to make next dies in the wake of my words. He pushes a hand through his hair and laughs without humor. "Jesus Christ. I can't believe I'm doing this."

If I wasn't already leaden with love for Jason, I would be now. Lord, would I ever. "The reason they couldn't get that final turn is because Birdie has a tendency to lead. There's no time now for a practice run. If she takes the lead, just let her have it. Considering the circumstances, maybe it's for the best. But you do know the steps. I've watched you count them off in the church basement. I know you can do it. Jason, even if you screw up spectacularly, it won't be for nothing. It'll be for everything."

I take his hand and lead him through the back exit, stopping him before he enters the changing section. "Wait here." Moving at a clip, I find Birdie our designated spot, holding up a staying hand when she starts to ask me where I've been. "Change of plans."

"Change of plans," she sputters. "Oh my God. Did that asshat not show up?"

"He did. I sent him home." I tug her through the throng of harried contestants—including one gymnast and two clarinet players—and reach Jason a few moments later. "Here is your new dance partner."

Jason executes a sweeping bow, making my heart go splat. "I'm as surprised as you are." He nods. "Let's do this, kid."

Birdie lets out a small sound, one that makes her seem so much younger in an instant. Then she covers a watery laugh with her hand. "They could have upped the price of admission for this." She's clearly trying to hide her happiness, but the smile she can't control tells me I did the right thing. Thank God. "Try not to step on my toes and crush them to dust."

He holds out his hand and Birdie takes it. "I make no promises."

"Bristow."

"Go go go," I manage after a gasping breath, shooing them toward stage right. "You're up next."

It all happens so fast. A river is rushing in my ears as I deposit Birdie and Jason in the waiting area at stage right. I make a mad dash to inform the pageant director of the change in partners, and thank heavens I buttered her up earlier, because she doesn't make a stink—and that is why you arrive early to a pageant, folks. By the time I return to Birdie and Jason, they're being called to the stage and I don't even have a chance to say good luck. They're already gone, although Jason sends me a look right before the music begins. I don't know what it means, only that it wraps around me like a warm hug and makes my knees weak at the same time.

"I'll miss you, Blackbeard," I whisper to myself when he looks away.

Because I'm already gone.

There's no reason to remain once the dance starts. I can see that right away. Birdie's expression is pure, open joy. A kind I haven't seen her wear before—and I know. I know as she smiles up into her brother's face and he nods back, executing the dance moves like a bull in a china shop, that Birdie found the sense of togetherness she was looking for. Even I can feel the spirit of their sister, never having met her. They honor her with every awkward turn and subsequent laugh. An unguarded melody mixed with a low rumble.

It's beautiful. I'll never forget it.

I'm in my car with the engine started before the last note plays.

CHAPTER TWENTY-SEVEN

ConspiracyCrowd.org
Username: UrDadsMyFave69
Ding, ding, ding. We have a wiener.
That's a woman who has been getting the business for
two months.
I accept accolades in the form of Tom Hardy GIFs.

Naomi

I F I'VE LEARNED one thing over the last seven days, it's that punishment comes in many forms. For example, this morning I'm a pincushion. And the entertainment.

The morning after I arrived back in Charleston, I immediately set out on my apology tour, hitting the wedding planner, catering company and pastor in the space of two hours. My closest relatives and bridesmaids each received a phone call and a wine basket. When it was all over and my list had been—mostly—checked off, I collapsed into bed and didn't get up.

It took me until today to leave my room again and I was immediately scheduled for a dress fitting. With three weeks to go until my mother's charity ball, I need some practice acting normal. I hate how weak I became at the drop of a hat, but it took all my strength to leave St. Augustine behind and drive back to Charleston. To walk through the door of my childhood home and have all the positivity of the last two months mean nothing to anyone but me. Did any of it really happen?

Right now, standing on a pedestal while the seamstress yanks my bodice tighter, it doesn't feel like any of it was real. I feel bloodless and half-asleep. Around me in a semi-circle, my mother's friends sit on cushy chairs sipping mimosas, suggesting different materials, new styles, dashes of bling here or there. Among them, my mother sits like a cat who caught the canary, allowing me to be on display. The object of curiosity.

"Naomi, you're looking so skinny," says Doris, one of my mother's oldest friends. "Maybe I should run away for two months."

The ensuing laughter carves another chunk out of me. In the mirror, I watch my mother calmly sip from her champagne flute, her eyes daring me over the rim to be anything but gracious. To do anything but fix the damage I've wrought by my absence. Oh yes, punishment comes in many different forms.

"You're perfect the way you are," I murmur to Doris. "There's no need."

"Speaking of running away..." says another woman while setting down her drink. *Clink.* It sounds like a starting gun. "Well, I'm sure we're all aware of the theories, but I'd love to hear it from you, dear. How were you occupying yourself in Florida?"

I was falling in love.

My tongue protests when I bite down on it too hard. Four minutes. That's the longest I've gone without thinking of Jason in weeks. I plummet back to the drawing board now, wishing I'd risked another lecture through the door from my mother and stayed in my room. What would Jason do if he walked in right now? He would pretend mimosas were for sissies, but he'd drink one, anyway. No, that's not right. He'd get these stupid pins out of me, one by one, and kiss any spots left behind. He'd kiss my mouth, damn the crowd. Everything would be all right if he was here. Birdie, too. She would kick up her heels on my mother's antique coffee table and demand some spikes be added to my dress. God, I miss Birdie to death.

They were real. They were real.

I'm the one who isn't real. I'm exactly where I started. In the place I ran from. Except now there is a stigma attached to me that I will probably spend my whole life trying to overcome. And I won't succeed. The conspiracy theories about my disappearance were mostly ludicrous, but some of them sounded credible. She was institutionalized. She had a nervous breakdown. She ran away with the gardener. I can see the women sizing me up in the mirror and I know their minds are already settled on whatever theory they chose on day one. This gathering is pointless. I wonder if my mother realizes that.

Even if she does, she's made it clear she plans to trot me out like a show pony, regardless. Through my door for the last several days—in between lectures—there has been optimism on her part. If I just meet with Elijah, he'll remember why good blood marries with good blood. He'll stop his ridiculous gallivanting with Addison Potts and see sense. It's what his parents want. It's what's expected.

Crazy enough, I feel more of a kinship for Elijah than I did when we were dating and engaged. I want to call him on the phone and command him to keep gallivanting, to hell with what our parents think. Yes, Elijah is the last stop on my apology tour, but I haven't been able to bring myself to make it. Going to see him seems unfaithful to Jason.

Jason.

Another pin jabs me in the hip and I wince, jarred back into the moment. What did that woman with the ugly brooch ask me?

How did I occupy myself in Florida?

A glance in the mirror tells me they're all watching me expectantly. "Well...I took some educational classes." On beer brewing. "I went scuba diving." After which I had the most mind-melting sex of my life on a boat. "And I did some consulting for a beauty pageant contestant..."

"Were you paid for it?" Doris sits forward. "Did you work in Florida?"

She says work like some people say *pus*.

"Not work," I say with a smile, even though I feel like I'm choking on every word. "More of a favor for someone who needed some guidance."

"Tina," my mother cuts in smoothly, addressing the seamstress. "Can you please add another half inch to the straps? We don't need to remind everyone why she has tan lines."

"Yes, ma'am."

I straighten my shoulders and hold still, giving Tina a reassuring smile as she works to widen the material and keep it in place. She's not jabbing me on purpose. It's clear that she's new to the job and I don't want to think that's why my mother hired her, because that would just be too much. More than anything right now, I want to rip this green silk off my body and wear the loose, casual clothing I grew accustomed to in Florida. They're still under my bed, locked in the suitcase I can't allow myself to open.

"Did you...meet anyone interesting in Florida, Naomi?"

That not so subtle question comes from Ugly Brooch and I ache—ache—to tell her I met the most incredible person on this planet. An honorable man who can also be a grouch but would die to protect the ones he loves. My throat aches with the effort to keep the truth trapped. Oh God, I can't stand here much longer. I want to scream.

No, I'm *going* to scream. It builds in my chest—

Elijah's mother walks into the room, escorted by a maid. I deflate.

"Mrs. DuPont has arrived, Mrs. Clemons."

"Thank you," sings my mother, standing to greet her.

I'm frozen on the pedestal, my gaze locked with Elijah's mother's in the mirror. She's another person I should have apologized to by now. For ruining her son's wedding day. I just needed more time to stop being in actual, physical agony. More time to stop missing Jason so bad my legs refused to move.

Elijah's mother doesn't look angry with me, though. Or even disappointed. If anything, she looks kind of…conflicted. "Welcome home, Naomi," she says. "You look well."

"Thank you, Mrs. Du Pont."

Between us, heads are moving like the crowd at Wimbledon.

"Mrs. Clemons," the maid prompts, handing my mother an envelope. "This came in the mail. It's addressed to Miss Clemons, but I thought you'd be interested since—"

"No need to go into detail," my mother clips out, taking out her glasses and perching them on her nose to study the envelope. Whatever she sees visibly flusters her. "It's from Elijah. For you, Naomi."

The gentle version of an explosion goes off in the room. Murmuring and hand fanning ensues. My stomach drops to the floor. No. No, I'm not ready to deal with this. Not ready to deal with anything. I turn on autopilot to accept the note from my mother, noticing Mrs. DuPont's confused expression and wondering what it means.

"Well, open it, Naomi," my mother snaps, laughing somewhat hysterically. With all eyes on me, I slide the note out of the envelope, my heartbeat deafening in my ears.

Dear Naomi,

I still love you. I know we can get past what happened. Please come see me.

Elijah

I almost fall off the pedestal, but Tina steadies me.

"Well," prompts Doris. "What does it say, dear?"

"Yes," drawls Elijah's mother. "I'm quite curious myself."

I'm unable to form words when shackles are tightening around my wrists and ankles. Deep down, I'm not sure I ever believed my eventual marriage to Elijah was salvageable. I didn't want it to be, I finally, finally confess to myself. Of course I didn't. I'm in love with someone else. Someone who knows me, through and through. I don't want to marry a stranger and live as a dutiful ornament the rest of my life. Elijah moving on was my only hope for having more. If I can't have Jason, can't I at least keep my renewed sense of self? I could build on that. With the reading of this note, however, all of those hopes are dashed. My choices are gone.

If Elijah wants a second chance and I don't give it to him, I'm as good as disowned, my financial security stripped away. There's nowhere to go but back to the start.

"It says...to come see him," I manage. "If you'll excuse me."

I leave the room full of pins.

I WALK UP the steps of the home Elijah and I were supposed to inhabit after our honeymoon. Lord, it's more intimidating than I remember. Needing to stall, I look up at the second floor at what I'd planned to make my meditation room. Why? I don't even meditate. My friends insisted mediation rooms were as essential as kitchens, that's why. Did I ever have a mind of my own?

Memories drift back to me. Renting my motel room in St. Augustine, food shopping in a strange place for the first time, the sensation of a paintbrush stroking down my ribcage. Telling Jason I wanted to be used hard. The carbonation of a beer tickling my throat.

Jason dancing with Birdie under a spotlight.

Those reminders that...yes, I do have the ability to make decisions and think for myself, to make a difference, send me up the steps to knock on the door. I'm braced to see the man I left at the altar. My apology is rehearsed and ready on my tongue. No one answers on the first knock, but when I lift my hand to knock again, the door flies open.

Whoa. This tall, suited gentleman is my ex-fiancé, but he's not the poised and polished Elijah of my recollection. His dark hair is in disarray, his tie knot pulled to one side. He's a man who never misses a step or looks anything but confident. Not right now, though. He's very clearly upset. Almost...haunted. What is going on?

"Elijah. Hello." I cling to my purse strap for comfort, waiting for the customary gentleman's greeting. A kiss on the cheek, a smile, a compliment. He says nothing back, though, simply staring at me like...he doesn't even know me. As if we've never met at all. I say his name again and he visibly shakes himself, fear moving into his expression. "Are you all right?"

"No." His hand slaps down on the doorframe, his knuckles turning white from gripping it so hard. "Naomi, I don't want to be rude, but this isn't the best time."

"Oh, of course, I—" Wait, what? He's the one who invited me here, isn't he? I search through my purse for the envelope. "I wouldn't have come, only you sent me the note."

He stares at me like I'm speaking in pig Latin. "Note?"

"It was in my mailbox this afternoon." The murk clears and reveals what should have been obvious the moment he opened the door, regarding me as one does a stranger. My chest expands with my first full breath of the day. With creeping, cautious relief. "I'm guessing you didn't write it," I breathe, handing him the unfolded piece of paper.

His eyes move one side to the other, reading—and the contents bring a sound out of his mouth. It's a tortured denial. If he didn't write the note, who did? Right now, that doesn't matter. What matters is that he very obviously does not love me or want me back.

Thank God.

"Naomi..."

I hold up a hand with a boldness I didn't always have. But I do now. "You don't have to explain." A bittersweet laugh puffs past my lips. "Engaged to be married and I didn't even know your handwriting. If that's not a sign, I don't know what is," I say, desperately trying to remember the words to my apology as more and more relief floods in. "Even so, I'm sorry about what happened, Elijah. How I handled it, especially. Driving like a bat out of hell to Florida until I couldn't go any farther. Honestly, I barely recognized myself—"

The memory of Jason opening the door to his house for the first time, his big shoulders spanning the frame, almost strangles me, so I rush to distract myself, rambling, needing to go. Away from this house that represents the past. Past Naomi. *Get the rest out.* "Gosh, I've been going around apologizing to just about everyone. My mother, the wedding planner. Something about us just never felt right." I shake my head. "Maybe I don't know what right is even supposed to feel like with another person. Maybe…that's what I learned in Florida. I'm not sure. I'm just sorry about the trouble I caused you."

"I'm sorry, too," he says, sincerity in his tone. "Someday, when all of this is long behind us, Addison and I would love to have you over for dinner. We'll laugh about it."

Happiness positively floods me at that confirmation that something good for Elijah and Addison came out of me fleeing the church. "I wondered if it was true. You and my cousin." I heave a final sigh for the past. The one Elijah and I built with the best intentions, trying to please everyone but ourselves. "Everyone thinks I'm crazy, and seeing you in this house where we were meant to live…I think they must be right," I say, trying to ease the distress radiating from him. "Hopefully Addison is smarter than me."

"I'm hoping for the opposite. The smarter she is, the harder it's going to be to convince her to forgive me." I laugh, but he doesn't join me, his gaze distant. "Naomi, I really have to go."

"I understand. But there's just one more quick thing." My revelation is unplanned, but it needs to be said. This secret has been kept far too long and as of this moment, I'm done letting my parents deal the cards of their choosing and still having the gall to dictate how they're played. "I overheard my parents arguing. A very long time ago." All of those tense meals trying to mediate arguments about my father's affair rush back to me, but one in particular stands out. One I wasn't meant to witness. "Addison…she's not just my cousin, she's my half-sister. She deserves to know that. Will you tell her, please?"

Elijah's chin snaps up, then all at once he looks weary. "Yes, I'll tell her," he says, attempting a smile, which I return. "Goodbye, Naomi."

"Goodbye, Elijah."

The door closes and I turn, floating down the steps. That's how it seems. As if there are clouds under my feet, carrying me forward. Forward is where I need to go. Not back. I came here believing marriage to Elijah and a lifetime of posturing was my only option, but it's not. It's very clear he loves someone else, and thus, I am free. I'm free. Even my parents can't maneuver past the love for another woman I just witnessed on Elijah's face.

A bolt of lightning streaks across the sky and I look up, allowing rain to land on my cheeks and forehead. I laugh up into the storm, absorbing the power of it. My own power.

Jason will always hold my heart. I love him and I miss him, but we were driven apart by the choices we made. He didn't ask me to stay in Florida. Wouldn't. Not when his military career is the most important part of his life. I chose a different kind of duty. Duty that I'm relinquishing as of now, so I can prove my own capabilities, with no fallback money this time. No home to run back to if the going gets tough. Yes, Jason will always, always have my heart. But I have courage. I have me. And I'm ashamed of myself for forgetting that when I set my mind to it, I can stand on my own two feet. That's exactly what I plan to do.

CHAPTER TWENTY-EIGHT

ColdCaseCrushers.com
Username: StopJustStop
Well, it's nice to see that sanity has returned to the Internet, but...
...an update on our Runaway Girl now that she's home wouldn't be too terrible.

ConspiracyCrowd.org
Username: IWant2Believe2000
Do not be fooled by New Naomi. She's a plant.
That said, I wouldn't mind an update, either.
Does she seem sad to anyone else?

Jason

IT'S NOT UNTIL Birdie comes home from school with her graduation robe and cap that I check the calendar and realize I've been numb for a full month. Completely, sickeningly numb. If it wasn't for Birdie, I'm not sure I would have had the wherewithal to get out of bed in the morning. Something went dark inside me when I walked off stage and Naomi wasn't there. Like a candle being blown out in a dark room, leaving nothing behind but the baseline of silence.

My sister does need me, though. I don't think I really believed I could be needed for anything other than protection, providing, until she smiled up at me on that stage. I'm more to her than I knew. She's more to me, too. I never let that in, because it would mean staying. Operating outside my capabilities. When I came home, I treated my care of Birdie like just another mission. Maybe I still look at it that way, in a sense, because you can't take the Army out of the man. But I do know my sister will always have been my most important mission.

And I wouldn't have figured that out without Naomi. Wouldn't have thought myself capable of living up to another person's expectations, should they go beyond providing. Protecting. Who knew letting my guard down or being there for Birdie when she does the same…could be its own form of providence?

Maybe I've never really felt like a hero until now and I was searching for this feeling over and over on the battlefield, underwater, all over the goddamn place but at home.

It's awful to have a sense of peace so deep, I couldn't dive far enough to find it…while also being sublimely miserable. I don't know which end is up anymore. Naomi came here and made everything so fucking right. But it was only right with her. Not without. Never without.

"Hey, bro." Birdie tosses her graduation cap on the mantle, alongside her third-place trophy, which sits in a place of honor beside a picture of Natalie. "How long have you been sitting here?"

I look down at my hands. They hold a letter from my commander formally welcoming me back to active duty, beginning in June. "I have no idea," I say in a voice rough from disuse. "A while."

Over the last month, we've started making arrangements for my upcoming deployment. After graduation, Birdie is going to Dallas to stay with our parents until she starts college in the fall. I can tell she doesn't want to go, but she isn't letting on. She probably thinks I'm too fucked up over Naomi to handle her fears and I hate that she's right. I barely got through this letter in my hands without dropping into mental blackness, replaying every single moment from the time Naomi knocked on the door to when she vanished into thin air. Jesus, I miss her. Half of me has been torn away, leaving the rest of me to rot.

More than anything, I want to put on a positive face for Birdie. I want to tell her my parents aren't going to treat her like a walking ghost of our sister, but it might be a lie. If they would abandon her when she needed them most, they're not strong or smart enough to see Birdie is her very own unique person and treat her that way. My sister deserves better and I don't know how to give it to her. I don't know how to do anything when it hurts to function.

Pull it together. I set down the letter and stand, wincing as blood rushes to my feet. Hours. I must have been staring into nothing for hours. "How about some of those bowls for dinner? What do you call them?"

"Poke bowls. And you hated them last time."

I have no memory of how they tasted or how long ago we ate them. "They were fine."

"Jason."

"I'll make the call if you want to test your blood sugar."

"Jason."

Her serious tone alerts me that I need to focus. I don't want to. I just want to make it through the next hour, guilty as it makes me for being less than Birdie needs. "Yeah?"

"Yeah," she drones, mimicking me. "I've been letting you mope because I could tell nothing I said was going to penetrate your big head. But I, uh…" Her eyes flick to the letter resting on the table, complete with Army insignia at the top. "I'm starting to get worried, okay? If you leave without settling this thing with Naomi, you won't think clearly over there. And I really need you to be thinking clearly so you don't end up dead. Okay?"

I'm still trying to recover from hearing Naomi's name out loud. It has been weeks of hearing it on a loop in my head, but having the vowels and consonants linger in the air has taken a blowtorch to my house of cards. "It's settled. It couldn't be more settled."

"Said the dying man."

I brace myself on the counter. "Birdie, please."

"Naomi's parents were going to disinherit her if she didn't come home. And like, kick her out of the family, which if you ask me, would be a blessing." She takes a breath and whistles it out. "I hate betraying a confidence."

The kitchen crumples like tin foil around me. "What?"

Birdie shrugs. "It doesn't matter, anyway."

"*The hell it doesn't*," I shout. "Why wouldn't it matter?"

"Because you're leaving. And her life is elsewhere."

"Yeah, but..." Fuck, my heart is going to beat out of my chest. That last day with her is replaying itself in a totally different light now. "Why wouldn't she tell me?"

"Oh my God, Jason. I just got home from school." She opens the fridge and ducks inside, coming back with a Diet Coke. "I get quizzed enough there."

"For the love of God, Birdie."

She points the can at me. "I'm only going to tell you the rest if you fucking do something about Naomi." The cracks begin to show in her casual act. "You love her."

"Yes." I swallow a lump of pain. "She doesn't love me back."

"Oh, come on." She stands up pin straight and pats her hair, speaking with Naomi's southern drawl. "Please don't tell Jason. He's so capable and strong and heroic...I don't want him to remember me as a poor little rich girl still dependent on her parents."

My skin is flayed from my body with every single word. "Is that what she said?"

"Yeah, more or less."

I pace the kitchen, my hands fisting at my sides ready to strike out. Needing to. Christ, I would like to drive to Charleston and wrap my hands around her father's neck. "How could she believe that bullshit? Before her...I thought I was trapped here. I was trapping myself, though. There's more here than anywhere. Without the fighting. There's you, Birdie. There's what we can be. What I can be. Does she think I would have figured any of this out without her?"

"Dunno."

"And Naomi. What she did at the pageant—what she did for us—aside...Jesus, she breathes life into everything she touches. This home. The apartment. Me, you, herself. She's not the same woman who showed up here. And she changed herself. She did that. Never could have done it unless there was already so much damn strength inside of her. It was always there. How could she compare herself to anyone and find herself lacking? It's..." I drop back against the counter, rocking my suddenly throbbing head in my hands. "She asked me. She asked if I thought she could have made it without my help."

Birdie is silent for a heavy moment. "What did you say?"

"The wrong thing."

"Okay." I look up to find Birdie looking concerned for the first time, and an anchor drops into my stomach. "Don't tell me what it was. You don't want a black eye when you go to Charleston to fight for her." Go to Charleston to fight for her. Is that even a possibility? The dusting of hope brings my surroundings into laser-sharp focus, makes my mouth go dry. While imagining Naomi opening the front door to a giant, Southern estate to greet me, I've failed to notice Birdie sitting down at the kitchen table and pecking away on her laptop. She pauses in the act of turning the device around to show me what's on the screen. "And Jason? I hate to tell you this, but I mean it when I say you'll have to fight."

Dread pummels me before I even see the picture. I'm not prepared, though. Nothing on this green earth could prepare me. It's Naomi on the doorstep of a white mansion, looking like a princess out of a storybook. She'll never look more beautiful to me than when she's got messy hair and a sunburned nose, but she's a vision in a pink sundress, her hair twisted up in the back, hands folded at her waist. I drag my eyes to the man who answered the door and a sound escapes me. It's Elijah. And he's ravaged at the sight of her. Of course he is. He hasn't seen Naomi in months. What man wouldn't look like a shell of themselves after having and losing her?

I stumble from the kitchen to the driveway, no idea where I'm going. The hope I experienced before is long gone. Buried, along with my chance of getting her back. *She went to him. She went back to him.* The stairs to her apartment creak under my heavy tread as I climb approximately one step an hour. Might as well drop that final league into misery while surrounded by reminders of Naomi, right? I have nothing left to lose.

When I swing the door open, I catch her scent. No. How is that possible? I have to be imagining it. But it's there. It's in the room. Birdie came in and collected the sheets weeks ago, because I couldn't set foot in the place. Where is the scent coming from? I lose the trail at her bed and reverse back to the kitchen, the closet—

The closet.

I throw it open…and find the wedding dress. Still hanging there.

She left it? Why? Didn't she keep it because she planned to wear it again? Yeah. Yeah, she confirmed it right in this kitchen. I could never forget that detail. It fucking haunts me.

Was she lying? If not to me, then to herself?

I yank the dress off the rack and hold it to my face, inhaling her, tasting her in my bones. Christ, maybe I'm insane to find hope in this discovery. I can't help it, though. I'm in love with a woman and I refuse to believe she felt nothing for me. Maybe those feelings won't be enough to let me keep her. If that's the case, I'll find a way to live with that.

Nothing worthwhile comes easy, though. Nothing worthwhile comes without a fight.

And I have just enough fight left in me for one more shot.

CHAPTER TWENTY-NINE

ReadtheComments.com
Username: TheRappingTheorist
My heart is spontaneously combusting.

Naomi

B EING DISOWNED AND disinherited was a lot less ceremoni-
ous than I expected. After parting ways with Elijah on his
doorstep three weeks ago, I simply went home—my hair and
clothes drenched from the storm, mascara running—packed my
bags and left my parents' home while my mother screeched
threats and insults behind me. There has been no formal letter of
banishment from the Clemons clan and I'm sure they know
where to find me. Thankfully, my former maid of honor, Harper,
had a strong enough yen for the official scoop regarding where I
went for two months. Strong enough to let me live in her
guesthouse while I figured out my next step. I delivered on the
truth and Lord, it felt good to tell someone about Jason and
Birdie. By now, word is all over Charleston and frankly, I don't
give a damn.

I've been busy over the last three weeks. Not only because I
don't want to live in someone's guesthouse for long, but because I
need action. Distraction. For just a split second every morning
before opening my eyes, I think I'm in Jason's bed in St.

Augustine. When reality strikes, my heart is sliced to ribbons all over again. How long is this going to last? Heartbreak doesn't get better. It doesn't grow manageable.

I find myself doing little things accidentally on purpose to remind myself of him. Ordering a Budweiser on the nights I go out to eat alone in restaurants. Going down to the ocean off Isle of Palms and sticking my feet in the water. Or searching for his name on a magnet at one of the many downtown tourist stands. I ache every moment of the day for his arms around me and there's no end in sight.

So I work.

And I crash parties, apparently.

I stare back at myself in the ornate mirror over the restroom sink, resisting the urge to splash cold water on my face and ruin my makeup. On the other side of the door, the swell of an orchestra rises and falls, the gala in full swing. Time to remind myself why I came here tonight. Why I borrowed this silver, floor-length ball gown and Tiffany earrings from Harper and took an Uber to the charity gala where I'm guaranteed to encounter my parents and an avalanche of speculation?

Because I can.

Mostly, however, because Charleston is my home and I'm not going anywhere. If Beauty Queens Unlimited, the pageant coaching business I've spent weeks planning and organizing is going to be a success, this town needs to know I have backbone and determination. Maybe I need to continually remind myself of it, too, until I never waver in that belief again.

I take a deep breath and push away from the sink, mentally preparing to show my face in the ballroom for the first time. To see my parents for the first time since leaving home for good. I don't fault myself for thinking of Jason, picturing how he would give that arrogant stare down at anyone who got in his way. That image causes my chest to pull painfully as I stride through the double doors and into the crowd, heads swiveling in my direction. I lift my chin and let them look. That's right. I'm not going anywhere. Get used to seeing me. Having Jason in mind is a blessing and a curse in this moment, because it hurts, but nothing thrown my way tonight can be worse than losing him.

The world seems to pulse around me as my mother and I make eye contact. She stands in a circle of friends near an ice sculpture, her mouth hanging open where she left it midsentence. I school my features and meet her leaden stare without flinching. I'm grateful for the tick of surprise, maybe even respect, she affords me before turning her back. Everyone witnesses the gesture and knows what it means. I do, too. With a nod, I let the last remaining veil of my old life whisper off my skin and pool on the floor.

A waiter passes and I take the offered flute of champagne, pausing in the middle of my first sip when I notice someone on the opposite side of the room. Someone that is both familiar and unknown to me at the same time. Butterflies unleash in my stomach as Addison's gaze lifts to mine and stays there. She wets her lips...nervously? No, I can't possibly make her nervous. She's at the gala of a woman who hates the very existence of her. Maybe that's why she's here. To face it head on, same as me. That possibility and yes, my own courage, pushes me closer.

"Hello," I begin, splashing a little bit of champagne onto my knuckles when I gesture too broadly. "So...it's an interesting few months we've had, right?"

A surprised laugh puffs out of her. "Oh God. Please don't make me like you."

"It's not a requirement. I promise." I subdue my smile, but

it's not easy. "Is everyone staring at us?"

Addison flicks a look over my shoulder and sighs. "Yeah." She leans in. "Fuck 'em."

We share a slow smile. It's the first time that I notice a resemblance between us, courtesy of us having the same father. Subtle. Just a stubborn chin. But she notices it, too, and we both take long swigs of our drinks. The polite socialite in me wants to change the subject to something more pleasant, but this new Naomi? She doesn't let opportunities pass. "I'm not going to make a big emotional scene or anything, Addison. Not when we're standing here like two bugs under a microscope," I say for her ears alone. "I do have a couple of things to say, though, and I hope you'll listen and know I mean every word."

After a moment, she nods.

I command my racing pulse to slow down, but it only seems to speed up. "We might not know each other, but you are my sister. You're family. And I just wanted you to know I acknowledge you and..." I shake my head. "More than that, I admire you. I don't know if you want this on your head or not, but you gave me the bravery to leave the church. One look through the window. I could tell you'd been through a trial and I wanted...one ounce of the courage you showed walking up those steps. I wanted to go out and earn it."

It takes her a long time to respond. "It appears you did," she says on a shaky exhale. "Thank you. I didn't know how badly I needed to hear that."

Elijah approaches, dapper in a tuxedo, and slides an arm around Addison's back, natural as breathing. Whispers whip around us like industrial fans. How it must look to everyone— the love triangle of the decade—when in reality, it's simply a man, the woman he loves, and another woman who unwittingly played a role in uniting them. Seeing them together inspires a yearning in me so deep for Jason, I almost can't speak. "Good evening, Mr. Mayor."

"Naomi. It's a pleasure." He trades a look with Addison, and whatever passes between them brings a rush of warmth to his eyes. Gratitude, I see, as he turns toward me. "Rumor has it you've started coaching pageant contestants full time. You'll be sure to let us know how we can help you along."

"Yes," Addison adds. "I'd love to help. I'm not too bad myself at sparkling things up."

Witnessing the way Elijah and Addison gravitate toward each other, the burden of missing Jason is too heavy all of a sudden. I'm back in this place where everything is so familiar...except I'm no longer the same. My crutches of popularity and family and banal small talk are no longer options. And while I would never wish for those things back in lieu of my new foundation, I go back and forth between a place of strength and feeling like a lamb in the eye of a hurricane, ready to be swept off. Lord, I'm just so lonely without him.

"Well," I say too loudly. "I've taken up enough of your time." Taking a chance, I lean in and kiss Addison's cheek. "I hope you know I wish nothing but the best of luck for you both."

"Thank you. I...believe you." Brows drawn together, Addison gives me a quick hug. "Dammit. I guess we have to see more of each other. It's going to be awful."

"The worst," I return on a laugh.

My half-sister steps back and Elijah comes closer, giving me a polite kiss on the cheek, a brief hug. It's the warm closure I wasn't even aware I needed, but all I can think of the arms I crave having around me. The ones belonging to the man who knows me better than anyone.

"I know that look," Addison murmurs to Elijah's right, her gaze ticking toward the door and widening, turning thoughtful. "And I wonder if the gentleman who just walked in has anything to do with it." Her lips twist in a teasing smile. "Am I crazy, Naomi? Or is he making it pretty obvious he's here for you?"

It doesn't even occur to me she could be talking about Jason. Maybe a tabloid reporter or an associate of my father's preparing to deliver a rebuke disguised as a compliment. I've been on the receiving end of plenty of those in the last few weeks. Because of that, I almost don't even turn around. Thank God I do, though. Thank God.

Just inside the double doors of the ballroom, Jason stands out like a bolt of lightning in an otherwise clear blue sky. My legs almost give out beneath me he's so beautiful. Lord. Oh Lord. He's wearing formal Army dress, the left side of his olive-green jacket decorated with colorful medals, hair combed back, beard trimmed. Gray eyes riveting. If possible, he's even more of a gravitational pull than he is in a wetsuit or jeans. He's just *so much*.

And he's looking at me as if he's just lost purchase and is sliding down the side of a cliff.

DEEP DOWN, I didn't believe she'd go back to him. Here it is, though. Confirmation of my worst fears. A nightmare so much worse than the recurring ones I've had for years, happening right in front of me. I have no choice but to face this headfirst, though. I came here ready to fight for my life—Naomi—so bring it on.

The fact that she looks elegant on a level I've never witnessed up close...and that fucker Elijah looks like he belongs by her side...does not help. Whatsoever. It's taking every ounce of restraint I possess not to storm forward and rip them further apart. She's mine. The fact that everyone in this fucking room doesn't know she's mine is so offensive to me, I want to bellow until the chandeliers shake.

"Jason?" Naomi whispers, turning. "I-I...what are you doing here? I..."

Her whisper of my name is enough to halt the room's motion and I vaguely notice heads turning our way, one by one. I don't care about any of it. I'm too busy soaking up the sight of her as I walk closer, counting the seconds until I can smell her, run my eyes over her skin up close—to hell with the fact that she belongs to another man now. I know she's mine. *I know it.*

When I get within reaching distance of her, I stop, the speech I practiced on my drive to Charleston forgotten. Completely lost in the presence of this woman I love beyond reason.

"You could have made it in Florida without me. You could have built a kingdom, ruled it and thrived. I was just the lucky son-of-a-bitch who opened the door and got to keep you for a while. You challenged me to be more. I'm more because of you, but I'm nothing—*nothing*—without you." Emotion clogs my throat, but I continue anyway. "That's what I should have said to you. That's what you deserved to hear and I'm sorry my weak moment brought you down, baby. Brought *us* down." My attention lands on Elijah and he raises an eyebrow at the probable hatred I'm sending him. "I've come to make her mine. You're welcome to try and stop me."

Naomi, Elijah and a brunette standing nearby all trade a confused look.

"Oh, Jason," Naomi breathes, her eyes closing briefly. "Please let me introduce you to Addison Potts. Elijah's girlfriend."

"His..." The concrete that has been filling every square inch of space inside me cracks and crumbles, the sudden loss of tension almost knocking me over. "You're not back together?"

She shakes her head and color infiltrates my world again, my lungs expanding with renewed breath. Not together. She didn't go back to him. My God. "No," she says with the hint of a smile. "No, he's with the person he was meant to be with."

"And what about you?" I say hoarsely. When I don't get an answer, I reach deep for the speech I've been working on for a week. No more fucking around. She didn't go back to her ex-fiancé and doesn't seem upset over the loss. Not at all. I'm afraid to translate that into her still feeling something for me. But I still have to take my shot. Look at her. *Look at her.* She's worth getting on my knees for. "Naomi, if I didn't fulfill my obligations, I wouldn't be a man worthy of you. I'm going back overseas, because I said I would. I committed, just like I'm committed to you. And there are men counting on me. But I'm asking you...no, I'm begging you to wait for me." She presses a hand to her chest, saying nothing. "I know I'm asking you for a huge sacrifice, baby. To give your time. To give up your family and security. So I'll make a sacrifice, too. Charleston is your home, so I'll make it mine, too. I'll move my business here. I'll do anything to make you happy if you can...if you can just wait for me. We will have family and security together. We will build those things *together.*"

Naomi's voice is feather light. "Why?"

In contrast, I'm all but shouting. "What do you mean, *why?*"

"Why would you do all of that?"

Awareness creeps over me, not a moment too soon. Leave it to my clueless ass to leave out the most important factor when writing my speech. "Because I'm in love with you, Naomi Clemons. I'm standing here half alive from being without you." I have to take a breath because my voice is shaking. "Come on, beauty queen. Revive me."

Her hands join at her waist, wringing together. "A-and Birdie?"

A pang catches me in the chest. "She's set to go live with my parents after graduation."

Naomi's forehead wrinkles, but she nods, shifting side to side in her silver shoes. Here it is. She's taking everything I offered into consideration and will either sentence me to live or die. I can do nothing but wait for my fate, like a man before a judge, the guillotine on one side, happiness on the other.

"No," she says, finally.

"No," I croak, blood draining from my head. "Please—"

"Birdie should come live with me while you're away," she interrupts. "Don't you think?"

I start to double over, pulled beneath an undertow of relief, but Naomi runs and jumps into my arms, staggering me backward instead. "I love you, too," she hiccups. "I love you, Jason. I'd wait decades for you. I *have* waited decades."

I'm barely capable of speech. "Is this happening? Did I get you back?"

"Yes. Yes."

"Mine for good? You're mine?"

"Completely. Irrevocably."

"Oh my God."

Our mouths meet in a hard kiss, and hell if my eyes aren't damp as I hold Naomi close as possible, crushing her against me and vowing to never let her go. Ever. When I become aware of our surroundings again, Elijah is escorting his girlfriend away, but not before stopping beside us to clear his throat. "I don't know if you'll find this information useful, but if you take a right out of the ballroom, there's an empty office around the corner and three doors down."

I give him a look. "Don't make me like you."

Naomi buries her face in my neck and laughs. I make short work of getting us to the doors, kicking them shut behind us and muffling the music...and applause. Yeah, there is definite clapping, some whistling, although I can barely hear it over the pounding of my heart. *Need to get her alone.* We're together and that fact still isn't sinking in. I don't think it ever will, but having her wrapped around me, her mouth on mine, will make this real. It's real, right?

"I missed you so much," she whispers into my neck, her legs sneaking up to rest on my hips, tightening in that way I've been dreaming about obsessively. "I can't believe you're here."

"You should. You should have known living without you wasn't an option for me." I have to stop to press her up against a wall as soon as we turn the corner, our mouths locking in a kiss fraught with shallow breaths. "I shouldn't have let you leave without making sure you knew I love you, baby. I've been so fucked up. Christ, I thought you were with someone else."

Her mouth forms the word *no*, pain coloring her expression. "And you still came."

"I couldn't be the only one who knew we were forever, Naomi. You had to know it, too. I had to believe that or I would have broken."

"I'm sorry," she murmurs against my lips. "I'm yours, Jason. I could never be anyone but yours. Take me somewhere so I can show you."

I carry Naomi into the empty office, locking the door behind me—and I send a silent *thank you, bro,* to Elijah even though it hurts. I'm searching for somewhere to put down the love of my life, but she surprises me by wiggling out of my hold, taking me by the lapels of my jacket and throwing me into a wooden chair. Okay, fine, I *let* myself be thrown, but I'm not going to tell her that. I'm too busy enjoying the slide of her thighs on mine and she straddles me, her fingers busy down below on the fly of my pants.

"Did you wear this uniform to drive me crazy?" The rasp of my lowering zipper sounds like an extension of her seductive voice. "You look so...so s-sexy. Why haven't I seen you like this?"

"Don't worry, baby." I groan as she wraps my cock in a fist, stroking light twice, then hard, hard, hard. "You sure as hell will now that I know how much you like it."

"Love it." My balls press high, tight when she slides off my thighs, and just like that, I have a goddess kneeling between my legs. My goddess.

"No. No, baby, baby. No." Ignoring me, she licks the tip of my cock, then throats it with a savoring whimper that shakes me head to toe. "Fuck." The sides of the chair creak where I hold on for dear life. "I love your mouth. God knows I love it, but I haven't touched you in a month. I've been miserable needing you. I can't handle this. Up. Come up here. Please."

Naomi must have missed me, too, because she can't stop sucking me. I plant my heels hard on the ground, demanding my hips to stop rolling toward her mouth, but I can't help it. She's relentless perfection, sinking me deep again and again, jacking me off in a tight hand.

"I'm going to come," I growl. "Stop." Of course, when she does let my dick go with a pop of her sweet lips, I want to cry. But then I don't, because she's climbing onto my lap, her incredible tits jiggling in the neckline of her dress. "Goddamn. I need you, baby. I've been hurting like hell."

"I need you, too, need you, Jason," she babbles in that Southern girl accent I missed so much, her eyes glazed with hunger. "I'm so wet."

Desperate to feel the evidence of that claim, I gather the material of her dress as fast as possible in my hands. "Condom in my pocket. Condom."

"It doesn't matter. I'm two weeks late."

My pulse clamors to a halt. "*What?*"

Naomi's eyes clear in a split second and she smacks a palm over her mouth. "Oh my God. I didn't realize until now, but…I'm two weeks late, Jason."

I haven't gotten this far. Kids. How could they have entered the equation when I poured all my hope and energy into just getting Naomi back? Surviving one day to the next? There's no mistaking the absolute joy that assails me now, though. It's nothing like I've ever experienced, my face inches away from the astonished woman I love with my whole soul. "A baby." My voice is hoarse. "You're pregnant with my baby."

Her hand falls away. "That night in the driveway…" Watching her lower lip tremble, I make a low sound. "I-I…was I trying to keep you with me somehow?"

My mind drifts back to that night. That moment when I sank into Naomi and that primal energy gripped me. That need to form an unbreakable bond. To keep her. "No. We were trying to keep each other. Trying to make sure we stayed connected." I finish bunching the dress around her waist and rock her closer. I work my hard flesh inside of her, biting back groans while simultaneously kissing away her beautiful gasps. Trying to keep myself from exploding. It's been so long. "We're going to have a baby, Naomi. Holy shit. I love you."

Her smile blooms against my mouth. "I love you, too."

"I love our baby."

"I love them, too. So much."

A knife cuts through my happiness, the reality of the situation dropping on my head. "Jesus, beauty queen. I'm leaving. I won't be here while you're pregnant." Dizziness lands hard, followed quickly by all out panic. "*Naomi—*"

"We'll be fine." She cuts me off with a kiss. Another. Another. "We'll be fine. I'm the girl who can build and rule a kingdom, remember? You said so yourself."

Without seeing my face, I can feel my expression is one of total suffering. My woman. My life. How can I leave her alone at a time like this? Still, she's right. I have to put my money where my mouth is or my words meant nothing. And she needs to know I'll never say anything to her I don't believe one hundred percent. I'll be one hundred percent for her or nothing at all. She can do this. She has my full faith. "I'll come home to you, do you hear me?" I manage around the lump in my throat. "I'll come back to you and the kingdom you build, Naomi. Tell me you know that."

"I know that," she says, my confidence causing her to bloom right in front of my eyes. "I know you'll come back to us. We'll be waiting."

She clings to the collar of my jacket and works her hips up and back, the chair creaking beneath us as we speed faster and faster toward the fulfillment we've both been missing. Needing. Craving. And groaning, helping her move with both hands on her backside, I'm lost. Lost in the beauty of Naomi, our future. Even the obstacles ahead are beautiful, because this woman will be on the other side of them. I can't wait to live every second of this life with her.

EPILOGUE

ConspiracyCrowd.org
Username: UrDadsFave69
Damn. Finally, a man even I would brave monogamy for.

Naomi

Seven months later

I PRESS A hand to my sore lower back, groaning in gratitude when Birdie takes over the task, pressing her thumbs into my ache and massaging in circles. I'm actually a very agile and active pregnant woman—or so my doctor tells me—but we've been standing on the airport tarmac for two hours now and my stamina is waning. My excitement, however, is not.

Jason is coming home today.

Lord, I'm actually a little nervous. I haven't seen my husband in person in six months. He's not going to mind that my stomach enters a room a full minute before I do. No, we managed to Skype him during my last sonogram two weeks ago and he told me several times that my mountainous belly and I were the most beautiful thing he'd ever seen in his life. That was so nice to hear, wasn't it? So sweet. It really was—

A tissue appears in front of my face. "You're crying again," Birdie says. "Get yourself under control, would you? Jason has seen enough water over the last six months."

I take the tissue and press it carefully beneath each eye, careful not to smudge my makeup. "It's a losing battle, I'm afraid. I cried at a cat food commercial this morning."

Birdie shakes her head, then sighs. "Aw, you know I think it's cute. Cry away."

I well up again on cue. "Thank you."

Seven months ago, Jason came to Charleston and brought me back to St. Augustine—still wearing my silver ball gown. We spent a week there…reacquainting, so to speak. Vigorously. There are still grooves in his bedroom wall behind our headboard thanks to the hours we spent vigorously acquainting.

While Birdie was in school, of course.

At night, while she was home, we planned. Jason and Birdie's parents genuinely seemed disappointed to lose their chance to make things right with Birdie, so visits were scheduled. Since Jason was deployed, Birdie and I have flown to Dallas a few times to see her mother and father, also known as my new in-laws. At first, there was awkwardness between them and their daughter. It took a visible effort for them to separate Birdie from Natalie and their grief, but Birdie impressed the heck out of me through it all. Something settled in her the day of the pageant and she's matured in a way that makes me prouder by the day. I don't know if I could have survived Jason's absence without her. And I'm not sure she could have survived it without me. We're a team.

All three of us.

As if summoned, my little man twists and turns inside my stomach, cozying into his favorite place—atop my bladder. I settle a hand on him, marveling at the miracle of life Jason and I created that night so many months ago. Lord, I miss my husband's touch more than I ever could have imagined. I reach for him in the night, talk to him under my breath during the day.

He's my missing half, and as happy as I am to have this new life growing inside me, I need him back. Now. He hasn't even landed yet and I'm already being stitched back together.

Jason. Mine. My husband.

That month before he left, we lived like we had all the time in the world, splitting our time between Charleston and St. Augustine. Since Beauty Queens Unlimited is based in Charleston, we rented an apartment, staying there on the weekends while waiting for Birdie to graduate. During that time, Jason took me scuba diving. To bed. A lot. And on dates. So many dates. Understanding my desire to experience new things, these dates were somewhat…unconventional. We went swimming with dolphins, drove to the Georgia State Fair and went on every single ride. Indoor rock climbing was my favorite date because of the feeling of accomplishment it gave me, and I've even been back several times since Jason left. Before he was deployed, I was *thisclose* to convincing him to participate in the next body art festival in Daytona Beach. My mission is still in the works, but I think he'll cave.

I can't wait to see my big warrior covered in pink butterflies.

Our wedding doesn't really count as a date, I suppose, but we did go dancing afterward. Or rather, I danced and Jason smoldered at me, his hands roaming over my hips, his skillful tongue sliding along that full lower lip…

Lord, pregnancy makes a woman horny. This day really could not come fast enough.

As a little girl, I imagined a fancy, elaborate wedding with doves and sparkles. A lot like the one I ran away from. Maybe I only expected an extravagant wedding because I was supposed to. Because that's what I knew was waiting for me. How could I have known that a civil ceremony on a Wednesday in city hall would be the most romantic wedding I ever imagined? Jason assured me he believed in my ability to provide for myself and care for our baby, but he wanted me to have the benefits of his military service should the worst happen. And I wanted to give him that peace of mind. I wanted him to have every single reassurance before leaving, so he wouldn't be distracted. It goes without saying that I wanted to marry the man more than I've ever wanted anything.

So we did. I married the love of my life. All because I reached for more within myself and found it. Found enough to offer someone and got more than I ever expected in return.

I've found my more. I ran toward an adventure and got one that will never end.

Beauty Queens Unlimited has taken on a life of its own. Contestants from all over South Carolina travel to Charleston for lessons and consultations. I make sure to keep a percentage of my schedule open for girls who can't afford the lessons and do the work pro bono. Birdie is living on campus in Tallahassee and sometimes she stays at the St. Augustine house, which I hope to still visit often with Jason, because of the memories it represents.

Birdie drives up to Charleston frequently on the weekends, too. She likes helping me with my pro bono contestants most of all, and it gave me the idea to start the coaching scholarship in Natalie's name. We're keeping the memory of Birdie's twin alive, but I watch Birdie become her own person a little more every time I see her. I think she might even have a boyfriend, but she's not giving up the goods.

"There he is."

At Birdie's words, every cell in my body lights up and I can't feel the pain in my feet anymore. I can feel nothing but an overflowing of gratitude to the universe for bringing my husband back to me. He's descending the stairs of the plane like an action hero, a gear pack strapped to his back. His hair is longer, his beard bushy, and there might even be some new lines on his face.

Everything about Jason makes him the most handsome, wonderful man I've ever seen in my life. My breath grows short watching him stride toward me, brow furrowed, cutting through other soldiers and members of the crowd. His expression is so intense, I wonder how I can stand when the ground is surely shaking.

"My God," Jason rasps, encompassing Birdie and me in the tightest, most welcome hug of my life. I wrap myself around him and cling, positive I'm soaking his uniform with tears and not caring. "My God." His voice shakes. "How am I the lucky bastard who comes home to this?"

"All right, all right, I feel the love," Birdie says, breaking the hug and slugging him in the chest. "Kiss your bride, man, before she expires."

Jason's mouth lands before Birdie finishes her watery command, his lips parting mine on a broken sound. His calloused hands cradle my jaw on both sides, sliding into my hair to tilt my head. His mouth is ravenous on mine, but there's so much underlying tenderness and awe, that I wonder if I'll ever be able to stem the moisture leaking down my cheeks ever again. His tongue flickers against mine, then dives back in for a more thorough taste, before he pulls away with a frustrated growl that echoes in my womb.

That's not all that's happening in my womb. I take Jason's hand and place it on my belly, so he can feel his son kicking, and I'll never forget the look of wonder on his face as I press our foreheads together, smiling up into my most beloved face.

"Welcome home, Blackbeard."

He releases an unsteady breath. "I'll never leave you again, Naomi."

THE END

ABOUT TESSA BAILEY

Tessa Bailey is originally from Carlsbad, California. The day after high school graduation, she packed her yearbook, ripped jeans and laptop, driving cross-country to New York City in under four days.

Her most valuable life experiences were learned thereafter while waitressing at K-Dees, a Manhattan pub owned by her uncle. Inside those four walls, she met her husband, best friend and discovered the magic of classic rock, managing to put herself through Kingsborough Community College and the English program at Pace University at the same time. Several stunted attempts to enter the work force as a journalist followed, but romance writing continued to demand her attention.

She now lives in Long Island, New York with her husband of ten years and six-year-old daughter. Although she is severely sleep-deprived, she is incredibly happy to be living her dream of writing about people falling in love.

Website: www.tessabailey.com

Instagram: instagram.com/tessabaileyisanauthor

Facebook: facebook.com/TessaBaileyAuthor

Twitter: twitter.com/mstessabailey

Goodreads: goodreads.com/author/show/6953499.Tessa_Bailey